RAIDER'S HEART

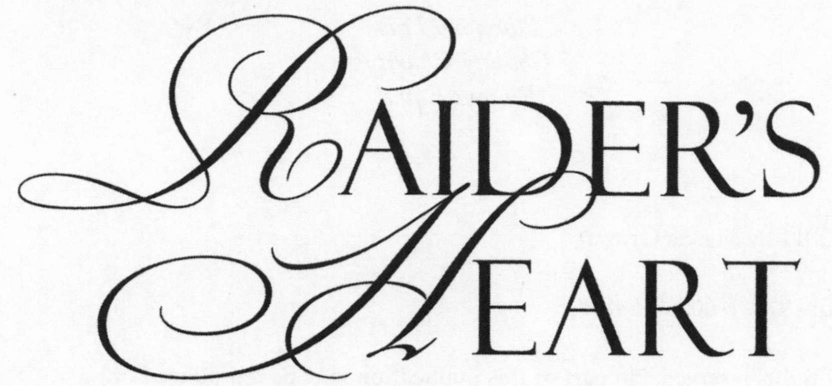

Raider's Heart

BACKWOODS
BRIDES

MARCIA GRUVER

Other Books by Marcia Gruver

Texas Fortunes Series:

Diamond Duo
Chasing Charity
Emmy's Equal

ISBN 978-1-60260-948-8

Scripture quotations are taken from the King James Version of the Bible.

This book is a work of fiction. Names, characters, places, and incidents are either products of the author's imagination or used fictitiously, except characters based on historical people. Any similarity to actual people, organizations, and/or events is purely coincidental.

For more information about Marcia Gruver, please access the author's Web site at the following Internet address: www.marciagruver.com

Cover design: Kirk DouPonce, DogEared Design

Published by Barbour Publishing, Inc., P.O. Box 719, Uhrichsville, OH 44683, www.barbourbooks.com

Our mission is to publish and distribute inspirational products offering exceptional value and biblical encouragement to the masses.

Printed in the United States of America.

Dedication/Acknowledgments

To Lisa Ludwig, for your giving heart, helping hands, and eagle eyes. This one is yours, babe.

My Heartfelt Thanks To:

My husband, Lee, who bears the weight of author deadlines on strong and willing shoulders.

My daughter Tracy Jones, a collaborator and plot consultant, in both writing and real life.

Janelle and Rodney Mowery, my experts on all matters related to seedtime and harvest.

Aaron McCarver, my copy editor at Barbour Publishing. Aaron, you make me shine!

Pembroke, North Carolina (Scuffletown), and the Lumbee Tribe of North Carolina for the fascinating story of their folk hero, Henry Berry Lowry.

Doug Hansen, president of Hansen Wheel & Wagon in Letcher, South Dakota, and Hugh Shelton of Texas Wagon Works in Gonzales, Texas, who kept the wagons rolling.

Author disclaimer: No chickens were harmed in the writing of this novel.

A bruised reed shall he not break,
and smoking flax shall he not quench,
till he send forth judgment unto victory.
Matthew 12:20 KJV

A bruised reed—A convinced sinner: one that is bruised with the weight of sin.

Smoking flax—One that has the least good desire, the faintest spark of grace.

Till he send forth judgment unto victory—That is, till he make righteousness completely victorious over all its enemies.

—Wesley's Notes on the Bible

Fayetteville, North Carolina, 1852

Silas McRae crashed through the moonlit cornfield and burst out the other side panting like a hounded deer. Free of the noisy stalks, he lit out at full speed then tripped and kissed the bottom of an irrigation canal. Cursing his foolhardy decision to return to Fayetteville in the first place, he lifted his mud-smeared face and took stock of the situation.

Not one soul of his band of misfits lurked across the wide expanse of newly mowed grounds, and no one hunkered along the tree line past the nearby manor. They'd cut out on him when the heat turned up. As simple as that.

A surge of warmth crept up his neck at the thought of the skirmish he'd just dodged. Every lead slug exploding from the end of a scattergun had missed him cold. Every indignant hand on the scruff of his neck had fallen away as he ran.

By thunder! He loved the thrill of the chase. The bulging knapsack of loot under his arm only topped the cake.

His roaming gaze eagerly swept the stately main house, and he closed his eyes for fear their sudden twinkle might be spotted from afar. It appeared his night of plunder wasn't done. What treasure lay behind those gilded walls? Beckoning. . .

As stealthy as a panther, Silas crept toward the siren's call. With any luck, he'd have a king's portion to lay at Odie's feet on his return. His lovely wife would be most proud.

He angled across the courtyard to the back side of the house and came to the first window. Squinting in disbelief, he watched the curtains gently sway. With a sense of destiny, he raised the sash higher and peered inside. Cocking his head, his trained ears strained for the slightest noise.

Nothing.

Smiling, he swung his lithe body over the sash and soundlessly touched the floor. When his eyes adjusted to the meager light, he gasped.

Trinkets and charms of every description lined the top of the polished dresser. On one side a solid brass bell, a fine kerosene lantern on the other. In the center, a delicate silver tray held an infant's brush and comb along with matching vessels of various shapes and sizes. Fanciful folderal, his for the taking.

He placed the lantern near the window to snatch up as he slipped out. But first. . .

Stuffing a crocheted doily into the mouth of the bell to silence the clapper, he opened his sack to add it and the silver pieces to his collection. Rubbing his hands together, he took inventory of the dusky room to see what might be next.

A glint of reflected moonlight caught his eye from across the room. He tiptoed toward it, amazed that the shimmer seemed suspended in midair. Closer inspection revealed an item displayed on a glass-topped table.

A chill shot up his spine. Had he stumbled across Aladdin's magic cave?

The curious low-slung lamp had a long spout and ornate handle—fashioned of gold, if he knew his business. Breathless, he hefted it to test the weight and smiled.

Worth a fortune!

Rustling in the corner spun Silas toward the sound. More startled by what he saw than what he heard, he crept close for a better look. Heart racing, he parted the mosquito net draped around the crib and gazed at the unforeseen windfall.

A baby sat up in bed, propped by legs so fat they creased in impossible places. A white nightdress tucked under one side of its bum made it difficult for the little mite to stay upright. Struggling to keep its balance, the child stared at him with round, questioning eyes.

Laying aside the lamp, Silas's hands inched forward, stopping when sudden creases feathered the delicate brow and the rosebud mouth puckered to cry.

Odie's words flew at him like darts from the shadowed corners. *"Promise me! Swear on your life you won't steal a babe and leave its mother with empty arms—not even for me."*

He straightened and patted the pudgy leg. "S'alright, snippet. Don't aim to hurt you none."

With practiced hands, he eased the child down on the mattress, tucking the cover into the folds of its chubby neck. The delicate threads of the blanket were so fine, they snagged on the tips of his calloused fingers. "There you are, little one," he cooed. "All snug in your bed."

The baby blinked up with wary eyes.

Silas chuckled. "Don't fret, now. Go on to sleep. Tomorrow's another day."

He carefully swept up the nearby bounty and bundled it into a spare knapsack. Satisfied, he nodded. "Your husband's a man of his word, Odell McRae. What I take from this room will leave no empty arms behind."

Crossing to the door, he cast one last glance at the sleeping baby in the cradle and nodded. "That's right, good wife. A man of his word."

Fayetteville, North Carolina, December 1871

Dawsey gasped and ducked behind the broad trunk of a live oak, her lovely mood snuffed like a hearth doused with dishwater.

Aunt Lavinia had charged onto the columned porch and stood peering down the tree-lined street, shading her eyes with both hands. "It's no good, child," she shrilled. "I've seen you."

So much for pride in a timely escape.

Dawsey hid her bundle behind her back and searched her mind for a fitting Psalm.

"Because he hath set his love upon me, therefore will I deliver him."

Whispering a prayer for strength, she stepped out onto the path. "Morning, Aunt Livvy."

Scowling, her old aunt scurried to meet her. "Dawsey Elizabeth Wilkes! Were you hiding from me?"

No sense denying. It would be a lie. Dawsey swallowed hard and fessed up. "Forgive me, dear. Not hiding from *you*, really, more from what you're about to say."

"Then I'll have it over and done. Did you keep your appointment with the dressmaker?"

Dawsey hung her head. "Not exactly."

Aunt Livvy caught her chin and raised it. "Kindly explain."

"I reached the door this time, Auntie. Touched the knob before a basket on display in the general store caught my eye." She pulled the package from behind her, attempting a winsome smile. "Sweet potatoes.

For the Christmas meal. Once I saw them, I forgot everything else. Father adores them sugared, and you know how he loves my holiday bread."

Aunt Livvy groaned and sought the heavens. "What is this fixation with the kitchen? Winney's a perfectly capable cook, dear."

"Yes, but I—"

"Young lady, I've tried to be patient, but sweet potato bread is hardly more important than your coming-out party."

This time Dawsey groaned. Inwardly, of course. "I respect your opinion, Auntie, but in this case, I can't agree." She softened her tone. "Father seems to love my special dishes, and I'm eager to offer him every comfort."

Aunt Livvy drew a breath, her lips moving as she counted on the exhale. She made it to number five before frowning and stamping her foot. "Your stubbornness in this matter is outright indecent. Your refusal to cooperate has positioned this family soundly beyond the pale. This is Fayetteville, North Carolina, Dawsey! General Sherman burned our buildings to the ground, but not our spirits. You must conform or be blacklisted." She tilted her head. "Don't you wish to marry well?"

Dawsey took her arm and started for the house. She dared not voice the thoughts swirling in her head. The truth was, after surviving the ravages of war, few citizens of the Old South concerned themselves with coming-out parties. Marrying well seemed the last thing on their minds, especially Dawsey's. Only the elders held fast to fading traditions. Sadly, no matter how stubbornly they clung, the old ways bore the stench of death and begged a decent burial.

Sadder still, stubbornness oozed from every pore of her well-meaning aunt. Lavinia believed Dawsey's standing as the only daughter of a wealthy planter would suffer crisis should she stay her meddling hand.

Despite Aunt Livvy's zeal, more pressing matters consumed Dawsey's heart. Her father's depression had worsened, if such a thing was possible. Curiously, her aunt seemed too busy to notice her only brother losing his mind.

When they reached the front porch, Dawsey found the courage to answer. "To be honest, Auntie, marriage hasn't entered my mind. I'd be perfectly happy to stay in this house forever, cooking for Father and tending his needs. Is he in his room?"

As always, when Dawsey mentioned him, her aunt grew flustered.

She sputtered and waved behind her. "In the den, I think."

"Is he alert today?"

Aunt Livvy promptly changed the subject. "Take those silly tubers to the root cellar or they won't be edible by Christmas. Then freshen up and meet me right here." She poked Dawsey's shoulder with her finger. "Don't keep me waiting. I only hope the seamstress will work us in after you've missed two appointments in a row."

As she spoke, the gangly boy who tended the grounds ambled up the walkway behind them. Barely out of knee pants, the lad made a vague impression of grimy overalls, tattered coat, tousled red hair, and a willful cowlick.

Aunt Livvy wiggled her fingers in his direction. "Yes, you're late. Don't waste my time apologizing. Get out back and weed the roses. We'll address your habitual tardiness when it's time to settle up."

Without a word or a missed step, the poor boy—Tiller, if Dawsey remembered his name correctly—lowered his head and crossed the lawn in a sulk.

When he disappeared, Aunt Livvy spun on her heels and entered the foyer still muttering under her breath.

Dawsey followed her inside. Dawdling at the coatrack, she waited until her aunt reached the top landing then placed her bundle on the hall table and crossed to her father's den. Sweet potatoes and dressmakers could wait.

Dreading what awaited her on the other side, Dawsey held her breath and pushed open the door. She strained to see her father in the dimly lit room, but the horrid smell reached her first. A mixed odor of stale cigars, musty wool, spoiled food, and unwashed body assailed her nostrils. Suppressing a retch, she briefly wished to step outside and slam the door against the foul smell and her heartrending pain.

Father coughed, the sound a damp rattle, and concern propelled her inside.

"What's this I hear? Are you ill?"

He jerked as if he'd been dozing then lifted shaggy brows, his gaze bleary. He grunted but didn't speak.

Dawsey felt his brow. Clammy, but blessedly cool.

Smoke saturated the oppressive air, providing an excuse for her watery eyes. The real reasons for her tears—dried egg on his tattered sweater, three days' growth of whiskers, and his vacant stare—she'd never allow him to know.

She lifted the pitcher and poured a shallow bowl of water. Dipping a rag, she wiped the sleep from his eyes and a spot of drool from his bristled chin. He didn't shrink from the cold cloth.

Squatting, she sought his face. "Are you hungry? It's nearly noon."

Eyes straight ahead, he responded with a cough.

"If you keep that up, I'll have to call the doctor."

This earned her a twitch in his cheek.

Laying aside the cloth, Dawsey sat next to her father, wondering how much deeper he could sink before losing his way back, how much further he could slip before she lost him forever.

The dark paneling and deep mahogany furnishings, meant to create a rich, impressive space, thrust the dismal room into shadow. A swirling beam of sunlight, the only bright spot in the room, pierced the gloom like a beacon of hope. Dawsey gazed at it, grateful for any hope she was offered.

She closed her eyes and leaned against his chair, longing for something she'd never known. Whatever force pulled her father into darkness by degrees had been tugging him away her whole life. There were stories about the brilliant man Colonel Gerrard Wilkes had once been, and Dawsey loved to hear them. She'd caught glimpses of that man in her early years but had never known him whole.

The door behind her opened with a flourish, drawing a rush of cold air from under the sash. Her aunt hovered on the threshold as if she couldn't bear to step inside. "I might've known."

Dawsey hustled to her feet. "I was just coming."

"Don't tell lies, dear. I know you forgot." She held up the package. "About these potatoes as well."

"I'm sorry, Auntie."

Aunt Livvy glanced at her brother and a grimace twisted her face. "I'll have Levi draw him a bath. Finish up here and meet me out front by the carriage."

"Yes, ma'am."

The door closed as briskly as it had opened.

Approaching the window, Dawsey shook her head and pushed down the familiar wave of sadness. She raised the sash higher, reached for the peculiar golden lamp on the sill, and came face-to-freckled-face with the boy, Tiller, kneeling in the flowerbed. Their eyes locked briefly before Dawsey snatched the lamp inside and lowered the pane.

She knew her efforts were wasted. The next time she entered the den, the window would be open, the lamp outside on the ledge. The pointless ritual had gone on for years.

Crossing the room, she placed the gaudy bauble in its proper place on the glass-topped table, resisting the urge to rub it and summon the genie.

It would take a grander wish than a genie could grant to help her understand what was happening to her father. . .and a God-sized miracle to save him. Fortunately, Dawsey believed in God-sized miracles.

Casting a hopeful peek over her shoulder, she slipped into the hall and closed the door.

Robeson County, North Carolina, December 4, 1871

Hooper McRae watched his hero's back until the low-lying mist and dense tangle at the edge of Bear Swamp swallowed him in silence. He wouldn't see Henry Berry again until Henry Berry summoned him and only on Henry's terms.

There wasn't another man Hooper respected more, not even his own father. Silas McRae gave his utmost in the fight for justice and was a notable man in his own right, but not equal to the likes of Henry Berry Lowry.

But then, who was?

Hooper turned his horse and headed through the quagmire to rejoin his brother Duncan and their weary band. Ears attuned to every sound, he picked his way along the same route he'd come.

The men of Robeson County took their first toddling steps in three inches of mud and knew every inch of the swamp by heart. Those unfamiliar with the area soon found themselves in trouble trying to navigate the marshy lowlands.

Many lost their lives in the maze of identical cypress. The mirrored trunks, jutting from the shallow pools that stretched for miles, tricked the mind and stifled a man's sense of direction. With no distinct markers, befuddled men rode in circles for days, never arriving where they were bound.

Outliers claimed Scuffletown hovered atop the water like a straddle-legged spider, its flooded roads and waterlogged houses floating free.

To Hooper and others like him, it was home, and he couldn't wait to get there.

He came to the clearing and found his men where he'd left them. Slump-shouldered and dozing, they seemed ready to topple from their horses, his bleary-eyed brother the worst offender.

Disgusted, Hooper shook his head. "Snap to, you sorry lot! I could've been Sheriff McMillan slipping up to cart you off to jail."

Duncan yawned and pushed back his soaking wet hair. "We've been riding all night in the rain. I'd welcome a cell in Lumberton with a dry cot to stretch out on."

Hooper snorted. "They'd stretch out your neck for you is all."

The memory of Henry Berry's proud back strolling fearlessly out of sight clashed with the sight of Duncan slouched in the saddle, a hollow-eyed, bedraggled mess. A sniveling ninny with no stomach for righteous vengeance, his brother suffered in comparison with Henry.

For that matter, their sister Ellie was a braver soul than Duncan. The little spitfire had more gumption asleep than Duncan did wide awake.

As if he'd read Hooper's mind, Duncan looked up and squared his shoulders. "What did Henry say?"

Hooper glanced away. "He said to hold our ground tonight. Go home and guard the folks. He sent word to the militia to stay out of Scuffletown business or suffer the consequences."

"And after tonight?"

The exhausted band of men crowded close to hear the answer.

"Henry promised to send word."

Wyatt, second in command to Hooper, whooped as loudly as he dared with the dogs on their heels. "That means we sleep in our own beds tonight?"

Wyatt's brother Nathan grinned. "And belly up to our mama's table?"

The rough-and-tumble brothers beamed so foolishly, Hooper might've smiled, too, if he remembered how. He nodded at the other two boys instead. "Jason and Richard will bunk at your house tonight. Until we get the all clear, it's not safe for them in Moss Neck."

Wyatt raised his brows. "Suppose Henry can't hold 'em off? Will we have to leave again?"

Hooper took up his reins. "We do whatever Henry says."

Duncan made a sound in his throat. "*You* will. I'm tired of lying out in this godforsaken swamp. I'm bound for Scuffletown, and once I cross the Lumber River, that's it for me. If I make it home in one piece this time, I won't be leaving again"—he squinted at Hooper—"no matter what Henry says."

A sour taste in his mouth, Hooper spat. "Suit yourself. If I were you, I'd steer clear of turkey blinds and watch the brush for the flash of arms."

"They're not looking for us, Hooper."

Richard, the youngest of their group, pulled a folded paper, tattered and well creased, from his breast pocket. "Sure they are, Duncan. It says so right here."

The boy's cousin, Jason, groaned and shook his head. "You're still carrying that around?"

Interested, Hooper nodded at Rich. "What have you there?"

"Old news," Jason grumbled. "Not worth your time, Hoop. It's an article the *Wilmington Star* ran a year ago."

"What does it say?"

Jason's face reddened. "It's nothing. The way Rich makes over it you'd think his own name graced the headline. He's read it so often the words have all run together."

Ignoring Jason, Hooper lifted his chin. "Read it to me."

Richard grinned. "Yes, sir." Clearing his throat, he pulled the paper close to his face and read in a halting voice:

> "October 15, 1870—If we were the. . .c–citizens, we should feel pretty well. . .satisfied that there is no law there and would favor Lynch law, ex–ter–extermination, tomahawking, anything else that would prove. . .effective in putting to death Henry Berry Lowry and his band of outlaws."

Wyatt tilted his head. "Didn't you hear, Duncan? They're gathering hunting parties to capture or kill us for the reward. The Conservative legislature in Robeson County offered two thousand dollars for the delivery, dead or alive, of Henry Berry, and one thousand dollars each for his men."

Nathan gave a hearty laugh. "Henry answered by offering one thousand dollars for the county commissioner's head. Ain't that a hoot?"

Duncan scowled. "If you think a nickel of that reward is pinned on our heads, you're fooling yourselves. They're after Henry's real gang, men like Steve and Tom Lowry, Boss Strong, and George Applewhite."

Jason squinted. "There ain't no truth to that, is there Hoop?"

Cutting Hooper off, Duncan raised his voice. "You may wish it to be different, but no one even knows we're helping the resistance. Half the time, Henry forgets who we are." He swiveled to Hooper. "You're lucky he didn't step out of that thicket back there and slit your throat."

Hooper whirled his horse to cut in front of Duncan. "Thunderation, man! What's your problem?"

Duncan met his charge with blazing eyes. "Hunger's my problem. Exhaustion, too. Living in swamps and doing without is my problem. Looting houses and bushwhacking men in their beds, and for what? To aid Henry and his men?" He tucked his chin and his tone softened. "Now that you mention it, my problem might be Henry Lowry himself." His anguished eyes sought Hooper. "What are we doing this for, brother?"

"How can you ask? You know why."

"Do I? All this stealing and killing ain't done the just cause a lick of good."

"You've killed no one, Duncan," Hooper said. "None of us gathered here have taken a life. We steal food and goods to distribute to Scuffletown's poor. But know this. . .if called upon to take a life in defense of my family, I wouldn't hesitate no more than Henry did."

Stillness settled over the men.

Duncan's eyes on him never flinched. "You didn't need to tell me, Hooper. There's bloodlust in your eyes."

"Is passion wrong, brother? You don't find our people worth fighting for?"

"Our people, yes. I'm not convinced they're the source of your passion. . .or your first concern."

Hooper tightened his grip on the reins, the sting of the leather a welcome distraction from his rage. "Tell me my first concern, since you know me so well."

"I fear you're using Henry's uprising as an outlet for your anger. An excuse to strike at the wind."

"What does that mean?"

"It means stealing from the Macks' fine houses helps you forget we're half-breeds scratching a living off the bank of the Lumber. It means burying your fist in a pasty-white Confederate helps you forget we'll never be counted as equals while there's a drop of Indian blood in our veins—even if our name is McRae."

Hooper lunged. His arm thrown around Duncan's neck took them both from their saddles and landed them with a splash in the musty-smelling water of Bear Swamp. As they rolled in four inches of swirling green slime, Hooper fought the urge to hold his brother's head beneath the surface until the traitor breathed his last.

Chapter 3

Ellie McRae perched like a wren at her papa's feet, basking in his cheery voice and warm smiles. The yarn he spun lifted her from the dirt floor of their two-room shanty and carried her to a faraway mansion whose walls bulged with treasure like a tow sack stuffed with corn.

She'd heard the story many times but never tired of listening. Each time she slapped her leg and howled at the part where he plowed through a cornfield and landed facedown in a ditch. She patted his hand and felt his pain when he claimed his carelessness robbed the family of the chance for a better life.

"Had I been in my right mind, I'd never have left that lamp behind. Blasted thing was worth a king's ransom." He held his head and moaned, and Ellie mourned with him.

"Was the magic lantern pretty, Pa?"

He stared over her head, a sparkle in his glazed eyes. "Prettiest thing I've ever seen." His head swung to Ma. "Besides you, Odie."

Mama turned from the hearth. "You've worn the shine off that tale, Silas McRae. The children all know it by heart." She sighed. "Like I've told you too many times, if you keep looking back at that golden lamp, you'll wind up going nowhere."

Pa lifted mournful eyes. "You're right, Odie, my love. No good comes of dwelling on bad fortune."

"Then why do you persist in brooding on it?"

He winked at her. "It gives me something to do, woman."

Mama came from behind and gathered Ellie's hair off her neck with cool fingers. "It's a marvel you can hold up your head, child, with the weight of these curls down your back. The good Lord didn't short you none on hair, did He?"

Never passing a chance to tease, Papa grinned, his eyes still moist from his recollections of the past. "Reckon you got befuddled and stood in the hair line more than once, Ellie?"

Mama chuckled. "I think you've hit on the answer, husband. That's why her locks can't decide on a color. Fresh out of bed in the morning, they look as brown as a coffee bean." She tugged on the horse's tail she'd fashioned. "Let the light hit just right and we have us our redhead."

Ellie craned her head to smile, and Mama leaned to kiss her forehead. She let go of Ellie's hair and lifted her coat from its wooden peg.

Cut from cypress knees and staggered in a crooked line along the front wall, there was one bumpy knob for each member of the family.

Papa's hook was the highest, though he wasn't the tallest. The boys' slots, empty far too often to suit Ellie, were about the same height, though Hooper stood a head taller than his brother.

Ellie measured close to Duncan's height, but her peg fell below the men's, right alongside her short little mama's.

Sliding her arms in the sleeves of her coat, Mama frowned. "There are chores to be done before the noon meal, Silas. Do you have plans in that direction?"

Ellie watched her fasten the row of buttons. "Where you going, Ma?"

Ma leaned to peer out of the cabin's only window, bobbing to see past the oily smears on the pane and the split logs stacked on the porch. "Nowhere yet"—she stifled a smile—"but I want to be ready when the boys ride up."

Ellie swung around. "They're coming?"

She nodded. "I feel it in my bones."

Never one to doubt her mama's bones, Ellie sprang off the floor and dashed to open the door. "*Wahoo!* From which direction?"

Recovered from his slump, Papa grinned and cocked his head. "I doubt she's privy to the details, honey." He blinked and swiveled in his chair. "Are you, Odie?"

She ignored him. "Ellie, shut the door. There's enough winter inside these walls without you inviting more."

Ellie grabbed her shotgun, reached for her coat, and stepped out on the rickety porch. The menfolk had thrown it together in a single day, stripping the bald cypress and cutting the jagged planks themselves, and it showed. She counted the creaky boards to the steps, skirted the soggy mess around the rain barrel, and perched on a stump to wait.

She loved big-hearted, childlike Mama and cheerful, blundering Pa, but after weeks alone with them in the cabin, she craved a dose of Duncan's booming laughter and Hooper's flashing eyes.

Watching the woods for any sign of her brothers, she let her mind wander to the reason they'd fled. Two weeks ago, word of the latest rampage by the Guard had ricocheted through the trees, bouncing off every cabin in Scuffletown and sending their men scrambling for the swamps.

Papa, bent on keeping their names off enemy lips, hustled the boys from the house before they'd properly dressed, with orders to hide out until the danger passed.

Ellie begged to ride with them. Knowing she had a keener eye, sharper ears, and a straighter aim than any man, Papa said she could go, but Ma's word carried in the end.

She laid her shotgun aside and watched him pick his way past the bog holes on his way to join her. Scuffletown was a muck swamp. Living within its borders meant wet socks and spattered britches, sodden cuffs, and muddy boots. Papa trudged up sporting the lot, his gaze sweeping the trees. "Ellie, my girl. . .you reckon your mama's on target?"

Ellie brushed off the stump beside her. "She seldom calls it wrong."

He sat with a groan then leaned close and lowered his voice, the spark of a smile in his eyes. "Don't let on I told you, but it's no hunch she's going by. A message came in the night from Henry's wife. Henry's sending them home today."

She spun and gripped his knees. "They're coming for sure then?"

He shot her a crooked grin and winked. "Don't be so hasty, Puddin'."

She jabbed his leg with a raised knuckle. "Stop that and answer."

He howled, part pain, part glee, and caught her hand before she delivered another blow. "If you're bent on pounding it out of me, I'd say it's only a matter of time." He rubbed his hands together. "It'll be good to see those two huddled around the table again."

By the light in his darting eyes, Ellie guessed what he was thinking. "You mean Hooper."

Pa's head swung around, his weathered forehead creased. "Duncan as well. I miss them both."

She met his shifty stare. "I know you love Duncan." Ducking her head, she thumped a loose piece of bark from the stump. "But Hooper's special."

Pa sniffed. "There's no man his equal."

Ellie cut her eyes to him. "Duncan doesn't seem to mind."

"No, and that's part of what makes him special in his own right." He slung his arm around her neck. "Remember the story of Jacob and Esau?"

"Yes, sir. From the Bible."

He shifted on the stump. "Old Isaac favored Esau for his rugged ways and his skill in bringing meat to the table." He held out his open palm as if Esau perched there. "Jacob was the quieter sort." He raised the other hand to hold Jacob. "He liked to hang about the house, so his mama liked him best."

Gripped by the story, Ellie wagged her head. "Like our boys. Brothers, but different in every way."

Papa "lowered" the biblical twins. "In our story, Hooper is my Esau and Duncan is Ma's Jacob. I suppose it's my nature to get on better with rugged men." Raising his brow, he shook his finger in her face. "It don't mean I hold less affection for Duncan. Don't you go thinking otherwise."

They sat in silence for a spell before he cleared his throat and spit off the side of his stump. "There's another likeness in our stories, Ellie. The Almighty knew His business about Jacob and Esau from the start. He saw both men's hearts, saw the greed in Esau, the potential in Jacob. Hence, the good Lord favored Jacob."

He worked his jaw as if dreading to come to the point. "If you were to weigh Hooper's heart against Duncan's"—he paused, ripping up a shallow root with the toe of his boot—"I'm not sure Hooper would come out on top."

Stunned, Ellie glared at his shaggy sideburns. "I don't know why you'd say such a thing."

He shifted his gaze to hers and lifted his hands in surrender. "Don't fault me for speaking my mind. You know how I love that boy. You just accused me of loving him too much." He drew a ragged breath. "But there's a dark side to him, Ellie."

She set her jaw. "You're wrong, Pa. Hooper pretends to be hard, but inside he's pulled taffy."

Pa widened his eyes. "You've never watched him on a raid. Or seen his hands tighten around an enemy's throat."

"Hooper believes in what we're fighting for, that's all. There's a fire inside that he struggles to harness, but he'll turn it to good. I just know it."

Papa patted her knee. "I hope you're right, honey. If not, we're bound to lose him."

A whistle trilled from the trees along the marsh to the east. An outlier would mistake it for the call of a winter bird, but Papa hauled to his feet. "They're here!"

Ellie shoved two fingers in her mouth and blew an answering blast before Papa could pucker.

Six men on horses parted the curtain of brush and struck out across the shallows.

Her heart soared to see Hooper and Duncan in the lead, but the sight of Wyatt Carter riding alongside them poured honey on the biscuit. As they approached, her brothers' drawn, sober faces afflicted with cuts and bruises dampened her pleasure. She bolted off the stump and hurried toward them. "What on earth happened?"

Papa followed her to Hooper's side and stared up at his battered son. "Did you boys meet up with an ambush?"

At his words, the men grew restless. Turning away, Wyatt fiddled with his saddlebag. Nathan quickly dismounted. Richard suffered a sudden coughing fit, and Jason wiped his nose on his sleeve.

Like Ellie, Papa was nobody's fool and noticed their silly grins. He glared around the circle of waterlogged men. "What the devil's going on here?"

Duncan snorted and jerked his thumb at Hooper. "The only ambush I met came at the end of his fist."

Pa's attention jumped to Hooper. "Is that so?"

Avoiding his searching gaze, Hooper dismounted and gathered his reins. "I showed him mercy," he growled, his eyes blazing beneath pitch-dark strands of hair. "The penalty for treason is death." His back stiff as a plank, he moved to lead his horse past them.

Papa clutched his arm. "There ain't enough enemies hiding in these woods to suit you, son?"

A bit of the swelling left Hooper's chest. His jaw clenched but he didn't speak.

"Whatever this latest squabble is over, you'll set it to the back of the hearth for now," Pa said. "I don't have time to stand between you."

He paused to watch Mama hurry down the steps. "The truth is," he continued, his tone grave, "I've an unsettling problem of my own, and I need your help."

Hooper studied his anxious face, one brow drawn to a peak. He finally nodded, his throat working with unspoken questions.

Lifting his steely gaze to Duncan, Papa scowled. "That goes for you, too."

Duncan nodded grimly and dismounted.

Ellie crowded between them. "Help with what, Pa?" She gave her brothers a worried look. "He's mentioned nothing to me."

Pa took the reins from Hooper. "It'll keep for now. Go greet your mama, boys. She missed you something fierce."

He slipped his arm around Ellie's shoulders and squeezed. "Wipe the worry off your face, Puddin'. We'll meet around the table tonight and talk it through. You'll know everything then."

He turned with a smile. "Meanwhile, let's go sample some fine rabbit stew. This poor woman has danced with the hearth all morning."

Chapter 4

Dawsey balanced on the dressmaker's pedestal, watching the gaunt widow pin the endless hem of her gown. The poor woman's knobby fingers moved so swiftly over the bright blue fabric, one might never know how grievously she ached when the cold weather stiffened her joints.

Yet Dawsey knew. With her skill in the healing arts, she wound up privy to the sufferings of most of Fayetteville's old and infirm.

"Stand straight, niece!" Aunt Livvy barked. "Lest we be here all day."

Mrs. Gilchrist's thin shoulders jerked, and she frowned at Aunt Livvy from the floor. "For heaven's sake, Lavinia Wilkes, I nearly rammed this needle through her legs. Hush now, or it won't be the girl's fault if this hem takes all day. You have me shaking like meal in a sifter."

Ignoring her rebuke, Aunt Livvy fingered the strap of the gown. "This is good work, Mary Gilchrist. The fabric beneath hardly shows. It's as if these delicate ribbons are holding up the dress." She ran her hand along Dawsey's side. "The full skirt and fitted bodice are very flattering on you, dear. Your waist looks as thin as a wisp." Staring at Dawsey in the faded looking glass, sadness doused Aunt Livvy's smile. "Ah, but you're so like your mother, dear. It's like gazing at Margaret through time."

The words pierced a tender spot in Dawsey's heart. She clasped her hands and beamed at her image. "Am I really?"

"It's true, dear," Mrs. Gilchrist said, pinching the straight pins from her mouth. "You bear her delicate frame, with the same lithe body and narrow hips. Except you're taller. A tiny little thing, she was."

Dawsey blinked down at the seamstress. "You fitted my mother?"

Mrs. Gilchrist lifted her chin and nodded. "Many times."

Aunt Livvy touched a strand of Dawsey's hair. "Margaret had the same tangled mane—chestnut colored like yours—and she wore it loose and flowing, same as you. You inherited her milky complexion and freckled nose, too." She looked closer. "In the same pattern, I believe."

Dawsey laughed. "Nonsense. How could that be?"

Hiding a grin, Aunt Livvy busied herself with the blue flowers on Dawsey's shoulder. "It's possible, isn't it? As for the other details, my memory is certain." She blinked away the brightness. "You're a replica of Margaret Wilkes."

Stepping off the pedestal, Dawsey stared harder at her reflection, trying desperately to see her mother. "Oh, Auntie, I wish I could remember."

Mrs. Gilchrist struggled to her feet, dusting her hands on her skirt. Hugging Dawsey from behind, she pressed her wrinkled cheek against her face. "You don't need to remember, dear. She's standing right in front of you."

The door opened and sunlight flooded the room, ushered in by Flora, Mrs. Gilchrist's daughter. She stopped short at the sight of Aunt Livvy and Dawsey then recovered from her displeasure enough to greet them with a frown. "Afternoon, ladies. Your appointment has run past the noon hour again, I see."

"Mind your manners, Flora," her mother said.

The girl carried a small bowl, balanced on a plate and covered with a dishcloth. Shoving aside scattered bolts and scraps of fabric with her elbow, she placed the food on a nearby workbench and turned with her hands on her hips. "If you won't come for dinner, then dinner must come to you." Concern flashed in her eyes. "Really, Mama, you must take better care of yourself."

Aunt Livvy patted Dawsey's shoulder. "Flora's right, of course. Let's get you out of this dress and into your own things. We've imposed enough on Mrs. Gilchrist's good nature."

Flora's manners grudgingly returned. "Forgive me, Miss Lavinia. Mama's aching joints have her down more than she lets on—especially the pain in her back. If she pushes herself, she'll wind up bound to the bed."

Alarmed, Dawsey spun and put her arm around Mrs. Gilchrist's waist. "You never mentioned your back. If that's the case, the blue cohosh I brought you won't do. You need windflower tonic and mountain laurel for sudden onset of misery. Does the pain move from one joint to another? Or travel down the body?"

Wide eyed, Mrs. Gilchrist nodded. "A little of both."

"Hot baths will work wonders then. Soak yourself once in the morning and again at night."

Flora rolled her eyes. "She could be shed of her affliction once and for all if she'd follow Grammy's advice."

"Oh?" Dawsey turned. "Please share. I'm always seeking new cures."

Flora smiled and stood a bit taller. "Of course, Dawsey. You take a dead cat to the woods. Stand near a hollow stump that still has some life in it. Twirl the cat overhead three times then toss him to the south. Walk away to the north and don't dare look back." She winked for emphasis. "Grammy swears by it."

Mrs. Gilchrist waved her off. "I'll have you know I tried that silly old cure. All I got for my trouble was a stiff shoulder and a second glance at my supper." She gathered Dawsey close. "But this dear lamb's advice brings relief every time."

She cocked her brow at Aunt Livvy. "You've a treasure stored in this one, Lavinia. I hope you realize her worth."

Beaming, Aunt Livvy crossed her arms at her chest. "I do indeed."

Cheeks aflame, Dawsey excused herself and scurried to the dressing room. Their praise embarrassed her and felt undeserved, considering the urge to help bubbled from within like a wellspring.

Before the door had closed behind them or Mrs. Gilchrist turned the sign, Dawsey knew the questions clawing at her insides were bound to come out and upset Aunt Lavinia.

They summoned the carriage, and Levi urged the mare past the rows of houses and shops, and then over the Cool Spring bridge. Rounding a curve, they made the turn toward home.

Breathless, dreading Aunt Livvy's reaction, Dawsey lost the battle with her tongue. "Tell me about the day Mother died."

The warmth and goodwill of the day swirled away like a mist, replaced by Dawsey's tight chest and Aunt Livvy's thin lips. "Again, Dawsey? The story won't change by the telling. I've grown tired of repeating myself."

"Please? It helps to hear the details, what few there are."

Aunt Livvy sighed. "Your mother was ill. Frail. She couldn't fight anymore. It's as simple as that."

Dawsey nodded. "Her heart, then?"

Her aunt paused. "In a manner of speaking. It seemed she lost the will to go on."

As always, the cruel words pierced Dawsey. She wrung her hands. "I simply can't understand what that means, Auntie. She had Father and me to live for. How could a mother, a new mother at that, lose the will to live?"

The haunted look in Aunt Livvy's eyes spoke of matters too deep, too far away for Dawsey to fathom. "I wish I could say, dear. It's an unanswered question for me as well."

"And you'd tell me if she really died. . .in childbirth?"

Aunt Livvy spun to face her. "I'll answer that question one last time, to put it to rest for good. *No,* dear. Birthing weakened Margaret, there's no doubt, but you were six months old when she passed." She gripped Dawsey's hands. "I'd never lie to you about a thing like that."

Years of frustration welled in Dawsey's chest. "Then why won't anyone talk about her death? Why do the locals in Fayetteville point and whisper, change the subject if her name comes up?"

"Calm down, dear. You're upsetting yourself."

"You're not telling me everything, and I know it. Why are there no photos on display of me as an infant and none tucked away in boxes? No baby clothes or mementos of my birth?"

She clenched her fists and pounded on her knees. "It's as if Father wants to forget I was ever born!"

Aunt Livvy turned on the seat and gripped her wrists. "Stop it, now. You'll do yourself harm."

Past caring about her welfare, Dawsey pulled away from Aunt Livvy and hid her face in her hands. "The most important question of all," she wailed, "what terrible secret about her death has driven poor Father insane?"

Chapter 5

Most meals in the McRae house passed in a blur of flying elbows and reaching fingers. The boys shared the appetites and manners of feral hogs, with Papa no better. To fill her stomach, Ellie had to stay poised and nimble, ready to grab a stray biscuit or overlooked chicken wing.

Tonight was different. No one would recognize the family seated around the table, their elbows grounded, fingers stilled.

Her brothers loaded bread on their plates and ladled rabbit stew in their bowls quietly, taking their share and passing the dishes. Ellie supposed an outlier would mistake their hushed tones and careful bites for manners instead of dread of what Papa had to say. McRae family meetings were seldom good news.

The thought of sharing a meal with Wyatt had pleased Ellie, but he and the boys were too anxious for their own hearths to accept Papa's offer of a meager bowl of stew. They'd ridden out of the yard a half hour ago, headed for home.

Though she called it to no one's attention, Mama held back from the table again, prepared to go without to see her family fed. Most nights, she'd go hungry if Ellie didn't smuggle her a few bites.

She started to clear their plates, but Pa raised a staying hand. "Leave it, Odell. Sit yourself down."

Settling into her chair, she watched him. For the first time, Ellie noticed her eyes were steady and calm. Whatever Papa was about to spring on his children, his wife already knew.

He peered at them, beginning with Mama and sweeping to look at each of them in turn. "Family. . ."

Ellie's breath caught in her throat. She clenched her fists in her lap.

"There's another place about to be set at this table and another sleeping mat spread before the hearth." He held up a hand in answer to their frowning faces. "Don't matter if we like it or not. We're about to have another mouth to feed."

Startled by the thought, Ellie's gaze shifted to Ma, and the question flew out of her mouth. "A new baby?"

Mama squirmed and blushed.

"Don't talk foolish!" Papa boomed.

He held up a folded paper. "A few days ago, this letter came from your aunt Effie in Fayetteville. It says she can't care for that boy of hers since my brother's passing." He glanced heavenward and crossed himself. "God rest him."

Ellie gaped. She had an aunt? A cousin? A now-departed uncle that Pa had never mentioned?

A thousand questions burned in her chest. She opened her mouth to ask them, but Mama motioned for him to continue.

"Effie's asked us to take in my nephew, so we will." He slammed the letter on the table with a grand flourish, as if pronouncing a sacred decree.

Duncan stood. "In a two-room cabin? Tell her no. It's hard times everywhere. Aunt Effie can care for him as good as we can."

Ellie's head swung around. Duncan knew about Aunt Effie?

Papa pointed his fork. "Hush up and sit. Effie's penniless. Besides, she claims Reddick's a handful. Gone wild as a buck and won't mind her."

Hooper put down his knife. "That's what a hickory switch is for."

Ellie's gaze swiveled to Hooper. He knew as well.

"Hard to spank a boy standing three heads taller than you," Pa said. "First she'd have to catch him."

Duncan grinned. "That never stopped you." He sobered. "Hooper's right. The boy just needs a good thrashing."

Papa shoved his plate aside. "I didn't call this meeting to ask permission. We're taking Reddick McRae into our house and that's final. I need you boys to go fetch him for me."

Duncan and Hooper shared a look, their brows arched to the rafters.

Hooper cocked his head. "You made us swear an oath never to go into Fayetteville. You said—"

"I know what I said." Papa gave a curt nod. "Just like I know what I'm saying now. You'll go to Fayetteville, and this is how you'll do it—you're to ride straight there and straight back, never veering from your path. Tell no one you're coming and no one you've gone. You'll see nary a soul, save Effie and her boy, and they'll know I've sent you when they lay eyes on you. Not before." He raised a warning finger. "Enter town after nightfall. Leave before first light." Sniffing sharply, he glared. "The most important thing to remember is this—tell no one you're a McRae from Scuffletown. Let neither fact pass your lips." He leaned to squint into each of their faces. "Have I made myself clear or will you be needin' a do-over?"

Mama cleared her throat. She didn't often utter her opinion at a family meeting, so every eye looked her way. Whatever she had on her mind, it must be important.

Biting her lip, Ellie waited.

"For too many years, we've kept you children out of Fayetteville. We raised you without benefit of family ties, your own blood relations." She gave Ellie a somber look. "I spoke of them often to Hooper and Duncan when they were young in the hope that if we ever returned, the family wouldn't seem like strangers." She sighed. "Over time, I let them fade to distant memories." A faraway look darkened her eyes. "The McRaes and Presleys are good stock with kind and generous hearts." She wiped a falling tear with the corner of her apron. "Especially my own dear parents." She glanced at Papa. "I don't even know if they survived the war, and if so, how they're faring."

"Don't do this, Odie." Papa moved to rise from the table.

She waved for him to sit. "Our children deserve to know their kin, Silas."

Duncan pushed back his chair and knelt at her side, caressing her hands. "Then why, Ma? Why have you warned us away from them all these years?"

Staring into his eyes, she drew a deep breath. "Because—"

"Odell!"

She shot Papa a weighty glance. "*Because* son. . .we had to." She patted Duncan's shoulder. "Take a seat, and let me have my say. I can't tell you the whole story, but you're about to learn more than you've ever known." Papa stirred and she lifted her hand. "It's all right, Silas. It's the only way."

He shook his head, but she swallowed and continued. "I met your pa in Lumberton while I was visiting distant kin. He followed me to Fayetteville where we started our lives together among my friends and family. Before long, he moved me seven miles south to Hope Mills and built me a fine house." She smiled with her eyes. "We were so happy there."

After a long pause, Hooper lifted his head in her direction. "Go on, Ma."

She tightened her lips. "Something happened that changed everything. On a trip into Fayetteville, poor judgment landed your pa in a pitiful stink."

Ellie's eyes flew wide. Now Pa would stomp and bellow for sure.

Shoulders bowed, he sat with his chin nearly grazing the table.

Unable to trust her own eyes or ears, Ellie shook herself and forced her attention back to what Mama was saying.

"I can't tell you what the trouble was, so don't ask." She sighed, a lost look in her eyes. "But the stench of it drove us from Hope Mills in the dead of night. Papa's folks had passed on by then, and his brother had followed him to Fayetteville, but our ties with the Lumbee Indians were still strong. We fled to Scuffletown, where the Lowrys swore to hide and protect us. They've kept their word all these years, especially dear Henry."

Hooper blew out a breath. "How did Aunt Effie's letter find us?"

Papa squirmed. "I felt someone in the family should know our whereabouts, for emergency's sake. So I got word to Uncle Sol."

"Against my counsel," Mama said, her face hard. "I knew it would be a mistake, and look where it got us. Now Effie knows. Who's next?"

Papa's jaw tensed. "I suppose Sol told her on his deathbed. Otherwise, he'd never have given me up."

Mama drew her chair closer to the boys, her voice so low Ellie strained to hear. "There's a powerful man in Fayetteville, one we've grievously wronged. If you make one misstep while you're there, you'll bring his wrath down on our heads." She shuddered. "His vengeance will be fierce, and there are no more places to hide. Even the Lowry gang won't save us from our due."

Ellie copied her shudder. "Who is this terrible man?"

Papa bolted to his feet. "That's enough. This meeting is over." Back in charge, he rested both hands on the table and barked orders at Hooper and Duncan. "There's an hour left of daylight, at best, so let's make good use of it. I patched the busted wheel, but the hitch needs fixing, so get to it."

Duncan blinked. "We're taking the rig?"

"Yes, in case the lad has no horse. Pack light; he'll want to bring his belongings. Besides, you won't need much. This will be a mighty short visit." He pushed back his chair. "Find your bunks early tonight. I want you on the road by daybreak. With a rest stop or two, that puts you outside of Fayetteville just before dark."

Ellie steeled her spine. "Can I go, too?"

Papa's gaze jerked her way. "Out of the question."

Mama stood and began stacking their plates. "It's too dangerous, Ellie."

"My brothers will protect me. I'd dearly love to see Fayetteville. . . and meet my family."

On the way to the door, Papa stopped and slid his arm around her neck. "Let it be, Puddin'. There's a better chance of you leaping off the barn and winging your way to Boston."

Chapter 6

Hooper pulled the pin and dropped the hitch, scrambling to catch it before it hit the ground. If he busted the evener, there'd be a price to pay, and he didn't relish a glimpse of Papa's temper. He'd set himself at odds with enough family members for one day.

The relative in question ambled into the barn, absently rubbing his battered face. The angry black and blue reminders of their scuffle stirred Hooper's regret until Duncan's eyes flashed a threat. "You stay on your side of the barn, and I'll stay on mine," he growled. "Maybe I'll let you walk out of here in one piece."

A surging band tightened around Hooper's head and blood pulsed a war cry in his neck. "If you'll check your likeness in a mirror, you might guard your words more carefully. It would be a challenge to find a spot I haven't pummeled to mush, but I don't mind trying."

Duncan's hand fluttered to his cheek before he clenched his fist and glared. "All the gals that trail you through town would turn aside today." A head shorter, he swelled his chest and lifted his chin to smirk. "They wouldn't find you quite so tempting with that pretty brown eye swelled shut."

Hooper cocked one brow. "I'm in no mood for reckless games. Can you really afford to try me?"

A step closer brought them toe-to-toe. "I can if you can."

Familiar aching fire lit the roiling pit of Hooper's stomach. The last clutching grasp on his unwelcome temper slipped as he glimpsed the challenge in Duncan's eyes. Balling his fist, he drew back to swing.

Papa's arm shot between them and caught Hooper's taut knuckles midair. "By crick, that's enough!" With his other hand, he tugged Duncan away from Hooper's rage. "Son, in most things you show fair good sense," he said to Duncan. "Why don't you know pulling your brother's trigger is akin to kissing a rattler?"

Struggling to control himself, Hooper took a backward step. "Put it down to ignorance, Pa. The boy don't seem to learn."

Papa glared. "No need to throw fuel on the fire, Hooper. I'll handle this."

Duncan pulled free, still poised for battle and bouncing like a restless fox. "You think I can't take him? Look at his face. I split that pretty lip for him."

Pa gripped his shoulder. "You caught him off guard, that's all. Got in a lucky punch. Have the sense to know it won't happen again." He sighed. "Persist in this foolishness, Duncan, and you'll find yourself hurt."

Clutching both of their sleeves, he dragged them to a bench along the wall and shoved them down. "We're going to have this finished here and now. I'm depending on you boys to ride to Fayetteville, but you won't leave the yard until you've buried the hatchet." He jutted his chin. "And not in each other's skulls."

Hooper snorted.

Duncan crossed his arms and swiveled on the seat, turning a frosty back to Hooper. "If you send us to Fayetteville together, only one of us will make it home."

Squelching a grin, Pa cleared his throat. "I hate to hear you say that, son. We'll miss you around here."

Duncan bolted forward on the bench. "What?"

Resting his hands on his hips, Pa gazed thoughtfully toward the ceiling. "It won't be the same around the breakfast table, that's for sure. We've gotten used to seeing your face."

If Hooper laughed, he'd undo Pa's efforts to smooth Duncan's feathers. He held his breath, squirming from the urge to bust loose and pound his knee. He didn't have long to wait.

"Pa!" Duncan's howl rattled the rafters. "You slippery old coot."

Shaking with glee, Papa shoved Duncan over and squeezed between them on the seat. When the laughter died, he slid his arms around both their shoulders and gave them a shake. "I won't have you two pounding on each other, you hear? Even with the chance it might knock some sense into you, it's flat wrong." He turned to Hooper, deep sadness in his eyes. "You're brothers." He switched his gaze to Duncan. "You'll always be brothers." Pushing off the bench, he stiffened his jaw and took a warrior's stance. "If you two come to blows again, I'll ask the both of you to leave. It won't matter who throws the first punch." He swallowed, his throat working hard. "So do me a favor, don't let it happen again."

Hooper bit his bottom lip. "Yes, sir. You have my word."

Duncan nodded. "Mine, too."

"Now you're talking." He offered them both a hand up. "How about giving an old codger a peaceful night's sleep? Shake on it like men."

Feeling foolish, Hooper made the first move.

Smiling shyly, Duncan took his hand and squeezed.

Meeting his brother's eyes with effort, Hooper returned his smile.

With a shout, Papa wrapped them in his arms like a charging grizzly. "There's the sons I raised. I knew I could count on you." He pounded on their backs with strength Hooper didn't know he had.

"I'll leave you boys to your work now. It's getting late. Finish up here and go to bed. I want you well along the road before the rooster crows."

Dawsey tossed aside the smothering weight of her comforter and flipped to her back. With her head propped on her arms, she could see past the mahogany footboard to the darkening window.

How odd to spend the day lolling beneath the covers when she wasn't sick. Yet "Shuck down and climb into bed" were Aunt Livvy's strict orders.

Dawsey's sigh produced a little hitch, the aftereffects of all her crying. She crossed her ankles and frowned at the high ceiling. Embarrassing hysterics had gained her no ground in the quest for truth. She'd wound up hoarse and puffy eyed but no wiser. It seemed profoundly unjust.

Her thoughts drifted to her father. By now, they'd trundled him off to his room, too—like a lad sent to bed without his supper.

Each evening, he'd start out in his four-poster bed, lying "meek-as-you-please" with the sheets drawn up to his chin. Each morning they found him in his study, dozing in a chair or standing with his nose pressed to the glass, staring out at the golden lamp.

She sighed. Always the lamp, glinting in the first muted rays of sunlight on the windowsill, a futile offering to his personal god of suffering.

Squinting at the ceiling, Dawsey riffled through the catalog of psalms she kept in her mind.

"Thou shalt increase my greatness, and comfort me on every side."

She let the ancient words sink in.

"Let, I pray thee, thy merciful kindness be for my comfort, according to thy word unto thy servant."

She touched her chin. So God's merciful kindness, which she found in abundant measure in His Word, was sufficient for her comfort?

Before she could settle on the right scripture to apply to her pain, the door opened with a squeal of hinges. "I heard you stirring, so I brought your supper."

Dawsey sat up and plumped the pillows at her back while her aunt slid the bed tray into position.

Despite the rousing *clink* and *rattle*, Aunt Livvy managed to unburden herself of her offering without sloshing a single drop from the delicate teacup. She stood and appraised the overflowing tray with a satisfied smile. "There now. Eat all of that, and you'll feel better."

Dawsey lifted the silver dome. "If I eat all of this, we'll need a wheelbarrow to cart me out."

Beaming, Aunt Livvy pointed. "Look under the saucer. It's your favorite."

Dawsey peeked beneath the china saucer, turned upside down over a steaming bowl of soup. The rich aroma of potatoes, onions, and butter swirled out on a puff of steam. "Umm. I love Winney's potato soup."

Aunt Livvy nodded. "Her spice cake, too. There's a slice for you under the napkin."

Cutting her eyes to her aunt, Dawsey cleared her throat. "Have I slept for three weeks? It's not Christmas, is it?"

Her smile too bright, Aunt Livvy perched on the side of the bed. "What do you mean, child? I don't need a special occasion to pamper my only niece."

Dawsey watched her closely. Furrowed brows and anxious, darting eyes gave her away. The thief caught red-handed. Moving the tray aside, she picked up her aunt's trembling hand. "I won't eat a bite until you tell me what this is about."

Aunt Livvy bit her lip and lowered her head.

Dawsey leaned to see her face. "You're keeping something from me, aren't you?" She waved at the tray. "All of this is because you feel guilty."

"Oh Dawsey." Aunt Livvy wadded her hands into fists and pressed them to her eyes. "I wish I could say something to make you feel better."

"Why can't you?"

"It's a secret, dear. And not mine to tell." She squirmed, twisting her skirt into knots. "I gave your father my word a long time ago."

Dawsey swung her legs over the side of the bed and gripped her aunt's trembling shoulders. "You must tell me, Auntie. So I'll know what to do for him."

Shifting her weight, Aunt Livvy turned her face to the wall and moaned. "I can't go back on my word. Please don't ask me."

Dawsey stared in disbelief. "Pain and grief are eating into Father's soul—destroying him—and you won't let me do one thing to help?"

Aunt Livvy lifted tortured eyes. "That's what you think? That heartache is killing him?" Dazed, she shook her head. "No dear. Neither pain nor grief has taken your father away from us." She paused, her eyes heavy with sadness. "It's hatred he battles, Dawsey. Pure, raw hatred has festered inside my brother for the last nineteen years of his life."

Ellie shivered on the porch in the gray dawn, watching Old Abe Lincoln, Pa's gelding, pull the buckboard up the lane. Her brothers didn't glance back or spare a wave, but why should they? They didn't know she hunkered there, pining to ride along.

"Where's your shawl, baby?"

The cool hand on Ellie's back startled her more than the sudden voice in her ear. She clutched her fists to her chest to settle her leaping heart. "You scared me silly, Mama."

"Guilty conscience?"

She snorted. "A body would need to live a little to have one of those. You and Papa don't give me the chance to be guilty of much."

Mama's chuckle hurled a white puff of mist in the air. "Be grateful. A sore conscience is hard to bear."

Ellie bent to read her face in the meager light. "Why do you carry the load for something Papa did? Your hands are clean."

She stepped forward and gripped the rail. "I allowed what he did to stand. Insisted on it, after a little time had passed."

"How could you have changed it?"

"I should've pressed him to go back to Fayetteville and turn himself in, made him do whatever it took to make it right."

Her head lowered so far, Ellie strained to hear.

"But I couldn't. Right or wrong, some things can't be undone."

The pain in her voice pierced Ellie's heart. "Was it so awful, Mama?

What he—what the two of you did?"

In a rush of emotion, Ma spun and gathered her close. "I wish I could tell you no, but I won't lie. What we done was plain awful."

Eager to comfort, Ellie slung her arms around her. "Hush now. Don't think about it if it makes you sad. It's a shame to be in such a state with the day not yet started."

Mama lifted her head and gazed over Ellie's shoulder. "It has started, I'm afraid. The sun's already over the horizon. In fact it's—"

She stiffened and pushed Ellie behind her just as Papa stepped onto the porch, his Winchester in the crook of his arm. "What do you want, mister?"

Scolding herself for letting the strange man catch them off guard, Ellie reached through the door and lifted her shotgun from the rack.

The uninvited visitor straightened in his saddle and cautiously lifted his hat. "Morning folks. There's no call for all that firepower. I come in peace."

Papa edged closer. "Slipping up so quietlike could get a man shot. Matter of fact, my trigger finger's twitching pretty bad." He jutted his chin. "What are you doing on our property?"

The dapper stranger smiled, slow and toothy.

Ellie stole a glance at his hands. "Might've known," she whispered to herself. "Never trust a man with back-bending thumbs."

"I have a message"—he leaned forward and lowered his voice, as if he and Pa shared a secret—"from Henry."

Pa never flinched. "Don't know any Henry. You got the wrong house."

Her pa was no fool. Henry always signaled first and never sent a grown man to their door. A messenger from Henry would be a woman carrying a tin cup, asking to borrow coffee beans. Or an Indian girl with a basket of corn on her head. Not a preening dandy reeking of foul play.

The man looked left then right, a smirk on his face. "The wrong house, huh?" He pushed back his hat with his thumb. "Well, I might consider that suggestion if there were rows of houses to choose from." His mocking smile widened. "But there aren't that many around, are there?"

Pa held his gun steady and didn't answer.

"So you claim you don't know Henry Lowry?" The dandy snickered. "You insult my intelligence, Mr. McRae." He craned his neck to peer through the door.

Papa took aim.

"Whoa there." He held up his hands. "I mean you no trouble. Just need a word with your boy, Hooper." He cleared his throat. "Unless you deny him, too."

Ellie's skin crawled and her mouth filled with sand.

Mama trembled beside her.

The Confederates had paid no attention to her brothers—seemed ignorant of their part in the resistance—until now.

The intruder didn't know Silas McRae well enough to hear the tension in his voice. Ellie heard, despite Pa's unruffled manner. He chuckled. "Best friends with Henry Lowry and acquainted with Hooper McRae, too? You get around some, don't you, mister? Considering those two don't wade the same ponds."

A hearty laugh exploded from the man. Wiping his eyes with his crooked thumb and forefinger, he gave Pa an amused grin. "Mr. McRae, I like you. Tell you what, let's get properly introduced." His saddle groaned as he leaned and stuck out his hand. "The name's—"

Pa advanced two more steps, cutting him off. "Not interested. I'll ask you to move on now. Give my regards to Sheriff McMillan."

The corner of his mouth twitched. "McMillan? The sheriff has no part in this."

"Mister, when you lie down with devils, you get up smelling of brimstone."

"Beg your pardon?"

"Won't do no good to beg. You'll get no pardon from me."

The mocking smile returned. "I'm offended, sir."

"You're offended?" Papa tilted his head. "You've got me standing on a drafty porch without my flannel drawers, and I think the wife's biscuits are burning. My daughter's teeth are clattering, but she won't lay down that shotgun and fetch her wrap until you head that filly's nose off my land."

Gathering his reins, the rascal sniffed. "In that case, I reckon I'll be on my way. It's plain I'm not wanted here."

Papa nodded. "You wore the welcome off your visit with the first lie you told. Now git."

Laughing, he tipped his hat, wheeled his horse, and trotted away.

Staring after him, Mama pushed down the barrel of Ellie's gun. "Cocky devil."

Dancing with impatience, Ellie waited until the stranger gained some distance then fumbled for her coat on the hook inside the door.

Mama frowned. "Where are you going, girl?"

"I have to warn the boys."

Papa clutched her arm. "Let them get to Fayetteville. They'll be safe there."

"That stranger may go after them," Ellie said, her voice shaking.

"If he knew where they were, he wouldn't have wasted time coming here."

Worry lined Mama's face. "Unless he came to throw us off while his men set up an ambush."

Papa flinched and his eyes widened. "You're out-thinking me this morning, wife. These woods could be crawling with snakes just like him."

"That's it." Ellie leaped off the porch. "I'm going to find my brothers."

Pa shouted her name.

Blowing an impatient breath, she turned. "Let me go. Time's wasting."

"Not so fast," he said, rubbing his chin. "The way I see it, we have two problems. We've got to make sure the boys are all right, and we need to get word to Henry."

Worrying his bottom lip with his teeth, he met her eyes. "I'm afraid you'll have to do both, Ellie. You're the only one who can slip through unnoticed."

She moved again, but he held up his hand to stay her. "Hear me out, girl. First, scout the situation with Hooper and Duncan. If they're in trouble, you'll know what to do. Once you're certain they're safe, slip away without them knowing you were there. If they suspect something's wrong, they'll turn back and ride into danger."

She nodded.

"Be careful," Mama called, wringing her hands.

Papa reached to comfort her, his burning gaze still on Ellie. "If all is well with the boys, hustle out to Henry's place and tell him what happened here today. Maybe he can shed light on what we're dealing with." He cast an angry scowl up the lane. "And who."

He barely finished talking before Ellie spun and bolted for the barn. She rode so hard her formerly chattering teeth rattled. She'd ridden Toby so often through the marshy woods, the young gelding seemed to know the way by heart. Rounding hawthorn brush and leaping quicksand bogs with hardly a nudge from the reins, he made quick work of catching up to the wagon carrying her brothers.

Ellie winced at how easy it was to find them. Old Abe Lincoln's unmistakable *clop*, along with the *creak* and *rattle* of the wagon, echoed so loudly through the trees the boys might as well have been shouting and pounding drums.

Eyes alert to any movement, ears attuned to every sound, she rode a few yards ahead and slipped off her horse. Ducking between thick poplar trunks and woody vines, she belly-crawled the last few feet, in time to watch the rig rattle past.

Hooper held the reins, eyes fixed on the road ahead. Duncan sang a quiet ditty, one foot propped on the front rail, the other keeping time with his song. He leaned to speak to Hooper, his words lost in all the noise, but Hooper's laughter boomed, rousing a nearby covey of quail.

She longed to leap from cover and chase them down, slap her hand over his mouth to quiet him. Remembering Pa's stern warning, she held her ground. She followed in the brush for close to a mile, watching the foggy tree line for movement and scanning the road for turkey blinds. A hastily constructed blind could mean an ambush at best. At worst, a stealthy shot between the eyes.

Knowing she'd taken far too long from her other task, Ellie hunkered in the bushes and watched the buckboard shrink to a wobbly speck in the distance. Papa said if all was well, she should hustle to Henry's house. Thankfully, all seemed well.

She found her horse where she'd left him and swung into the saddle. Leaning to pat his neck, she whispered in his ear. "If you get me to the Lowrys' as fast as you got me here, I'll steal you a nice juicy apple."

Toby must've understood. He wound his way along much the same track he'd come, only this time tighter and faster. Ellie reined him away from the trail home with its promise of pilfered apples and urged him into the dank, murky mists of Bear Swamp.

Long past the point where most folks dared to go, the track grew so muddy and dense, Toby's clumsy gait slowed her down. She tied him to an island of Doghobble shrub and continued toward Henry and Rhoda's cabin on foot.

She couldn't remember a single instance when she'd made it to the front door unchallenged. This time was no different. The soft *crunch* of leaves said she had company.

The dim figure of a man appeared in the corner of her right eye, and she froze midstep. Heart pounding, she waited. By the time he reached her, gun drawn, three others had sidled up behind him.

"She's all right," a soft voice called from the shadows. "Take that gun out of her face."

Warmth washed over Ellie at the sight of Boss Strongambling toward her. Boss, Rhoda Lowry's younger brother and Henry's second-in-command sported lighter skin and shorter hair than most Scuffletown men, not counting Duncan. In the sunlight, his dark waves had an auburn cast like the hair of his sideburns and the soft curling tuffs around his lip. Sweet faced and quiet, Boss could turn mean at the nod of Henry's head.

She released her breath. "Hello there."

"Ellie McRae." He flashed a gentle smile and hugged her neck. "How are things up your way?"

"Not good. I need to see Henry."

His brows crowded together. "Trouble?"

She nodded.

"Henry's up at the cabin. Follow me." Barely out of his teens, but a better man than most, he pushed past his men and led her through the twisted brush to Henry's weathered shanty.

Chapter 8

Dawsey's heart leaped in her chest.

The boy, Tiller, stood beneath the window of Father's den with the gold lantern in his hands. Staring with rounded eyes, he held it above his head, turning it this way and that to catch the light.

She jabbed his shoulder. "Put it back!"

Tiller jumped as if she'd popped him with a dishrag. The lantern flew into the air, but he caught it before it hit the ground, juggling a bit to regain control. Scrambling to the ledge, he replaced the lamp, working with shaking fingers to restore its balance.

"Just what do you think you're doing?"

He turned, his bottom lip protruding and his arms harmlessly crossed. "I didn't hurt it none. Wanted to see it up close, is all."

Breathing hard, she pushed past to stand between him and the window. "Did you have a good look? Because it will be your last." She pointed over his shoulder. "You may take your leave. And don't bother coming back."

Fury darkened his face. "Suits me fine, since I planned on quitting today anyway." He shoved out his hand. "You owe me three dollars."

"Three whole dollars? For what?"

He hitched up his pants and scowled. "A sore back and a passel of blisters."

Dawsey gave him a sideways look. "My aunt's not here at the moment. Come around later, and she'll decide your wages for you then."

His bottom jaw jutted to the side. "Uh-uh." Stubbornly shaking his head, his hand shot out farther. "I need it now."

She jammed her fists on her hips. "Why do you need it so soon?"

"To buy food for me and Ma. We ain't got nothing to eat."

Dawsey twisted her mouth and squinted. "Are you telling the truth?"

He squinted right back and nodded.

"And your father?"

"Dead."

She winced.

"Last May," he said. "Consumption."

"I'm awfully sorry." She sighed, sympathy and regret tugging at her heart. "All right, meet me out front in five minutes."

She turned on her heel and started for the back door. Thinking better of her trusting nature, she stalked back and snatched the lamp. Trying to look as fierce as possible, she leaned close to his face. "If anything ever happens to this lantern, I'll know you're the culprit. You understand that, don't you?"

He smirked and ducked his head.

Dawsey gripped the front of his collar and forced his chin up. "I'll find you, wherever you are. I'll sic the dogs on you. Am I clear?"

The cocky swagger disappeared. He swallowed hard and nodded. "What use would I have for the dusty old thing?"

"Don't bother trying to figure it out." She thumped his ear. "Just keep your hands off."

He clutched his reddening ear and howled. Pulling away from her, he rounded the house, still mumbling under his breath.

Fishing the jangling key ring from her bodice, she made her way to the back door. On the stoop, she slipped the key into the lock and entered the hall. Smiling in anticipation, she hurried into the brightly lit kitchen. Winney's stove smelled of bread and cast a warm glow over the cheeriest room in the house.

Dawsey fought the urge to roll up her sleeves and bake something. No matter the dish, elbow-deep in mixing, stirring, or kneading were the only times she felt at peace.

Winney grinned over her shoulder. "Saw them pretty sweet potatoes in the larder. I told Levi we ain't to touch 'em. They must be for Christmas dinner." She turned, smiling. "What you aiming on making, missy? Sure do hope it's your special bread."

Returning her smile, Dawsey winked. "How'd you guess?"

Winney cackled, her dark cheeks round with glee. "It's the colonel's favorite, that's how."

Dawsey lifted the towel draped over a row of bread pans and poked her finger into one. The soft dough sank in, leaving a small dent in the loaf. "Speaking of bread, we can't possibly eat this much. Why do you make so many?"

Winney clutched the front of her apron. "My old mama taught me to bake, Miss Dawsey. She cooked for her masta's family all her life. Six boys amongst his brood, and they was always hungry." She hung her head. "I tried cuttin' the recipe in half, but that don't always turn out right."

Dawsey motioned at the loaves. "So where does all of this wind up?"

Winney brightened. "Oh, I puts it to real good use. I bake some hot and fresh for supper then slice a loaf for breakfast next day. I toast extra and keep a mess for crumbs to coat my fried chicken." She touched her bottom lip. "Oh, and I shred a loaf for baking." She grinned. "Where you reckon all that bread pudding you like comes from?"

Dawsey crossed to pat her shoulder. "I'd call that thrifty thinking." She motioned at the pans. "But that still won't make use of all this."

"Well. . ." Winney ducked her head again. "The rest I wrap up and send off to Widow Douglas." She blinked. "And Widow Gilchrist."

Stunned, Dawsey studied her glowing face. "You do that, Winney?"

Winney squirmed, one of her plain leather shoes turning inward. "Yes'm, I do. I sure hope you don't mind."

"Mind?" Dawsey leaned to hug her. "On the contrary. It's a lovely gesture."

Levi opened the door into the front hall. "Miss Dawsey, there's a boy dancing a jig on the porch. Never saw the like for fidgeting. He say he's waiting for money."

"Oh my goodness, Winney. Your kitchen has cast a spell and robbed me of my senses." She lifted her chin at Levi. "Tell him I'll be along shortly."

Levi held the door, and she scurried through.

Dashing to Father's den, she stopped outside and knocked. No answer came, as she expected. He never answered.

She entered, surprised to find no sign of him, and hustled to his desk. Reaching inside the shadowy hutch, she opened the bottom drawer where Aunt Livvy kept the household funds. If the cashbox was locked, Tiller would have to wait until morning. Dawsey didn't have a key.

Lifting out the small silver box, she tried the lid. It stuck a bit at first then popped open. Lucky for Tiller.

Dawsey counted out three dollars' worth of coins and dropped them into her pocket. She reached to close the lid when a curiosity caught her eye and stopped her cold. Bending closer, she peered inside the box.

The tip of a yellowed slip of paper peeked out from what appeared to be a false bottom. She pinched and tugged, pulling out the wrinkled square.

Two ragged edges and two straight meant that someone had torn the snippet from the top corner of a writing tablet. In the center, smudged but legible, a single word was written.

On closer inspection, she realized the writer hadn't merely scrawled the word but dug it into the paper with great force, as if spelling it out in a fit of passion.

In a rage perhaps?

She turned it over and stared at the inked word, bled through, upside down and backward.

McRae.

Was it a name?

She jumped and clutched the paper to her chest as the door squealed open behind her. "Levi! Please knock next time."

"Sorry missy. Didn't mean to spook you." He hooked his thumb behind him. "Only that boy outside's in a frightful hurry about somethin' and he's gettin' mighty antsy."

Her heart still pounding, Dawsey's charitable mood slipped. "Well, he can be patient if he wants his money."

Levi frowned. "He don't seem to have much patience. No manners either, and that's a fact."

The sympathy she'd felt for Tiller returned in a rush. "I suppose he's afraid I won't pay, and he needs his wages awfully bad. Go tell him I'll be right along."

Levi turned to go, but Dawsey lifted her finger. "Have Winney wrap a few loaves of bread to send with him, along with a jar of blackberry jam. Tell her to add the boy's mother to her list. She's the Widow—"

She lifted her brows. "Goodness, I don't know his family name."

Levi nodded vigorously, looking pleased to be of service. "Well, I do. It's McRae."

Dawsey's fingers closed around the slip of paper in her hand. "What did you say?"

"I said McRae." Still grinning, he backed out of the door. "His name be Tiller McRae."

There were no fellow travelers along the quiet stretch of road for Hooper to tip a hat to or bid a good day. Most Scuffletown folks avoided a wagon ride to Lumberton by hopping the train into Moss Neck every Saturday to lay in supplies for the week. A shame really, since the trip was so pleasant.

They wouldn't see Lumberton proper. Duncan snickered and called it a needless precaution, but Hooper planned to slip past without showing themselves. With a sigh of satisfaction, he leaned against the seat and propped the heel of his boot on the dash.

Beside him, Duncan gazed into the distance, grinning like a dolt.

The silly smile was catching, tickling the corners of Hooper's mouth. He nudged his brother from his thoughts. "What's so funny?"

Duncan's grin widened. "Just thinking about our rear guard. What you reckon Ellie was up to, skulking about in the brush?"

Hooper chuckled. "There's an easy answer. She sorely wanted to join us, so she tagged along as far as possible without setting off Pa's temper."

"You think she followed us the whole way?"

"Sure she did. Ellie could tail us clear to Fayetteville and never be spotted. She's a fine tracker." He jutted his chin. "I taught her myself."

"Ha!" This time Duncan nudged him. "Except we did spot her."

Hooper frowned. "She got careless this time. Left in such a hurry, she assumed we weren't watching our backs. I'll have to teach her to be more careful."

Duncan gazed toward Chicken Road, an ugly scowl replacing his smile. "Then teach her to be less like you before she gets her head shot off."

Familiar irritation crowded Hooper's throat. "That's senseless talk. Learning to survive in the swamp will keep her head where it belongs."

Duncan faced him and blew out a breath. "Ellie watches your every move, Hooper. I fear she'll follow your reckless path to an early grave."

Frustration from years of constant tugging with Duncan swelled Hooper's chest. "Ellie and the rest have no problem with who I am. Why do you have to be different?" He leaned toward Duncan and raised one brow. "But then, you always were the odd duck, right, brother?"

Duncan stilled and shrank in the seat.

Hooper felt bad for goading him, but the boy stuck out like a chokecherry on a cornstalk.

Shorter than Hooper, he had a wide, stocky build where Pa and Hooper were narrow at the hips and broad shouldered. He sported pale gray eyes under busy brows, and his hair tended toward light brown. Unlike the warm, toasted skin of the other McRae men, Duncan's legs were pale where the sun never shined.

The outside trappings were only half the story. Inside, he was nothing like a McRae. Duncan marked these differences and they bothered him something fierce.

Guilt settled over Hooper's heart. "What I mean to say is you're the sensible one in the family. Without you around to corral me, Pa, and Ellie, I suppose Ma would pack up and leave home." He patted Duncan's rigid back. "Speaking of Ellie, don't worry. With Henry and Boss watching the swamp, we left her in capable hands."

Ma always said men were like candy. Past the crackle and crunch, most had mushy, sweet insides. Some were taffy and needed a bit of stretching to turn out right. Others were toffee, nice but a bit hard to manage. She warned Ellie to cut a wide swath around the pralines, dainties that fell apart under pressure, and the brittles, nutty with sharp edges.

Henry Berry Lowry was a chocolate buckeye kiss. Soft enough to yield, but never dainty. Firm, yet far from brittle, Henry was the finest, bravest, most handsome man Scuffletown had ever turned out.

Ellie watched him from under her lashes as they drew near the cabin. He sat on the lopsided porch, a king in woolen overalls and a faded beehive hat.

She took care not to watch too closely because Rhoda, his Scottish-Indian queen, perched at his side. She caught Ellie's eye and nodded.

Henry stirred and dipped his head.

Boss urged her forward then slipped away to resume his watch.

Henry's legend was far reaching. Brave men quivered like pork jelly in his presence. As he leaned forward, gracing her with a sunny smile, fear was the last thing on her mind. "What brings you?" A man of sparse words, his voice oozed like melted wax—despite his straight back and tense shoulders. Even surrounded by his army, letting his guard down for a second could cost him his life.

"A stranger came around this morning asking for Hooper." Saying the words aloud bumped her heart into motion. "Claimed he had a message from you."

Interest flickered in Henry's eyes. "Militia?"

"Not sure. Papa has him lumped with Sheriff McMillan, but he hopes you know something different." She shifted her weight to the other foot and glanced toward home as if she saw it through the trees. "The sneaky devil slipped up on us."

"He come alone?"

She nodded.

Henry arched his brow. "Don't mean he was. Did he mention Duncan?"

She shook her head.

Henry gnawed on his cheek. "Silas worried?"

"Pa has sorely dreaded this day," she said. "Once they link a man's name with the resistance, he don't last long in Robeson County. Up to now, they've been so careful, but I'm afraid their lives may never be the same." Why was she chattering like a rousted squirrel? Unclenching her fists, she drew a breath, embarrassed when her nostrils flared.

"Hooper got away then?" Henry asked.

"He wasn't home."

Frowning, he leaned to study her face. "I sent them there."

"They came, all right." She shuffled her feet. "But a family matter called them away."

Nodding thoughtfully, Henry picked up a river birch twig and ran it sideways through his lips.

Rhoda uncrossed her legs and stood. "You must be cold. I'll fetch some scuppernong wine."

Ellie's breath caught in her throat. "Umm. . .thank you, ma'am, but—"

"Ellie's folks don't allow strong drink, honey. Brew a pot of sassafras tea." His eyes, always tender when they lit on his wife, tracked Rhoda to the door.

She stepped through the shadowed entry and disappeared.

Ellie thought back to July when the Guard captured Rhoda and held her hostage in the Lumberton Jail. The Wilmington *Morning Star* printed the warning that Robeson County had "aroused the lion."

They were right.

Henry, who never breathed an idle threat, sent word to the county commissioners to release Rhoda or he would capture their women and carry them off to the swamp. He added that they wouldn't be so eager to return.

Rhoda was on the next train home.

Henry stirred, drawing Ellie from her ponderings. She glanced up and he motioned.

"Come. Sit."

She closed the gap and settled on the edge of the steps. Rhoda's black cat peeked from beneath the porch then glided in and out through her legs, mewing softly.

"The woods may not be safe just now." Henry grinned. "Even for you."

Ellie glowed from his praise.

"We'll have our tea then Boss will see you home. Before nightfall, your pa will know who came sniffing around your place."

Relief flooded her limbs. "Thank you, Henry. For this and for being so good to my family."

He gazed over her head, his eyes bright with pain. "They've made it a crime for a man to take up arms in defense of his own." Grief sagged his cheeks, smudging charcoal circles under his dark lashes and etching deep grooves between his brows. "I'll be tried and sent to the gallows for what they claim as a right."

An ache swelled Ellie's heart, and she choked back a sob.

Henry ran his hands over his handsome face from forehead to chin, blotting out the ugliness of sorrow in one fell swipe. His eyes softened, and a smile rounded his cheeks. "I suppose if they catch me, I'll meet the hangman without benefit of a trial."

Ellie lifted her chin. "They won't catch you."

His gaze swung her way so fast she sucked air. Wiggly hairs danced on her arms, but she resisted the need to squirm and watched him.

His hand slid to the gun belt slung over his shoulder, determination churning his blue gray eyes. "You're right about that, little girl. They never will."

CHAPTER 10

Dawsey argued with herself on the way to the door, Tiller's three dollars clutched in her hand. What good would it do to ask the boy about the slip of paper? The chance that he or his mother had something to do with the scribbled name in Father's cashbox seemed ludicrously slim.

Still. . . Coincidence or not, there were a few things to clear up, and Tiller McRae could be the very one to ask.

Dawsey spied him through the front window, slouched against the porch rail with one foot cocked behind him on the slats. Muttering to himself and impatiently tugging the brim of his hat, he held the wrapped loaves Winney had given him under one arm.

Drawing a deep breath, Dawsey opened the door.

At the sight of her, his hand jerked to his thumped ear. Then he straightened and wiped his nose with the back of his hand. "About time, if you don't mind my saying."

She drew up to full height and squared her shoulders. "As a matter of fact, I do mind. That's no way to speak to your elders."

Easy, Dawsey. You need to gain his favor.

She relaxed and smoothed her skirt. "However, I do apologize for keeping you so long."

Ignoring her apology, his customary frown deepened. "You don't look like no elder to me."

Dawsey huffed. "Then look again. I happen to be the mistress of this household."

Aunt Livvy's face loomed, pulling her down a notch. "Well, practically. Besides, anyone older than you is your elder. I certainly qualify."

He jutted his chin. "How old are you?"

She wiggled a warning finger. "You must never inquire of a lady's age."

Tiller shrugged and stuck out a grimy palm. "Suit yourself. I'll take that money off your hands now."

Dawsey drew the jingling coins out of his reach. "Not so fast." She summoned a winsome smile. "I thought we'd have a nice chat first."

Suspicion darkened his eyes. "Chats are for grannies at tea parties. I know you ain't that long in the tooth." He scowled. "Are you planning to pay me or not?"

She extended her open hand. "Certainly."

"That's more like it. I've wasted too much time here already." He scooped up his wages and spun to go.

Dawsey latched onto his arm. "Of course you have. What with you being the man of the house now. Your mother must be as proud as a peacock. I suppose she counts on you for everything."

His tense body eased. Shifting the bread to his other arm, he tucked the thumb of his free hand around his suspenders. "That she does, ma'am, that she does."

"And you shoulder the burden alone? With no family to call on?"

A thoughtful look crossed his face. "Well there's Ma's brother, Uncle William, for all the good he does. He can't tell corn from oats." He tapped his temple. "Soft in the head. Come back from the war that way. Old codger slumps in a corner all day, whittling Union soldiers and catching them afire."

"Oh Tiller, I'm so sorry to hear it."

He shrugged and grinned. "Don't be sorry. Uncle Willy don't realize the state he's in."

"So you're the only McRaes left in Fayetteville?"

His bare nod and tight lips wouldn't do. Dawsey needed to draw out more information, but she'd fare better pulling teeth.

"Have you always lived here in town?"

Another nod.

She hid her clenched fists behind her back. "Where does your family hail from?"

He squinted. "Don't know what you're asking."

"McRae. It sounds Gaelic. Are your ancestors Scottish?"

He pulled away. "Say, what's all this? I've never worked harder for a measly few dollars."

"Whatever do you mean?"

"Why are you drilling me?"

"I'm sorry. I didn't mean to pry. I'm concerned about your mother's welfare, that's all. With her shortage of help, she's quite lucky to have you."

The suspicion in his eyes dimmed, and his chest swelled like a turkey's. "You speak the truth, ma'am. Can't see how she'll manage without me."

Dawsey cocked her head. "Are you going somewhere?"

"Reckon I am."

Her mind soared to the poor Widow McRae, left alone and destitute. She patted the boy's thin shoulder. "Well, don't you fret. We'll look after her while you're gone."

He grinned, spreading the freckles on his cheeks. "That's mighty Christian of you, ma'am."

"And you can forget what I said earlier about not coming back to work. Your job will be waiting when you return."

He stuck out his bottom lip. "Won't be returning. I'm leaving town for good."

Dawsey's brows shot to the vaulted eaves. "How can you leave for good? Your mother needs you."

"Too bad she don't have sense enough to know it."

Reams of information lurked in the pain shining from his eyes. Dawsey longed to draw him out, but she didn't have the time.

"Who'll be left to care for her?"

His scowl darkened. "She wanted shed of me, didn't she? I reckon she'll have to fend for herself."

Dawsey rested gentle fingers along his jaw. "Where are you going?"

He pulled away. "To live with my uncle Silas."

Her heartbeat quickened. "Would that be Silas McRae?"

"How'd you know?"

"Only a guess. Where does this uncle live?"

He scratched his head. "Come to think on it, I never heard nobody say."

"You're going to stay with family, but you're not even sure where they live?"

"Don't know and don't care, as long as I can get out of here." He gazed around with flashing eyes and tugged on his baggy trousers. "Yes, sir. I'm on the way to better things than Fayetteville, North Carolina. Can't wait to see what's around the bend." Despite the false posturing, fear lurked on the edge of his broad smile.

"When do you leave?" she asked softly.

He shrugged. "They'll be fetching me soon. That's all I need to know."

"Your uncle Silas said this?"

"Nah. He never answered Ma's letter."

"Then how do you know they'll come?"

He jutted his lips and nodded. "They'll be here. Ma says Uncle Silas won't dare rile her with all he has at stake."

Dawsey's stomach tensed. "What did she mean?"

"Who knows?" He sniffed. "Old folks' ways are too knotty for me to cipher."

She opened her mouth to question him further, but Aunt Livvy's carriage rattled up the lane, stopping in front of the house. Levi scurried down from the driver's seat to open the door, but he was too slow. Aunt Livvy stood outside the carriage smoothing her skirts before his feet ever hit the ground.

"There you are, Dawsey," she said. "You saved me the breath to call you. Help me with these porcelain dishes, dear. I don't dare trust Levi. Such delicate pieces require a woman's careful touch."

Dawsey hurried forward. "Certainly Auntie."

Aunt Livvy unpinned her hat and tossed it on the seat. "Bring that insufferable contraption, too, will you?" She glared at the tall, feathered cap. "I can't imagine what the milliner lines his hats with these days. The silly thing makes my head sweat in the dead of winter." She started up the walk, wiggling her finger at Tiller. "Stand there, boy. I'll bring your wages."

Dawsey gathered the bundles and closed the carriage door. "It's all right, dear. I've paid him."

Aunt Livvy cocked one brow. "Oh?" Pulling on the fingers of her gloves, she continued for the house. "Very well. Did you mark a dollar off the ledger?"

Tiller hustled off the porch and down the brick path, but Dawsey moved in front of him, blocking his way with the packages. "One dollar, Auntie? Not three?"

Aunt Livvy chuckled over her shoulder. "What fool would shell out three dollars for weeded flower beds?"

Stopping short, she slowly turned. "Dawsey, you didn't."

Dawsey's gaze flashed to Tiller. "Why, you deceitful little—"

He bolted, knocking Aunt Livvy's packages from Dawsey's grasping hands. The delicate chinaware landed at her feet with the *crash* of broken glass. As the scoundrel ran, he lost his hold on the wrapped loaves. The bread fell, rolling end over end across the yard. Weaving side to side, he snatched them up at a dead run then streaked across the lane.

Dawsey watched until he ducked into the woods and disappeared.

"Go after him, Levi," Aunt Livvy shrieked.

Levi hitched up his britches and poised to sprint.

Dawsey caught his arm and hauled him around. "Leave him be."

Her aunt stalked to where they stood. "What are you saying?"

"Let it go, Auntie. What can you do to that wretched boy any worse than what fate has dealt him?"

"I'll take back the two dollars he stole." She waved her arms in a frantic circle over the broken dishes. "I'll make him pay for this damage."

Dawsey shook her head. "You'll squeeze precious few pennies from him, dear. He simply doesn't have it. Anything you manage to get will only pluck food from a poor widow's mouth." Taking her arm, Dawsey gently led her toward the house. "Let's forget about him, shall we? They need that two dollars worse than we do, so let them have it."

She glanced in the direction the boy had gone and sighed. "After today, young Tiller McRae's shenanigans will be someone else's problem."

Basking in the glow of Henry's company, and especially his flattering remark, Ellie allowed Boss and his men to shepherd her home. The family liked to brag on Ellie's knack for vanishing in plain sight, but knowing Henry took note of her skill swelled her heart to bursting.

Yes, Henry had called her "little girl," an offensive term another man would swiftly regret, but his tone was free of teasing or haughty airs. The warmth in his voice and the fire of shared passion turned the simple words to sweet gum sap, binding their wounded hearts.

Ellie smiled to herself in the darkness. Wyatt Carter had once called her "little girl," but she hadn't minded then either. The fire in his eyes when he said it had little to do with the zeal of a shared cause.

Henry Lowry was a chocolate buckeye kiss, but he was Rhoda's kiss. Ellie knew Wyatt was destined to be hers. No man quickened her heartbeat or dried her throat the way he did. The music in his voice was livelier than the strumming of Pa's banjo, and the way he spoke her name was as close to a man's caress as she had yet to know. She spent hours pondering the challenge shining from Wyatt's dark-eyed glances.

Boss whipped his horse into a thicket. "This way."

The hoarse whisper pulled Ellie from her guilty thoughts in time to rein Toby sharply into the scrub behind Boss and the others. The warmth of Henry's confidence in her faded to a scalding vat of dishonor. Angry with herself for mooning when she should be watching, Ellie scoured her surroundings for a glimpse at what had forced them deeper into the swamp. Though she heard rather than saw them, it didn't take long to find out.

A band of riders passed behind them on the road, doing a pitiful job of keeping quiet. Six, maybe eight horses, if she counted the hoofbeats right. She'd bet her last dollar the cocky man who came asking about Hooper rode with them.

Boss reined up and motioned at two of his men. They split off to tail the riders, careful to keep a healthy portion of trees between themselves and the strangers. Without a backward glance, Boss skillfully led Ellie and the rest away from the intruders. None spoke a word until they reached the edge of her yard and heard Pa's answering whistle.

They broke through the trees, and he hurried to meet them, flashing a welcoming grin. "Look what the hound dragged in."

Boss laughed and swung his leg over the saddle. "I admit I'm as gaunt as a gnawed bone, Silas, but I hope you ain't calling Ellie a dog. She's way too pretty for that."

Turning away to hide her blush, Ellie slid to the ground. "He knows better, Boss. I'd skin his wrinkled ears."

The men laughed uproariously, worsening Ellie's embarrassment. Thankfully, they turned their attention to more serious matters.

Boss laid a sympathetic hand on Papa's arm. "I hear they're sniffing around after Hooper."

A shadow crossed Papa's face. "I knew this day had to come. Thought I'd be ready." He raised sad eyes to Boss. "I thought wrong."

"You reckon your uninvited guest was sent out here by the sheriff?"

Pa snorted. "I did right at first. Now, I'd put my money on bounty hunters."

Frowning, Boss spat on the ground. "Vultures. Lining their pockets with the flesh of innocent men." He looked up with a light in his eyes.

"Don't worry, Silas. The situation's bad but not hopeless. Hoop will have to leave home to stay alive, but he will stay alive."

Ellie touched his arm. "Where will he go?"

"He can join us at the cabin. Henry's told him a dozen times he's welcome to hide out with us in Bear Swamp."

Papa grimaced. "The most dangerous place in Scuffletown is at Henry's side. At the same time, it's the safest. Don't make sense, does it?"

Boss laughed softly and gave Pa's shoulder a shake. "Henry would lay down his life to keep Hooper out of harm's way." He motioned toward his men. "Any one of us would."

Tears moistened Papa's eyes. "I reckon I know that."

Ellie dreaded asking but had to know. "What about Duncan?"

Pa's sorrowful look broke her heart.

"Duncan won't leave, honey. No matter how dire the risk, he'll dig in his heels here at home."

Tugging on his bottom lip, Boss stared toward town. "Silas, they'll come and blast him right out the front door."

"Boss,"—a grim look aged Papa's haggard face—"I'm afraid they'll have to."

Under cover of darkness, slipping into Fayetteville unseen was a simple task. Even the silvery slip of a moon lent a hand, casting meager beams to light their path. Hooper kept to the back roads, skirting the town square and more crowded streets, until they crossed the bridge over Cool Spring near the old mill.

Past the graveyard, as gloomy and misty as he remembered as a child, Hooper turned the buckboard down the narrow lane to Uncle Sol's place. As pleased as the plodding horse must be to see the outline of the barn in the distance, Hooper was more grateful to see flickering lights behind the thin curtains.

He felt a stab of sadness when he realized Uncle Sol wouldn't be greeting them with his rousing laughter and booming voice. The house and all its memories now belonged to Aunt Effie—a woman he couldn't recall, no matter how he tried—and her wayward seed, their scalawag cousin, Reddick McRae.

Hooper grinned at the thought of his troublesome relation, the sole reason for their unscheduled journey. He figured a spell wallowing in Scuffletown's mud and trouble would smooth young Reddick's ruffled feathers.

From what Hooper could make out in the dusky moonlight, the ramshackle dwelling had fallen into serious disrepair. It appeared the roof buckled in places. The windows sagged. A felled tree blocked the broken brick path, and no one had bothered to cut it away.

Pa had taught them to always park the rig facing the way out so they'd be ready for a quick getaway should the need arise. Hooper made a sweeping circle in Aunt Effie's front yard and set the brake. Leaning over, he shook Duncan awake.

He came up sputtering with ready fists.

Laughing, Hooper punched his arm. "Keep it down, you dolt. You'll get us shot." Watching the house for movement, he lowered his stiff body to the ground.

Grumbling his displeasure, Duncan eased down on the other side. He joined Hooper at the tailgate, blinking to focus his bleary eyes. "Hasn't changed much, has it?"

Hooper gaped at him. "Are you still asleep? Look again. The place is falling down." He gazed at the entrance and sighed. "The biggest change is the worst, I'm afraid. We won't find Uncle Sol behind that door." He glanced at Duncan. "Do you remember Aunt Effie at all?"

"I think she was sort of loud."

A piercing scream from inside the house brought them up off the ground. A startled look passed between them before they hurdled the downed tree and lit out for the porch.

Hooper teetered on his toes, one hand on the knob, the other poised to knock, when a string of angry curses poured from within the house. Foul threats and ugly promises scorched his ears, aimed at a poor soul named Tiller.

Blushing at the bad language, especially distasteful in a woman's voice, Hooper raised his brows. "It appears she's gotten louder. What do we do?"

Duncan shrugged.

Gritting his teeth, Hooper pounded hard enough to be heard over the ruckus.

Without a break in her rant, the woman's screaming voice approached the door. ". . .then I'll split your lousy skull with my broom and won't bother to mop up the mess, you wretched. . ." The door jerked open with a boisterous *rattle*. "What the devil do you want?"

Hooper caught the vague impression of large bare feet, wide hips, and a tall wispy bun atop a broad, sloping forehead. The face below the glaring eyes was mottled and red.

"Don't stand there with your tongue in your mouth," she shrilled. "I asked you a question."

Duncan took a backward step.

Hooper jerked off his hat, wishing it was big enough to hide behind. Clutching it tightly in his fists, he cleared his throat and tried to answer. "Ma'am, we—"

"How dare you knock at a decent widow's house at this hour." She squinted. "You'd best have a stinking good reason."

Not sure she'd find their reason good, stinking or otherwise, Hooper retreated to join Duncan.

Jerking her head to the side, she fixed them with bulging eyes. "Wait a minute. You boys are McRaes, ain't you?"

Hooper cleared his throat. "Yes ma'am, we. . .um, Aunt Effie?"

"Took you long enough. I'm ready to string up your no-account cousin." She spun on her heel and left them on the porch, as if rattling hinges was an invitation to enter.

Hooper shot Duncan a knowing glance. "Uncle Sol didn't die. He escaped."

Duncan poked him in the side. "Lower your voice or we'll join him."

Pointing past the entrance, Hooper grunted. "Look's like we turned up just in time to help that poor fellow make a getaway."

Every ounce of Scottish blood still residing in the McRaes had found its way into the skinny, freckled body lurking in a corner across the room, his face the image of Uncle Sol.

Elbowing his way closer, Duncan stared. "That's Reddick?"

"Has to be."

"Then who's Tiller?"

"Not sure." Hooper grinned. "I'm just glad it's not me."

Aunt Effie swept past in a huff. "Why are you still outside? Get in here. You're letting in the cold."

Flinching, Hooper stepped cautiously past the threshold, a reluctant Duncan in tow.

Aunt Effie had disappeared, likely to the kitchen, given the rattle of pots and pans coming from the other room.

The slender lad in the corner stood, wiping his hands on his pants. "Are you two my cousins?"

Hooper nodded. "That's right. You Reddick?"

The boy hitched up his sagging britches. "Name's Tiller."

"No it ain't!" Aunt Effie bawled from the other room. "It's Reddick, like you said."

Reddick's back straightened and he scowled. "I won't answer to it."

Stepping closer, Hooper offered his hand. "Nice to know you, Tiller."

Duncan winked at him. "Tiller, huh? What sort of name is that?"

Aunt Effie appeared in the doorway, drying a plate with her grimy apron. "It ain't no name at all. Folks call him that on account of he's right good with the soil." She sneered at her son. "This silly thing took a shine to it."

Hooper shot him a sympathetic look. "How old are you, son?"

"Sixteen."

His mama cackled. "No he ain't."

Red faced, he whirled on her so fast he nearly dropped his drawers. "Almost, and you know it."

"You're barely fifteen." She sneered then grinned at Hooper. "Don't believe him. His birthday's in May."

Hooper squeezed Tiller's shoulder. "Five more months, huh? You're better than halfway there." He beamed at the upturned freckled face. "I reckon that counts."

The deep lines between the boy's brows relaxed, and the hint of a smile lit his eyes. He opened his mouth to speak, but whatever he was about to say was lost when his mama caught his arm and propelled him toward the kitchen.

"Get in there and finish those dishes. Then go pack your things. You don't want to keep your cousins waiting."

Color drained from Duncan's face. With a smattering of freckles, his complexion would match Tiller's. He lifted a faltering hand. "Ah. . . Aunt Effie? I mean, well, we've just ridden an awfully long way. We're hungry and—"

Her bug-eyed glare closed his mouth. "Leave it to Silas McRae." Each syllable rose in pitch until McRae came out a sharp bellow. "He's supposed to take Tiller off my hands. Has he sent me two more mouths to feed instead?" Fuming, she flapped her dish towel. "I don't have food enough for my own empty stomach. Nor for Tiller's. How can I be expected to fill yours?"

Duncan gulped like a catfish but made no sound.

Hooper pushed him aside. "Don't fret, ma'am. We're not here to eat." Ignoring the added shock on Duncan's face, he flashed a winsome smile. "All we need is shelter for our horse, and a few oats if you can spare them."

Aunt Effie brightened. "I can provide you with that much, but you'll have to share the barn with your animal." She took in her surroundings with a scornful glance and a backhanded wave. "As you see, extra room is as scarce as bread." Again, she whirled without another word and left the room.

Duncan grabbed Hooper's arm. "What are you doing? We've ridden all day. I'm tired. And *hungry*!"

Hooper chuckled. "What are you complaining about? I got you a nice pile of hay for a bed. And a portion of oats, if the horse is willing to share."

"I don't think this is funny," Duncan fumed. "Now I see why Pa sent us instead of coming himself."

"Stop moaning." Hooper jerked his thumb toward the kitchen. "Just be glad you're not that poor lad. Can you imagine the misery his life has been? The sooner we get him free of this dung pit, the better."

Duncan flicked his hand, his shoulders rounded in defeat. "Have it your way. . .as usual." He cut his eyes toward the kitchen. "Besides, I'm not all that eager to eat from those filthy dishes. I'd sooner stick my muzzle in Old Abe's feed sack."

Grinning, Hooper patted his back. "We'll rest a few hours in the barn then get on the road. I'll drive first then we can relieve each other on the way." He patted the pack tied around his waist. "I still have a piece of jerky. Maybe some hardtack in the rig. With any luck, we'll be home in time for breakfast."

"No need to fret about food," Tiller said. "I'll fetch you some after Ma goes to bed."

Hooper's gaze bounced to where he slouched near the kitchen door. "Don't let your ma hear you say that or you'll be in trouble."

The lad straightened and pulled his pants higher. "She's out back with the hogs." He sneered. "Feeding them leftover grub she could've fed you."

A sudden grin lit his boyish face. "You fellows like bread? Fresh baked and spread with jam? I have all you could eat stashed in my room." He nodded, eager to strike a deal. "If you let me bunk with you in the barn, I'll share."

Duncan rubbed his hands together. "Sounds like a bargain to me." He paused. "I don't suppose you have a slice of cheese to go with it?"

Tiller snorted. "You funning me? We ain't had nothing as tasty as cheese since Pa died."

Duncan's brows lifted. "You've had a hard time of it then?"

The boy poked out his lips and nodded.

Hooper beckoned him closer. Laying a hand on his neck, he peered into his eyes. "Are you sure you don't want to leave some of that bread here for your ma to eat?"

He stiffened and backed away. "You can't tell her. If she knows I have food, she'll skin me good then feed every crumb to the hogs." His desperate gaze bounced from Hooper to Duncan. "I'm telling you, we won't see a bite."

Duncan cocked his head, his top lip pulled up in disgust. "She'd do that?"

Tiller's nostrils flared. "Get that look off your face, mister," he warned. "Ma wasn't always like this." He swiped the back of his hand over his shining eyes. "She used to be nice. When I was little, she held me on her lap and stuff." Embarrassed, he tugged on the waistband of his trousers. "When Pa died, times got hard and she changed."

Hooper unbuttoned his suspenders from the waistband of his pants. Gathering them in his hand, he started toward Tiller.

The boy ducked and flinched, his hands thrown up like a shield. "No don't," he cried. "I didn't mean to sass."

Hooper froze. With a sharp pang in his heart, he patted Tiller's arm. "Stand up, son. I'm not going to hit you."

He stood, fear and distrust shining from his eyes.

Slowly, gently, Hooper slipped the suspenders over his shoulders and fastened them to his pants. "There, now. No more losing your drawers."

He took Tiller's shoulders and sought his frightened eyes. "You listen to me. I give you my word that no one will strike you again if I'm around to stop it, not with suspenders or anything else. Do you understand?"

His eyes round with surprise, Tiller nodded.

Hooper patted his back. "Good man." His stomach growling, he hooked his arm around the boy's neck. "What do you say we head to the barn and feast on jam and bread?"

He twisted to grin at Duncan. "I think we'll leave the oats for you and the horse."

Chapter 12

Dawsey opened the oven door with her dish towel and bent to slide in the popovers. Before they made it safely in, her father bellowed her name from somewhere inside the house. She leaped, sending the gem pan one direction, the popovers another.

"For goodness' sake," Aunt Livvy said from inside the larder. "I do wish he'd stop that."

Her head appeared around the pantry door. "Are you all right, Dawsey? I heard a ruckus."

Before Dawsey could answer, she gaped at the mounds of dough scattered over the floor. "What a shame. So sorry, dear."

Father howled again, and Levi stuck his head inside, panic lining his face. "Colonel Wilkes crowing for you, Miss Dawsey."

"We're well aware of it, Levi. We can hear for ourselves." Aunt Livvy motioned with her chin. "Go and settle him down, please."

Levi backed away then popped in once more. "How, Miss Livvy?"

"Tell him Dawsey will be along soon." She covered her ears when Father cried out for the third time. "Tell him anything you wish, as long as you silence him. Now go."

Dawsey bent to scoop up the ruined dough with her dish towel. Aunt Livvy picked up the muffin tin and tossed it on the counter with a clatter. "I truly loathe this brutish conduct. I much prefer his silence."

Dawsey swallowed her irritation. Aunt Livvy could be quite insensitive at times. Struggling to keep her voice even, she untied her apron and placed it near the sink. "What do you suppose has gotten into him? I'd become used to his sullenness, but this. . ."

Aunt Livvy walked to the window. Dawsey recognized the angle of her shoulders and set of her jaw. Her aunt had something to say. She turned and met Dawsey's watchful eyes. "It's not the first time your father has behaved badly. Even as a child, he was gloomy and pouting." She frowned. "When he wasn't being stubborn and willful."

Anger shot through Dawsey. She bit her bottom lip. "That can't be true. People recall my father as a kind and generous man, a brilliant leader, and a doting husband. I've heard wonderful stories."

"Of course you have. All of them true." Aunt Livvy leaned her weight against the back of a chair and stared at the floor. "Your dear mother brought out the best side of Gerrard. When she died, I lost my brother to bitterness." Her bosom rose and fell with a sigh. "Then that wretched war came along to finish him off."

Aunt Livvy crossed to Dawsey and took her hands. "Forgive me, dear. I shouldn't unburden myself to you. Especially when you carry your own dreadful load. I suppose I've lost patience with the stranger in the den. I miss the man he used to be."

Dawsey's shoulders sagged. "What happened to him, Auntie? Other men lose their wives. . .go to war without losing themselves."

The wall Aunt Livvy used to protect her brother's past rattled into place. Eyes veiled, she waved a dismissive hand and crossed to the pantry. "Your father has suffered many losses, dear, crushing blows every one. But the truth is Gerrard lost himself when he lost his faith."

Dawsey let the truth she'd suspected settle over her heart. Despite her own sorrow, the love of God filled her with peace and hope. Her father seemed devoid of either emotion. Surely, if he had yielded his burdens, they wouldn't have affected him so deeply.

Sadness swept over her. "Then we must help him find his way back to faith. If I knew his terrible secret, then I could—"

Both heads turned as Levi pushed open the kitchen door. "Someone here to see you, Miss Dawsey."

"At this hour?" She frowned. "Who is it?"

"Flora, that's who. Miss Gilchrist's girl. She say her mama down in the back. Sufferin' something fierce." He rolled his eyes to Dawsey. "She needs you to come along right away."

"Poor Mrs. Gilchrist. Levi, fetch my medicine bag and bring the carriage around."

He left to do her bidding, but Aunt Livvy snatched her sleeve as she passed. "You can't go, honey. Not with your father like this. You're the only one who can quiet him." She tightened her grip. "He'll be calling for you all through the night, Dawsey, and I simply couldn't bear it."

"But Auntie. Mrs. Gilchrist. . ."

"I'll go tend to Mary myself. I know just what to do. I've watched you enough times to learn."

Dawsey rubbed her temples. "Oh my. Are you sure?"

"Quite sure. Stay here with your father. If I can't ease Mary's suffering, I'll come straight home and relieve you."

Before Dawsey could open her mouth in protest, Levi hurried in with her medicine bag. "Miss Dawsey, the colonel tuning up to squawk again, and I got no more tricks to hush him."

She shot her aunt a helpless glance. Without a word, Aunt Livvy swiped the bag from Levi's hand and hustled out the door.

Tiller droned like a pestered hive.

The boy had yammered throughout their meal of crusty bread and slathered jam, through Duncan's lengthy nap, and during the three hours of swapping memories and family gossip. He didn't seem inclined to wind down anytime soon, so Hooper decided Duncan should have a turn.

He spread his coat on the floor of the barn then reached for an armload of hay. Rolling the coat tightly around it created a fair pillow. Shoving his hat down over his eyes, he lay back to rest.

The hat wasn't enough to shut out the flickering lantern, so he turned over and buried his face in the straw pillow. Sadly, nothing could shut out Tiller.

"Why do you call that old mule Abe Lincoln?"

Duncan feigned an offended gasp. "Why, that's a horse, boy. Don't let him hear you say different. We call him Abe Lincoln on account of he's faithful and dependable." He laughed deep in his throat. "And ugly as mud."

Hooper grinned to himself when Duncan and Tiller howled.

"But he does lean a tad toward crazy at times," Duncan said. "We don't spend a lot of time within reach of his teeth."

"Our Uncle Willy's crazy, too," Tiller informed Duncan. "Matter of fact, he's just as batty as a loon. The old coot sits in a corner all day playing with toy soldiers."

Duncan grunted. "Is that a fact?"

"Gospel truth. But come to think on it, he's Ma's brother, not Pa's. I reckon that means he's no relation to you boys." He whistled. "Lucky for you." The little fellow heaved a deep sigh. "No, sir. When it comes to family, me and Ma are in short supply. We're the last of the McRaes in Fayetteville. And now, I—"

Duncan cleared his throat. "Mark your place in that story, little cousin, and toss me another hunk of that bread."

"It's *good*, ain't it?" Tiller's laugh echoed in the barn. "I told you so."

Paper rustled behind Hooper.

"And look here. She gave me three whole loaves."

"It's good, all right," Duncan agreed. "Some of the best I've ever tasted." He paused. "Pass me that blackberry jam while you're at it."

"You know, it's funny," Tiller said, his voice strained from reaching. "The lady who gave me this food has crazy kinfolk, too."

"You don't say?" Duncan mumbled, his mouth obviously full.

"I ain't lying. It's Miss Wilkes's pa, but she calls him "Faawtha." He tittered like a girl. "Only he's worse off. At least Uncle Willy plays with something fun like toy soldiers." His laugh rang so loud, Hooper jumped. "That poor codger stares all day at Aladdin's magic lamp."

Hooper sat up so fast he left his hat in the straw. "What'd he say?"

Duncan had thrown his sandwich aside and come up on his knees in front of Tiller, gripping his skinny arms. "You heard right. He said magic lamp." He gave Tiller a shake. "Didn't you, boy?"

Tiller had paled as white as sugar and his eyes bulged with fear. "Y–Yes. . .m–magic lamp."

"Have you seen it?"

Tiller's frightened eyes hopped back and forth. "Did I say something wrong?"

"Just answer the question."

"Lots of times!"

"Then you can describe it."

"S–Sure I can. It's shaped funny. Has a long skinny spout and a sissy handle. It looks to be made of solid gold, but it ain't, of course."

"How do you know?"

"Well, it cain't be, can it? They leave the fool thing sittin' on a windowsill."

Duncan released Tiller and sat back on his heels. "It's Pa's lamp, ain't it?"

Hooper swallowed hard. "Has to be."

Free of their frightening questions, Tiller scooted to the corner, watching them.

Swiping his hand over his mouth, Duncan stared at the barn wall, his eyes glazed over. "But that would be crazy, wouldn't it? After all these years?"

"You heard the boy. Aladdin's lamp. That's what Pa always called it."

A grin split Duncan's dazed face. "I'd give my right arm to see that blasted thing."

Hooper chuckled. "Wouldn't that be something?"

Tiller scrambled toward them on hands and knees. "That's easy. I can take you."

Both their heads swung around to stare at him. Excitement surged in Hooper's chest. "You know where it is right now?"

The boy's chest swelled importantly. "I know exactly where. Sitting in the window of the biggest house in Fayetteville."

Hooper's eyes met Duncan's over Tiller's head. "More proof. Pa said the same about the house he raided."

"I do yard work for the family," Tiller continued. "At least I did before she ran me off"—he grinned and nodded for emphasis—"for touching the lamp."

Hooper shot to his feet. "What are we waiting for?"

"Are you serious?" Duncan scrambled off the floor. "We can't, Hoop. You know what Pa said."

"This is different," Hooper said. "It's all he's talked about for years. He'd understand." He chuckled. "If he was here, he'd be the first man in the wagon." He walked to pick up his hat. "The horse is rested. No sense lying about in this barn. We'll see the magic lantern then head for home."

"I don't know. . . ." Duncan scratched his head. "You've had no sleep at all, and we still have a long ride ahead."

"I'm too excited to sleep. You've snoozed a bit, and like I said before, we'll take turns at the reins."

"What's your plan? It's the middle of the night. We can't just sashay up to the door."

"We won't have to. The boy said they leave the lamp in a window." He nudged Tiller. "You know which window, right?"

Tiller nodded.

"There, you see? We'll just take a look, and then we'll go. They won't even know we were there." He clapped his hands and rubbed them together. "What a story we'll have to tell Pa."

Frowning, Tiller tucked his thumbs in his new suspenders. "Say, what's all this about anyway?"

Hooper tugged his ear. "Gather your things while we hitch up Old Abe. On the way I'll delight you with the tale of young Silas McRae and his magic lantern." He chuckled. "I think you'll find his adventure far more exciting than Aladdin's."

CHAPTER 13

There are moments when I see the rush of the Indians, hear their war-whoops and terrific yells, and witness the massacre of my parents. . . .

Dawsey frowned and skipped ahead.

The little girl whom I before mentioned, beginning to cry, was immediately dispatched with the blow of a tomahawk from one of the warriors. . . .

She shuddered and laid the book aside. *Memoirs of a Captivity among the Indians of North America* turned out to be a poor choice of reading material while seated alone in Father's den in the dead of night.

How horrid to watch the murder of your parents, the pillage of your home. Then to be bound against your will and carted off to a strange place? Another shudder took her, mostly from the terrible thought but partly because of the draft blowing in under the window.

Dawsey had given up on sleep hours ago. Father had never been more restless, and she wondered what new evils plagued him. Each time she dozed off in her room, he called her name. Each time she ran to meet his needs, he seemed only to want her company.

She hadn't talked to him or held his hand. She'd just brewed more chamomile tea and perched at the edge of a chair by his bed until he slept again. The last time he drifted off, this time more soundly, she'd slipped downstairs to his study to wait for Aunt Livvy.

Sighing, Dawsey glanced at the eight-day clock as it chimed the eleventh hour. Apparently, Aunt Livvy decided to stay overnight at the Gilchrists'.

Crossing to the window, she parted the heavy drapes and peered out. By the dim light of the backyard torch, the shadowed front wheels of the carriage were visible inside the shed.

Her gaze jumped to Winney and Levi's quarters. If Aunt Livvy had left instructions to return and fetch her, Levi would be nodding at his kitchen table until time to go, but no lanterns burned inside their house.

Poor Mrs. Gilchrist! She must be suffering something awful if Aunt Livvy felt compelled to stay. Guilt pricked Dawsey's conscience. She shouldn't have let her aunt outsmart her when sweet Mary Gilchrist needed her help. What Dawsey had done for Father, Aunt Livvy could've managed quite well.

Drowsiness pulled at her heavy lids. Jumping awake, she rubbed her eyes and contemplated another cup of tea. Thinking better of it, she snuggled into the soft fabric of the sofa and pulled a blanket over her lap.

Staring idly at the wall, she counted the plaster mounds covering the holes left by four tenpenny nails. According to Aunt Livvy, the nails once held a small quilt stitched in fanciful, prancing lambs. She insisted Father's den had once been the nursery, though Dawsey found the news impossible to fathom. If so, hidden nail holes were the only evidence that the dark, gloomy room had ever housed an infant.

A brisk wind howled beneath the window, driving her to tighten her dressing gown and hurry to pull down the sash. Huffing her frustration, she shoved it up again and pulled the golden lamp inside the house. In no mood for anything related to her father's suffering, she tossed it on the floor behind her.

The lamp was nowhere in sight when Dawsey turned to head up to her bedroom, so she assumed it slid beneath the corner table. *A fitting place for the irksome thing!* No doubt, she'd be on her knees fishing it out the next morning, but it could stay where it was for the night.

Hooper pulled the rig off the road about a hundred yards from the dim glow of lights in the distance. There was little chance of anyone passing by so late at night, but just in case, he drove a ways behind the trees before he stopped the wagon.

Laughing like loons, the three of them scurried to the ground and ran into the woods. The moon overhead shone just enough to keep them from slamming into each other or plowing into a tree. They didn't stop running until they came upon a towering wall of shriveled cornstalks standing between them and the house.

Duncan clutched Hooper's sleeve. "Do you realize where we are?"

Laughter bubbled up Hooper's throat. "This is Pa's cornfield. . . which means there's a ditch we need to dodge on the other side." He peered at Duncan in the moonlight, wide grins on both their faces. "I think we should go find out, brother."

Duncan tipped his head at the stalks. "Let's go!"

Tiller at their heels, they barreled into the field.

With a brisk wind whipping past his ears, Hooper bounded like a two-legged deer. Shoving aside withered leaves and jumping broken stalks, he relived his pa's adventure. For all he knew, Silas McRae had trod the same ground, breathed the same air. He could almost hear the braying dogs and the roar of a shotgun behind him.

His heart swelled to bursting when they reached the far edge of the corn and hit their bellies. Scouring the ground, disappointment welled in his chest. "Where is it? Where's the ditch?"

Gasping for breath, Tiller crawled up between them. "Don't remember seeing no ditch around here. I reckon there ain't one."

Hooper strained to see Duncan's face in the meager light. "Were we wrong? This isn't the right cornfield?"

Duncan gnawed his bottom lip. "It's been years, Hoop. They could've filled the trench in by now." He sniffed. "It could still be the right house."

"Right or wrong,"—Tiller piped up, pointing his finger at the line of rear windows—"there's a lamp sittin' right over there. That much I know for sure."

Grinning again, Hooper nodded. "Good enough for me."

Bent low and skulking like thieves, they broke through the stalks and scurried for the back side of the house. Tiller crouched under the first window and pointed overhead.

Hooper bobbed up to look then dropped down again. "Not there."

Throwing caution aside, Tiller rose and felt along the ledge. "Huh?" he whispered. "It's supposed to be here."

"Well, it's not," Duncan hissed.

"It's sitting just inside then." Tiller strained to see past the darkened windowpane. "The lady takes it in sometimes. I've seen her."

Duncan fell back on the ground. "That's it then. Let's get out of here before this boy gets us shot."

Hooper joined Tiller at the glass. "I'd risk the mean end of a pistol to see that lamp." Without thinking it through, he worked his fingertips under the sill and the window squeaked open a crack. Excitement churning his stomach, his eyes searched Tiller's. "Little cousin. . .is there a gold lamp inside this room?"

Tiller slapped one hand over his heart. "I swear on my life."

Duncan scrambled to his feet. "Hoop, are you crazy? This ain't Scuffletown, and these folks ain't Macks. If you break in here, it's not to feed the poor and hungry. It's just plain wrong."

Hooper grabbed his collar and jerked him to the ground. "Lower your voice. We're not going to steal from them, Duncan. We'll take a look and then climb out the way we came—empty handed."

Duncan wagged his head. "No, sir. I want no part of it."

Hooper stood. "Then sit there. I'm not passing up this chance."

He looked left and right then slowly raised the window. Tiller squirmed anxiously beside him, but Hooper held up his hand. "Stay with Duncan."

He scrunched up his face. "Aw!"

"Be quiet, and do like I say."

Hooper strained to pull himself up to the ledge, but it was too high. He nudged Duncan's foot with the toe of his boot. "If you give me a leg up, I'll show you the lamp when I find it."

Grumbling under his breath, Duncan made a sling with his hands and hoisted him up to the sill.

Hooper went through headfirst, catching himself with his hands and rolling silently to the floor. Kneeling, he felt around on the ledge, then under it, but found nothing. "It's not here."

Tiller poked his head inside. "Sure it is." He pointed. "Look on that table yonder."

Hooper groped his way across the room, wincing and covering his mouth when he stubbed his toe on a chair. Shaking off the pain, he felt his way to the table, where his searching fingers found only a fringed lamp and a large book. He turned to grumble but choked on his words.

The shadowy outline of a pleasing apparition hovered near the window facing Tiller, a breeze billowing her nightdress and lifting long strands of her hair.

Stunned, Hooper rubbed his eyes and looked again. His disbelief vanished when the dreamlike figure doubled her fists and shrieked with all her might, "Tiller McRae!"

A *thud* shook the ceiling. Footsteps echoed overhead, then a man's voice bellowed from the top of the stairs.

Snatching a blanket from the couch, he threw it over the woman's head and lifted her struggling body. Racing to the window, he threw one leg over the sill. "Here! Take this!"

Duncan hurriedly reached for the bundle. "What is it?"

The man roared behind Hooper. With no time for his brother's questions, he tossed her at them and jumped.

They caught her, grunting under the weight. She wiggled, and Tiller screamed and let go. Duncan cursed and dropped her.

Struggling on the ground, she screeched and clawed at the blanket twisted around her head.

Before she could escape, Hooper snatched her up and slung her over his shoulder.

"Rrrrun!"

They bolted for the cornfield, Hooper going as fast as he could manage carrying the extra weight. With anguished bellows echoing from the window behind them, they crashed headlong into the merciless stalks.

Chapter 14

Dawsey fought to breathe.

The suffocating blanket flattened her nose, and the man's shoulder pounded her stomach each time his running feet hit the ground, forcing air from her lungs in little gasps.

Short of oxygen.

Arms pinned cruelly to her sides.

Swift feet carrying her into the night.

Dawsey violently sucked a breath of air and exhaled on a scream.

The man beneath her jolted and lost his stride. He stumbled, and she prayed he'd fall. Recovering his footing, he swatted her hard on the behind. "Hush! You'll send us sprawling."

Indignant, Dawsey flailed her feet, hoping to knock him down, but he was too strong for her. The effort only increased her need to breathe. Gasping, panting in terror, she cried out to God for deliverance as white dots swirled past her eyes.

She vaguely sensed being carelessly tossed and rolling into a lifeless heap. Hands pulled her, twisted her, jerked on her arms as disjointed voices floated overhead.

"Are you mad, Hooper? What the devil are we doing?"

"Hooper! Why'd you take her?"

"Be still, both of you. What choice did I have? She called Tiller's name."

The frantic quarrel faded as the white dots sped up and swirled her away to darkness. She dreamed of tomahawks, baby quilts, and fields of rotted corn. Of Mrs. Gilchrist hunched over a stump, twirling a yowling cat.

Dawsey's eyes flew open, and she gasped for breath. Blinking against a wall of blackness, her heart pounded as she remembered. She smelled the musty scent of cornhusks on the blanket, and the heavy wool blocked her sight. Mercifully, someone had folded the cover away from her mouth. Terrified, but thanking God to be alive, she hungrily gulped the air.

She lay very still, desperate to get her bearings. Feeling every bump and shift beneath her, hearing creaky wheels and rustling grass, she figured out that she lay bundled in the bed of a jostling wagon. Stunned, she realized they'd tied her hands behind her back. Struggling against her bonds, she tried to sit up. Without her arms to brace her, she fell hard on her shoulder with an anguished cry.

"She's awake!" Tiller shouted. He sounded close, maybe seated right behind her.

"I told you she wasn't dead," a strange voice called. "Give her a drink from the flask."

Tiller scrambled about in the wagon bed then scooted around in front of her. "Here you go, Miss Wilkes. Some water for you."

She turned her head. "If you touch me, I'll scream."

Silence followed, then Tiller's desperate plea over her head. "What do I do? She says she'll scream if I touch her."

"Let her. We're too far out for anyone to hear."

"I don't want her to scream."

"Then leave her be. If she gets thirsty enough, she'll ask for water."

Tiller shifted and sighed, making little mournful sounds in his throat. He leaned so close she felt his breath on her face. "I'm real sorry, Miss Wilkes," he whispered. "Please tell me you're all right." He heaved another sigh. "If I'd known they'd take you, I'd never have showed them your house. I swear it."

Tiller brought them! She might've known. The boy had been nothing but trouble. "Just go away."

"No," he whimpered. "I won't."

"Then make yourself useful. Help me sit up."

He scurried behind her and lifted her by her shoulders.

"Now cover my legs."

He dutifully tugged her nightdress down over her exposed calves.

"Will you untie my hands, please?"

A squirming pause. "Hey, fellows. She wants her hands untied."

"Sorry, ma'am. I can't do that," a clipped voice replied. Obviously the leader.

"Aw, come on," Tiller said. "What would it hurt?"

"I don't like it either, but we have no choice."

Irritation spiked through Dawsey. "At least take this ridiculous blanket off my head." In the pause that followed, she dared to hope he might be considering her request.

"Hand me a knife, brother."

Hope turned to choking fear when he swept close and tugged at her. He cut off most of the cover, fashioning a heavy blindfold of sorts, then moved away again.

Braver with some distance between them, she lifted her chin. "Oh please. . .can't you take it off? I can't see a thing."

"Miss, that's sort of the point. If you need food or water, we'll be happy to oblige, but we can't untie you or uncover your eyes. Don't ask again."

Her heart sank. What a horrible human being. Yet what other sort of being would seize her from her home and hold her against her will?

Though she couldn't see him, she twisted her head his direction. "Mr. McRae?"

Saying the name aloud reminded her of the yellowed slip in the cashbox—this man's name viciously ground into the paper. Remembering made her even more afraid. "May I ask why you're doing this to me?" Her heart hammered while she waited for him to answer.

After a tense silence, he cleared his throat. "What makes you call me by that name?"

"You are a McRae, aren't you? Tiller's uncle Silas, come to fetch him?"

Tiller laughed. "Nah, he ain't my uncle. He's my—"

"Hush, boy!" the stranger growled. "Come away from her. Haven't you done enough damage?"

Tiller's boots scraped against the rough boards as he scooted to the front of the wagon.

Determination surged through Dawsey. "Won't you answer my question, Mr. McRae? What are you planning to do with me?"

The harsh answer she expected didn't come. Instead, defeat laced his words. "Just lie back and rest a bit, miss. There's a long stretch of road ahead."

Exhausted, Dawsey longed to lie down, but with her hands tied, she couldn't manage by herself. She gritted her teeth. She'd sooner perish than ask for help.

"There you see, brother?" The low hiss, floating to her on the brisk night air, jolted her alert and struck fresh terror in her heart. "Whatever happens, that woman can never return to Fayetteville."

Chapter 15

Ellie opened her eyes and blinked at the cypress slat inches from her nose. She gingerly felt her face. No bumps or soreness this time. Relieved, she stretched and rolled off the bed.

Mama claimed Ellie wrestled gators in her sleep. Waking up with scraped arms and busted lips from thrashing against the wall made her tend to agree.

When she turned thirteen, Papa announced that a budding flower needed a private space to grow. So he built her a bedroom, set off from the main house, on the last available patch of high ground. Ellie spent most of her time inside with the family, taking her meals and playing table games with the boys, but she loved her time alone to daydream. And to moon over Wyatt Carter.

She washed her face and dressed then peered outside her little bedroom door. Light flickered in the window of the big house, and smoke streamed from the chimney. Mama would soon have breakfast on the table.

Sailing off the highest step to the ground, she trudged through the mud to the cabin, pulling up short at the corner.

Wyatt himself leaned on the porch talking to Pa.

Ellie crouched behind a patch of dead weeds to watch.

Wearing no shirt or shoes, despite the cold December morning, Papa stood with his back to Ellie, rubbing his tousled head. "You're up and about early, boy."

Wyatt nodded. "Hope I didn't disturb you folks. I have business that won't keep."

Pa sniffed. "The missus has breakfast about ready." Thankfully, he slid into his dangling suspenders before he lost his droopy britches. "I'll go tell her to lay a place for you."

Wyatt had lost the smile that usually graced his downright pretty face. "Don't need food, sir. Just conversation."

Papa scratched where he shouldn't in public.

Embarrassed, Ellie squirmed.

"The boys ain't here this morning. I expect them later today."

"Mr. Silas, it's you I've come to see."

The side of Pa's jaw worked, chewing on Wyatt's words. "Son, I won't pretend I don't know why. You're here about my Ellie."

Wyatt flushed but held his gaze. "I'm keen to court her."

The hoot that surged inside exploded past Ellie's lips in an unexpected squeal. She ducked and covered her mouth, hoping they hadn't heard.

Papa had the nerve to chuckle. "Are you right sure you're the man to skin that bobcat?"

Wyatt squared his shoulders. "Reckon I am."

"You may as well know we've spoiled her putrid."

Wyatt nodded firmly. "Yes, sir."

"Ellie ain't prone to girly pursuits. She'd sooner skin a rabbit than fry one."

"I know that, too."

"She can't sew a lick."

"Don't care."

"She's a mite shiftless, too." Pa pointed over his shoulder with his thumb. "Here it is pushing seven o'clock, and she's still out there piled in bed. The girl's used to having her way."

Anger fired through Ellie. With Pa doing the peddling, she'd rot on the shelf.

Wyatt shook his head. "I don't mind bending to Ellie's whims a bit… right at first."

This brought her to her feet. *Right at first?*

Shifting around, her pa leaned beside Wyatt, staring as if taking his measure. "You might be good for my little girl, Wyatt Carter. You're bound to do a better job than her ma and me did. The little scalawag has us bound around her finger."

Wyatt grinned for the first time. "A mighty cute little finger, too."

Papa's chin shot up and he glared down his nose. "Say again?"

Hanging his head, Wyatt cleared his throat. "Sorry, sir."

Easing his harsh stare, Papa folded his arms. "Well, then, my answer is yes. You can court my Ellie." He pounded Wyatt on the back. "Now, if that's all you've got. . .my eggs are cackling for me."

In a blinding flash of teeth, Wyatt found his smile again. He watched Pa amble inside then turned to go. Catching sight of Ellie skulking beside the house, his eyes softened and his smile turned tender and sweet.

Ellie grinned and ducked her head, her cheeks ablaze. When she raised her eyes, the cocky rogue winked and gave her a jaunty wave. She wiggled her fingers—her cute little fingers—and Wyatt turned away whistling, his thumbs hooked around his suspenders. She watched until he slipped past the trees and disappeared.

Spinning on her heels, she dashed up the steps to her room. Breakfast could wait. Ellie needed time alone, to leap and twirl, to fall across her bed and moon.

She wasn't Papa's budding flower anymore. Beneath the light in Wyatt's eyes, she'd blossomed into a fully grown woman.

Hooper moaned with relief when Duncan turned down the lane toward home. He had cocked back against the seat and dozed through the last long stretch of road then paid for his folly with painful cricks in his neck.

He longed to be home yet dreaded getting there. His mind couldn't conjure the conniption they'd face when Papa laid eyes on the woman.

What he'd done seemed the only way in the black haze of night. By the light of a new day, he wasn't so sure.

They'd driven straight through, switching up drivers when needed and taking regular short breaks for Abe Lincoln. Wracked with guilt, Hooper longed to untie the girl's hands, but he didn't dare give into her pleas. Not after her last stunt.

Hog-tied and blinded, she'd thrown herself from the wagon into an overgrown field. After twenty minutes of beating the brush, they'd finally found her. Thankfully, she didn't break her neck.

The blindfold seemed to bother her most of all, but Hooper wanted no chance she'd recognize her surroundings or sort out the direction they were traveling. Ellie could chart a path by the moon and stars, but then Ellie wasn't like most girls.

Tiller hovered by her side the whole way, talking her ear off and giving her sips from the canteen and bites of jam and bread. He finally gave in to sleep, but not until his self-appointed charge drifted off.

Glancing over his shoulder at the huddled bodies, shame cut through Hooper like buckshot. He should probably fear his mama more than Pa, once she saw the poor girl in her nightdress.

Duncan pulled up to the house with Hooper still rehearsing what he'd say to them both.

Tiller sat up rubbing his eyes. "Where are we?"

Easing his aching body to the sodden ground he loved, Hooper limped to the tailgate. "You're home, little cousin."

Tiller gazed around with an ugly scowl. "I'm too tired for teasing. What is this place?"

Hooper saw the ramshackle cabin with its dirty windows, rickety porch, and waterlogged yard through Tiller's eyes and grinned. "You'll have time to get used to it. Don't worry, it's cozy inside."

Duncan hobbled to join them. With arched brows, he pointed at their reluctant visitor, her thin nightdress hugging her back so closely Hooper could count the bones of her spine. "What do we do with her?"

"We show her to Pa. He'll decide."

The door burst open behind them, and Pa blustered out with a welcoming shout. Hooper cringed. "Here he is now. Hold tight to your backside."

Duncan turned with both hands in the air. "I had nothing to do with this, Pa."

Hooper shot him a glare.

Papa's stride slowed, and his broad smile wilted. "Nothing to do with what, son?"

Mama hurried onto the porch, drying her hands on her skirt. "Welcome home, boys!"

"Not so fast with that welcome, Odie," Pa called over his shoulder. "These two have been up to something again." He pushed between them and stilled, his hand tightening on the tailgate. Murder in his eyes, he spun, his low growl chilling Hooper's blood. "There'd best be a blasted good explanation for this one."

Hearing the rage in his voice, Mama grabbed the handrail and made her way to the ground, her eyes huge cisterns of dread. "For heaven's sake

Silas, what's wrong?" She scurried over to squeeze in amongst them, and a hush fell over the yard. Lifting her head, she searched Hooper's face, her unspoken question searing his heart.

"Ma, it's not what you think."

Pa slammed down the tailgate. "It don't matter what we think. Get that poor girl out of there."

With a sigh, Hooper nodded at Tiller. "Help her to sit up."

Leaping into action, he lifted the woman from behind. She sat hunched over with her chin buried in her chest, a forlorn captive in a dark blue headdress. "I won't climb down," she whispered. "Not until all of you turn your heads."

Pa handed Tiller his knife. "Cut her loose and come away from her."

Tiller freed her hands then scrambled out of the wagon.

"All right," Pa said. "Turn around, all of you."

Hooper cleared his throat. "I don't know, Pa. She's pretty slippery."

"Turn your heads!" he roared.

They spun like dancers on cue.

"Just tell us when you're ready, ma'am," Papa called over his shoulder in a far more civilized tone.

They waited.

Hooper began to fidget. "Pa?"

There wasn't a sound behind them.

Pa glanced nervously at Hooper. "You ready, miss?"

No answer.

Hooper whirled. The blue headdress lay on the ground at their feet.

"Yonder she goes!" Tiller cried, pointing.

Hooper sprinted to where she'd slipped in the mud, too weak to run far. He caught her around the waist from behind and spun her about. "See? I told you she was slippery."

As he carried her, kicking and squealing, Pa stared like a man possessed, and a strangled sob tore from Mama's throat.

Her eyes wide pools of fear, she backed away, nearly tripping on the bottom step. "Get it out of here!" she screamed. "Hooper, turn it loose. It's a changeling."

Dumbfounded, he watched his ma scramble onto the porch while he fought to keep his grasp on the squirming body in his arms.

"Let her go!" Mama shrieked. "She's a witch."

Ellie's bobbing head rounded the corner of the house, catching Hooper's eye. She walked with a merry step, and a big smile lit her face.

Tiller turned at her footsteps, his jaw going slack. "M–Miss Wilkes?" he said to Ellie, rubbing his startled eyes. Then his head whipped around to stare at the woman in Hooper's arms. "Take me home this minute," he whined. "This place is cursed."

Moaning, Mama rushed down the steps to head off Ellie before she reached the wagon.

Dazed from all the commotion, Hooper carried the struggling woman to the wagon and plopped her down. She raised defiant eyes, and his blood drained to his feet.

The girl glaring at him with dreadful hatred was his sister, Ellie. A certainty made impossible by the fact that Ellie stood five feet away, clutched in her mama's arms.

Dawsey's abductor—her bitter enemy—released her and backed away.

Circles of fire burned her wrists, and her arms tingled. The dim morning light tortured her eyes after hours swaddled in a thick wool blanket. The scraped knees she earned by jumping from the wagon stung like salted wounds. And if these indignities weren't enough, she sat on display for a half dozen strangers in nothing but a torn cotton nightdress.

Yet none of these atrocities were foremost on her mind. She was too busy memorizing every shadow, curve, and line of her captor's face.

She'd never hated another person, never wished a man dead, but with every ounce of burning fury in the pit of her stomach, she wished violent harm to this one.

Squinting through streaming eyes, she sneered and lifted her chin. "Stop gaping at me. It's your fault I look a fright."

He drew farther away, his mouth ajar.

Among the odd mix of people, shuffling feet drew her eye. A stocky man took two steps closer, his eyes bulging like a bullfrog's. "Brother? Do you see what I see?"

Her captor gulped and nodded. "She's hexing us."

Tiller shoved between them, his voice high and shrill. "Who, Miss Wilkes? She ain't hexing nobody." He wiggled his finger at a tousle-haired girl dressed in trousers and boots. "That one's the witch."

The older woman, her pale face streaked with tears, clung to the boyish girl. "Take it away from here, Silas. It's a doppelgänger. An omen of death."

The man beside her placed a steadying hand on her arm. "Now, Odie. . ."

"I mean it. Take her far off before she finishes casting her spell on our daughter."

He gave her a shake. "Calm down, Odell. There's no witchery afoot." He glared at the two young men. "All we have here are a couple of sons who've been where they weren't supposed to go."

The girl pulled free from the woman's desperate grasp. "Stop it, Mama. Will somebody please tell me what going on here? Who's that in the rig?" Ignoring her mother's frantic pleas, she approached Dawsey. Two feet away, she stopped cold and gasped.

Dawsey's gaze swung to the stranger's face, a mirrored reflection of her own horror.

They jumped away from each other.

Dawsey drew in her legs and crab-crawled to the front of the wagon, the words *changeling* and *doppelgänger* tearing through her mind. Scared speechless, she huddled in the corner and watched the frightening image of herself shivering in her mother's arms.

The man called Silas—Tiller's uncle?—clutched his head. "This is my fault, every last bit. Oh blast it, what have I done?"

He pulled the crying girl from her mother and held her to his chest. "I'm sorry, Puddin'. Don't be scared. That girl's no threat to you. No threat at all."

"How can you be sure, Pa?" her captor asked.

"Oh I'm sure." He took a deep breath, his nostrils flaring. "Because the truth is"—he cast a fearful glance around the circle of anxious faces—"the little gal in that wagon is Ellie's own sister."

All eyes swung to Dawsey then back to the open-mouthed girl.

The man's wife spun to face him. "What are you saying, Silas McRae?"

He squared his shoulders. "I'm saying I left no empty arms in Fayetteville, just like I promised."

The woman stared at Dawsey but directed her dire words at him. "Husband, what have you done?"

"I told you I left a sister behind."

"A sister! You never said she was Ellie's twin."

"But don't you see?" His eyes begged understanding. "That's what made it right. Why should they have two little girls and we have none?" He nodded as if to justify himself. "Take one, leave one. It's fair."

Glaring, his wife shook an accusing finger. "Now our boys have taken the other." She gathered double handfuls of her hair atop her head and pulled. "It's a curse come back to haunt us. Our just desserts for what we've done."

The stocky young man clutched the old one's sleeve, his head cocked like a befuddled hound's. "Wait a minute, Pa. Are you saying Ellie's not really our sister?"

The girl cried out and tore free of her father's arms. Sobbing pitifully, she bolted around the corner of the house.

Stricken, he reached a trembling hand. "Wait, Ellie, I can explain."

Dawsey's captor scowled. "Let her be, Pa. There's nothing you can say to her now."

The mother lifted the hem of her dress and rushed after her daughter.

Dawsey watched, no longer concerned about her own welfare. Her heart had followed the fleeing girl.

Turning, she found her adversary watching her, his eyes troubled behind fallen strands of pitch-dark hair. She scrambled for the remnant of the blue blanket and tugged it up to her chin.

Blushing, he lowered his gaze. "What do we do with her, Pa?"

"Pa" lifted dazed eyes. "Lock her in the shed then meet me around the table. There's some reckoning due—and it's judgment day."

Ellie flung her body across the bed where a lifetime ago she'd mooned over the promise of courting Wyatt. Now that childish girl didn't exist.

She gazed at the rough-hewn wall that she often wrestled in her sleep. If not the scrapes and bruises, at least the details of her struggle always faded with the dream. Never in her waking hours had she felt so battered and spent.

Mama opened the door without knocking. "Baby, it's me."

Ellie buried her head in the pillow. "Go away."

"Not until we talk."

"Don't want to."

Mama pushed her over and sat down beside her. "Then listen." Ellie's broken heart ached at the light touch on her shoulder, the cool hand of the woman who'd been "Mama" her whole life.

She eased away. "I want to know everything. Don't leave nothing out."

"Very well." Mama's answer seemed to rise from a deep well of sadness, and her weight shifted to the edge of the bed. "Lord knows, you deserve that much."

Ellie's heart sank. Where was the outrage? The shocked denial? "So it's true?"

A ragged sigh. "Yes, honey. It's true."

Her answer tossed Ellie's life in the air like a scattered deck. Breathless, she waited for the cards to fall. "So the powerful man in Fayetteville, the one who's looking for you and Pa. . .he chased you here because of me?"

"That's right."

"You let me call him a terrible man."

"I know," Mama said. "We shouldn't have done that."

She touched Ellie's arm. "Do you remember asking why I share the load for Papa's sin?"

Ellie tried to answer, but she couldn't form the word. She turned over and sat up, searching her mama's tortured eyes.

"I told you that I allowed what he did to stand." Her voice grew husky. "It's because I couldn't bear to let you go, Ellie. You filled a need in me." The barest smile touched her lips. "You were the cutest little thing. . .with your apple dumpling cheeks and tiny spit curls." Her smile deepened. "And such a good child." She tilted her head at Ellie. "You still are." She bent to dab her eyes on her skirt. "And now you know the truth." Her voice broke and she wiped her nose on her hem. "Papa and I had nothing to do with your goodness."

Ellie wanted to shake her, to cover her mouth and blot out the terrible words. Instead, her shaking fingers closed over Mama's hand, the only comfort she could manage.

Mama lifted sad eyes. "I'm so sorry, baby."

"Can you. . ." Ellie's chin dropped. "Can you tell me why?"

The mattress sagged, as if Mama's burden of guilt weighed her down. "I'll do my best to explain, but you might find it hard to understand since you've never ached for a child of your own." Pulling one knee on the bed, she scooted closer. "You see, your papa carries an uncommon passion for me, Ellie. The need to keep me happy wrestles inside him. He's toiled for nothing less since the day we met."

Ellie watched her. "You weren't happy?"

Mama looked at the floor. "I needed babies." She drew a deep, shaky breath. "Always have. As a girl, I dreamed of walls bulging with rowdy children."

"You had the two boys."

She nodded. "I wanted me a girl." A tear fell on her folded leg. "Your pa couldn't accept our plight. He blamed himself for my grief." With a trembling hand, she caressed Ellie's cheek. "I longed for a daughter, so he brought me one."

Ellie sat quietly, trying to make sense of her story. It seemed ruthless at the core. They wanted something, so they took it. Told those hurt by their actions to go hang themselves. People like her real parents, whoever they were. And the girl in the wagon. People like Ellie herself. "Is that all, then?" She didn't intend the harshness in her voice.

Mama blinked then raised her brows. "There's one other thing." She stood and held up her finger. "Wait here." Shuffling to the door, she pulled it closed behind her.

Ellie tried hard to think, worked her mind to sort out all she'd heard, but seething anger blocked her thoughts.

Returning with a somber look on her face, Mama sat down in front of Ellie with a delicate wisp of cloth in her hands.

Ellie stared at the tiny white dress. "Mine?"

Mama bit her lip and nodded.

Ellie took the soft fabric and ran her fingertips over the tiny crocheted flowers. Cross-stitched letters on the hem spelled out a name, the threads puckered and faded with time.

Sounding out the letters, she glanced up. "You're mistaken. This dress wasn't mine."

Tears welled in Mama's eyes.

Shaking her head, Ellie squinted at the stitching again. "This says D–Dilsey Elaine Wilkes." She peered into Mama's sorrowful eyes, and the truth pierced her heart.

"That's me." Her lips felt numb. "So even my name is a lie?"

Mama gripped her hands, still clutching the dress. "Of course not. We took Ellie from Elaine, your middle name."

"But my given name is Dilsey." The strange word sounded hollow in her ears.

"Yes, but we couldn't call you that. It was too risky. You understand, don't you?"

Ellie watched her.

"People were looking for you, baby. And Dilsey is so. . .unusual. We couldn't make it easier for them to find you."

"Them?" Ellie nodded. "My parents you mean."

Scowling, Mama squeezed her fingers. "Ellie McRae, Pa and me are your parents. That hasn't changed a whit."

She pulled her hands free. "So they looked for me?"

Mama cleared her throat. "Well he did, but the woman—" Her gaze flickered and she lowered her voice. "We heard the woman died before your first birthday."

Ellie crawled to the comfort of her pillow. "Please go. I've heard all I care to."

After a time, Mama's weight lifted from the bumpy mattress. Eight steps later, she closed the door behind her.

CHAPTER 17

Dawsey cowered in the dirt beneath a low shelf in the shed, too broken to care about spider webs or darting creatures. Whether due to a lumber shortage or sheer laziness, the uneven floor stopped at the row of shelves, two feet shy of the wall. Sitting on the floorboards would be warmer, but fear kept her huddled in the corner.

The cotton gown wasn't enough between her and the cold ground, so she crawled out of her den long enough to grab the folded blanket and stack of clothes they'd tossed through the door. She fumbled into the flannel shirt and tattered trousers then pulled the cover around her shoulders.

The clothing smelled of lye soap, and the old quilt felt stiff and scratchy from hanging too long on the line. Still, they comforted her greatly and warmed her frigid bones.

The shouting in the house had gone on for what seemed like hours. After one last bellow and a slammed door, all had gone silent.

Dawsey leaned her head against the wall and stared at the beam of light coming through the slats they'd nailed over the entrance. The shed had a single window, also covered in planks, lined up like the bars on a cell.

Of one thing she was certain—if they kept her too long in the confines of the tiny space, she'd go mad. For now, two spellbinding matters held her mind captive. First, she must escape and find her way home to Aunt Livvy and Father. Second—no matter how she tried, she couldn't shake the thought of it—she had a sister.

A sister!

The knowledge brought sense to her life in a rush. How could her father display baby pictures when two faces smiled from the photos? How could he keep infant things about when there had been two pairs of booties, twin hair bows, and identical dresses? Somewhere along the way, Father had decided he didn't want Dawsey to know. Most likely to shield her from the grief. What power and influence he wielded over his friends and neighbors, as well as Aunt Livvy. They'd kept his secret for nineteen years.

McRae.

The bitterly scratched name in the cashbox.

Father had known or suspected who broke in and stole her sister. He must have searched for years before giving up. No wonder his mind couldn't cope. Especially after losing his wife.

Her stomach lurched.

Aunt Livvy said Mother lost the will to live, an explanation Dawsey had never understood until now. Knowing she was sick, frail, and bereft of a child made all the pieces fit.

Such a twisted fate! Dawsey had uncovered the greatest mystery of her life, only to face a more frightening question.

Why had the kidnappers returned for her? What had they hoped to gain? Clearly, her sister knew nothing, so it wasn't for her sake. Even the older folks were surprised to see her.

Why would the two young men come to Fayetteville and drag her away to such a godforsaken place?

Approaching footsteps jolted Dawsey's heart. Had they come to do away with her?

Tears sprang to her eyes as shadows lurked outside the door. The wood planks cracked and splintered, and light burst inside the shed. Wincing, she shrank deeper into the dim cranny.

"Thou art my hiding place; thou shalt preserve me from trouble."

A figure loomed, outlined by the bright sunlight.

"Thou art my hiding place and my shield."

Pitiful cries escaped her throat. Blackness threatened as her heaving lungs struggled to keep up with her heartbeat.

Her kidnapper ducked under the low door, both palms raised. "Whoa there. We mean you no harm. Just thought you might be hungry."

The ordinary words sounded odd to her terrified mind. His slow, easy manner didn't fit her expectation of a cruel executioner. She struggled to control her fear.

From under the shelf, Dawsey watched the sinister man.

Wispy strands of black hair hung in his face, and whiskers shadowed his chin. His eyes appeared sunken in the low light, his cheeks hollow.

The crazy mother followed him inside. Her eyes were red and swollen like she'd been crying, and she wore a pinched frown as though she were in pain. Ducking her head, she stared at Dawsey as she passed.

Dawsey lifted her chin in defiance.

The woman looked startled then dropped her gaze, busying herself with balancing a laden tray on a squatty three-legged stool. After one more glance, she spun for the door in tears.

The concern in the man's eyes as he watched her go surprised Dawsey and gave her courage.

"Mr. McRae," she called from under the shelf, "you must take me home right away. My poor father has withstood enough loss at the hands of your family. There's no telling what my disappearance will do to him."

Ignoring her request, he bent to lift a cloth off a steaming bowl. "There's soup here and a slab of venison roast. Corn bread, too." He took a square and offered it to her. "With butter and wild berry jam."

Dawsey's hand snaked out and dashed the food to the floor. Frightened by what she'd done, she shrank from his reaction.

He merely sighed and pointed behind him. "Water in the canteen over there."

"I want to go home."

Crossing his arms, he gazed at something over her head. "If there's anything else you need, best tell me now. You won't see anyone for a while."

She leaned so her face would be in the light. "Please Mr. McRae, won't you please let me go?" Tears sprang to her eyes, and hope hastened her words. "There's no need to take me back to Fayetteville. If you'll just point me in the right direction, I'll make my own way. I'll—"

Spinning on his heel, he took two long strides to the door. "I'm sorry," he said over his shoulder. Without another word, he nailed the wood planks into place and then he was gone.

Dawsey moaned with frustration and withdrew as far into the

corner as the splintered wall allowed. A shiver took her body, but not from the cold. Pressing her head against her knees, her fists closed around handfuls of dirt.

The idea came like a whisper, taking form as she gouged holes in the soil. Flipping over, Dawsey ran her hands along the wall. Her probing fingers followed the boards deep into the soft ground until she found the splintered bottom. Excited, her thoughts grew bold.

The uncouth brutes had forgotten this bare patch of floor when they'd pitched her inside like rubbish. Or they underestimated her.

Dusting her hands, she darted to the tray and devoured the hot bowl of soup. Wrapping the venison to take with her, she spread jelly on a thick square of corn bread and shoved it in her mouth. She ate to fill her aching stomach, but more importantly, she ate to keep her strength up. Strength she'd need when the sun went down.

Dawsey would see Fayetteville again. She would escape these lunatics and find her way home to Aunt Livvy and Father. She would live to see his face when he learned she'd found his missing daughter at last.

Hooper's best sweet talk hadn't convinced Ellie to come to supper. Neither had Mama's tears. When he told her Pa had called an after-supper meeting to decide the fate of Miss Wilkes, Ellie said she didn't give a fig what happened. Yet there she stood on the threshold with the door banging against the wall, daring them with her eyes to say a word.

Mama said more than one, just not directly to her. "Move down, Tiller, if you don't mind. That's Ellie's seat."

Tiller scooted, staring so hard at Ellie that his skinny body slipped between the chairs and hit the floor. Blushing, he scrambled up and sat, his gaze still fixed on her.

Ellie ignored him, sitting tall as she took the platter of roast from Mama's hands and shoveled some into her dish.

Beneath the table, Hooper reached across and tapped Tiller's ankle with his boot. Tiller jerked around, and Hooper frowned and shook his head.

The boy got busy filling his plate.

Except for the scrape of forks and an occasional quiet cough, they finished the meal in silence.

Papa wiped his mouth and laid aside his napkin. "We have three matters to ponder tonight, so let's get at it."

With a rustle and scrape of chairs, the family shifted around to face him.

"First off, we haven't properly welcomed young Reddick"—at Tiller's scowl he cleared his throat—"young Tiller, I mean, to the family."

He nodded toward the boy. "I regret that you turned up in the midst of a whirlwind, but we're mighty glad to see you." Dabbing the corner of his eye with his napkin, he sniffed. "You're the spitting image of my brother, son. Did you know that?"

Tiller bit back a smile and lowered his head while all but Ellie mumbled a welcome.

Pa blew his nose then sat forward in his chair. "Next on the list, we have the question of Hooper's and Duncan's safety."

A grim look crossed his face. "Henry checked out the scoundrel who came sniffing around for Hooper. Sheriff McMillan turned a pack of no-account bounty hunters and trumped-up deputies loose in the swamps." He sneered. "The cowards are too scared to go after Henry, so they've set their sights on some of our local boys. They're all greedy and trigger-happy men, so these are perilous times in Scuffletown."

Fear shone from Mama's eyes. "How can we protect them, Silas?"

Duncan reached for her hand. "Don't fret, Ma. Nothing will come of it."

Papa frowned. "We won't be making light of this, son. Your mama's got every reason to worry." He shoved aside his plate. "We'll make no proud or stupid mistakes. Mistakes will get you boys killed."

His anxious gaze swung to Hooper. "You're both headed into the swamp to stay with Henry."

Hooper shot Duncan a startled look. "But Pa, we—"

Pa's hand shot up. "Henry swore to protect you. That's banked money in my book, and a sight more than I can promise." He banged his fist on the table. "It's settled. We'll hear no more on the subject."

The legs of Duncan's chair squalled as he jumped to his feet. "I'm not going, and you can bank on that. I won't be run out of my own house."

Hooper sprang up beside him. "Duncan's right. I say we hold our ground. We're not youngsters anymore. We can protect ourselves."

A threatening hush stilled the room. Papa stood with a loud *crack* from his bad knee. Bracing his meaty hands on the table, he leaned with an angry stare. "You'd place our womenfolk in peril before you'd abide by my wishes?" He dipped his chin for emphasis. "Because that's what it amounts to. As long as they get their reward, those dogs don't care who gets in their way."

Not so sure now, Hooper glanced toward his ma.

She leaped up and stood between her sons. "They'd best care if I get in their way, old man. I'm a McRae, too, and I can still aim a shotgun. These boys stay right here with me."

Outmatched, Pa's head drooped. "That's it then. I've done all I can." He plopped down on his chair with a weary sigh. "Sit, you reckless knotheads. We have one more pressing quandary."

Clearing his throat, he glanced at Ellie. "Puddin', you may not want to stay for this part."

Her face paled. "Why?"

"It might be best if you didn't, that's all."

Color rushed to her cheeks, washing away her pallor. "Since when am I not welcome at a McRae family meeting?"

"It's not that, honey. It's just. . .well, the matter at hand is sort of delicate."

Tears sparked her eyes, and she clutched her napkin with white-knuckled fingers. "You're going to talk about that girl, and I have a right to hear." A tear spilled from one corner and slid down her cheek. "She shows up, and all of a sudden I'm not welcome?"

Pa's jaw went slack. "Now Ellie—"

She bounced up so fast, her chair clattered to the floor. "Go on and have your *family* meeting."

Her mournful cry pained Hooper's stomach.

Mama clutched Ellie's arm, but she pulled free and bolted. Opening the door with a *crash*, she glared from the threshold, her eyes menacing slits. "Listen up, you blasted McRaes. Ellie McRae is dead and gone thanks to you, and I'll never answer to her name again. If my name is Dilsey Wilkes, then by thunder you'll call me Dilsey Wilkes."

Mama reached a trembling hand. "Now Ellie."

She shook her head so hard her hair flew out at the sides. "I'm Dilsey!" Throwing her napkin across the room, she sailed into the night without closing the door behind her.

Silence hung like pork in a smokehouse. A soft sob from Ma as she whirled to her room broke the stillness like a hammer on glass.

Pa hung his head. "Well boys, have a seat. I reckon it's down to us to decide the fate of that poor little gal in the shed."

Dawsey dreamed of little girls in white dresses. Two happy little sprites, glowing and giggly, wearing identical blue sashes and feathered hats. Knee-length pantalets peeked from beneath their hems, pulled on over black leather shoes.

The two frolicked. Skipped rope. Played chase in a green meadow. They laughed over cups of make-believe tea and ate pretend biscuits. They held hands, smiling into each other's faces, and saw their own.

She sat up gasping. Shivering. Every inch of her body ached.

With nightfall, the cold earth beneath her had turned to ice. The December chill seeped into her bruised muscles and battered joints. Moaning, teeth chattering, she rolled onto the rough plank floor.

A muffled cry came from the window over the door. The girl, Ellie, stood outside, staring through the slats.

Dawsey guessed she'd been peering inside, searching the candlelit shed for her, never expecting her to spin out of nowhere.

Their eyes met and held, and the dream returned. Dawsey sought to reconcile the blissful little twins with the pitiful wretch on the floor and the wild-eyed wraith at the door.

Then Ellie was gone.

Dawsey shook her head to clear it, thinking she must still be dreaming.

She tugged the blanket around her shoulders and prayed for strength and courage to carry her through the coming task. Comforting herself with thoughts of her warm bed in Fayetteville, she crawled under the shelf and set to work.

The topsoil came away easily until she reached the frigid, hard-packed dirt beneath. Dawsey dug until her fingernails ached from clawing.

The longing for her bed became an aching desire to see her father's face, and the thought of him grieved her to tears. She clenched her teeth and scrubbed them away with a grimy palm, which only ground stinging, gritty dirt into her eyes.

Setting her jaw, she went at her digging with renewed vigor. Tears may wet her cheeks, but no matter what happened, she wouldn't cry.

It seemed hours before she sat back on her haunches and surveyed the gap she'd made. Satisfied that it appeared large enough, she tried to wriggle through. After several grunting attempts to squeeze past the boards, she sat up with bloody scratches on her cheeks and went at the stubborn hole again.

On the second try, she slid through with no problem—no problem soap and a hot soak wouldn't cure. Greeted by a gust of cold air, she fumbled behind her and pulled the blanket through to wrap around her shoulders.

Both a blessing and a curse, the vast moon sitting atop the trees swallowed most of the sky and lit the yard as bright as daylight. She'd have to lie low at first to avoid being seen, but once she cleared the yard, the moon would light her way. She needed rest, but the urgency to flee tightened her chest. She pushed off the ground, poised to run.

"Hold up there miss." The deep, rasping growl stopped her cold.

Dawsey didn't need to spin around. She knew his dreadful voice. In a burst of strength, she shot across the soggy yard.

Splashing footsteps approached from behind, jogging her heart. "Don't make me chase you."

Shedding the blanket, Dawsey sped up.

He closed the distance.

She screamed as strong arms encircled her waist. Flailing blindly, she dug in with heels and fists.

"Be still."

"Take your hands off me."

"I can't do that."

"Oh please. Haven't you hurt me enough?"

His sigh stirred her hair. "Likely so, but right now I'm saving your life."

Helpless against his strength, she fell limp.

Leaning to retrieve the discarded blanket, he carried her to a rise and sat her on her bottom.

She scowled up at him from the ground.

Handing her the cover, he tilted his head toward the woods. "Ten steps past those trees would've landed you in a quicksand bog."

He leaned to pick up a shotgun and Dawsey stiffened.

"If you were lucky enough to miss the bog, you'd like even less what came next. Scores of critters roam the marsh at night searching for their supper."

She sneered. "I should think scores of critters feasting on my flesh would serve your purpose well, Mr. McRae."

The horrible man squatted beside her. "You'll have me looking over my shoulder for my pa. Call me Hooper."

Tiller's voice rang in her head. *"Hooper! Why'd you take her?"*

Sliding away from him, she snorted. "I'll do no such thing. I despise you."

He shrugged. "Suit yourself. I suppose you call all of your enemies mister."

Dawsey bit her lip and raked him with her eyes. "Have you enjoyed sitting here watching me dig for hours?" She held up bruised and blistered hands. "If you'd made your presence known, you might've saved me from this."

Before she could react, he laid down the shotgun and took her hand, studying it in the moonlight. "You need salve on this."

"Stop that!" She jerked free and scooted farther away.

He motioned with his finger. "On that cheek, too. You're bleeding."

She reached for her face but otherwise ignored him.

Hooper sat on the grass and wrapped his arms around his knees. "If it makes you feel better, I didn't sit here and watch you dig. You were worming your way under when I showed up." He grunted. "And lucky for you I did. You'd be gator bait by now."

Anger roiled in Dawsey's gut. "Suppose I believed you, which I don't, why were you skulking about?" She dipped her head at the shotgun. "And with that thing, no less?" She shot him a distasteful look. "I hardly think such measures are necessary to subdue me. As you've proven numerous times, I'm no match for your brutish strength."

The horrid Hooper reached behind him and slid the gun onto his knees. "What, this?" He had the impudence to laugh. "I assure you, this has nothing to do with corralling you." Raising his head, he scanned the distant tree line with a curious mix of sadness and determination. "Like I said, there are all sorts of critters lurking in these woods." He patted the barrel. "Old Bessie here evens the odds."

Dawsey's head throbbed worse than her cheek. She'd used up all her nastiness and scorn trying to get a rise out of him. . .to no avail. Fed up with pretense, she spun on the ground to confront him. "I have the right to know how you plan to dispose of me." She waved toward the swamp. "If not the alligators, then what?"

Hooper tilted his head. "Dispose of you?"

"I heard what you whispered to your friend. You'll never allow me to return to Fayetteville." Her eyes bulging with dread, she paused to swallow. "We both know there's only one way to stop me from finding my way home."

He nodded, watching her. "Yes ma'am, I reckon so."

Heart pounding, Dawsey tried to read his expression. When he casually leaned to pull a blade of grass and poke it in his mouth, she lost control. Leaping to her feet, she stood over him with her hands on her hips. "If you're going to kill me, I'd just as soon have it over." She pointed behind her at the shed. "It's positively cruel to lock me in there alone to await my fate."

Throwing the grass aside, he jumped up and grabbed her arms. "Wait a minute. Kill you?" He narrowed his eyes. "That's crazy talk. Nobody wants to hurt you."

She gaped at him, fighting for the strength to pull away. "But you said—"

"What I said, I spoke in haste. Pa reminded me of the same thing. There's only one way to keep you from running away, and we never once considered it."

"Then. . .what?"

His gaze flickered over her face. "Pa said when the trouble in Fayetteville dies down, me and Duncan will take you home."

His words released a flood of gratitude in her heart. A pardon granted to the condemned.

"Oh thank you. Thank you so much." Relieved tears spilled onto her cheeks, and she drew her first easy breath. "How long?"

Smiling down at her, Hooper tilted his head in thought. "A couple of months ought to do it. Four at the most."

Stunned, she backed away. "Four months?"

"It'll take at least that long for the stink to fade. Otherwise it won't be safe." He spoke calmly, as though he expected her to find his explanation remotely reasonable.

Aghast, Dawsey stared. "You can't be serious. You see, my father is quite ill. Mentally frail, I'm afraid." She took a step closer. "He'll think I'm never coming home. His poor mind won't be able to cope."

Hooper lifted his hands to his sides. "It's the best we can do."

Something inside Dawsey shattered. Rushing him, she pounded his chest.

An immovable wall, he held his ground and gripped her arms. "Whoa there. Settle down."

Her fists still clenched, she moaned. "I don't understand why you took me in the first place. What do you want with me?"

"Miss, if you'd stayed in your room last night, you wouldn't be here now."

She opened startled eyes. "If you'd stayed out of my house, I wouldn't be here."

His jaw tightened. "Believe me, it's a mistake I regret."

She lowered one brow. "If you didn't come for me, why *were* you in my house?"

He released her arms. "It's a long story that has nothing to do with you."

"If it has nothing to do with me then release me."

"I'd love to oblige you, but I can't."

"That's a ridiculous answer," she said, thrusting her chin. "My father needs me. Why won't you let me go to him?"

Looming over her face, his eyes begged understanding. "Because I love my pa, too. Turning you loose will put him in harm's way. I won't do that."

She stared vacantly. "Your father should pay his due for hurting so many people. My father is the victim here."

Anger flashed on his face. He bent to snatch the shotgun off the ground. "It's time for you to go inside. You want to squeeze under again or try the door this time?"

She eyed the gun nervously. "You're not throwing me back in that horrible shed?"

"Just for tonight."

"But it's cold." She lifted one shoulder, reluctant to beg compassion from him but too desperate to keep still. "And overrun with creeping things."

"I'll board up this hole and bring you extra blankets. The creeping things won't be a bother. They're more afraid of you." He stilled. "Except for snakes. Watch out for them. They'll crawl right into your bedroll."

Cringing, she glanced over her shoulder at the warm lights flickering inside the house. "There's no place else?"

"After Ma breaks the news to Ellie that you're taking her room, you'll sleep out there from now on."

Her breath caught. "You mean I–I'll be rooming with her?"

Hooper chuckled. "I don't see that happening. You'll have her room to yourself." He motioned with the gun. "Enough talk. Go ahead now."

Dawsey crawled beneath the wall and peeked out. "Your boards can't keep me inside, you know." She smirked. "I got out once. I can do it again."

He scowled. "If you lack the sense to fear these swamps, then fear me." He patted the gun over his shoulder. "I'll be keeping watch tonight."

Shame chafed Hooper like a woolen shirt. Each time the girl's eyes lit on his scattergun, they sparked with fear. His troubled stomach already ached from the dreadful wrong he'd dealt her. Having the frail, delicate woman afraid of him didn't hardly sit right.

Still, better that she fear him and stay put than perish in Bear Swamp's belly.

He smiled picturing her thin shoulders wiggling from under the shed but flinched recalling her battered cheek and blistered hands. She fought the ground until it yielded and almost made good her escape. How could a woman with so much pluck seem so fragile?

He picked up the hammer and nails then grabbed a sturdy cut of lumber left over from boarding up the door. Kneeling beside the hole she'd dug, he wedged the wood into the ground.

"Miss. . . ?" He struggled to remember her name. *What had Tiller called her?*

A pale face appeared at the gap. "Wilkes. Miss Dawsey Wilkes. You see, I have a name. I'm a human being, endowed by my Creator with unalienable rights. Rights you've selfishly trod asunder."

He groaned. "Just shove some of that dirt around the plank, will you?"

Gaping at him, she stilled. "You want my help to entrap me? Sir, I think not."

He couldn't see her in the daylight without thinking of Ellie. The glow cast by the full moon and her fancy words almost made him forget that she was Ellie's twin. He blew out a puff of air. "Fine. Have it your way."

He dropped to his belly to peer inside the shed.

Miss Wilkes didn't retreat.

"Move aside, please."

She set her lips and shook her head.

If Ellie acted so pigheaded, he would scoop a handful of dirt on her. With Miss Wilkes, he dare not.

She had spunk, but not the same kind as his sister. With Ellie a man got spit and sass, a knot on the head with a broomstick. He could punch her in the arm and laugh when it raised a lump. When this girl hit him, he'd clutched her arms for fear she'd hurt herself.

"Miss Wilkes, if you don't let me get at that dirt, I'll have to pry open the door."

She tilted her head. "That sounds like a fine idea."

Seething, he moved to push off the ground then froze and sprawled again. "You're going to crawl out, aren't you?"

She raised her brows.

Hooper threw down his hammer. "Blast it!"

He stretched his arm past her to scoop dirt in the hole.

She rose to her knees and hauled armloads out of his reach.

Beat at his own game, Hooper sat up and scratched his head. Maybe a handful rubbed in her hair wasn't such a bad idea.

Jerking the board loose, he stood and tossed it aside. "Miss Wilkes, come out here, please."

She peeked through the slats. "Why?"

"Just do like I said."

Disappearing again, she called in a timid voice, "Not while you're angry."

He gulped fresh air and worked to control his tone. "I'm not angry. Now come out."

Her face appeared, watchful eyes staring at him before she slithered into the open and stood up brushing her hands. "Where are you taking me?"

He gripped her arm and pulled her along beside him. "Where do you think? We'll have to tell Ellie ourselves. Her room is the only place left to put you."

With surprising strength, she jerked her arm free. "Don't touch me."

Hooper exhaled through pinched lips and nudged her with the butt of his gun. "See to it you walk a straight line, and I won't have to."

Chapter 19

Smiling through tears, Ellie covered her mouth and hunkered deeper into the brush. She didn't think anything could be funny on the most dismal night of her life, but laughter bubbled in her throat, threatening to give her away.

Not many folks got the best of Hooper McRae. Ellie was pleased she had the chance to watch.

Sobering, she gazed after them. It had been impossible to squelch the thoughts scurrying through her mind since the morning. She'd replayed her first sight of the girl countless times, though in the memory she had no features, as if Ellie's mind refused to share her likeness.

It was easy to watch her in the moonlight with her face muddled by long hair and shadows. A bit trickier facing her in the shed. Startled, Ellie had bolted. Now if only she could stay away.

Wondering where Hooper was taking her, Ellie tailed them, surprised when they stopped in front of her room. She peeked around the corner and watched.

Hooper knocked as if afraid someone might actually answer. "Ellie?" he called in hardly more than a whisper. "You in there?"

Pa rounded the main house and lumbered toward them. "What are you scalawags up to?"

Hooper spun on his heel, dragging his prisoner with him.

Pa laughed. "Didn't mean to startle you, son. I was looking for my Ellie."

He slunk toward the strange girl, his hat in his hand. "I'm sure glad Hooper found you, baby. I need to talk to you."

Hooper tucked the girl behind him. "Hold on, Pa. This ain't Ellie."

Pa looked like Hooper had dashed him with the rain barrel. He mumbled under his breath then frowned at Hooper. "What's she doing out of the shed?"

"The shed won't hold her. She dug out under the wall. If I hadn't showed up to stop her, she'd be gone."

Pa tapped his leg with the brim of his hat. "Well, I'll be. . ." He peered closer. "You sure are a ringer for our Ellie. Especially dressed in her clothes." He dropped the hat on his head. "What do we call you, missy?"

The girl stood with a stiff back toward Pa, her eyes cast down. Only Ellie could see her biting back tears. Setting her jaw, she turned and spoke to Pa in an uppity manner. "My name is Dawsey Elizabeth Wilkes. Miss Wilkes, to you."

"Dawsey Elizabeth," Ellie whispered to herself. The stitching on the infant gown swirled past her eyes. *And Dilsey Elaine.*

The girl—Dawsey—took a bold step forward. "Mr. McRae, you must release me. My father has suffered much over the injustice you've dealt him. I fear he won't survive another blow."

Pa pouted his lips, the first sign of irritation. "You're some kind of fancy talker, ain't you?"

She squared her shoulders. "I demand to know why you brought me here. Wasn't stealing one daughter enough for you?"

"A little sassy, too." He shook his head. "I take it back. You're nothing like my Ellie."

Ellie bolted from her hiding place. "Stop it, Papa! She's nothing like me because she ain't me." She folded her arms over her chest. "And I'm not your Ellie. I've told you what to call me."

She shot a warning glare at Hooper. "Don't take my stand for weakness. I don't care a thing about her, but she's right. You two have wronged her family, and I'm ashamed of you."

Wilting like spinach in hot fat, Papa hung his head. "Baby, I know what I done was dreadful bad. But I swear to make it right."

Ellie's stubborn head persisted in turning toward Dawsey. With each stolen glance, she met Dawsey's darting eyes.

Ellie pointed at her. "How do you reckon to make this right, Pa?"

He squirmed like a naughty youngster. "I aim to take her back to Fayetteville. Just as soon as it's safe."

One finger beside her nose, Ellie pretended to ponder his answer. "That plan just might work." Hands going to her hips, she shifted her angry gaze at him. "If her pa lives that long." She patted her chest. "What about me? How will you make *me* right again?"

A frustrated exhale puffing his checks, Papa turned to Hooper. "Put Miss Wilkes inside and guard the door. I'll help you rig a latch when I'm done talking to Ellie."

Ellie raised a threatening brow. "Paaa. . ."

"When I'm done talking to your hardheaded sister."

He clutched Ellie's arm and hauled her toward the house. Over her shoulder, her gaze locked with Dawsey's until they turned the corner.

"Where are you taking me?"

"You're coming inside with your ma and me. It's time we chewed the fat."

When he pulled her onto the porch, she caught sight of Ma through the window, hunched over the table with her head in her hands.

Ellie's heart stirred with pity.

Mama only sinned by loving Ellie too much. Who could fault her for that?

Ellie's conscience tugged. *The Wilkes family, that's who.*

As they gathered around the table, Ellie pondered the fact that the folks with the odd name were her real family. The people she called "Ma" and "Pa" were meant to be strangers. Yet the two dear faces gazing at her with loving eyes were hardly strangers. She loved them fiercely.

Her heart throbbed as Mama shyly touched her hand. "Can you ever forgive us?"

Ellie's "yes" came out on a sob. She lowered her face to her hands and cried like a foolish child.

Papa stood behind her, kneading her shoulders. "We never meant to see you hurt by what we done, Ellie." His voice quavered. "You weren't supposed to find out."

She sat up and clutched her ears. "I didn't want to know. Not ever."

Mama stretched her arms across the table and pulled Ellie's hands down. "Your pa and me, we lost sight of one thing. The Good Book says nothing's covered that won't be revealed, nothing hid that won't be known." She shook her head. "I wish we'd paid more heed."

Ellie wiped her eyes with her palms. "I just need to know why."

Mama handed her a dish towel, and she blew her nose. "I already told you why, honey." Her gaze flickered to Pa. "You see, we—"

"I'll answer for myself, Odell," Pa broke in. "This whole tangle is my doing."

He came around and sat beside Ellie at the table. "I didn't plan to take you out of your crib that night." He pointed over her head. "The girl out there had the same pluck then that she has now, sitting up in bed watching me, daring me to touch her."

His mouth softened. "But you? Well, you were another story."

Papa stared into the past and chuckled. "Laying there beside your sister, jerking and twitching in your sleep just the way you do now." He grinned. "Smiling one second, frowning the next. You were the cutest little thing."

He laid his hand over Ellie's. "I gazed at you and saw you in Mama's empty arms, as content as a fat pup. I forgot the reason I crawled in the window. Forgot the sack of loot. I even forgot the gold lantern."

Her jaw dropped. "You left the magic lamp because of me?"

Rubbing his forehead, he nodded firmly. "Given the chance, I'd do it again. I didn't have another sensible thought until I carted you in the house and eased you in Mama's arms."

Mama sighed. "And I couldn't think straight once I saw you. I touched your chubby face, and you opened your big, button eyes and smiled." She held up her hands. "And that was that."

Pa's gaze jumped from Mama to Ellie. "From that moment, we knew we'd give up everything for you. We left home, family, and common sense behind in Hope Mills and fled to Scuffletown."

Mama squeezed her hand. "And I've never regretted one loss." She lowered her head. "Until I saw we broke your heart."

Ellie slapped her palm on the table. "What you done was wrong. I need to hear you say it."

Papa hung his head. "I'm starting to see just how off the beam it was."

"It was dead wrong," Mama cried. "It's haunted us for years."

Ellie bolted from the chair and rushed to her side.

Papa hurried around to wrap them in his arms. "I know you asked us to call you Dilsey, but you'll still answer to Puddin', won't you?"

Biting her lip, Ellie nodded.

He smiled through his tears. "We'll call you whatever pleases you, Puddin'"—he sniffled—"but some things don't change. Until I draw my last ragged breath, you'll still be my Ellie."

CHAPTER 20

Dawsey curled into a tight ball of misery. By her count, it was Wednesday morning. A full week had passed since her capture. It seemed she'd spent each minute plotting her escape and praying for her father.

Every Wednesday afternoon, Aunt Livvy and her tittering cronies gathered in the parlor for a ferocious game of whist, Levi swept the fireplaces, and Winney baked bread. Dawsey pined to see Winney bustling about the stove, longed to tease her and poke holes in her dough. Her heart ached to see them all, and she wondered how they fared without her.

Ellie's bedroom was better than the shed, but not by much. A little roomier at least, with a small, corner fireplace to warm one's toes. Gazing at her surroundings in the first morning light, Dawsey decided it had less character than the drafty shed. There she at least had the possibility of escape. Here, there'd be no digging out, and Hooper had boarded up the only window.

She flopped to her back and tried to shake the oppressive cloud of despair. *"My voice shalt thou hear in the morning, O Lord; in the morning will I direct my prayer unto thee, and will look up."*

"Good morning, God," she whispered, staring past the low ceiling toward heaven. "Hear my prayer and deliver me."

Her gaze shifted to the door. Over the last week, a curious parade of kidnappers had filed into the tiny room bringing food, water, a basin for washing up, and clean clothes.

Dawsey dreaded Mrs. McRae's visits. She was a pleasant-looking woman, lovely in fact, with a kind face and soft brown eyes, but she always wore a meddling stare and usually left in tears.

Duncan, the elder brother, always came along to make sure Dawsey didn't escape. He brought with him sweet smiles and heartening words and never crossed the threshold without his mother. If he came alone, he'd rap softly on the door and wait for permission to open. Then he'd pass his offering over the doorstep and leave. At times, he lingered on the steps to chat awhile—long talks she'd come to enjoy. Duncan seemed genuinely repentant for his family's indecent behavior.

Unlike Hooper, who lacked his brother's attention to proper manners. He barely knocked before lifting the bar and bursting into the room, oblivious to her scowling irritation. Hooper had no qualms about entering without a proper chaperone and never stayed longer than necessary.

Mr. McRae hadn't shown his face, and Dawsey was glad. Neither had Tiller, and she couldn't help wondering why.

Once, Ellie came. She stood in the entrance staring into Dawsey's eyes for long seconds, neither of them blinking. When she opened her mouth to speak, no words came. Before Dawsey could stop her, she backed out of the door and barred it behind her.

At the thought of her sister, Dawsey rolled off the bed and sat on the edge of the mattress.

Her given name was Dilsey. Duncan complained about how hard it was to remember, and how angry she became when he forgot. Insisting they use her rightful name said a great deal about the girl's mindset.

Dawsey and Dilsey. How clever Mother had been.

The thought gave Dawsey pause. The pain of never knowing the one who gave her life wasn't hers to bear alone. Dilsey was a living link between Dawsey and her mother and joint heir to Dawsey's loss—whether she realized it or not.

Life had cheated them, especially Dilsey. Instead of growing up side by side, sharing laughter, love, and secrets, Dilsey had been forced to live in muddy squalor while Dawsey enjoyed the comforts of their father's house.

Dawsey slipped from her borrowed nightshirt into Mrs. McRae's housedress, embarrassed at how much ankle showed below the hem. The tiny woman's frocks were inches too short, but Dawsey preferred them to Dilsey's coarse shirts and scruffy britches.

Hooper had belly-laughed when she'd asked for one of Dilsey's dresses. Dawsey took it to mean such a thing couldn't possibly exist.

A polite rap on the door signaled a visitor. Lonely for conversation, Dawsey prayed for Duncan. She hurriedly tied the yellow sash behind her back and called the all clear.

After enduring the scrape of the heavy beam lifting from its hooks, followed by the *squeal* of rusty hinges, Duncan's wide grin was her reward. More pleased than she should be to entertain a McRae, Dawsey gave him a shy smile. "What's this you've brought me?"

His lowered the plate for her to see. "Eggs, grits, and ham. The ham is a gift from our raiding Lowrys. Ma found it on our doorstep this morning and fried a few slices. I hope you like it"—he grinned and offered the food—"just not too much. The rest she's saving to roast for lunch."

The smell of crisp ham wafted from the plate to Dawsey's eager nose. Steaming grits swam with butter and the edge of a fluffy biscuit ran yellow with busted yolk. She blushed when her stomach moaned with anticipation.

Her blush deepened when she spotted Mrs. McRae crossing the yard behind Duncan. Dawsey knew the purpose of her mission and hoped she knew to show discretion in front of her son.

She huffed up the steps puffing wispy clouds of mist into the cold morning air. "What are you about, son? I told you to wait till we got back from the outhouse."

Dawsey shrank to fit the dress. So much for discretion.

Duncan tipped his hat and backed away, turning on the bottom step and loping for the house.

Laying her breakfast aside, annoyed that it would be cold when she returned, Dawsey wrapped the musty shawl around her shoulders and followed Mrs. McRae out the door.

The first time the woman took Dawsey to the crude little building with the carved-out crescent moon, her heartbeat quickened at the prospect of escape. She'd combed the woods, charting her getaway, until her gaze landed on Hooper, perched on a distant stump.

Dawsey's heart sank seeing him there to make sure she didn't run, and she kicked herself for letting him outsmart her. She cut her eyes and gave him a sullen look.

He bent to pluck a twig from the ground, pretending not to notice.

As Mrs. McRae led her back along the path to her prison, her sister's voice rang out through the wooded hollow. Eagerly searching, Dawsey spotted her through the tangle of trees. She had joined Hooper, sprawling on the stump facing him, her back to Dawsey.

As they passed, Hooper laughed at something Dilsey said, his voice a low rumble.

Dilsey stood to ruffle his hair then bent to kiss his cheek.

Dawsey's mind jumped to the book in Father's den, the frightening account of the boy abducted by Indians. Hadn't the same fate befallen her and Dilsey? They'd been bound and carried from their homes by a ruthless and arrogant tribe—Dilsey while tiny, innocent, and too weak to resist.

Watching them, Dawsey's jealous heart squeezed her chest. It grieved her to see Dilsey teasing and caressing the savage enemies who took her.

Determination surged. The blasted McRaes had duped, hoodwinked, and swindled Dilsey out of her God-appointed destiny. Dawsey would beat them at their own game and steal her sister back.

Furthermore, she knew exactly how to do it. When Dawsey set her mind to something, she could be quite persuasive.

Fighting a smile, Hooper watched over Ellie's shoulder as Miss Wilkes passed. She hopped and dodged the mudholes with the nimble feet of a woman born in Scuffletown. As they started up the rise to the house, she stiffened and raised her chin, as if she'd settled the answer to a pressing matter.

Shrugging, Hooper allowed his attention to return to Ellie, as he should, since her words had her pixie face twisted and troubled.

"I can't say why I'm so drawn to her when I honestly wish she didn't exist."

Hooper gave her a tight smile. "I wouldn't fret over it, Ellie. It's only natural for you to be curious." Remembering, he slapped his leg. "Sorry, honey. It's hard to think of you as anything but Ellie."

She waved him off. "It's hard for me, too. Why should I expect more from all of you?"

Ellie propped her elbows on her knees and gripped both sides of her head. "The truth is I'm not Dilsey *or* Ellie." She raised teary eyes. "I don't know who I am anymore."

Hooper scooted closer and took her hands. "What do you mean? Nothing about you has changed. You're still my little sister."

She pulled her hands free and wrapped her arms around his neck. "That's the thing, Hooper. I'm not at all. I never was."

Hooper's heart lurched when his rough-and-tumble sister laid her head on his shoulder for the first time in her life.

Ellie sniffed. "Dawsey's so different from me, and such a lady. I look at her and think, 'Is that what my life should've been?'"

Burrowing deeper in his neck, she started to cry. "Why'd you bring her here?"

His pain turned to guilt. "I wish I had it to do over, honey. Everything happened so fast that my mind was a muddle. When I heard Miss Wilkes call Tiller's name, I lost my head. I thought I was protecting Pa. I just didn't know, Ellie. I didn't know." He wrapped his arms around her and let her cry out her grief.

When she slowed to a sniffle, he set her up, wiping her tears and brushing the hair from her eyes. "I think I know what you have to do. It won't be easy, mind you, but you have to talk to Miss Wilkes. It's bound to help you sort things out." He ducked his head and caught her eye. "Might even help you find our Ellie again."

She searched his face. "Are you sure it's the right thing?"

He nodded. "I reckon I need to have a talk with her myself. It's time I followed my heart and apologized for what I've done to her." He jutted his chin at the trail. "But you first. Your time with her is more important."

Big eyed, Ellie stared. "Now?"

"Can't think of a reason to put it off. Now go."

She stood on shaky legs, staring up the trail and rubbing trembling hands on her britches.

He swatted her leg. "Have I ever steered you wrong?"

Ellie bit her lip and shook her head.

With a last desperate glance over her shoulder, she made her way up the path.

Watching her go, Hooper's hands began to sweat. Had he offered bad advice?

At best, she would come back with a clear head. If their chat turned sour, Ellie could wind up more confused than ever.

Leaning to snatch up another twig, he groaned at his own stupidity. Dawsey was Ellie's twin, for heaven's sake. He'd heard of strong bonds forming between twins. What if his hasty advice cost them Ellie's loyalty?

Regretting his folly, he threw the twig on the ground. Worse, suppose it cost them Ellie?

Dawsey sat on the bed with her hands in her lap, gazing at the dismal furnishings in Dilsey's room. She wondered again how the girl slept in such dingy, meager surroundings.

The quilt on the bed was clean but tattered and gray, the single window bare of curtains. There'd been no effort to decorate the walls with photos, pictures, or plaques. The only thing adorned with the slightest woman's touch was a pretty cane basket in the corner, painted white and trimmed with lace.

Dawsey wrinkled her nose. It overflowed with muddy clothes. She laid back on the musty-smelling bed, missing her room at home, the model of feminine decor.

All at once, she longed to see Tiller's familiar freckled face. The boy was her closest link to home, the only person for miles she felt she knew. He'd been so attentive during the horrid wagon trip, so worried Dawsey would blame him. Of course, she had until Duncan told her why Tiller brought them to her window that night.

Father's ridiculous magic lamp, that golden burden and bane of her existence, had brought her untold grief for years. Now its shadow had crossed many other lives and landed Dawsey in her present dilemma.

A tapping, so light she almost missed it, set her upright. It sounded different from any knock she'd heard before. Might it actually be Tiller?

Bolting from the bed, she hurried to stand in front of the door. "Come in," she called, her heart pounding.

The bar lifted and dropped. The hinges squealed. She stepped back as the door swung toward her, and. . .

Hooper stood on the top step, his impossibly black hair slicked back, his hat in hand.

Dawsey slumped with disappointment. "What do you want?" She hoped she sounded rude enough.

On closer inspection, she realized he'd changed into a clean shirt and scrubbed his face until his nose shined. Sleep had erased the dark circles from under his eyes, and a fresh shave had lifted the sinister hollows of his cheeks into pleasing, smooth valleys.

Her once-over reached his eyes. He smiled and lifted his brows.

Embarrassed, she glanced away.

Instead of strolling in without an invitation, his usual behavior, he tilted his head and looked behind her. "Is—" He looked again. "Am I interrupting?"

Dawsey gaped at him. "What on earth might you be interrupting? A garden party? My sewing circle, perhaps?" She walked to the window, feeling foolish when there was nothing to look at but crisscrossed boards.

Behind her, the door soundly closed.

She turned and pointed. "I'll thank you to leave that open."

He glanced over his shoulder. "I'll open it. After I've had my say."

"You can talk with the door open."

"If you don't mind, I have a private matter to discuss." He frowned. "Where did Ellie go?"

She blinked. "If you mean my sister, Dilsey, I wouldn't know." Curious now, she watched him. "Why?"

Hooper stared at the floor, scratching his temple. With a shake of his dark head, he seemed to dismiss the topic of Dilsey. "Never mind. I'll find her later. Right now, I need to see you."

Dawsey crossed her arms. "I'm standing right in front of you."

Usually so frustratingly self-assured, the man seemed jittery. What mischief might he be pondering?

He motioned her toward the bed. "Sit down, would you? I need room to pace."

Aghast, Dawsey looked over her shoulder at the lumpy mattress. "I will not. It would be highly improper, especially with the door closed."

Fidgeting in the narrow space, Hooper waved his hand. "Fine, just listen."

He strode past her a few more times before he spoke. "I've been doing a lot of thinking over the past few days, and I have something to say to you." He cleared his throat. "Miss Wilkes, I've broken into houses to steal money and goods. I've ambushed men, threatening some so fiercely they fled the state. I've rebelled against sworn officials and stirred the passions of local folks to do the same."

He flicked his wrist. "I'm guilty of many things I'd rather not mention"—he whirled to face her—"but I lay down in peace each night because every deed was against a sworn enemy, to further a just and honest cause."

With two strides, he closed the distance between them. "Lately, I'm not sleeping so well. I know I've grievously wronged you, an innocent woman who didn't deserve it." He took a deep breath. "So I've come to ask your forgiveness."

Stunned, Dawsey backed up and plopped on the bed.

Hooper squatted in front of her, pleading with sincere brown eyes. "I hope you can find it in your heart to forgive me."

Ellie shouldered Pa's Winchester and kicked her way through the canebrake, eyes and ears trained for the rattlers that used the switch cane stands for cover. Eager to join Tiller and Duncan's hunt and even more eager to run from Hooper's harebrained idea, she'd left the trail and cut across the dense underbrush.

She whistled when she caught sight of Tiller's light red hair bobbing over a young grove of hickory. Duncan whistled back as she broke past the trees to the trail.

Ever mindful of Papa's warning, she scanned the edge of the clearing for lurking bounty hunters. Satisfied they were alone, she hustled to join the boys.

Duncan grinned. "I should've known you'd be on our tails. Can't keep you home once you catch wind of a hunt."

She laughed, and it warmed her insides. "Reckon not."

Tiller, who could finally look at her without frowning and scratching his head, smiled as brightly as Duncan. "Did you bring us something to eat?"

Ellie nudged him and pointed at Duncan's forty-four caliber Henry. "You've got that backwards, don't you? You two are supposed to bring me something to eat."

He chuckled but rubbed his stomach. "I sure could use a bite. I'm as hollow as a gourd."

Duncan tucked in his chin. "After the breakfast you put away?" He rested his arm around Tiller's shoulders. "Four eggs and six biscuits should last you past suppertime."

Tiller's eyes glazed over. "That sounds mighty fine. I could go for seconds." He feigned pouring from a ladle. "With another big dollop of grits."

Tightening his arm around Tiller's neck, Duncan pulled him along the trail. "Hush, boy. You'll have us turning back to the kitchen."

Ellie leaped for them, catching the backs of their shirts and pulling them into the brush. They tumbled over each other in a tangle of arms and legs, with Tiller landing hard on his bottom.

Red faced, he shoved Ellie off his lap. "Hey! What are you—"

Duncan jumped him, slamming a hand over his mouth.

Tiller stared at him with wide, frightened eyes.

Pulling his freckled face closer, Duncan frowned and shushed him with a finger pressed to his lips.

Tiller nodded, so Duncan took his hand away.

Ellie rolled to her belly and carefully parted the brush.

Duncan crawled up beside her. "Where?" he whispered.

She nodded in the direction she stared.

"Can't see them."

She elbowed him. "Just wait."

Tiller scrambled up the other side, his head bobbing to see.

Might as well wave a red flag, Ellie thought, shoving his bright head lower. She stiffened and pointed. "There."

The forelegs of three horses appeared briefly though a break in the scrub, along the back side of a far stand of trees.

Duncan followed them with the barrel of his Henry.

Tiller's thin body trembled beside Ellie as they passed out of sight. "Who were they?"

"Trouble," Duncan answered. "Looked like patrolling Guard to me." He rolled over on his back. "At least they're headed away from the house."

The rustle of wilted cane jolted Ellie's heart. She spun and raised Pa's gun.

Duncan whirled to his knees, his rifle aimed at the brush.

A familiar chuckle dropped her heart to its proper place but sped up the pounding tenfold.

Wyatt.

Somehow, in a haze of pain, she'd forgotten he existed. Hadn't years passed since he'd asked permission to court her?

That girl who twirled about her room had been a giddy child, free of heartrending calamity. Searing truth had doused her joy and ended foolish daydreams. What could she offer Wyatt Carter? He wanted Ellie McRae, not Dilsey Elaine Wilkes.

Wyatt crawled out of the canebrake grinning like a fool.

Duncan lowered his gun. "That's a good way to air out your gizzard."

Still laughing, he scuttled over the high grass and swung up beside them. "The Guard?"

Duncan nodded. "Had to be. They were riding high and proud. Bounty hunters creep about like egg-sucking dogs."

Wyatt's gaze slid to Ellie, and he smiled their secret smile.

She looked at him and felt nothing. Her heartbeat slowing to normal, she rolled over to scan the far trees.

Duncan sighed. "I suppose that marks the end of our hunt. Can't venture a half mile off the place these days without running into bad business. We'd best lay low for a spell."

Tiller sat up and crossed his legs. "Fine by me. It's bound to be lunchtime."

"We need to warn Henry," Ellie said over her shoulder.

Wyatt snorted. "It's more likely that Henry has already warned your folks. Not much happens in this swamp that he's not the first to know."

Ellie remembered the man who'd come searching for Hooper. "Not always." She pushed to her feet and brushed off her behind. "It's safe to move on now. They're gone."

Her glance flickered to Wyatt.

He watched her with a troubled frown. "You feeling all right, Ellie?"

Tiller's head jerked around. "I wouldn't call her that if I was you."

Duncan cleared his throat. "She don't go by Ellie no more, Wyatt. Best to call her Dilsey."

A frown spread over Wyatt's forehead. "Who?"

"Dil–sey," Tiller offered from the ground.

Fuming, Ellie brushed past them and started up the trail. "Don't call me nothing. How about that?"

Furious with the lot of them but not sure why, she ran ahead, feeling their eyes on her back. She reached the place where her shortcut hit the trail and ducked out of sight. Tears seared her eyes, making her madder than ever. Brushing them away with the backs of her hands, she picked up her pace.

Why hadn't she listened to Hooper? The only thing left was to see Dawsey Wilkes.

Talking to her would either heal Ellie's heart or worsen her pain, but it was a chance she'd have to take.

To go on shunning her was madness.

Chapter 22

Realizing he'd dropped to one knee in front of Miss Wilkes, Hooper shot to his feet. He hadn't come to beg, after all, and he sure wasn't proposing. He had asked the pouting woman sitting on the bed to forgive him. The rest was up to her.

She sniffed delicately and cocked her head to the side. "Mr. McRae, are you serious?"

He grinned and held up his finger. "Not so polite. We're enemies, remember?"

She cleared her throat and tried again. "Hooper. . .as a rule, I'm a very tolerant person." She gazed around the room. "But in these circumstances, a mere apology will not do."

"A mere apology? You don't believe I'm sorry?"

One brow cocked scornfully, she shifted on the bed. "That I'm still trying to decide. But don't you see? No matter how sincere you are, it doesn't lessen the damage you've caused."

Hooper rested one hand on his hip. "Such as?"

Anger flashed in her eyes. "Such as my father, for one. Your coming to me spouting so much flummery won't relieve his suffering. Or lesson the threat to his health."

He squinted. "So much what?"

"Flummery," she repeated. "Flattery. Empty talk."

Hooper glared. "That's what you call my apology? Empty talk?"

Lifting her chin, she challenged him with her eyes. "Are you prepared to unbar the door? To take me home, perhaps?"

Swallowing hard, he backed off his anger. "It's not that I wouldn't like to."

"But you won't."

"I can't. Not yet, anyway."

She snorted and crossed her arms. "Flummery."

Warmth crept up Hooper's neck. He reached to loosen his collar. "You're hardly being fair. You're asking me to trade my father's safety for yours."

She drew herself up proudly. "My father is a fine Southern gentleman. A decent, law-abiding man."

Hooper seethed. "Unlike mine? Miss Wilkes, my pa makes no secret of his shameful past. He was a bandit and a scoundrel in his youth, but that was a long time ago. Now he spends his days helping our people carve out a life under the harsh rule of an unjust government. I think that more than makes up for his past crimes."

She shook her head. "You'll pardon me if I don't agree, at least concerning his most notable and heinous offense."

Hooper turned his back, struggling to control his temper. His apology wasn't going so well. He needed to find a way to start over.

Behind him, Miss Wilkes released her breath in a rush. "If you don't mind my saying, even the just and honest cause you speak of sounds like criminal behavior to me."

He spun on his heels and stared.

She leaned away from him but kept right on talking. "A moment ago, you confessed to stealing, ambushing, and rebelling against sworn officials. I've never heard of a just cause that required such reprehensible conduct."

"Then you've never been oppressed."

They glared, pecking with their eyes like a pair of rival roosters.

"Miss Wilkes, my people are Indians without a tribe, proud folks forced to live like poor men. They branded us 'free people of color' and pulled us into a war that had nothing to do with us, using us for free labor and a place to lay blame."

"Hooper, the war's over."

"Not where I live. Some days I wonder if it will ever end." A dull ache slammed Hooper's chest, and his nose flared. Shame surged through him when his eyes watered. He blinked furiously, but a tear spilled onto his cheek. "Every day a mother's son disappears in Bear

Swamp. She knows she won't see him again, unless he bobs up before the gators get him. Elderly women, left without husbands or sons to provide for them, are starving. Still, they're the lucky ones. The young girls are beaten and used." He wiped his eyes with his sleeve. "If I don't help them, who will?" He steeled his voice. "I'll die to keep Ma and Ellie from such a fate."

"I had no idea," Dawsey said, compassion softening the stubborn set of her jaw. "It appears it's my turn to apologize."

Hooper waved her off. "You don't have to say you're sorry for something you don't understand." He sighed. "Just be thankful you'll never have to." Settling his battered slouch hat on his head, he hooked his thumb. "I'll be leaving now. I've wasted enough of your time."

"You haven't."

"You were right to say mere words aren't enough. I wish I could give you what you want. Only it's out of my hands. But I do aim to prove my apology was more than empty talk."

"How will you do that?"

He shrugged. "I still need to work that part out." Saluting, he started out the door.

"Wait, please."

He paused.

"Why do you insist I call you Hooper, yet you still call me Miss Wilkes?"

Hooper nudged his hat off his forehead. "First off, you haven't given me permission to call you nothing else." He grinned. "And second, I don't consider you my enemy."

Dawsey leaned against the door, her mind whirling. Seething fury warred in her heart with a newfound respect for Hooper McRae. He deserved to suffer for what he'd put her family through, but the sight of his flooded eyes and swollen nose had touched her heart.

She'd never met a man with such passion. Of course, the only men in her life were meek and docile Levi, and a weak, useless father who'd given up on life.

Dawsey slapped her hand over her mouth, and tears filled her eyes. Shocked at her own conduct, she whispered a prayer for forgiveness. It wasn't like her to be hateful. She needed to draw closer to God in her current distress, not struggle with sins of the flesh.

Hurried feet pounded up the steps, jolting her away from the entrance. It seemed like time for lunch, so she expected Mrs. McRae and Duncan. Only why would they be running?

The door clattered open, and Tiller stood on the threshold, watching her with a hopeful expression. He held out his arms, as if he meant to block her escape. "Please don't try to run off, Miss Wilkes, else you'll land me in terrible trouble." He glanced over his shoulder. "I ain't supposed to be here."

In a rush of excitement, Dawsey tasted freedom. Tiller couldn't hold her and probably couldn't catch her, though he'd squeal like a pig when she ran. If Hooper was inside the house, she had a chance.

She took two determined steps, her heart pounding. Two more, and she reached the doorsill with Tiller's arms around her waist and the sweet smell of liberty in her nostrils.

Dilsey sailed around the corner of the house like a girl on a mission. Barreling toward them, she glanced up and nearly tripped over her feet coming to a stop. She stared at Tiller, a mixed hash of emotions on her face—surprise, irritation, and then longing—before she bolted down the trail toward the outhouse.

Tiller tightened his grip and dragged Dawsey inside. Sticking his head out for one last look, he shut the door and plastered his body against it. "What'd you go and do that for?"

Gnawing her cheek, she watched the floor.

"Promise you won't try it again?"

She nodded, and he pried his hands from the knob.

"Are you all right, Miss Wilkes? I've been so worried, I can't even eat."

Fondness pricked her heart. Smiling, she wound a lock of his hair around her finger then pushed it from his eyes. "That's awfully sweet of you."

He flashed an angelic smile.

"But you needn't fret so." She gazed around the room. "Though I'd much rather be home, they're taking good care of me."

"They feeding you and stuff?"

She smiled down at him. "Yes they are. In fact, I expect Mrs. McRae any minute with the noon meal."

His face lit up. "You'll like it, too. She cooked the best roasted ham I ever tasted." He gave a hearty nod. "Savory greens, too, seasoned with pork fat. If you drop your corn bread in to sop up the juice, it makes for some mighty fine eating." He paused to belch. "Repeats on you, though."

Dawsey narrowed her eyes.

Catching himself in his own lie, Tiller held up his hands. "Don't go giving me evil looks. I choked down enough to keep my strength up, that's all."

He burped again and glanced at the floor. "I really have been powerful worried about you."

Laughing, Dawsey pulled him close and kissed his cheek. "I'm sure you have. You were very kind to me in the wagon."

He blushed and brushed off her kiss. "If I'd known what Hooper was about to do, I swear I'd never have brought him to your house."

She patted his shoulder. "You couldn't have known, because Hooper himself didn't know." She paused, excitement building. "Can you tell me something, for my own peace of mind? How did Hooper know the lamp existed?"

"That's easy. You see, Uncle Silas—"

"Tiller McRae!" Mrs. McRae stood just inside with a tray balanced in one hand.

Duncan peered from behind her, a huge grin on his face. "Caught in the chicken coop, huh?" He swatted at Tiller as he ran past. "Git, boy!"

Tiller yelped and scurried down the steps.

Dawsey steeled her spine. The time had come to begin working her plan. As long as she acted angry and eager to escape, the McRaes would watch her too closely.

She smiled brightly at Mrs. McRae. "Thank you so much, ma'am. Whatever you have under that cloth smells divine."

A startled frown creased her brow. "W–Why, thank you, honey."

Dawsey lifted the dish towel. "Oh my, it looks even better. You're a wonderful cook, you know." She rolled her eyes. "Breakfast was delicious."

Blushing now, Mrs. McRae tittered. "I'm real glad you liked it."

"Do you keep a recipe box, Mrs. McRae? Because I'd love to riffle through it."

She waved her hand. "Please, call me Odell." Her bottom lip protruded. "There's no box, I'm afraid." She tapped her temple. "I keep my recipes right up here."

Dawsey took the tray and placed it on the bed. "What a shame. I'm quite the cook, too, if I say so myself." She hooked her arm through Odell's and walked her toward the entrance. "Have you ever made sweet potato bread?"

Her eyes widened. "No, but I tasted some years ago in Hope Mills. It was delicious."

"You must let me teach you to make your own."

Flashing a doubtful glance at Duncan, Odell began to stammer. "W–Well, I d–don't know. Silas, he. . ."

Winking at Dawsey, Duncan slid his arm around his mother's shoulders. "I think it'll be just fine, Ma. I'll stay right there in the kitchen with you two. You know. . .just in case?"

His mother cut her eyes to him. "Are you sure?"

He nodded, his expression solemn.

Odell smiled and clasped her hands. "All right, then. I'll send for you this afternoon."

Dawsey squeezed her fingers. "Wonderful. I'm looking forward to cooking with you. I may even jot down some of your secrets."

Odell chuckled until she reached the bottom step. "That'll be just fine, honey. I'm pleased to share."

Grinning, Duncan paused on the threshold. "You're as smart as you are pretty."

He closed and latched the door, and the jolly tune he whistled as he crossed the yard made Dawsey smile. "You're fairly wise, yourself, Duncan McRae."

Ellie huffed and fumed for a quarter mile before she doubled back and started for the house.

Blast that hollow-legged Tiller for gobbling three times more grub in half the time as anyone else at the table. When he excused himself, still chewing a mouthful of corn bread, Ellie had no inkling where he aimed to go or she'd have found a way to beat him to the bedroom.

Of course, that meant getting past Mama without cleaning her plate, a next to impossible trick. If the stubborn little woman had ever taken no for an answer, Ellie would've skipped the noon meal outright. Instead, she wolfed down food she hadn't the slightest interest in eating then hurried out back to find Tiller had gotten the jump on her.

By thunder! Before the day was out, she'd find a way to talk to Dawsey without a passel of prying eyes.

She trudged into the yard with her mind settled on her favorite stump and a quiet think. Too late, she noticed Pa and Wyatt perched at the edge of the porch like roosting hens, cackling as if they'd both laid an egg.

"Here she comes," Papa hollered. He had the bothersome habit of announcing her like she was Mary, Queen of Scots.

Pretending not to hear, Ellie veered toward the shed.

"Hey, gal, scoot yourself over here," he called.

Snared. Shoulders drooping, she slumped their way.

Pa greeted her with a big smile. "Where you been, Puddin'? This is your second walk since breakfast. Before long, you'll wear out your boot leather."

Troubled by Wyatt's presence, she crossed her arms and sat tight lipped on the other side of Pa.

Hooper's horse, stretching his neck to nip at a weed near the rain barrel, stood saddled and tied to the rail. Ellie longed to know why, but she wouldn't ask since she didn't care to speak.

Wyatt leaned into sight at the corner of her eye. "Where'd you run off to so quick after vittles?"

She gritted her teeth and took a sudden interest in the bank of dark clouds forming in the distance.

Pa cleared his throat. "Wyatt's speaking to you, girl."

"Nowhere at all," she said quickly, staring straight ahead. "Just felt like a stroll."

His hazy figure seemed to fidget. "I'd sure like to take a stroll sometime."

She flicked her wrist. "It's a big swamp. What's holding you?"

Wyatt's laugh sounded strained. "I meant with you."

She felt the urge to push off the porch and run headlong into quicksand. Instead, she gripped the splintered cypress and swallowed her rising tears. Grinding holes in the dank soil with the toe of her boot, she shrugged. "I may go again someday."

Two sets of eyes bored into her so hard she felt lashes tickle her skin. If Hooper hadn't stepped out of the door, she'd be darting for the swamp.

"Where's Ma and Duncan?"

Pa peeled his stare from Ellie and lifted his chin. "Right there in the cabin, last I saw."

Hooper grabbed the rail and lowered his lanky body to the ground. Squeezing between Ellie and the post, he sat down on the porch. "Well, they're gone now."

Pa grunted. "Must've slipped out while me and Wyatt were in the barn." He pointed beyond the shed. "Might be in the chicken yard"—he grinned—"wringing and plucking for supper."

Hooper rested his arm around Ellie's shoulders and gave her a little shake. "Where've you been all morning?"

She read the gentle question in his eyes. "I've been sorting out some things."

He nodded, his lips pressed together. "Did you get them sorted?"

She smiled shyly. "I reckon so."

Wyatt, with the dunderheaded reasoning and poor timing of most men, picked that moment to scoot around in front of her, offering his hand. "Come along, Ellie. Your pa won't mind if we take a little walk." He grinned stupidly. "Ain't that right, Silas?"

Her pa—curse his wrinkled hide—flashed as many teeth and little sense as Wyatt. "You two go on and spend a little time together. Just be careful, and don't go too far."

Wyatt stuck his hand out a bit farther, their secret look shining from his sick-cow eyes.

It was the last blow Ellie's busted heart could bear.

Ellie stiffened beside Hooper, and he knew trouble would follow. Wailing, she sprang to her feet, nearly shoving Wyatt to the ground, and tore out past the shed, most likely headed for the chicken yard and Mama's comforting arms.

Wyatt spun on his heels, but Hooper clutched his arm. "Let her go."

The rattled boy pulled free. "I need to go after her, Hoop. You saw what she was like."

Hooper grabbed the back of his collar and pulled him around. "Not just yet. Ellie needs to simmer for a spell."

The worry on Wyatt's face boiled over into fury. "I want to know what's happening here."

He whirled from staring after Ellie to pin Pa and Hooper with an angry glare. "First, Duncan tells me to call her by a different name. Now she's acting like a different girl." He stomped his foot like a pouting child. "I want answers, and I want them now. What happened to my Ellie?"

Hooper watched his ears for puffs of smoke. "Wyatt, calm down."

Fire in his eyes, Wyatt's chin jutted. "I'll kill any man that hurt her."

Still seated, Pa raised his hand. "Since you'd have to start with me, let's hold off on that killing talk." He gazed at the spot where Ellie disappeared. "At any rate, the ache in my old heart may do the job for you."

Wyatt's mouth parted. "What do you mean? You hurt Ellie?"

Standing with a chorus of creaky joints, Pa patted him on the shoulder. "Let's finish my work in the barn while I tell you the whole story." He brandished a finger. "I warn you, it's a right fanciful tale."

Hooper touched his arm. "Before you go, there's something I need to say."

Pa arched his brows. "Sounds serious."

Tightening his mouth, Hooper nodded. "You're going to think so."

"What is it, son?"

After a deep breath, he took the leap. "I'm going to ride out and see Henry, ask him to send Boss with me to Fayetteville."

Pa's head shot forward, one ear toward Hooper, as if he couldn't believe what he'd heard. "You what?"

"I want to get word to Dawsey's folks that she's in one piece." He shifted his jaw. "It's the least I can do."

"Dawsey?" Wyatt took a step closer. "Is that the name Duncan told me to call Ellie?"

Pa pushed him out of the way. "No, it ain't. Stand there and be quiet while I sort out my lunatic son."

Hooper held up his hand. "I know it sounds crazy, but I have a plan. Boss Strong's as slippery as Ellie. He could get in and out faster than you can spit, and no one in Fayetteville would ever tie him to us."

Pa swung his arm, brushing the idea aside. "It's foolishness, Hooper. If you're going to take the risk anyway, load the girl in the wagon and haul her home, set her out on the edge of town and be done with her."

Hooper braced his hands on his hips. "Don't think I haven't considered it." He hooked his thumb in the direction of the shed. "It's not that simple now. We made a mess we still have to clean up. Is that the Ellie you want to live with from now on?"

Pa's eyes widened. "No, sir."

"All right then. Send me and Boss to Fayetteville."

Pa stared at the ground for a long time then shook his head. "Can't do it, Hooper. The last thing we need is a tie between Fayetteville and the Lowry gang." He raised determined eyes. "Son, if just my hide was at stake, I'd say go. If you bring a firestorm on our house, your ma and Ellie will burn with the rest of us." He spat across the yard. "It's a bad idea."

Hooper's steely gaze challenged him. "I won't be responsible for bringing harm to Dawsey's pa."

Gnawing his bottom lip, Papa studied him. "That feisty little gal cast a spell on you?"

Hooper scowled but didn't answer.

After a bit, Pa blew out his breath. "Whatever happens to Mr.

Wilkes is on my head, like it's been from the start." He rested a hand on Hooper's shoulder. "Rest easy, son. None of this is your fault." His usual smile in place, he dipped his head at Hooper's horse. "Unsaddle that nag and you can help us in the barn." He turned to Wyatt. "How skilled are you at shoveling manure?"

Wyatt scrunched his face. "It don't take much thought. Why?"

Pa took his arm and herded him up the muddy path. "You can show me what you mean while I tell you my story."

Still uneasy, Hooper took the horse's reins and followed.

Chapter 24

Ellie sat with her back propped against a black gum tree, moisture from the cold ground seeping through her britches to her skin. Papa had steered her wrong. The chicken yard was empty, unless she counted clucking hens, skinny pullets, and one strutting rooster.

She wiped her nose on her sleeve but left the persistent tears to drip. She didn't remember crying so hard her whole life and couldn't seem to dry up.

When she ran toward the coop, bawling for Ma, the chickens had scattered to the four corners. Now that she'd settled to hiccups and sniffles, a curious hen ventured forward, her head bobbing as she planted one spindly leg in front of the other. She reached the fence and stood craning her long neck toward Ellie, muttering softly in bird-talk as if asking if she was all right.

Ellie smiled through her tears, thinking it downright sad that chickens didn't have a face. All eyes and beaks with no lips or cheeks, they had good reason to be mad at their Creator.

As a child, Ellie sat at Mama's feet and listened to her read the scriptures. Her favorite mentioned God's thoughts toward them of peace and an expected end.

Ellie had long since given up on the God of Mama's Bible, certain He'd turned His back on Scuffletown. Had He planned the awful thing that happened or just allowed it?

Either way, He'd hardly kept His word about an expected end, which meant her case against Him rivaled that of the chickens. The only thing left was to learn what sort of life she'd been born to live. Maybe then she could survive the one fate had handed her.

"Don't fret about me, little speckled hen." She pushed off the ground and swiped at the muddy circle on her backside. "I reckon I know what I have to do."

She hurried to the shed and peeked around the corner. No one sat on the porch, and Hooper's horse was gone. Muted laughter drifted to her from inside the barn.

Lying low, she scurried to the house and sidled along the wall to the rear. Busting past the corner, she ran toward her room. Halfway there, she slowed to a walk, the hair on her neck crawling. Near the bottom step, she came to a full stop, gaping at the open door.

With slow, cautious strides, she made her way to the threshold. Holding on to the frame, she leaned to peer inside, sure of what she'd find.

Dawsey was gone.

Spinning, Ellie hurled herself off the porch and landed with a *thump* on the uneven ground. Turning her ankle, she limped a few steps then dashed for the house. Taking no time for the front stoop, she threw her legs over the side rail and hit the door so hard with the palm of her hand, it slammed against the wall, rattling the front window. "She's gone, Ma! Dawsey got away. She—"

Three sets of eyes gawked at her. Duncan from the table where he held a knife and a knotty potato. Mama from the counter, sifting flour into a wide metal bowl. Dawsey, with a dishcloth in her hand and Mama's apron tied around her waist, blinked at her from the sink.

Ellie blinked right back. "W–What's going on here?"

Ma beamed. "Dawsey's teaching us to make sweet potato bread."

Sweet potato bread? Ellie fought the urge to rail, to storm at Duncan and rake potatoes to the floor, to dash the bowl from Mama's hands.

The only one without a simpering smile was Dawsey. She lifted an apron toward Ellie. "Would you like to help?"

"I don't cook." The witless answer fell from her mouth. Blushing, she ambled to the hearth to stir the fire. She longed to flee their staring eyes but refused to run again.

Duncan went back to peeling, Mama shook her sifter, and the kitchen sounds took up again.

Ellie sat on the stool near the fireplace, feigning interest in the flames. Hefting a split log from the box, she balanced it cut side up on the burning stack.

A wood beetle slipped from a narrow crack and scurried over the flat surface, desperate to find a way out of his fix. Wavering heat drove him from the back side, black smoke from the front. Ellie offered him the poker to escape, but it frightened him. He bailed off the edge and soared into the flames, meeting his fate with a *pop* and *sizzle*.

Look before you leap!

In a frantic effort to save himself, the bug took a death-leap off the wrong side of indecision. Ellie worried she was about to do the same, but going up in flames would be better than her frenzied dash around the truth.

She stood so fast, the legs of the stool squealed against the floor.

The three unlikely bakers stilled, watching her.

Wiping moist hands on her britches, she nodded at Dawsey. "I need to talk to you."

The girl across the room, so like her yet utterly different, nodded back. "All right."

Ellie started for the door. "Alone."

"Go on, honey," Mama said softly to Dawsey. "This batter will keep."

Ellie took the steps on stilted legs. A cool afternoon breeze blew up and chilled the beaded sweat above her lips. Turning the corner, she made her way to her bedroom with Dawsey dogging her heels.

Duncan followed at a distance, his heavy footsteps swishing in the grass.

At the entrance, Ellie stepped aside and let Dawsey go first. She motioned to Duncan. "Lock this door. Don't let anyone in or out until I say."

He nodded. The bar slid into place with a jarring clatter.

Ellie swallowed hard and turned. No sense dancing around, her feet were too tired from running. "I want to know everything. Don't leave nothing out."

In her innocence, she'd asked for the same on the night Dawsey came then stumbled under Mama's unburdening. This time she sensed the weight she'd asked to bear. Her back pressed to the door, she steeled herself and motioned to Dawsey. "Go on."

"What do you want to know?" Dawsey whispered.

Ellie tipped her chin. "What are they like? You know. . ." She bit her bottom lip. "The Wilkeses."

Dawsey flinched. She settled on the bed, arranging her skirt around her legs, and patted the quilt. "Come sit down, please."

Fists clenched, Ellie perched at the edge of the mattress, as far from Dawsey as she could get without falling off the end. Heart pounding, she waited.

"I'll tell you everything," Dawsey said. "But first. . ." She reached a trembling hand toward Ellie's face. "Do you mind?"

Ellie shook her head.

Dawsey scooted closer, a look of wonder on her face. Brushing the hair off Ellie's forehead, her roving eyes traced her features while her fingertips lightly touched her chin then smoothed her cheek. She tweaked both their noses at once and giggled.

Fighting a smile, Ellie brushed her away.

Dawsey caught her hand, measuring Ellie's palm against her own. Lacing their fingers, she closed her hand, and Ellie did, too.

Staring at their matching fists, crazy, cleansing mirth bubbled up Ellie's throat. Pulling free, she covered her mouth and howled until she wept. Without warning, the riotous tears became aching sobs that threatened to burst her heart.

Dawsey, her own wild laughter silenced, gathered Ellie in her arms and rocked her. "There's only Father, Dilsey. Our mother died. . .shortly after you disappeared."

Ellie stiffened against her shoulder. "Yes, Mama told me. Do you remember her at all?"

"Nothing. I was far too young when it happened." Dawsey set Ellie up and smoothed her hair. "Father raised me the best he could, with the help of an only sister." She smiled. "You'll like Aunt Lavinia. Aunt Livvy, I call her. She's stern but only on the surface. At heart, she's fluffy meringue."

Ellie had spent hours picturing the woman who birthed her, giving her kind eyes and a handsome face. It grieved her to think she'd never feel her touch or hear her voice. "I can't help wondering how she looked."

Dawsey hummed thoughtfully. "That much is possible. Simply look in the mirror." She laughed softly. "Or at me. Aunt Livvy says we're her image."

Trying to imagine, Ellie stared at Dawsey's face. Sudden sympathy pricked her heart. "It must've been hard growing up without her."

Dawsey nodded.

"Our father never remarried?"

Dawsey studied her freshly scrubbed nails.

Embarrassed, Ellie slid hers beneath her legs.

"I'm afraid not," Dawsey finally said. "Your disappearance, followed so closely by Mother's death, changed him, and not for the better. He grew quite distant over the years, leaving the burden of raising me to Aunt Livvy."

Ellie frowned. "Why would he do such a thing when you'd already lost your ma?"

Their eyes met. "I believe he blamed himself."

"For what?"

"For not finding you in time to strengthen and encourage Mother. She was frail and ill, but they say she lost the will to live." Dawsey sighed. "At last, I understand why."

"At last?" Stunned, Ellie watched her face. "You didn't know about me?"

Dawsey shook her head. "They hid the truth behind a shroud of secrecy. I knew something was terribly wrong but had no idea you existed."

Ellie leaned to grip her forehead. "You must despise my family. They've caused yours such dreadful heartache."

Dawsey touched her shoulder. "Don't you see, Dilsey? My family *is* your family. The same blood runs in our veins. You're a Wilkes, not a McRae. You belong with us."

Ellie slid from under Dawsey's hand and stood. "Mind your tongue. I am so a McRae."

Standing with her, Dawsey clutched her arm. "But you're not. By an act of cruel fate, Silas lifted you from our crib instead of me. A different role of the dice, and I would be living in this mudhole and you with our father in Fayetteville."

Ellie furiously shook her head. "You're wrong. Papa chose me."

Gazing fondly, Dawsey stroked her cheek. "Now that we've met, I almost wish it had been me so you'd be spared this life of hardship."

Ellie pushed her hand away. "That's what you think? That I'd trade lives with you?" She stamped her foot. "I don't live in a fine house or wear fancy clothes, but unlike you, I have two parents who love me."

Dawsey winced and fresh tears filled her eyes.

Ellie stormed to the door and pounded with her fists. "Duncan, unlock this blasted thing."

The door rattled open, and Duncan gaped at her. "You look like death. What happened?"

Ignoring him, she pushed past, stopping fast on the bottom step.

Wyatt leaned against the back of the house, a determined glint in his eyes.

Dawsey followed her out and clutched her wrist. "I didn't mean to hurt you, but whatever happens now, we're sisters, Dilsey. We have to stick together."

Moments before, Dawsey's hands exploring Ellie's face had filled her with joy. Now the grasping fingers seared her flesh.

She yearned for Ma's soothing strokes to blot out Dawsey's hateful touch, Pa's familiar yarns to dim her words. As usual, Hooper was right. A talk with Dawsey had settled her mind at last.

She squirmed free and lifted her chin. "I'm not your sister, Miss Wilkes." Her jaw set, she bounded to the ground and glared. "And don't call me Dilsey no more. I'm Ellie."

Dawsey stared after Ellie until Duncan moved in front of her, blocking her view.

He took her shoulders and gently guided her over the threshold and closed the door. "Are you all right?"

She nodded vacantly.

"What stung Ellie?"

Dawsey pressed her palm to her forehead. "I'm afraid I did. How could I have been so stupid?"

"It can't be that bad. What did you do?"

She met his laughing gaze. "I said she wasn't a McRae."

His laughter died. "That's bad. You can steal Ellie's horse, kick her dog, but don't ever say she's not a McRae."

Dawsey nodded. "I just learned that lesson firsthand." She searched his eyes. "Will she ever forgive me?"

Duncan lightly touched her arm. "Don't worry about Ellie. She'll come around as long as you don't make the same mistake twice."

She bit her tongue.

No matter how stubborn the McRae mind-set, they couldn't alter the facts, but it would do no good to argue the point with Duncan. There was wisdom in biding her time.

He glanced over his shoulder then pulled her away from the door. "There's something I'm itching to tell you."

Intrigued, she sat on the bed and felt only a brief pang of impropriety when he sat down beside her. "Goodness, what now?"

He smiled. "I had me a little talk with Wyatt just now."

She frowned. "The man outside?"

"He's Ellie's beau."

Her mind reeled at the news. "Ellie has a suitor?"

He shrugged. "Well, she did. Wyatt's still sweet on her, but she has no use for him lately."

"I see," Dawsey said. Only she didn't.

Duncan took off his hat and mangled it. "Dawsey, I'm trying to tell you something important."

She patted his hand. "I'm sorry. Go on."

He wiggled around to face her. "So Wyatt wanders up looking for Ellie, and he commences to talking. Seems Hooper came up with the idea to ride into Fayetteville, to get word to your pa that you're all right."

Remembering Hooper's promise to prove himself, Dawsey's breath caught in her throat. "He did?"

Duncan nodded. "Yes, but he let Pa throw cold water on his plans."

Her heart sank with a thud. "Then why bother telling me?"

Looking like a cat in a canary cage, he winked. "Because I'm going instead."

She gasped. "To see my father?"

He chuckled. "I won't exactly knock on his door, but I'll find a way to leave him a message. I've muddled it over in my mind, and I don't see how such a kindness could hurt."

"And your father?"

"He told Hooper not to go." He grinned. "Never said a word to me."

She sat back and stared. "You'd ride all the way to Fayetteville for my sake? Why, that would be wonderful."

Duncan dropped his hat on his head. "That's exactly what I aim to do."

She scooted closer and clutched his hands. "Oh, Duncan! Can you go before Christmas?"

He frowned. "That's a bit soon, but before the first of the year for certain." He squeezed her fingers and stood. "When you hear I've left for a couple of days, you'll know where I've gone."

Filled with gratitude, she walked him to the door. "I don't know how I'll ever repay you."

He chucked her under the chin. "No charge for my services, ma'am. Just keep it under your hat or it won't work."

Thrilled, she leaned to kiss his cheek. "You've made me so happy."

Beyond his broad shoulder, Hooper strolled across the yard, his troubled eyes fixed on them. Warming to her toes, she pulled away from Duncan and stepped inside.

Long after the door slammed shut and the bar rattled into place, she stood with a wobbly smile on her face. Tears sprang to her eyes as waves of relief flooded her shaky limbs.

Could she trust Duncan to keep his word? The very man who'd helped to kidnap her?

Something told her she could, and the bands on her heart loosened.

Father wouldn't receive the good news for Christmas, but soon after, his anxious mind would be put to rest. After that, despite Dilsey's reaction to the truth, Dawsey would find a way to take her home.

Chapter 25

Ghostly mists swirled in the faint yellow glow of the lantern, adding a touch of magic to Silas McRae's long-winded tale. Like most of his stories, the latest centered around Henry Berry Lowry, his mysterious tribe's only hope. Hero to the downtrodden Indian, scourge to the Scottish farmers scornfully dubbed "the Macks" by their sworn enemies, Henry sounded one part champion and two parts whimsical figure.

Dawsey couldn't wait to hear more.

Tightly wrapped in his own story, Silas peered closer at the spellbound listeners gathered around his chair on the front porch. "Henry's bulletproof, you know. They've wanted him dead for years and not one day closer to killing him."

Silas's fervor drew Tiller to his knees. With his hair rumpled to spikes in front and his bulging eyes aglow, he tipped so close to Silas they almost bumped noses. "You're funning us, ain't you Uncle Si? Henry Berry's just a man, after all. Flesh and blood, like the rest of us."

Silas cocked his head, his eyes gone to narrow slits. "You're sure about that, are you?"

Tiller's throat bobbed like a mole in a hole. "What are you gettin' at?"

"I'll tell you by thunder," Silas crowed. "You've heard of giants, ain't you? Like Goliath of old?"

Tiller swallowed again and nodded. "He's that fellow from the Bible."

Bug-eyed, Silas nodded. "I'm saying there be giants among us today, Henry Lowry the biggest one of all."

Tiller cocked his head. "Uncle Si, King David felled Goliath with a little old slingshot."

Silas slapped his leg. "Son, I'm glad you brought that up." He squinted at the sky. "The truth is, Henry is more of a giant in the way David was—able to take down his biggest foes with little more than his bare hands."

With every day that passed among the McRaes, Dawsey felt less like a captive and more like a visiting friend. Since that fateful day a week ago, when she'd mixed sweet potato bread with Odell, Dawsey spent most of her time puttering in the kitchen or huddled around the table with the family. Each evening they gathered for one of Silas's stories before Duncan walked her to the little room and locked her inside for the night.

Dilsey still danced a wide circle around her, refusing to look up or answer when Dawsey called her name.

Despite constant brooding over her sister, she had come to enjoy Duncan's company, and she blessed sweet-faced Odell for surrendering her hearth and allowing Dawsey to cook to her heart's content. Odell taught her to fry rabbits, stew venison, and roast a wild boar, foods Dawsey seldom saw back home.

Hooper sat across from her beside Duncan, silent as usual. On frequent raids with Henry, he had ducked in and out over the last few days. One day he'd be a brooding presence at the table, the next his chair sat empty.

Dawsey pretended to get along with him as well, but in the deep places of her heart, she found it hard to forgive him for taking her out of Fayetteville against her will.

Silas still avoided her eyes when they spoke. At breakfast that morning, he'd offered her the last golden biscuit with a soft smile on his face. Far from an apology, but Dawsey sensed his repentant heart. She told herself that being kind to Silas furthered her plan of escape, but the inscrutable truth was she found him hard to resist.

Returning her thoughts to the story, she leaned toward him. "How has Henry avoided capture for so long?"

Silas winked. "He's smart, missy. Bold as a bull and slick as a slug. He once dressed like a Confederate and hopped the train, shared lunch with the soldiers and listened while they told tales about the fugitive they were hunting." His eyes twinkled and he grinned. "That fugitive was Henry himself."

Dawsey laughed along with the rest of the family. "He sounds fascinating. And brave."

"Henry has to be brave with all he's up against."

"What started the uprising, Mr. McRae?"

Silas scratched his bearded chin and gazed into the past. "During the war, the Confederates started rounding up men to build Fort Fisher." His jaw tightened. "A fate that turned into a death sentence."

Dawsey's father spoke often of the effort at Fort Fisher, but he'd never mentioned forced labor. "Go on."

"After watching their brothers starve, drown, or die of the fever, our people hid out in the swamps to steer clear of the Home Guard, the devils appointed to round up the work crews. A rogue conscription officer rounded up and killed two of Henry's cousins, so Henry and his men killed the officer. They struck back by executing Henry's father and elder brother. That grave mistake began a war between Henry and the Macks that's lasted all these years."

Odell stood, dusting the back of her dress. "You've told enough stories for one night, old man. It's getting late." She hugged herself and gathered her shawl under her chin. "Besides, it's cold out here. I need to get inside by the fire and warm my feet."

Despite her striking beauty, only slightly beginning to fade, Odell McRae seemed naturally innocent and childlike, with a tender, loving heart. Swaying playfully in front of Silas in the moonlight, she looked like a teasing girl.

The effects of her spell shone from his adoring eyes, and he grinned at his timeless wife. "Are you trying to say it's time for me to hush?"

Her smile meant just for him, she shook her head. "I'm not trying to say it, I did."

Tiller spun her direction. "Not yet, Auntie. I want to hear more stories about Henry."

Silas offered his hand and Odell pulled him to his feet. "Your uncle has a dishpan to empty and a fire to bank."

Silas groaned. "Now, Odie, that's the reason I keep these boys around. It's too costly to feed them otherwise."

They all laughed merrily, except Hooper, who seemed preoccupied with his thoughts.

Dawsey yawned, hiding it with the back of her hand. She glanced at

Duncan, hoping he'd be ready to take her to her room.

Instead, Hooper jumped up and held out his arm. "I'll walk you, Dawsey, so Duncan can help Pa with those chores."

The look on Duncan's face made his displeasure clear, but Hooper gave him no chance to object. He quickly led Dawsey away from the family and around the side of the house.

Near the bottom step, he paused and cleared his throat. "Do you mind if we sit a spell before you go in? There's something I need to tell you."

Dawsey patted his arm. "Be a gentleman and let me jump ahead of you. I have something pressing to share."

He took her hand and helped her to sit. "What I have to say is important, too."

"Me first," she insisted. "It won't take long."

He smiled and dipped his head. "Go on then."

"Your father's story opened my eyes, Hooper. I'm afraid I've held a narrow view of the war. North against South—very cut and dried in my mind. I never considered the impact on those who chose to remain neutral." She raised her head and sought his eyes. "You must be honored to know Henry."

Hooper nodded, a frown teasing his brows. "Henry's a fine man, but don't be misled. He's done some ruthless things." He sighed. "Some folks call him a cold-blooded murderer."

"What do you think?"

Hooper tensed. "I don't hold with all of his deeds, but I know his heart. They pushed until he pushed back, and. . .well. . .Henry pushes hard."

She glanced at him in the moonlight, her mouth twisting. "So do you—when you think you have the right."

The foolish man preened, taking her angry words for a compliment. He jutted his chin. "None of us struck first, but my people won't accept sprawling in the dirt."

Dawsey tilted her head to study his dark eyes and hair. "Just who are your people, Hooper? With a name like McRae, I would expect your loyalties to lie with the Scots, and yet you don't resemble them in the least."

A flush darkened his face in the moonlight. "My grandpa was a Scottish immigrant. He settled here on the Lumber River and married an Indian girl." He smiled. "Grandpa never held with the ways of his people. He'd say, 'Don't mind the Mc before my name. I ain't no lousy Mack.'"

Hooper studied his hands, flicking his thumbnails together. "Sometimes I feel I'm the only McRae left to bear the weight. Pa's getting on in years, and Duncan. . . Let's just say Duncan doesn't share our passion."

"You don't have to bear your burdens alone, you know." The words fell unbidden from Dawsey's lips. Already out on a limb, she decided to flap her wings. "There are strong arms waiting to lift the weight off your shoulders."

He stilled. "And whose would they be?"

She held up her finger. "Wait." Closing her eyes, she strained for the words. "Oh, yes, I've got it now. 'Some trust in chariots, and some in horses: but we will remember the name of the Lord our God.'"

He folded his arms and leaned against the door. "What was that?"

"Comfort for the downtrodden."

He squinted at her.

"A scripture, Hooper."

He laughed. "I may be a backwoods heathen, Miss Wilkes, but I recognize Bible words. I meant that I don't see how scriptures can help."

"Then you haven't spent much time reading them."

He shrugged. "Not as much as you, I suppose. Ma reads to us sometimes."

"She does?"

"Well, she used to, when we were young. It's the only book she owns. In fact," he said, "I've patterned my life after two of the Psalms."

She shifted toward him on the step. "Really? I dearly love the Psalms. Please quote them for me."

He swelled his chest. " 'Defend the poor and fatherless: do justice to the afflicted and needy.'"

She clasped her hands. "One of my favorites."

" 'Deliver the poor and needy," he said, clearly waiting for her reaction. "Rid them out of the hand of the wicked.'"

She tightened her lips. "I fear you've taken the verses out of context, Hooper. David is calling on the Lord for deliverance. The Creator is our champion. It's His place to avenge."

She took a deep breath. " 'O God, to whom vengeance belongeth, shew thyself.'"

Hooper snorted. "It wouldn't do for God to show Himself around here unless He's a Mack. The Scots show little patience for outliers."

Dawsey tensed. "Please don't make light of spiritual matters."

A sheepish look crossed his face. "You sound like our ma."

Pouting, she straightened her skirts. "If so, your ma gives wise counsel."

Hooper grinned. "I didn't mean to offend you." His teasing mood turned solemn. "My people are penniless, hungry, and scared they'll be cast into irons. They need a real reason to hope. If God could end this war, His help would be most welcome." He lifted one shoulder. "Since He doesn't seem inclined to lend a hand, I'll do what I must to relieve them."

Dawsey huffed impatiently. "I know your desire is to render aid, but the scripture says, 'Happy is he. . .whose hope is in the Lord his God.' It doesn't say, 'Whose hope is in Hooper McRae.'"

He stood, gaping at her. "There's no talking to you about this." Spinning on his heels, he clenched his fists and stalked away.

Shame crept up Dawsey's neck. Her advice was spiritually sound and every scripture true, but she'd been harsh with Hooper, needling him on purpose. Worse, she'd thoroughly enjoyed seeing him squirm.

Watching him round the corner of the house, Dawsey wondered if she should call him back. The urge to run after him and apologize took her three steps across the yard before the truth enveloped her in a wave of excited disbelief.

She smiled at the irony. The blundering man who'd brought her to a godforsaken swamp had just unwittingly released her.

With utmost quiet and lightning in her steps, Dawsey whirled and hurried inside her room. She threw on layers of clothes then picked up a chunk of leftover bread from a plate on the bedside table, wrapping it in a white embroidered napkin. Her fingers itched to take the lantern, but she couldn't risk the light giving her away. Instead, she snatched several matches, shoving them in the pocket of Dilsey's trousers.

Pausing at the door, she stared toward the darkened house, thoughts of her sister tugging her heart. "I'll come back for you, Dilsey," she whispered. "I promise."

The shadowy outline of the shed became the needle for Dawsey's compass. The cavernous bog lurked directly in front of the loathsome building, waiting to swallow her whole. To get her bearings, she checked the position of the moon then lit out for the trees.

She knew where she was and where she was going. Forgetting to lock her in Dilsey's room wasn't Hooper's first mistake of the night. He'd let it slip that his people were Lumbee Indians, living along the Lumber River—which meant she must be near Lumberton in Robeson County.

Her heart a throbbing lump in her throat, she hunched lower and darted into the woods, kicking a tangle of thorny vines off her foot as she ran. The stand of trees broke sooner than she expected and she paused, but only briefly, before wading into ankle-deep water.

Tasting freedom, Dawsey's determination surged. It would take more than quicksand, alligators, and the Lowry gang to keep her a prisoner of Hooper McRae for another minute.

If she had to crawl from there to Fayetteville, no one could keep her from going home.

Hooper stretched out on his bedroll in front of the fire, Dawsey's offense like burning embers in his throat. For reasons he couldn't comprehend, he longed for her to understand about the injustice forced upon the Lumbee people. Stranger still, he craved her approval.

He'd explained his feelings to her the best he knew how to no avail. With a haughty air and a sassy mouth filled with Bible words, she'd taken him by the ear like a naughty child.

Turning over, he kicked his covers so hard his toes shot out and hit the woodbox with a clatter.

Across the room, Ellie sat up and stared with bleary eyes. "Hooper? What on earth?"

"Pipe down, you two," Duncan growled over his shoulder. "I'm trying to sleep."

Hooper mumbled an apology and pulled the blanket up to his chin, his mind consumed with Dawsey. The ill-mannered girl hadn't given him a chance to speak his mind, to tell her he at least tried to send word to her pa.

He wished he'd never heard about Papa's golden lamp and regretted the day he'd ever set eyes on Dawsey Wilkes. He saw only one way to rid his family of the blight he'd brought down on them. He'd have to find a way to take her home.

Chapter 26

Hooper awoke to the bitter smell of burned bacon. Groggy and confused, he buried his nose in his quilt and tried to go back to sleep.

Papa nudged him none too gently with the toe of his boot. "Up there, boy."

"Cut it out, Pa. I'm awake." He rolled onto his side and blinked sleepy eyes toward the hearth.

Ma stood beside Ellie, guiding her hand over the skillet.

The soft murmur of their voices almost lulled him back to sleep.

"Like this, sugar. Slosh the fat real careful-like over the yolks. Make sure they're floating free before you try to turn them or you'll bust the yellow. Nothing makes a man madder than sopping a biscuit in a hard-cooked egg."

Duncan groaned and turned over on his mat. "You've got it wrong, Ma. Nothing makes me madder than burned bacon. What'd she do, turn it to embers?"

Mama angled toward Duncan with her hand on her hip. "Hush, or you'll find them on your plate while the rest of us enjoy Ellie's do-overs."

Duncan laughed and sprang to his feet, crossing to the steaming basin to slosh water on his face. Spinning, he shook his wet hands toward Tiller, asleep in the corner.

The boy yowled and sat up swinging his fists.

With a grunt, Papa returned to his place at the head of the table. "Careful with them do-overs, Ellie. Good bacon's hard to come by."

Mama swung the metal arm holding her teakettle into place over the fire. "There may be more mistakes before Ellie learns, but there won't be any wasted food, Silas. I'll eat it myself."

Ellie scowled. "I will, Ma. I burned it."

Pulling out a chair, Duncan sat down to pull on his boots. "That sounds fair to me. Just so I never have to eat the stinking mess."

Tiller sat up rubbing his eyes. "I'll eat it," he mumbled. "What are we talking about?"

Duncan ruffled his hair. "No-account bacon, boy. Can't you smell it?"

"It's not all that bad," Ellie said.

He laughed. "Worse. I know ruined when I smell it."

Ma blew a strand of hair from her eyes and gave him a blistering look. "We'll do what we have to do to help your sister learn."

"Don't worry, Ma," Hooper said. "I can get you more bacon."

Duncan laughed. "I reckon you can, straight off the hook in a Rebel smokehouse." He glanced up from folding the cuff of his shirt. "Or will you crawl into Sheriff McMillan's kitchen window and lift it from the breakfast table?"

"That's enough, Duncan," Pa growled.

Ma expertly flipped two eggs onto a plate with a biscuit and held it toward Duncan. "Set this on the table then fetch Dawsey. It's late. She must be starved."

Snatching the plate from her hand, Duncan slid it in front of Papa then hustled for the door.

Ellie's head jerked up. "She's not going to help us cook, is she?"

Ma's brows arched, but she bit back whatever she thought to say. "We're about done anyway."

Ellie shot her a satisfied smile. She shoved the spatula under one of the eggs, frowning when it came up smeared yellow.

Mama bumped her with a hip. "That can be mine, honey. I like 'em hard-cooked and stuck between slices of bread." She gave her a heartening nod. "You know, like a sandwich."

Grinning, Hooper stretched then pushed off the floor. He rolled his mat and placed it against the wall. Steeling his resolve, he glanced toward the table. "There's something we need settled first thing this morning, Pa. It's about Dawsey."

Pa's eyes widened over the top of his coffee. He finished taking a sip and lowered his mug. "Before we belly up to breakfast? You ain't even washed your face."

Hooper hitched up his pants. "This won't keep. I think it's time we took Dawsey home."

Pa frowned and leaned back in his chair. He opened his mouth to speak, but the door blasted open with a *crash*.

Hooper spun and Tiller dove under the table.

Duncan tripped over the threshold and stumbled inside gasping for breath. "Pa!" he managed before he doubled over, panting for air.

Upsetting his coffee, Papa bolted from the table and ran to his side.

Hooper and Ellie reached the rack at the same time, readying their guns. Ellie sidled to the window, carefully peering out while Hooper's gaze jumped from the door to his winded brother.

"What is it, son?" Pa shouted.

"Sh–She's gone." Duncan glanced at Ellie. "Really gone this time." He held on to his knees and took several ragged breaths before he continued. "The door's wide open. I checked everywhere—the outhouse, the chicken yard—everywhere. She's nowhere to be found."

Bewilderment wrinkled Pa's brow. "How can that be?"

Duncan straightened and pointed an accusing finger. "He didn't bolt the door."

All eyes swung to Hooper. The room spun as he wracked his mind, desperate to remember. He'd walked her back. Sat with her on the porch. They'd quarreled.

He gripped his forehead. "It's my fault. I left her standing by the steps."

Ellie drew in sharply. "What were you thinking?"

Tiller crawled from under the table, freckles jumping off his chalky face. "We have to find her."

Hugging herself, Ma stared over their heads. "That poor girl, wandering through the swamp all night." She gasped. "Oh Silas! She might've stumbled into the bog."

Rage flashed in Papa's eyes. "If anything happens to her, it's on your head, son."

Hooper nodded. "None of you could blame me more than I blame myself."

Ellie stared with glazed eyes, gripping her gun with white fingers. For the first time in her life, she seemed small and unsure of herself.

He took a step toward her. "I'm sorry, honey."

She flinched and shook her head. "Just find her."

He squeezed her shoulder. "You have my word."

Duncan snorted. "You may find pieces. She's gator bait by now."

Tiller balled his fists and scowled. "No, she ain't."

Pa punched Duncan's arm. "Hush that kind of talk, and go with your brother to search. Dawsey has eight or nine hours on you, at least."

Ellie lifted her coat off the peg. "I'm going, too."

"Me, too," Tiller said, starting for the door.

Pa pulled him up by the collar. "No, sir. You'll stay right here with us."

"Aw, Uncle Si."

"Scoot," Pa said, and Tiller slunk away to sulk at the table.

Ma caught Ellie's sleeve. "Wait just a minute." Hovering near the table, she dumped biscuits and bacon into a napkin and tied it into a bundle. "Take this. You'll be hungry later."

Pressing it into Ellie's hands, she gripped and held them. "It's enough for Dawsey, too."

Ellie took the food and spun for the door. Duncan followed her out.

Grabbing his coat, Hooper paused on the threshold. "I'm sorry, Pa."

He tipped his chin toward the woods. "Just find her, son."

"When I do, I'm taking her home where she belongs."

Pa's jaw tensed. He glanced at Tiller then lowered his voice. "Let's hope it's not in a pine box."

Dawsey dragged herself clear of the crisscrossed branches only to have an identical wall of brambles spring up in front of her face. She moaned but not aloud. The last thing she wanted was to give away her position in the brush. Not out of fear of the McRaes; she'd give her dowry to see one of their familiar faces. She hid from whatever had stalked her all night in pitch darkness, the frightening noises only lessening as the light of dawn pierced the thick canopy.

She ran her tongue over her dry, cracked lips. Water surrounded her, so murky and covered in scum she feared trying a sip, despite her burning thirst. A rumble deep in her stomach made her long for the chunk of bread she'd shoved in her pocket, but she'd lost it somehow during the night.

Fighting her way through the dense vegetation took every ounce of her strength. Desperate for sleep, she released her breath on a sigh and lay down to rest her head on her arms.

Jerking awake, she swatted a slimy, clinging lizard from her hand. The creature wriggled beneath a layer of flattened grass, his horrid tail the last part to slither out of sight. Near tears, Dawsey pushed to her scraped, stinging knees and forced her head and shoulders forward into the brush. After crawling through the woods all night, help should be just a little farther. She had to keep moving.

She prayed, straining her eyes for a glimpse of a road, a campfire, or a cabin. She stared so hard, her eyeballs stung. Reaching to wipe away her frightened tears, she stilled with a gasp.

Just ahead, a white cloth hung, snagged by a thorny branch. The blue embroidery around the edges stood out like a lighthouse beacon. Shaking her head and denying furiously under her breath, her aching heart knew the truth from ten feet away. She scrambled for the muddy napkin she'd carried with her from Dilsey's room.

The bread was gone, every crumb. Animals and insects had eaten her breakfast while she circled in the dark like a blundering fool.

She wiped her eyes and raised her trembling chin. Suddenly, her confinement didn't seem so bad. The locking bar clattering into place became the sound of security in her feverish mind.

If she knew the way to the McRaes' cabin, she'd scramble there as fast as she could and lock the door herself, but every way she turned, the same thick-trunked cypress towered overhead. The same branches hung with mossy gray beards. Most upsetting of all, the same three inches of foul-smelling water covered the ground as far as she could see.

Forcing herself to stand, she peered around, desperate to get her bearings. Across a shallow pond was a slight rise covered by a field of tall yellow cane. If she could make it to the other side without plunging into quicksand, and if the rise was dry, she'd hollow out a place in the cane to rest.

After a little sleep, she could decide what she had to do next.

For the first time, Ellie's actions felt driven by her heart instead of good sense. Reason said, "Move slowly, listen closely, read the ground for signs." Her burning heart cried, "Run! Beat the brush. Shout Dawsey's name until your throat aches."

Hooper rode alongside, his horse's easy gait a balm to Ellie's jangled nerves. Duncan had branched to the left in front of the house. She and Hooper would ride together until they passed the bog then split off, Ellie to the right and Hooper down the middle.

Feeling his gaze swing her way, she glanced up. "I'm scared, and I don't mind saying it."

He gave her a tight smile. "Dawsey's tough and ornery. If anyone can last the night in a swamp, she can."

Ellie's eyes grew round. "She's as stubborn as a deep root, but she's hardly tough. Dawsey's downright girly, Hooper. She cooks and sweeps up and darns socks." She wiggled her finger at the gloomy clutch of trees. "What could she know about lasting ten minutes out there?"

Hooper shifted toward her in the saddle. "Settle down, honey. She's not you, and that's a fact, but she's sturdier than she looks."

Ellie sighed, the sound closer to a strangled sob. "I hope you're right, because her life depends on it."

He didn't seek to reassure her. If Hooper declared Dawsey as good as dead, it couldn't have scared Ellie more than his brooding silence. Dread seeped into her gut when they reached the outer rim of the bog.

Hooper lifted and settled his hat. "I'll search in a line straight to the Lowrys' cabin. If I reach there without finding her, I'll ask for their help."

"Good." She stared past him toward the woods. "I'll take all the help we can get."

"Be careful," he said. "Watch out for McMillan and his paid assassins. They're as thick as ticks in these woods."

"If that's so, then maybe they'll find Dawsey." She caught his eye. "You be careful, too, you hear?"

He winked and gave her a crooked smile then spurred his horse up the middle of the swamp.

Ellie rode on, forcing herself to pay attention to her tracking. In the summer, she'd watch for crushed or bent blades of grass, the greening of broken twigs, or leaves flipped to their dark bellies. In the heart of winter, with no sap flowing, she'd have to scour the ground.

Hooper's bass fiddle voice throbbed in her head.

Deep toe marks in short steps means a man bears a heavy load. If widely spaced, he's running. Water in a fresh footprint stays muddy for about an hour. In time, the water seeps away, and the outline of the print fades a bit. Turned-over rocks look dark and wet with yellow green patches on the other side.

Remembering the next part, she shuddered.

Stains spilled on the leaves and underbrush may be blood—red when fresh, brown with the passage of time. Low-lying drops are usually from minor wounds. High splatter is more serious. Low or high, a lot of blood spells trouble.

Blood was the last thing Ellie wanted to find. Squinting against the thought, she shook her head. No, a lifeless body would be far worse.

She longed to give up the hunt, to whirl her horse toward home and seek the comfort of Mama's arms. Dawsey's guileless eyes, pleading for forgiveness, kept Ellie's nose to the ground, searching for signs of her sister.

The breath caught in her throat. Just ahead, streaks of mud painted the dry grass a speckled brown. Not the miry muck they saw by the house—this was the soupy, light-brown sludge near the pond. A little farther, she found a rounded, knee-sized hole pressed into a line of deer tracks left before sunrise.

Her heart thundered in her chest as the facts lined up in her head. The soupy sludge and recent knee print told her Dawsey had gone deep into the swamp then circled back. An hour ago, maybe less, she'd come within half a mile of the house. Dawsey was lost and crawling in circles.

Ellie nudged Toby's side with her boot and hurried him through the brush until she reached the edge of a shallow pond. Instead of marking the end of the trail, the widening streak of rippled water quickened her breath. Dawsey's crossing had painted a muddy arrow from one reedy bank to the other.

She rode across, her gaze locked on the other side, searching for the next sign pointing to her sister. It came far sooner than she expected.

Beyond the lapping water, a tunnel opened into a stand of bent and broken cane. She pushed Toby into a gallop and closed the distance in the space of three heartbeats. In even less time, she was on her knees peering into the shadowy den. Fear shot up her throat, and she bit back the cry that sprang to her lips.

Dawsey sat against the back of the wallow sobbing piteously, both hands clutching her leg. She had shed her boot and torn strips from the leg of her britches to tie above and below the white-rimmed, oozing bite.

Not a rattler!

Sensing her there, Dawsey's head jerked up.

"Oh Dilsey, thank God." Her sobs became a whimper, and she stretched out her hand. "Help me?"

Ellie whirled away from the cane and hurled herself on Toby's back, turning him before her backside touched the saddle. She drove him across the pond, slinging water in her wake as Dawsey's hollow cries echoed through the swamp.

Dawsey slowly counted backward from ten, drawing deep breaths between each number. She had to settle her frantic heartbeat and hold very still to keep from spreading the venom.

Her head hurt and her mouth filled with moisture, the way it did before her stomach emptied. Weakness drained her strength, and her insides trembled.

She scoured her mind for a snakebite remedy. She'd read of cutting the wound and applying salt and gunpowder, but she didn't have a knife or either ingredient. Frightened, she realized she'd already done all she could remember from her books on the healing arts.

Seeking just as hard for a psalm, she could only come up with, *"He made a pit, and digged it, and is fallen into the ditch which he made."*

What had she been thinking? Hooper warned her repeatedly with terrible stories of wandering men found dead in the swamp. With insufferable arrogance, she'd counted herself stronger and smarter than all of them. Now, her reckless determination to get home had landed her in a desperate fix.

The thought of Hooper strangely saddened her and pricked her heart a bit like a touch of homesickness. Confused, she brushed away the silly notion.

"Please, God? I'm not ready," she whispered, gazing toward heaven. She'd left too much unsaid, too much undone. If she died miles from home, Father would never know. He'd go to his grave haunted by the mysterious disappearance of both of his daughters.

Feeling quite unladylike, Dawsey leaned over and spit to rid her mouth of a foul taste. Overwhelming drowsiness jolted her with fear. Unsure if the venom caused it or simply fatigue, she refused to give in to her whirling head.

Wasn't it pointless to sit and wait for rescue? What help could she expect after Dilsey had come and gone? If her own flesh and blood had abandoned her, what hope did she have?

Her bottom lip began to quiver. She knew her thoughtless words had angered Dilsey. Still, hadn't the impossible happened? Without a second glance, her sister had ridden away and left Dawsey to die in a backwoods swamp.

Henry Berry shifted his weight to one foot and jutted his chin at the marsh. "How long?"

Hooper gnawed the inside of his cheek. "Ten hours. Maybe more."

Twisting his mouth to the side, Henry shook his head. "It don't sound good, Hooper."

"You're right, but I'd lay a wager we'll find her breathing."

Plucking a long grass straw from beside the lopsided porch, Henry placed it between his teeth. "What makes you think so? She's not a Lumbee woman."

"She's powerful strong-willed, that's why. Not in the same way as Ellie. This one's thickheaded strong. Too stubborn to let the swamp win."

Boss Strong grinned. "We'd best find her quick then and spare some hapless gator."

Henry motioned with his head.

Boss hustled to where the rest of the men slouched around a firepot in wooden chairs. He reached them, barking orders at their upturned faces.

Eager to help, they unfurled their lanky bodies and quickly found their feet.

Beside Hooper, Henry tensed. He gave a sharp whistle and raised one long arm overhead, his slender finger pointing at the woods.

Snapping to attention, Boss whirled and scanned the staggered trees. One hand on his gun, the other shading his eyes, he glanced over his shoulder. "It's Ellie."

Hooper's head whipped around. "She must've found Dawsey."

Ellie wove through the trees like a shot, ducking low branches and launching off sugarberry trunks. Skirting Boss and Henry's men, she ran full out for the porch.

Hooper caught her at the bottom step and spun her to a halt.

She struggled against him, her breath coming in panting gasps, her eyes wild with fear. "Let go. I need Rhoda."

Hooper's stomach lurched. "Dawsey's hurt?"

"Snakebite." Ellie spat the distasteful word.

"Moccasin?"

"Maybe rattler."

Hooper groaned.

Ellie's gaze jumped to Henry. "Please get Rhoda. There's not much time."

Henry reached the door in three long strides, speaking in a voice too low to hear. When he turned, Rhoda followed him out, her medicine bag in her hand.

Hooper followed Ellie to where they'd tied their mounts. They were barely in the saddle before Henry, Rhoda, and Boss rode out of the shadowy brush.

"Follow me," Ellie called and laid her heels to Toby's side.

They rode single file behind her, first Hooper and Henry, followed closely by Rhoda, then Boss, their rear guard. The riders knew the land, so they swiftly covered the distance to the pond.

The horses splashed across, parting the scum and sending snakes slithering to the bank. Hooper pulled up and dismounted then passed Ellie, already running for the hole in the canebrake. She caught up and slid into the opening beside him, a moan escaping her lips.

Dawsey lay just inside, staring up at them with glassy eyes.

"Don't move, honey," Hooper said. "We're here now."

Delirium must have settled in Dawsey's fevered mind. Hooper's stern face swirled above, promptly joined by Dilsey's, her familiar brows crowded in concern. Dawsey opened her mouth to apologize for not heeding Hooper's warning, but he and Dilsey faded to the background while two stately angels hovered into view.

The male, the most glorious being Dawsey had ever seen, leaned over to look at her, his gray blue eyes softly smiling. The sun glinted off his long black hair and graceful goatee, and his nearness stifled her shallow breath. A dark crescent scar under his left eye was the only blight on his beauty. When he summoned the other angel, his rich voice floated through Dawsey's thick haze like a pleasant song.

The woman, small and straight with a billowing halo of hair, hurried forward and knelt at Dawsey's side, touching her throbbing leg with cool hands.

Dilsey scrambled up to squat beside her head. Their eyes met, and Dilsey reached hesitant fingers to smooth her hair. The unexpected gesture pierced Dawsey's heart with unspeakable grief, and tears muddled her sight.

The beautiful woman produced a leather pouch and riffled through the contents. Pulling out packets and vials, she barked orders at the men to gather roots and wild herbs. Dawsey knew some of the plants she called for, but most of the names she'd never heard before.

They jumped to her bidding while she fashioned a splint with sticks and strips of cloth. When the healing herbs came, she crushed them and mixed them with powders from her bag. She tied the poultice to Dawsey's aching calf then bound up the splint. Finally, she duckwalked to Dawsey's side and raised her head, tipping a bitter liquid into her mouth.

Dawsey sputtered and coughed but choked it down.

When the woman stood and nodded, Dilsey moved aside and Hooper swept in and gently lifted Dawsey. He carried her from the stand of cane, cradled in his arms.

Too weak to resist, too limp to sit upright, she lay against him, her cheek pressed to his chest.

The night he'd taken her from the window returned in a rush. Hooper had been anything but gentle, roughly tossing her over his shoulder like a sack of feed then swatting her on the behind. She found it hard to believe the same man held her now, his careful hands a fond caress.

"Keep her warm," the healer said, running along behind them to the horses.

Hooper passed Dawsey to the mysterious man long enough to strip off his shirt and wrap it around her shoulders. In one quick motion, he mounted his horse and waited while the man lifted her to the saddle.

Dawsey groaned when her dangling leg shot fire past her knee.

"I know it hurts," Hooper crooned in her ear. "We have to keep the wound below your heart."

Dilsey sprang onto her horse. "I'll ride ahead and tell Ma to ready a bed."

"I'll go, too," the healer said.

Reining sharply, Hooper pulled in behind them. He rode carefully, she suspected to keep from jostling her, so before long the others passed out of sight.

They picked their way slowly through the swamp. Holding tightly around her waist, Hooper dodged low limbs and dripping moss and swatted vines out of her face. Weak and dizzy, she lurched forward, her chin grazing her chest. Hooper wrapped his long fingers around her forehead and drew her head back to nestle against his shoulder. She rested next to the searing warmth of his bare skin, feeling safe for the first time in weeks.

Floating high and free like a dandelion seed, she stretched to press her face into the hollow of his neck. Nuzzling close, she breathed the earthy smell of him and felt his thudding heart against her back. He tipped his head, and her searching lips found the corner of his mouth.

When his trembling hand came up to smooth her hair, it broke the spell. Embarrassed, she shrank away and closed her eyes.

The next time she opened them, she lay on Hooper's mat in front of the fireplace, with Odell's worried face hovering overhead. She didn't stay awake for long but drifted dreamily until she couldn't tell which parts of her blurred memories were real.

Several times the woman who had bound her leg—Dawsey heard them call her Rhoda—braced her up with one arm and trickled more of the foul-tasting tonic between her lips.

Dilsey flitted close by, and Hooper seemed never to leave her side.

Once, she awoke to the sound of hushed voices. Turning her head, she found Dilsey and Odell hovering near the sink, Duncan, Tiller, and Silas clustered around the table. The window was a dark square on the wall, and Rhoda was nowhere in sight.

Someone touched her hand, and her head lolled to the side. Hooper sat cross-legged beside her mat, his shy fingers caressing hers beneath the quilt. She gazed up at him, and his dark eyes softened, a look of surprised wonder in their depths.

Joy welled inside of her as the fog in her head chased his face into shadows. She closed her eyes, hoping her smile reached her lips in time.

Chapter 28

Dawsey's snakebite had come to her fairly. At least the serpent played a gentleman's game and shook a warning rattle. Dawsey had quietly lifted her head and struck a blow to Hooper's heart with the barest touch of her lips.

He hadn't forgotten the harsh words she'd said to him on the night she fled. In fact, his newfound affection made her lack of sympathy all the harder to bear. But the swell of feelings he felt for her left no room in his heart for anger.

He'd just have to sway her, convince her to understand—a challenge that kept him staring at the ceiling in Ellie's room half the night, where he and Duncan would sleep until Dawsey was well again.

The day had dawned clear and dry, and now the sun shone high overhead. Hooper should've been riding a raid with Henry or tracking bounty hunters. Instead, he hunched beside Pa on the porch, working a deer hide to make it soft enough to drape around Dawsey's shoulders.

Papa sat beside him with a carving knife, whittling a cypress knee into a trinket for Ma. "These stiff old hands need greasing," he said. "I hope I get your ma's present done in time. Only three days left till Christmas."

Hooper raised his head. "Only three? It don't seem possible."

Twisting his mouth, Pa grunted. "Christmas has a way of sneaking up on a feller. I should've remembered that before I chose cypress. It's a hard wood to cut." He leaned to peer at the hide. "That's turning out real nice. Who's it for? Ellie?"

Warmth flooded Hooper's neck. "Um...no, sir. This one's for Dawsey."

Understanding flickered too quickly in Papa's eyes. "Dawsey, huh?"

Hooper nodded and went back to his work. "What do you think of her, Pa?"

Pa's hands stilled, and he stared past the shed. "A brush with death brings your true nature to the surface." He hooked his thumb toward the house. "That little gal has a pure heart."

"But she tricked us all into trusting her, and then she ran."

"She used what she could to try and get herself home." He shrugged. "Wouldn't you do the same in her place?"

Hooper gnawed his bottom lip and nodded. "I suppose so."

Blinking back tears, Papa shook off his thoughtful stare. "I don't deserve it, but both girls seem inclined to forgive an old fool his worst mistake."

Hooper sought his eyes. "You've done all you could to make it up to them."

Wincing, he stopped whittling and flexed his fingers. "It will never be enough. I often wonder if God Himself could set my sins to right."

They sat together in silence until Papa turned his head and gazed toward the barn. "I haven't seen Tiller all morning. Where'd that rascal sneak off to?"

Unease pricked Hooper's stomach. "He rode off with Nathan Carter and two of his cousins. They've taken quite a shine to Tiller."

Pa lowered one brow. "Which cousins?"

"Jason and Richard."

"Ain't those three boys a little rowdy?"

Hooper shrugged. "No worse than most, but I worry about their lust for adventure. They're not afraid to try anything, as long as there's a loose dollar or a good time to be had."

Pa nudged him. "Look yonder."

Ellie cut out of the woods holding two rabbits by their hind legs, her shotgun slung over her shoulder.

"On the outside, those girls are like two wrens on a rail," Pa said. "Under the skin they're as mismatched as you and Duncan."

Hooper studied his words. He remembered thinking the same, that Ellie and Dawsey looked just alike. Now when he gazed at Dawsey, he never thought of his sister. Ellie was indeed a perky little wren. Dawsey was more of a redbird.

Pulling Hooper from his thoughts, Papa chuckled and pointed at Duncan, creeping up behind Ellie. "Watch this."

Ellie spun, but she was too late. Duncan snatched the rabbits from her hand and ran for the porch.

Holding them aloft, he taunted her. "Thanks, Ellie. These will make a fine rabbit stew for Dawsey. She'll be grateful I'm such a good hunter." With a sinister laugh, he sailed around the house with Ellie's kill.

Her face a mottled red, she tore out after him, screeching like a hag.

The way his brother spoke of Dawsey, as if he held certain rights to her, pounded drums in Hooper's temples. It vexed him something fierce when Duncan hung around her sickbed, spouting jokes and singing foolish songs, but he'd almost forgiven him the first time Dawsey smiled.

She'd grown stronger through the night as Rhoda's drawing poultice pulled the venom from her leg. This morning, Mama warmed her three more cups of Rhoda's healing soup. Dawsey had bravely downed the last dregs before lunch, her face puckered to a point.

Too weak to sit up for long, she rested on his mat in front of the hearth.

Hooper's spine tingled with pleasure at the thought of sitting beside Dawsey, holding her delicate hand. With one tender smile, she had answered the burning question in his heart.

Rhoda said she'd been lucky. . .or blessed. By the close, shallow marks he left, the snake had been small and hadn't looked on Dawsey as a meal. Meaning only to defend himself, he left very little venom in her leg.

Hooper thanked God for sparing her life.

A whistle shrilled across the backyard. Papa whistled back and Wyatt rode out of the brush. He trotted close and dismounted. With an answering salute aimed at Pa, he sat on the bottom step.

"Ain't seen you in a while," Papa said. "What sort of courting you call that?"

Wyatt snorted. "Last time I came around, Ellie wouldn't even talk to me."

Papa cut two curling slivers of wood before he glanced up. "Ellie's been going through a baffling time, but she seems to be coming around." He nodded. "I reckon you'll find her a little more agreeable soon."

"I reckon I'd better." Wyatt's jaw clenched. "This time I won't leave until she talks to me."

Pa blew a puckered breath. "I admire your determination, son, but

I'd tread more careful if I was you. You don't want to spook her again."

Leaning against the rail, Wyatt swung his feet up on the wide step and crossed his ankles. "You got any advice for me, sir? On what I should say or do?"

Pa hooked his thumbs in his suspenders. "Since you're asking, I know a thing or two that might help." He peered at Wyatt's earnest face. "First off, go easy on the mush. Sweet talk's like salt. You can add some later, if need be, but if you pour out too much, you can't sift it out again."

Big eyed, Wyatt nodded.

Pa aimed his pointer finger. "Ellie's too spirited to be led around by the nose. Keep a gentle hand on the reins if you want to break her. Before you know it, she'll be eating right out of your hand."

Two skinned and gutted rabbits slammed on the porch so hard they bounced. Wyatt leaped like he'd been stuck, and Papa shouted an indecent word.

Ellie stood behind them glaring, her hands on her hips. "I ain't no blasted workhorse."

Wyatt jumped to his feet. "Ellie—"

"I'll tell you another thing, Wyatt Carter. I happen to like a little salt."

A slow grin lit his face.

She took his arm and pulled him up beside her. "The next time you need advice on romancing a woman, you'd be wise to start with me."

They disappeared around the corner, and Pa slapped his leg. "Now, don't that take the bacon?"

Hooper stood up laughing. "Better stick to whittling, Pa, and leave courting to the young folks."

Duncan ambled around the opposite corner, smiling and rubbing his shoulder. "That's a mean little gal you raised, Pa. She nearly twisted my arm clean off." He swiped at Hooper, just to be ornery, and ducked inside the house.

Rolling the hide under one arm, Hooper leaned and gathered the rabbits. "I'll take these fine plump hares to Ma."

Leaving poor Pa still shaking his head, he opened the door to the cabin. The sound of Dawsey's feeble laughter strummed his heartstrings—until the sight of Duncan by her side twanged in his head like a busted banjo.

His brother appeared entirely too content sidled up next to Dawsey.

She glanced up at Hooper but quickly lowered her gaze.

Duncan beamed like a drunken man. "Afternoon, little brother. Come see how much better Dawsey feels." He stroked her hand. "All she needed was a good dose of my humor."

Dawsey turned the warmth of her smile on Duncan, leaving Hooper in the cold. " 'A merry heart doeth good like a medicine.' The Good Book says so."

Squeezing her fingers, Duncan gulped her down with his eyes. "See there? I told you."

Hooper's stomach curdled. He couldn't deny what he'd long suspected. Duncan was sweet on his girl.

He balled his fists. Duncan could peddle his goods elsewhere. Dawsey Wilkes made her choice when she kissed him.

"Before long, she'll need Pa to cut her a walking stick," Hooper said, despising the strain in his voice.

Dawsey's chin came up. "Nonsense. I could get up and walk right now."

Mama turned from the hearth. "You only think you can. Rhoda's rattleweed tea makes you feel you could turn cartwheels."

"Rattleweed tea?"

"Rhoda brews cohosh with elderberry wine to make a pain tonic."

Dawsey gasped and pushed up on her elbow. "Wine? You mean strong spirits?"

Ma poked out her bottom lip. "Not too strong."

Shock then fury flashed in Dawsey's eyes. "That won't do! Alcohol has never once passed my lips."

Duncan grinned. "It has now."

She sputtered like a doused fire. "Well, I'll thank you all to make sure it doesn't happen again."

"It wasn't enough to corrupt you, honey," Ma said. "Just a little to ease your pain and help you sleep."

"I don't care. I won't take another drop."

The urge to protect her surged in Hooper. He squatted beside her and lifted her chin. "It won't happen again, Dawsey. I'll make sure of it."

She gazed at him, surprise widening her big eyes. For mere seconds, something else flickered there. Tiny lines creased the smooth skin above her nose, as if her mind fought to remember something important.

Ducking her head to free her chin, she whispered a hoarse, "Thank you," then eased her head against the pillow.

Mama leaned to pull up her covers. "Go away, you two. You've tuckered her out."

"Me?" Duncan squawked like a scolded girl. "I had her laughing. You're the one who spilled the news about the liquor."

Papa cleared his throat from the doorway. "Mind your ma, son. And watch how you speak to her." He crossed the room and held out his hand.

Grumbling, Duncan allowed Pa to pull him off the floor and herd him to the table.

Hooper squatted near the hearth and placed another log on Dawsey's fire. He could handle not talking to her for a spell, as long as he could stay close—and especially if it meant Duncan would leave her be.

CHAPTER 29

Drowsiness hovered, but Dawsey fought sleep. Before she allowed herself to rest, she had to sort out her muddled thoughts.

Uncertainty plagued her about Hooper. One man had stalked away from her after their spat; a completely different man had taken his place.

Gazing into her eyes and caressing her chin were not Hooper's usual behavior.

A compelling force drew Dawsey, pulling her thoughts, her eyes, her longing heart to him, in a way it hadn't before he'd rescued her in the cane.

She'd found his coal tar eyes and laughing mouth attractive from the beginning. But he was her captor! Entertaining silly notions about him was unthinkable.

Until now.

Dawsey didn't need to look past her feet to the hearth. Every nerve in her body felt him stooping there. She didn't need to peek beneath her lashes to know he watched her. His longing looks burned her flesh.

What had the rattlesnake done to them? Was there a primitive charm in the venom? An irresistible potion they were powerless against?

The sputtering fire pulled his attention.

Breathless, Dawsey studied his face, her eager eyes tracing his handsome nose, the strong line of his jaw—until pretend sleep turned the trick on her and she began to drift off.

Powerless to resist him? She smiled dreamily. *So be it.*

Stirring, she warmed with shame at her scandalous thoughts. No matter what, she'd stand firm against Hooper McRae, her reckless abductor. He'd kidnapped her body and invaded her mind, but he wouldn't win her heart, no matter how he tried.

More importantly, she'd never let him know how close he came.

A brisk wind rattled the bare limbs overhead, the haunting clatter like sparring antlers.

The breeze, mild for three days shy of Christmas, lifted and stirred Ellie's hair, tickling her cheeks with long strands. She gripped her knees and leaned forward on the stump. "You're going to marry me, Wyatt Carter."

Grinning, Wyatt scooted to the edge of his seat. "You have it backwards, don't you, gal? It's my job to ask that question."

Ellie cocked her head and pretended not to hear. "Yes, sir. You'll marry me and be my chocolate buckeye kiss."

Wyatt laughed and grabbed her hands. "If that means I'll be your sweetie, it's fine by me." His eyes twinkled. "I'd sure like to have a kiss before you reel me in."

She tilted her chin. "Pa would knot your skull for such talk"—she smiled and batted her lashes like she'd seen Mama do—"but I don't mind."

His fingers crawled up and gripped her wrists. Pulling her toward him, he closed his eyes. They met in the middle of the two stumps, suspended on bended knees. His face closed in and Ellie retreated an inch then swooned to meet his puckered lips.

The jangling branches overhead swept her up in a quick-rising cyclone. Wyatt's gentle kiss was the only steady point in the world spinning about her. Her trembling legs weakened, so she tried to sit, missing the stump by a foot.

Wyatt caught her in time and eased her to the weathered seat, his laughing mouth releasing her too soon. Chuckling, he held her face between his hands. "You almost sat in the mud."

She grinned. "If you ever drop me in the mud, you're going in with me."

They laughed together with only inches of space between them.

He kissed her nose. "It was just the way I dreamed it."

A picture came of Wyatt sprawled across his bed, mooning over her. "You dream about us, too?"

He nodded soberly. "Every night."

She reached for his hands. "Tell me what you see."

He blushed. "You mean when it's not about kissing?"

Giggling like a girl in pantalets, she nodded.

Wyatt backed up to his stump. "I see us sitting at opposite ends of the table, with a whole slew of little Carters lined up between us."

She gaped. "A slew?"

"At least."

She lifted one finger. "All boys then. I don't know enough things to teach a girl."

His eyes softened, and he stood to smooth her hair. "Don't fret, honey. Your ma can teach our daughters. Mine will pitch in, too."

She narrowed her eyes. "Only if they want to learn."

"That's right, sugar." He pulled her head to his chest. "Only if they want to."

The sound of sloshing feet sprang them apart with the force of a trap.

Nathan, Wyatt's brother, and their cousins, Jason and Richard, stood ten feet away with rifles slung over their shoulders.

"Look here! We caught them spooning. Kiss her again, Wyatt, so we can watch."

Fisting his hands, Wyatt spun toward Nathan.

Ellie caught his arm and held on.

"Nate, that's enough." Jason scowled and shoved Nathan in the chest.

Tiller crept out of the brush, his face darting between a grin and a grimace.

Ellie motioned him over, and the scowl won out.

He sauntered toward them, his thumbs hooked in his suspenders.

Ellie rose to meet him. "Why are you slipping up on people?"

His face flushed crimson. "We didn't go to slip up. I swear."

She swatted his arm. "Do it again, and you'll answer to me." She glared at the others. "That goes for the lot of you."

They mumbled and shuffled their feet.

"Where have you been all morning?" she asked Tiller.

"Nowhere special. Hunting with the boys."

Glancing around, she raised her brows. "Didn't bag much, I see."

More muttering and uneasy glances.

Gnawing her bottom lip, Ellie studied each guilty face. She shot Wyatt a glance.

His clear blue eyes studied the boys, settling on his brother. "Nathan, if Henry catches you boys stealing to line your pockets, he'll grind every nickel out of your hides."

Nathan glared. "Who told you?"

"No one had to," Wyatt said. "You're that bad at hiding the truth."

Ellie spun on Tiller. "If Pa hears you're taking needless risks, he'll run you clear out of Scuffletown. Do you want to go back to your ma?"

His mouth fanned like a fish's gills. The fear on his face said more than his silence.

Nathan's mouth twisted, and his eyes flashed in defiance. "You're starting to sound like an old woman, Ellie." His gaze jumped to Wyatt. "In fact, so are you."

Wyatt swooped on him and took him by the scruff. "Let's go see Pa. Maybe his strap will convince you to change your thinking."

With the memory of Wyatt's first kiss still fresh on her lips, Ellie watched him cross the yard and disappear into the brush. He didn't even say good-bye.

Angry with the boys, feeling scorned by Wyatt, she stood over Tiller and planted her finger between his eyes. "What about you? Do you care to explain your shenanigans to Pa?"

Tiller's eyes rounded to full moons. He shrank onto the stool, shaking his head.

Ellie poked him hard on the forehead and he yowled.

"See to it that you mind your steps, so he'll never have to know."

He gulped and nodded.

Grumbling, Ellie spun on her heel and stalked toward the house.

"You ain't near as nice as Miss Wilkes," Tiller called in a sullen voice.

"No, I ain't," she flung over her shoulder. "A fact you'll do well to remember."

Chapter 30

Dawsey flipped to her back in her four-poster bed, pulling the soft quilt under her chin. She blinked sleepily, stretching her toes toward the crackling warmth. She must ask Aunt Livvy to praise Levi for his diligence. He'd banked a hearty fire in her room that had burned through the night.

Rustling skirts meant Winney or Aunt Livvy had come to wake her for breakfast. Dazed by sleep, she peered up at the dim figure hovering over her bed.

"You awake, sugar?"

Dawsey's heart jolted, startled by a voice she couldn't place. She squinted and rubbed her eyes. Bright delusions of fresh bedding, sunny windows, and frilly curtains darkened into a lumpy mat on a plank floor in a dim, cluttered cabin. Her peace and contentment swept up the chimney with the dancing blaze.

"It's suppertime, honey," Odell said. "You've slept the day away."

Leaning closer, she grinned. "You must be plain tuckered if the smell of my fried chicken didn't rouse you. You slept so still and sound, I considered holding a mirror to your nose."

Duncan chuckled behind them. "Dead folk don't snore, Ma."

Tiller laughed wildly.

Odell twisted around to scowl at them. "Hush up, boys."

Dawsey rubbed her face with both hands, trying to chase the cobwebs from her head. "Did I really snore?"

Dilsey came and squatted beside Odell. "Don't listen to Duncan. He's a simpleton. Are you feeling better?"

Warmed by her concern, Dawsey nodded. "I think so."

"Would you care to sit up for a while?"

"I'd love to."

With the stealth of a cat, Hooper appeared. Before she could protest, he had his arms around her, lifting her up to lean against the wall.

For the first time, Dawsey realized someone had washed her and dressed her in a clean nightshirt.

"Adjust her pillow," he said.

Dilsey scurried to slip the lumpy cushion behind her back then covered her modestly with the blanket.

Blushing, Dawsey whispered, "Thank you," to Hooper; then, fearing the state of her breath, placed her hand over her mouth.

He dipped his head and smiled sweetly, his tenderness further jumbling Dawsey's mind. "I'll go fix you a plate."

Duncan rose halfway out of his chair, both hands stretched across the serving dishes. "I've got it, Hooper."

Hooper took the dish and ladle from his hands. "That's all right, brother. I can manage."

Swiping the plate again, Duncan loaded on a drumstick and a biscuit. "See, I have it. Now hand me the ladle."

Crossing behind him, Hooper relieved his brother of the job again, flipping his offering onto the table. "Dawsey likes light meat best and prefers crispy edges on her biscuits." He made the proper adjustments then dipped the ladle in a nearby bowl of corn.

Duncan snatched up his own food and dashed around his chair, headed for Dawsey. "Here you are, darlin', take mine."

Dawsey jumped a foot when Hooper dropped the heaping plate with a *crash* and charged after Duncan.

Before he reached him, Silas dropped his fork and stood up with a roar. "Freeze!" he bellowed.

They did just that, Hooper mid-dash with murder in his eyes and Duncan crouched to flee.

Fury singed a dark path from Silas to where they stood. "You boys ain't dogs and Dawsey's not a bone."

Tiller giggled, ending on a snort when Silas glared his way.

Dawsey hid her red-hot face with the cover.

"Duncan McRae, march over here and sit. Bring your supper with you, if you plan to get any."

His angry gaze swung to Hooper. "Clean up the mess you made of my table and make quick work of it."

Hoarse from shouting, he cleared his throat. "Dawsey's sister will fetch her supper. Left up to you two, we'll be sweeping her vittles from the corners."

Dilsey delivered the tempting plate with a rueful smile and the family settled down to eat in silence.

After a steady diet of broth and tonic, Odell's fried chicken delighted Dawsey's senses. The smell set her mouth to watering, and she couldn't wait to sink her teeth into the crispy brown coating. She swooned over the first bite, which soon became her last since she finished the chicken before touching anything else.

Casting a furtive glance at the serving dish, she felt certain of the answer before she looked. There wouldn't likely be an extra piece. Food was hard to come by for the family. Without Odell's skill in stretching flour into biscuits and quick breads, they'd all leave the kitchen hungry.

It felt good to sit up and eat solid food, but the longer she sat, the worse her leg throbbed. Rhoda's spirited tonic had gradually worn off, leaving unexpected pain behind. She laid aside her dish and glanced toward the others.

Hooper's gaze met hers across the room. She tried to look away, but the concern in his eyes held her. "Would you like to rest now, Dawsey?"

She sighed. "I suppose I should, but I'm not ready. It's nice to be able to see all of you. It's a bit lonely over here by myself."

He pushed back his chair and came to squat beside her. Taking her hand, he placed a golden fried wing in her palm.

Dawsey's heart swelled. He'd given her his food, and it might have been treasure. She smiled at him through damp lashes.

Hooper tugged at his bottom lip with his teeth, a pleasing motion that flipped her middle. "Rest now so you'll feel up to watching Ma and Ellie tomorrow."

She swallowed the lump in her throat. "Watching them?"

Odell clasped her hands. "We're going to decorate the hearth for Christmas. You can help if you'd like."

Dawsey's eyes widened. "Will you be trimming a tree?"

Hooper gave his head a little shake. "I've heard rich folks do, but we never have."

Dawsey gasped. "Never?" She couldn't believe her ears. Aunt Livvy's lavish trees were the centerpieces of every Wilkes Christmas. She couldn't imagine the season without one. "Then you must." She gripped his hand, forgetting her painful leg in her excitement. "I'll help. We can string garlands of pearls and silk roses then group brightly colored birds and candles on each limb." She could see Aunt Livvy's lively tree in her mind. "Oh, I can't wait. It will be wonderful."

The room had stilled.

The excitement building in Dawsey's chest deflated as her gaze bounced to each somber face. "Oh my. . .have I said something wrong?"

Odell shrugged. "Not wrong, exactly. It's just that we don't have all those"—she waved her hand about—"pearls and roses and birds." Her brows lifted hopefully. "I suppose the boys could shoot us a passel of winter birds to string up." She tilted her head. "But won't they start to stink?"

Embarrassed, Dawsey cringed. How could she be so thoughtless?

"We don't need pearls and birds," she said. "They're too gaudy, really. We'll link paper chains and hang apples instead. I'll bake cookie stars and make bows from the ribbons in your sewing box. The tree will be just as beautiful. Better, in fact, with handmade decorations."

Hooper took her shoulders and guided her down to the mat. Plumping the pillow beneath her head, he gave her a stern look. "You won't be doing anything until you get some rest." She winced, and he lifted one brow. "Are you sure you won't take a swig of Rhoda's tonic?"

She firmly shook her head.

"Ornery woman," he mumbled then went back to his supper.

Dawsey watched the fire, thinking of Levi and Winney, Aunt Livvy and Father, wondering if they would celebrate Christmas without her. She pictured her sweet potatoes, bought to make holiday bread to cheer her father, shriveling in a bin in the basement.

Tiller's strident voice pulled her from her lonesome thoughts. She craned her neck to see what had upset him.

"You can't mean it, Uncle Silas. They're the only friends I've got in this sinkhole."

In her dreamy daze, Dawsey hadn't heard what Silas told the boy. She could tell by Tiller's angry scowl and mottled face that he didn't like it one bit.

Silas leaned over his plate, matching Tiller's glare. "Defy me, and see how much I mean it."

Tiller turned a hateful look on Dilsey. "You told."

Still chewing, Dilsey's head shot up. "I never told him nothing." She wiped her mouth on her napkin, her outrage turned to sudden amusement. "But I reckon you just did."

Silas struck the table, rattling the utensils. "Now you're hiding things from me?"

Tiller jumped and stiffened.

Softening his voice, Silas touched his arm. "I'm trying to save you from yourself, nephew. The blunders you make as a youth can chase you into old age. Don't make a mess of your life while you're still damp behind the ears."

The boy jutted his chin. "I ain't no blasted baby."

"You're four years shy of Richard Carter, and he's the youngest. You've got no business hanging about with those older boys."

Tiller huffed. "They ain't so bad."

"They're young bucks full of mischief." Silas raised a warning finger. "Mischief can turn sour under the right conditions. I don't want you with them when it happens."

Tiller shoved away from the table but didn't get far before Silas grabbed his wrist.

"Rein your horses." He tugged, and Tiller plopped in his chair. "I mean you no grief, son, but these are troubled times in a dangerous land. We'd hate to see anything happen to you."

Tiller's slight body heaved with rage. Staring straight ahead, he released his white-rimmed mouth enough to speak. "Can I be excused?"

With a ragged sigh, Silas released his hand. "You might as well."

Stiff armed, fists clenched, he stormed for the door, tears glistening in his eyes.

Dawsey held out her hand as he passed. "Tiller?"

He didn't slow down or spare her a glance. Reaching the door, he slung it open then slammed it behind him.

"*Whooee!*" Duncan hooted, reaching for a biscuit. "Now we know why Aunt Effie wanted shed of him."

"Button up, boy," Silas said, pushing away his plate. "If being a pain in the rear was ample reason, we'd be shed of you by now."

Hooper coughed, choking on his food and his laughter.

"Let me help you, brother." Grinning, Duncan rounded his father's place to pound on Hooper's back.

Laughing harder, Hooper leaped up and shoved him, then slid an arm around his neck and tugged him close.

Dilsey ran around and squeezed between them, kissing both of their cheeks while Odell and Silas looked on with wide, beaming faces.

Dawsey watched in awe. She'd never known such warmth, never experienced such free expressions of love.

For all of their faults, the McRaes were a family. They taunted and teased, sparred and cried, but in the end, they sought each other for comfort.

In a make-believe game, Dawsey pretended to trade places. She saw herself as Dilsey, surrounded by affection, and saw Dilsey in Fayetteville, with a stern maiden aunt and self-absorbed father.

An ache hit her chest, so sudden and fierce it took her breath. Two babes lay in a crib that night, one lucky and one ill fated. The lines had blurred on which was which.

Guilt stabbed her heart, but she couldn't push away the truth. Covering her ears to block out the McRaes' merry voices, Dawsey rolled to the wall and shed bitter tears on her pillow.

Shivers roused Hooper from a sound sleep. Angry with his shiftless brother, his mouth tightened with irritation. Pa told Duncan to lay a fire in the hearth before bedtime, which meant the freezing cabin was his fault. Ma and Pa would be even colder stuck off in their room.

Groggy, he rolled off his mat to throw a log on the dwindling coals—and tumbled from Ellie's bed to the unforgiving floor.

Feeling foolish, he groaned and bit back a curse. Duncan, asleep on his mat on the other side of their sister's room, grumbled in his sleep and turned over.

Hooper sighed and pushed off the floor. He'd forgotten Ma had banished them to Ellie's room so she could keep Dawsey close enough to tend. It seemed his family played games in the night, swapping beds more often than they changed their underwear. Was it any wonder he awoke confused?

Yawning, he placed a log on the grate for Duncan then pulled on his trousers and washed his face. Grabbing his coat from the doorknob, he stepped outside. Since he was up early, he'd tend the horses for Pa, feed the chickens for Ma, and save them the trouble.

At the thought of his own chores, his stomach moaned in protest. He supposed his list of daily tasks could wait until after breakfast.

Early or not, Old Abe and the other horses seemed sorely glad to see him, and the hens and roosters didn't squawk none, not about the early breakfast, at least.

By the time Hooper loped up the path from the henhouse, Pa stood shivering on the porch, shading his eyes against the rising sun. "What are you doing up and about so early, son?"

Hooper grinned. "If you'd ever slept on Ellie's short bed, you wouldn't have to ask. Besides, neither of us thought to bank a fire." He rubbed his arms at the memory. "That little room gets colder than it does outside."

Pa sniffed. "That's right chilly, then, because it's freezing out here." He nodded toward the barn. "I'll grab my coat. I reckon the old man is eager for his oats."

"No, sir. I fed him for you," Hooper said, smiling. "The chickens, too."

"Well, I'll be." Pa pounded on Hooper's back as he mounted the steps. "You're a mighty fine lad. My aching joints salute you." His eyes twinkled. "Since we're handing out surprises, I've got a nice one for you." Clutching Hooper's sleeve, he herded him through the door.

Hooper paused then nudged him and winked. "Yours is by far the better gift."

The kitchen glowed with light from the flickering lanterns, the blazing hearth, and the bright smiles of three busy women.

Ma stood over a yellow bowl, beating eggs. Ellie hovered beside the table, cutting biscuits with a tin can.

Dawsey, Pa's big surprise, sat beside Ellie, folding scraps of paper into tiny linking chains. She glanced up and beamed, putting all other sources of light to shame. "Good morning."

He took a few steps closer. "Same to you. You must be feeling better."

She nodded, the pretty coil of hair on top of her head dancing. "Oh, yes, I'm much improved." Picking up the carved stick beside her chair, she shrugged. "I still need this to get around, but at the rate I'm healing, I'll soon be running."

Ellie glanced up from her dough. "Please, Dawsey. . .can't you find a better word? Running put you in that fix."

"It's a true Christmas miracle," Ma said from the hearth. "She's been better since we first mentioned decorating the cabin."

Dawsey held up the long paper chain. "See? It's nearly finished. Next we'll dip it in beet juice for color and hang it to dry."

Hooper's glowing praise died on his lips. He crossed angrily to the table and picked up the chain, rolling it around in his hands. "What is this?" He turned to Ma. "You gave her newspaper?"

Wide eyed at his tone, Ma put down the ladle and wiped her

hands on her apron. "Well. . .yes, but they're old newspapers, son." Her surprised look turned to worry. "Did I do something wrong?"

Hooper strode to her and motioned for Pa to join them. "What were you thinking, Ma?" he demanded in a low voice. "If she'd thought to read any of it, she'd know exactly where we are."

Ma pressed her fingers to her mouth. "Oh Hooper, I wasn't thinking."

He squeezed her shoulders. "You have to be more careful."

Pa put both hands on his hips and released a shaky breath. "It's all right, baby. What's done is done."

Behind them, Dawsey cleared her throat. "What's done was done before I ever laid eyes on the *Robesonian*."

Ma gasped and Papa groaned.

Hooper spun to face her. "What are you saying?"

"I'm saying"—she fairly simpered—"I've known for days that I'm in Robeson County, somewhere along the Lumber River. Most likely near Lumberton, considering that's where your paper is printed."

Hooper's nostrils flared. Stalking to her, he lifted her to her feet by her arms. "Who told you? Was it Tiller? I'll wring his skinny neck."

"Stop it, Hooper," Ellie cried. "Don't you dare hurt her."

Fear flashed across Dawsey's face, but her chin jutted in defiance. "Turn me loose this instant."

Hooper struggled to control himself, his breath coming in gasping pants. "Not until you tell me what fool put my family in danger."

Her long lashes swept down, and the corners of her mouth twitched.

He gave her a little shake. "You find this funny?"

"I'm afraid I do."

Bewildered, Hooper stared. What was she up to?

Tilting her head back, she raised her face to him. "You asked which fool?" She batted her eyes. "Why, it was you, Hooper. You told me yourself."

The surging blood at his temples turned to ice. "Me?" Cursing himself for croaking like a frog, he laughed harshly to cover his discomfort. "That's pure nonsense. I'd die before I'd tell you."

She laughed. "Oh but you did. You said your Scottish grandfather married an Indian girl and settled on the Lumber River."

As she spoke, he heard his own voice repeating the words in his head. He'd felt so free with Dawsey that night, so safe to speak his heart. Denial was pointless. Unbridled passion had gotten the best of him again.

Silence rang in the rafters. Tiller, asleep in the corner throughout the tempest, sat up scratching his head. "Why's it so quiet in here?"

Hooper's hold on Dawsey loosened. He caught her before she fell and lowered her into the chair while they sparred with flashing eyes. Resting his fingers on his hips, he blew out a shaky breath. "Well done, Miss Wilkes. You outsmarted me."

The smile disappeared and her brows crowded together.

"Women have snookered men since time began," Hooper sneered. "Never thought I'd be stupid enough to fall for a female's tricks."

Her mouth parted slightly. "What do you mean?"

"Was the kiss part of your plan?" He spun and slapped his leg. "What a muttonhead. Of course it was."

"Kiss?" The shouted question came from four directions at once. Mama, Papa, Ellie, and Tiller all gaped at them.

Hooper waved an accusing finger. "She kissed me. On the neck first then on the lips."

Dawsey groped for her walking stick and shot out of her chair. "I did not!"

Her shrill voice rang in Hooper's ears. "You're going to deny it?" He marched over to her again. "I suppose we never held hands under the covers."

Mama gasped. "For pity's sake, son. Not in front of Tiller."

Grinning, Tiller pushed off his mat and loped across the room. "It's all right, Aunt Odie. I've seen my share of sparking. Just yesterday, Wyatt and Ellie—"

He squealed as Ellie latched onto the back of his neck. "It's past time for you to hush, cousin."

Papa's eyeballs looked ready to pop. "Any more talk of holding hands and kissing, and I'll be fetching my shotgun to plan a wedding."

Outraged and disgusted, Hooper brushed the wretched paper chain to the floor. "She's used every swindle she knows against this family. I'd rather have a backside full of lead than marry this wily trickster."

Dawsey's face paled. "I don't remember proposing marriage to you." She looked ready to spit. "I'd sooner perish."

Papa crowded between them, a peculiar sadness lining his face. "That's enough, now. There's no need slicing each other to pieces." He laid his hands on Dawsey's shoulders. "My jig is up. It's time to take you home, and I know you're ready." He ducked his head. "I'd like to ask a favor first, though I know I don't deserve it."

She watched him with wary eyes, casting several hurt glances at Hooper. "Go on."

Papa went down on one knee in front of her. "If I promise to deliver you myself and confess my guilt to your Pa, will you give me one last Christmas with my family?"

Tears sprang to Mama's eyes. "No Silas. He'll turn you in. . .if he don't kill you."

Ellie draped herself around him. "Papa, don't—"

Hooper clutched his arm. "That's crazy talk. They'll never let you leave Fayetteville."

"Now, family, I've been thinking about this for a while." He shook his head sadly. "The past catches up to us all, whether here or in the hereafter. I'd just as soon have it over with now. I'm closer to the grave than I was yesterday. When I go, I'd like to go down at peace with God."

Dawsey's head drooped. "I don't know, Silas. You're asking to celebrate Christmas with your family, a gift my father will do without."

Papa sighed. "I suppose I am, honey. I'll understand if you say no."

She gazed around the room, tears shining in her eyes. "I suppose a few more days won't make a difference."

Papa beamed at each of them in turn then blinked tearfully at Dawsey. "I'll be forever grateful."

She held up one finger. "Not yet. I want to strike a bargain."

He cocked his head. "Name your price. Nothing's too precious to trade for more time with these dear ones."

"I have your solemn word?"

Hooper touched his shoulder. "Be careful. She's tricky."

Dawsey cast him an angry look.

Pa shrugged off Hooper's hand. "Throw in Hogmanay and you have my word."

She frowned.

"New Year's Day," Ma provided.

Dawsey returned her piercing stare to Pa. "Then we have an agreement. You'll have your Christmas celebration. New Year's, too. I'll even do what I can to keep Father from naming you to the sheriff. . . ." A determined glint in her eyes, her gaze jumped to Ellie. "As long as she returns to Fayetteville with me."

Hooper's stomach lurched as bedlam erupted in the cabin.

Dawsey met Hooper's glare, his eyes twin kettles of rage, across his father's shoulder. She held up her hand. "I don't mean for good. Just long enough to meet my father."

"It's too risky," Hooper growled. "Once he has her, he won't let her go."

Dawsey shook her head. "No one will hold her there. I'll see to it."

"I don't believe you."

She glared. "After all I've been through at the hands of your family, do you really think I'd make a prisoner of my sister?"

He blushed and turned away.

"Suppose I say no," a small voice asked.

Dawsey swung toward her sister. "I won't force you."

Silas brightened. "And the bargain?"

Casting a wistful look at Dilsey, her shoulders fell. "If she won't go, I'll remove the condition. You'll have your time with the family, and I'll still try to sway my father."

Hooper grinned. "That's it then. Ellie won't—"

"I'll need time to think about it."

Hooper spun toward Dilsey. "No, honey, you can't."

She touched his arm. "This is my decision."

Dawsey gave her a sweet smile. "You have until after New Year's Day to decide. I pray you'll say yes."

Tiller moaned and clutched his stomach. "If everything's settled, can we have a little less talk and a little more bacon?"

Odell and Dilsey moped toward the kitchen, salvaging breakfast while Dawsey cleared her Christmas project to make room at the table. Bending to pick up the folded links of newspaper, she felt a little sad that the merry little streamer meant to bring joy had stirred so much trouble.

Hooper shot her a dark look then went out mumbling that he'd lost his appetite.

Dawsey stared at the door, feeling sick.

Over the last few days, the hateful man who'd whisked her out of a window became a sweet-faced charmer. Had the scoundrel returned or never left?

She stared at the hands Hooper said he'd held, touched the mouth he claimed had kissed him. Her lips seemed to burn with a memory of their own. Had she done such a shameless thing?

Her gaze slid to the mat by the fire. His mat, filled with the musky scent of him.

One thing she remembered clearly. As the haze of Rhoda's tonic faded from her mind, Dawsey had watched Hooper near the hearth, irresistibly drawn to him.

Had he told the truth?

With her eyes closed, she could almost feel her lips nuzzling his. Shivering, she yanked her lids open to the sight of Duncan's looming grin.

She leaped and he hooted with glee. "Mornin', Dawsey. Dreaming about me again?"

Blushing, she glanced away.

"Nice to see you up and about. Did I startle you?"

"Leave her be," Silas growled from the head of the table. "Did you figure to sleep all day?"

Duncan whirled to sit next to him. "I gave it a good try, but the sun came pestering me through the boards on Ellie's window."

Odell shoveled a rack of bacon onto a platter and set it between him and Silas. Duncan snatched one, juggling and blowing on the crispy strip before shoving it into his mouth.

Tiller, who had gaped at Dawsey from the time Hooper said she kissed him, picked that moment to display the tactlessness of youth. "You missed the whole thing, Duncan. We had us a big old ruckus while you slept."

Silas lifted his bushy brows high over the rim of his cup. "Hush, boy."

The warning came too late.

"I missed a ruckus?" Duncan stared around the table then over his shoulder at Odell and Dilsey. "What sort? Was it bounty hunters?"

Dawsey's cheeks warmed. They must've colored, too, since Duncan's wandering stare landed squarely on her face.

"Nothing like that," Tiller said, flaunting the tactlessness of males in general. "Dawsey kissed Hooper."

Silas slammed down his cup. "Say another word, and you'll be doing chores on an empty stomach." His eyes rose to his wife, scurrying toward him from the hearth. "Can't you manage your household, woman? Is a peaceful table too much to ask?"

She smoothed his hair. "Breakfast is ready now, darlin'. It's hard for a boy to talk with food in his mouth."

Duncan scowled at Dawsey, an angry fire building behind his eyes.

Odell nudged his chair with her hip, so hard he scooted, and pressed a fluffy biscuit to his lips. "Ain't that right, son?"

He tugged his gaze from Dawsey and took a dutiful bite. "Yes, Ma," he mumbled with bulging cheeks.

"Here." She tossed one at Tiller. "I reckon your yap needs filling the most."

Dawsey was grateful to see his mouth busy with something besides her business.

Shaking her head, Odell took her place at the table. "I swear, Tiller McRae, with you around, the *Robesonian* may as well close their doors."

Hooper hoed the last six inches of the trench and watched the muddy water rush past his plowed rows then downhill to the stream where it belonged. He loved Scuffletown, but more for its sturdy, hard-wearing people than its soggy-bottomed land.

The rivers, creeks, and streams seemed determined to reclaim every inch of ground. In the dry season, the waters crouched, gurgling quietly, waiting for the rain. With very little invitation, they pounced from their banks, gobbling up crops, animals, and hapless people, sweeping them away without a trace.

Hooper spent so much time routing water from the fields, he had little time for anything else. On that particular morning, he welcomed the backbreaking work. It gave him a good excuse to pound on the ground with a stick.

Dawsey's taunting face flashed through his mind. With a furious grunt, he laid his shoulders into attacking the next furrow.

She'd denied their kiss. The idea made his head spin more than her dizzying lips. The kiss he'd replayed in his mind a thousand times—surer with each recalling that he'd lost his heart forever—Dawsey wouldn't even admit.

There was no one to blame but himself. The girl had spun her web then languished on the sticky strands, waiting to lure him in. Like a witless fool, he'd blundered willingly into her net.

He could accept his defeat, even admire her skill, but he'd never allow her to take down his family. If he had to lock them in the shed, he'd fight against Pa and Ellie going to Fayetteville.

He'd get rid of Dawsey if it meant tossing her over his shoulder again and carrying her all the way home.

One at a time, the McRaes filed out of the cabin—Silas to his chores, Odell to pull beets for their dye, and Dilsey with a hunting rifle slung over her shoulder.

Duncan waved off his father's invitation to the barn with a vague promise to be right along.

Tiller stood near the fire, running the last biscuit along the bottom of a skillet.

"What are you doing, boy?" Duncan growled. "Rubbing a hole in the iron?"

Tiller shot him a guilty glance. "I'm sopping the rest of this bacon grease for Aunt Odie. Makes the pan easier to clean."

He shoved the soggy bread in his mouth, and Duncan shuddered. "That bottomless stomach must be made of solid lead. Don't you have chores to do?"

Tiller wandered to the scrambled egg pan, to peel the papery slivers from the sides and nibble them. "Not right now."

Duncan cleared his throat. "I think you're mistaken. In fact, Pa's calling you now."

The boy tilted his ear. "I don't hear nothin'."

Duncan cocked his head, listening. "Wait, that ain't Pa. It's Saint Peter." He made a threatening move. "You'll be answering, if you don't scat."

With a shout, Tiller bounded for the door, stretching his arm to snatch his coat off a peg.

Laughing, Duncan sat across from Dawsey. "I guess that takes care of him." He sobered. "Now we can talk in peace."

Dawsey studied her hands, folded on the table. "What do you want to talk about?" Foolish question. She already knew.

Duncan closed his fingers over hers. "I want to know more about the uproar you and Hooper caused."

Dawsey glanced at his earnest face. She had to tell him something. Careful to avoid any mention of a kiss, she told him what had happened before breakfast.

She reached the part about the bargain she'd struck with Silas, and he withdrew the warmth of his hands. "Pa can't go with you, Dawsey. You know that, don't you? He'll spend the rest of his life behind bars." He blew out an anxious breath. "They might even hang him."

She pulled her rejected hands to her lap. "I didn't ask him to go. That part came from him, and he's very adamant. I only want the chance to show my father that Dilsey's alive."

Worry creased his brow. "Can't you just tell him?"

"It wouldn't be the same." How could she explain that she needed a miracle, one only Dilsey could provide? "Besides, he deserves the chance to see for himself."

"He'll want her back for good."

She nodded. "I'm certain of it, but he won't try to force her."

Duncan stared thoughtfully over her head. "What does all this have to do with Hooper?"

She lowered her lashes. "He feels the way you do, that neither of them should go." She shrugged in the midst of her half truth. "So he raised a bit of a. . .well, a ruckus."

Duncan quirked his mouth. "And you kissed him?"

She slapped the table. "No! At least I don't think so." She blushed. "I don't remember."

"Really?" He bit one side of his lip. "Poor old Hoop."

"Stop that. It's not his fault."

He leaned to cup her chin. "If you kissed me, you'd remember."

She swatted his hand. "Not with a snoot full of Rhoda's tonic."

Understanding dawned in his eyes. He laughed and straightened. "Fair enough."

A pang struck Dawsey's heart. "I'm beginning to regret my bargain. It would be wonderful to make it home in time for Christmas."

Duncan's gray eyes shone with an idea. "We could outfox the old man and put an end to the whole thing."

"How?"

He slammed his hand on the table. "I'll take you to Fayetteville myself. If we leave now, you'll be home in time for supper."

Her head whirled at the thought of walking through the high arched doorway, strolling past Winney's fragrant kitchen and into Father's den. "I'd dearly love to go."

He stood. "I'll hitch the wagon."

She caught his arm. "It's out of the question. I won't leave without

Dilsey, and she'll only agree to go if she thinks she's helping your father."

He gave her a solemn nod. "Then I'll do what I've already promised. I'll go to Fayetteville and get a message to your pa. At least he'll have the promise of your return to get him through."

She tilted her head. "You'd do that?"

He dropped to the chair and took her hand. "I would."

"But why?"

"For you, Dawsey," he said. "I'd do anything for you."

The door slammed, rattling the windowpane.

Dawsey leaped, but no higher than Duncan.

Hooper stood snarling at them. "Well, this is sweet. What has she suckered you into, brother? Hacking off your right arm? I see she's already cut the legs out from under you."

His harsh tone chilled Dawsey's spine. She stared in shock as he sauntered toward them, his dark scowl raising the hairs on her arms.

Duncan glared at his brother. "You can't talk about Dawsey like that."

"I need to speak to you, Miss Wilkes. In private."

Duncan held his ground. "You'll have to say it in front of me, because I'm not going anywhere."

Hooper opened his mouth, his chest like a swollen rain barrel. The shout he suppressed seemed to pain him. He winced and started over. "I need you to git, brother, so I can have a little chat with Dawsey before the house fills up again."

Duncan looked at her. "It's up to you."

Hooper leaned close to his face. "Duncan. . ."

His forehead arched in a plea, Duncan persisted, "You don't want to talk to him, do you, honey?"

Dawsey crossed her arms. "No, I don't." Breathing in sharply, she exhaled through her nose. "I'm afraid I must, at least one more time." She glowered at Hooper. "To defend my honor."

Launching himself from the table, Duncan stormed to the door. "I'll be right outside."

The second he left, Hooper swung into his chair, waving a threatening finger. "You won't take my pa to Fayetteville."

She closed her eyes. "Hooper, you're behaving like a lunatic."

"I won't allow him to go."

"The trip to Fayetteville was your father's idea. You were standing right here when he said so." She let her head fall back. "I'm tired of denying things I haven't done."

He smirked. "Just not the things you have?"

The room stilled. Every sound grew louder. The fire spit and crackled in the hearth. The wind whistled outside the cabin.

Hooper's labored breath rasped and a pulse pounded in her ears. She straightened and gazed at him. Unruly strands of hair hung in his eyes, dancing each time he blinked. Shadowy whiskers colored the soft skin of his cheeks, and zeal burned from his warm brown eyes. He'd never looked more handsome.

"Did I kiss you, Hooper?"

He flinched. "You know you did."

"Do I?" She struggled for words to explain. "Strong drink and dizzying herbs had never passed my lips before that day. The two together are quite potent, it seems."

His chin came up. "Rhoda's tonic?"

She nodded grimly.

Lost in thought, he studied the tabletop. The angry frown melted slowly as he blinked away his doubt. "You really don't remember."

Her cheeks warmed. "There's a foggy sense of *something* happening between us." She tilted her chin. "A pleasant memory, but it's only a vague shadow in the back of my mind."

He crossed his arms on the table and rested his forehead. "I said terrible things to you," he confessed to the crook of his arm. "Accused you in front of my folks."

"Yes, you did." On this score, she wouldn't go easy. "You humiliated me and brought my honor into question."

He sat up and squared his shoulders. "I'm sorry Dawsey, though an apology won't be enough. How can I make it up to you?"

"Will you tell your parents the truth? I don't want them thinking the worst."

He nodded. "Anything else?"

She ducked her head. "Will you accept my apology?"

"Yours?"

"Your accusations weren't far from the mark. I did use trickery and wiles against your family in order to escape. I purposely sought to gain your trust so you wouldn't watch me so closely." She struggled to hold back her tears. "Along the way, I began to care very much for you McRaes." She laughed. "As addlepated as that sounds."

Hooper whistled through his teeth. "I don't suppose there's a fitting

Psalm for that one." He grinned. "Am I the only one you kissed?"

They laughed together, and he shyly reached for her hand. "Please help me keep my pa at home where he belongs. Ma would be lost without him."

"I think his mind is made up to go." She squeezed his fingers. "It may be possible to convince my father not to bring charges though. I promise to try."

Hooper stood, pulling her into a gentle hug. "I couldn't ask for more."

Pleased with the number of whole pieces Papa had pried from the stubborn shells, Ellie took his full bowl of black walnuts and handed him an empty. "Keep going. You're doing a fine job."

Focused on Duncan, he took the bowl with fumbling fingers. "You going somewhere, son?"

Duncan stood beside Ellie's horse with a saddlebag over his shoulder. "Yes, sir. For just a day or so."

"Where to?"

"I. . .well, I'm not sure yet. Not exactly."

Pa leaned in his rickety chair and set the bowl on the porch. "Who's going with you?"

Something big had wiggled up Duncan's craw. It took several minutes of coughing to clear it out.

"The details are still sketchy." His eyes jumped to Dawsey. "A friend's in trouble and I offered to help. That's all I know right now."

Bent over a pail of beet juice, stirring handmade ornaments with Mama, Dawsey seemed as fidgety as Ellie's squirming brother. No doubt about it, they were up to something.

Mama stood with her hand on her hip. "Do you have to go now? Tomorrow's Christmas Eve. We're going to decorate Dawsey's tree."

Duncan grinned and patted the horse's neck. "Don't worry. Ellie loaned me Toby. He'll have me back with time to spare."

Mama scowled. "Suppose you don't make it?"

"Then I'll be home in time for presents, but only if you stop asking questions and let me get down the road."

Still smiling, he settled the bag on Toby's back and fastened it down with leather straps. With a jaunty salute, he reined the horse toward the lane.

Shading her eyes with her hand, Dawsey stared after Duncan with a tender smile on her face.

The breath caught in Ellie's throat. *She's sweet on him!* What else could her moony-eyed glances mean?

Hooper swung around the house and flung his body over the rail, landing with a *thud* next to Dawsey. She leaped and squeaked like a mouse. Mama screamed and clutched her heart. Papa laughed so hard his belly shook.

Grinning, Hooper slid his arms around Mama's waist. "May I have this dance?"

She poked him with her elbow. "You scared the soup out of me."

He kissed her cheek and let her go. "Guilty conscience?"

"Oh, you." She swatted him. "My sore conscience has nothing to do with it."

Hooper waltzed around Dawsey, jabbing her in the side as he passed. She yelped and sloshed him with her dye. He spun to dip one finger and touched the tip of her nose.

"Oh, Hooper!" She dropped the stirring stick and covered her face with both hands. "My nose will be red for days."

"You'll make a fetching ornament. We'll let you top the tree."

Batting her lashes like a silly schoolgirl, Dawsey blushed and looked away.

Ellie felt like scratching her head. Was Dawsey sweet on both of her brothers?

Papa fetched his bowl of walnuts and started peeling again.

Love shone from Mama's eyes. "You'll get an extra slice of brown sugar pie for your trouble, Silas."

"I'd best get an extra pie." Raising his head, he gazed toward the barn. "Anybody seen Tiller?"

Hooper snatched two fat walnuts and squeezed them together with a loud *crack*. "Not since breakfast. Maybe he's with your other son"—he smirked—"the homely one."

Papa jabbed a thumb, stained brown with nut sap, in the direction Duncan had gone. "No, the smart one just rode off, and he didn't have Tiller with him."

Hooper chewed his pilfered walnut and stared down the lane. "Where'd he go?"

Pa shrugged. "Can't say." He laughed. "And neither could he. The boy didn't seem to know where he was headed or with who."

Frowning, Hooper hooked his arm around a post. "That could be risky, Pa. Outright dangerous. Why'd you let him go?"

A concerned frown wrinkled Papa's nose. "I figure he's off with Henry or Boss. Maybe the Carter boy."

Hooper scratched the side of his head. "It's not like him to go off without saying a word to me, but he's grown enough to take care of himself, I reckon."

Mama laid aside her half-red stirring stick and wiped her brow. "Don't fret, Hooper. He promised to be home tomorrow evening. Christmas morning at the latest."

Deep in thought, Hooper nodded. "All right then."

Papa shifted his bulk in the chair. "It's Tiller who has me vexed." He gazed toward the swamp with a puckered scowl. "He's not roaming out there alone, no matter what he claims. The lad has deliberately disobeyed me by linking arms with young Nathan."

He looked ever his shoulder at Ellie. "For the Carters' sake, I hope Nathan matures with half of Wyatt's sense."

She nodded. "He will. Wyatt will see to it."

In better spirits again, Hooper rubbed his hands together and looked at Dawsey. "Are we still going for that ride?"

"I'd very much like to," she said.

"Then it's settled. We'll leave right after lunch, so eat hearty."

"Wait a blasted minute," Papa said, raising his hand. "Where do you think you're taking her?"

"Along Drowning Creek to search for holly."

"And greenery," Dawsey added.

"Bring me some possumhaw boughs," Ellie said. "The red berries are ever so pretty."

Pa slumped in his chair. "Did I die, and you lot forgot to bury me? I'm the last to know everything around here."

Ignoring his sulk, Mama peered at Dawsey's eyes. "Are you sure you're strong enough?"

"Oh yes, ma'am," Dawsey assured her. "Stronger every day."

"Besides," Hooper said, "we're taking the wagon."

Rising with a groan, Pa handed his basket to Ellie. "I'm more concerned about a chaperone."

Holding one finger aloft, Hooper cleared his throat. "All tended. We're taking the pest."

"Tiller?" Papa snorted. "What sort of chaperone is he?"

Mama leaned to pat his arm. "The very best kind. He's so afraid to miss them sparking, he won't take his eyes off for a minute."

They all laughed, except for Pa. "No telling where he is. You'd best hope he comes home in time."

Ellie grinned. "He'll be here before Ma sets the table. Tiller won't miss a meal."

Hooper ducked his head at Dawsey. "Speaking of Tiller's appetite, you'd better pack a biscuit or two. If hunger sets in, he'll squawk the whole time we're gone."

Crossing the porch, he took her arm. "Why don't you go inside and rest until we leave?"

He led her to the door with Mama fussing behind them. "He's right, Dawsey. It's an hour yet before the noon meal. I'll help you lie down."

They slipped inside the dim cabin and shut the door. Papa held his shushing finger to his lips and scooped out a handful of walnuts. Tossing his head back, he poured them into his mouth. "Picker's profit," he explained, his eyes twinkling.

Ellie hugged him around the waist. "There went a slice of your pie."

Still chewing, he shook his head. "Tastes more like Duncan's slice."

Giggling like naughty children, they followed the others inside.

CHAPTER 34

Ellie knelt beside the chicken fence, holding the picket still while her mama wired it into place. Without the plank, the fence had a snaggletoothed grin. Now it smiled in gratitude.

Giving the wire one last twist, Mama stood up, dusting her hands. "Blasted greedy 'coons. They eat more than Tiller. You wouldn't think they could squeeze those fat bellies through such a slim opening."

Ellie laughed. "That's what busts the wood."

Mama swatted the empty air. "I'll bust them, if they don't stay out of my feed."

Ellie shouldered her shotgun and Mama gathered the tools. On the way to the house, she listed the chores she expected Ellie to do before Christmas.

Ellie moaned. "Why on earth do you insist on sweeping the yard? It don't make sense."

"Don't mock things you don't understand," Mama warned. "All the best families in Fayetteville sweep their yards every Saturday. Once more if company's coming."

Baffled at her logic, Ellie took in their surroundings. "This ain't Fayetteville, we never have company, and what little yard we have is mostly underwater."

Mama scowled. "The part that's dry is getting swept." She poked Ellie's nose. "By you."

"Where's Papa? He can sweep."

"He won't. He calls it women's work. Besides, he's taking a nap."

Ellie whined. "Can't I wait for Dawsey? She should help. This fancy Christmas was her idea."

They reached the steps, and Mama swiveled on her heels. "Dawsey will be helping me in the kitchen."

"Why can't I? All the jobs you gave me, the men could do."

"And so can you." Mama shot her a rueful look. "I need Dawsey in the kitchen, honey. She's a wonderful cook."

Ellie followed Ma onto the porch. "And I'm not? You said my last biscuits turned out better than yours."

Her eyes softened. "It's true. You're getting much better, but Christmas is a special occasion."

Ellie opened her mouth to demand she explain, but Mama's hand shot up. "Did you hear something?" Tilting her ear toward the house, she searched Ellie's face.

Swallowing hard, Ellie nodded. The cold fear in Mama's gaze slithered under her skin. "Don't be scared. It's just Papa rattling firewood."

Ma's eyes were as big as wagon wheels. "It's not your pa," she hissed, "unless he has ten feet."

"Hooper?"

"Gone with Dawsey to fetch holly."

Ellie raised the shotgun. "Stay here."

She eased the door open a crack, wincing when the hinges creaked. Placing one eye to the narrow slit, Ellie's heart shot past her throat.

Long shadows, visible through the open door to Papa's room, danced a curious waltz on his wall. She held her breath and pushed inside then crept across the floor, past the hearth and the table, past the counter, to the door of her parents' room.

She had little time to decide her next move. Papa's yelp of pain fired heat to her chest and life to her hands and feet. With a war cry, she burst inside the room.

Two men held her pa against the wall, one with his hands around his throat, squeezing with a white-knuckled grip. The other was the bounty hunter who'd come looking for Hooper.

"Turn him loose," Ellie bawled, blinking away angry tears.

The one choking the life out of Papa wore a badge. He turned, his cruel face twisted with spite. "Well, look here. It's a little gal." He leaned close to Papa's ear. "Is this pretty little thing your daughter, Silas McRae?"

Ellie's gaze jumped from his pale fingers to Papa's bug-eyed plea for help. "I said turn him loose!" she screamed.

Mama plucked the gun from Ellie's hands. The look on her face was one Ellie had never seen before—one she hoped she'd never see again.

Her soulless stare had the same effect on the bounty hunter. He backed away from Pa, his hands held high. His pitiless friend tensed, loosened his grip enough for Pa to suck air in a rattling gasp. Then his shoulders relaxed and he leered. "Go ahead. Pull that trigger, ma'am. You'll scatter lead over half this wall and cut Silas down with me."

Mama cocked one brow and raised the barrel. "Just as well. I can't abide the old fool."

Mucky swampland and scum-covered ponds were all Dawsey had seen in Scuffletown, the place she'd lived for endless weeks. As the wagon rolled toward the river, a different side of the North Carolina countryside danced past.

His eyes glowing, Hooper leaned to point out a black-water stream that flowed in and out of sight around twisted bends. Moldy mushrooms jutted from thick loblolly pine trunks like fairy stairwells wending to tiny houses in the branches.

Ellie had loaned Dawsey a pair of slacks for the occasion and a woolen shirt that made her uncomfortably hot in the sunlight. With Tiller tugging on the sleeves, she pulled off her borrowed coat and rested it over her lap. "Much better. Thank you."

He smiled and ducked his head. "Sure thing, Miss Wilkes."

She turned on the seat. "Please, call me Dawsey. Everyone else does."

Grinning, he picked at his cuff. "I'll try. Course I might slip a time or two, since I ain't never called you nothing else."

She patted his hand. "If you forget, I'll remind you."

Hooper reined Old Abe near the riverbank and turned with a smile. "This is it. The place I told you about."

He'd stopped in a clearing too small to call a meadow but with all of the same charm. Surrounded by towering pine and wide oak, a quaint trail led across the browning grass. Holly trees, bright with berries, grew in clustered groves around the rim.

Dawsey stared in awe. "It's lovely."

"I knew you'd like it."

She crossed her arms to keep from clasping her hands and squealing. "I simply love it, Hooper."

Scrambling to the ground, he hustled to her side and helped her down.

She stood with her hands on her hips, surveying the clearing. "I don't know where to start. There are so many."

With one hand on her shoulder, he leaned close and pointed. "Plenty of evergreens, too."

Tiller pulled a long, thick-handled knife from the wagon bed. "Want me to start cutting?"

Sucking in his stomach to dodge the blade, Hooper relieved him of his weapon. "Don't be waving that thing about, boy." He ruffled Tiller's hair then grabbed the back of his neck. "It's best to let a man do the cutting."

"Can't." Tiller sniffed. "Duncan ain't here."

Hooper swatted at him, but Tiller was too fast. He tore across the field with Hooper on his heels.

Halfway across, Hooper doubled back for Dawsey. Bowing, he offered his arm. "May I?"

Feeling like a debutante, she curtseyed. "Sir, you may."

For the next half hour, they cut bushels of holly branches, picking only the reddest berries to stack inside the wagon.

On their way up the path for the last time, Tiller groaned. "I've never seen so many cuttings. What are you planning to do? Cover the walls?"

Dawsey tweaked his ear. "Yes, I am. Inside and out."

He squinted up at her. "Why?"

"Because holly trees are very important at Christmastime," she said. "Do you know what they signify?"

"Huh?"

"Signify," she repeated slowly. "It means suggest or be a sign of."

Gnawing his bottom lip, Tiller nodded. "So what do they s–signify?"

"Very good." She patted his back. "Well, the thorny leaves"—she plucked one off to show him the tiny curved spikes—"suggest the crown of thorns on Christ's head."

Hooper took it from her hand. "They do?"

"Yes, and the red berries bring to mind drops of His priceless blood."

Making a face, Tiller took the leaf from Hooper. "Why is His blood so priceless?"

Dawsey tilted her head. "I can best answer your question with my favorite carol." Drawing a quick breath, she began to sing:

"Cedar and pine now cheerily twine:
Crown every scene with evergreen:
Now is the reign of darkness o'er:
Jesus is king for evermore!
Boughs of the holly this day adorn:
Sharp are the leaves as crowns of thorn:
See, in the berries all blood red,
Blood that, for us, this babe shall shed."

Silence filled the woods around them, as though nature had hushed to listen.

Hooper seemed stunned. "That was beautiful, Dawsey."

"He's right, Miss Wi—I mean, Dawsey. You sounded real pretty. What does it mean?"

"It means that Jesus shed His blood, so we might live. This makes the blood precious indeed."

He frowned. "A babe shed his blood?"

She smoothed his hair. "No, but a babe born to that very purpose."

"Oh." His interest fading as fast as it had sparked, Tiller punched Hooper's arm. "Race you to the rig."

Dawsey longed to finish the story, both for the boy and for Hooper, who seemed to be listening carefully. Sadly, the mood was broken.

They reached the wagon and she placed her sticky evergreen branch atop the rest.

Tiller tossed in his holly. "Can we go now? After all that work, I'm powerful hungry."

Hooper handed his branch to Dawsey. "We expected you to say that."

He stretched to reach under the seat and pulled out a bundle tied with string. "How about one of your aunt Odie's biscuits?"

Tiller hunched over the food and sniffed. "My nose tells me there's more than plain old biscuits in there." He lifted the edge of the towel and smiled. "I knew it. Bacon."

Dawsey spread a blanket while Hooper pulled out a jug of sweet cider. They sat under the clear blue sky and finished Odell's simple fare in no time at all, especially with Tiller's help.

Dawsey hugged herself and shivered.

Watching her, Hooper wiped his mouth. "Are you cold?"

"A little. There's a hint of a chill in the air."

He pushed off the ground. "I'll fetch Ellie's coat for you."

Tiller lay back on the blanket and wrapped himself with the corner. "It's 'cause we worked up a sweat."

Back with the coat, Hooper bumped him with his foot. "Mind your manners."

He gaped. "What'd I do?"

"You're not supposed to mention things like sweat in front of a lady."

"Why not?" He rose up on his elbow. "Ma says she can sweat like a washerwoman."

Hooper cringed.

Caught off guard, Dawsey laughed, spewing biscuit crumbs. Horrified, she clutched her mouth, the laugher dying in her throat—until Hooper doubled over, howling.

"I told you." Tiller cackled, his high-pitched voice echoing through the trees. "There ain't nothing special about a woman. They burp and spit just like we do."

Hooper sat up wiping his eyes. Sobered, he swung toward Dawsey with tears of glee caught in his lashes. "You're dead wrong, cousin." He pressed so close, his breath warmed Dawsey's cheek. "Some women are very special."

Tiller pulled a face. "Aw, there you go spooning. Just when we was starting to have fun."

Dawsey whirled. "There is no spooning happening here, young man. Don't you go telling stories to Silas."

Hooper stood, pulling Tiller up by his collar. "Come on, you. Get this blanket folded and in the wagon. It's time to get Dawsey home."

Shading her eyes, she turned her face up to him. "We can't go yet. We forgot Dilsey's boughs. She made a special request."

Hooper's hands went to his hips. "She did, at that." Turning, he searched the edge of the clearing with darting eyes. "I think I saw a possumhaw tree a little past those pines."

He loped to the wagon and pulled the knife from the bed. "Let's go, Tiller. I'll let you cut this time, if you promise to come back with both legs."

They shuffled away, jostling against each other as they trudged up the beaten trail.

Dawsey stood, shaking the embarrassing crumbs from the blanket and folding it small enough to tuck under the seat. Smiling to herself, she stared at the wagon bed, mounded high with deep red berries over a bed of cedar green. The lovely sight seemed so Christmassy, it brought happy tears to her eyes.

Recalling the beautiful story she'd shared about the holly, Dawsey closed her eyes and basked in God's love amid the quiet calm of the clearing. Despite her recent trials, she'd never felt such peace.

On the way home, she realized Hooper had left her alone in the clearing with a horse and wagon, the perfect opportunity to escape, but it hadn't occurred to her to do so. Frowning, she searched her heart for the reason.

Pushing aside the outrageous idea that it had anything to do with Hooper, she told herself she didn't run because she couldn't leave Dilsey behind.

Chapter 35

Mama motioned to Ellie, crouched behind her. "Stand back, honey, and plug your ears."

Fear pooled in the hateful man's dark eyes. He heaved Papa on the bed and bolted, barely clearing the room before the blast of the gun rang Ellie's ears like a gong.

Mama whirled on his friend who seemed to have wet his pants. "I think you were just leaving."

Nodding, he slid along the wall until he reached the opening then shot through with Mama on his heels. He sailed through the cabin, knocking over chairs in his haste, and bolted from the house.

She slammed and barred the door behind him then whirled to gape at Ellie. They stared at each other in silence until Papa groaned from the bedroom. Heaving great gulping sobs, Mama ran past Ellie to kneel beside him on the bed. "Oh Silas! Please tell me you're all right."

Papa clutched her hand, reaching a clumsy finger to wipe her tears. He tried to speak but only managed to croak, so he nodded instead.

Mama stretched out beside him, gently caressing his hair.

Smiling through her tears, Ellie slipped out and closed the door. She knew in her head that the men weren't likely to return, not without more hired guns. Still, she set up a watch near the window, alert for any movement, while her heart willed Hooper to hurry home.

Mama appeared, rattling her pots.

Ellie abandoned her post to throw another log on the hearth then sat down in front of the fire. "Chicken soup?"

Mama nodded.

No matter the ailment, in her mind, chicken soup was the cure. Ellie couldn't figure how steaming broth might ease a near strangling, but if it promised a cure for jangled nerves, she'd gladly sip a cup.

Mama finished her healing brew and sat beside Papa's bed, blowing the heat off bites and spooning them into his swollen mouth.

He tried to speak, but Mama hushed him. "Rest, darlin'. Let the warm soup loosen your throat before you try to talk."

This nugget of wisdom shed light on Mama's claim. Ellie resolved to try a bit of soup on the pesky lump in her own throat.

Waving away the cure, Pa stared at Ellie, his eyes troubled.

She settled on the other side of the bed and took his hand. "I know, Papa. You're worried about Hooper."

His head bounced up and down.

"Do you want me to ride out and find him?"

He nodded faster.

Mama stood, sloshing soup on the mattress. "She'll do no such thing."

"But Ma—"

"Forget it, Ellie." She bore down on Papa. "There are lunatics in those swamps, Silas. One of them almost killed you. I won't risk my only daughter, not even for our son."

Concerned for Hooper, Ellie girded herself for battle. Before she decided her best line of attack, three loud raps on the door, followed by persistent hammering, threatened to loosen the hinges.

Papa swung off the bed, reaching for Ellie's gun. The fresh terror shining from his eyes tore at Ellie's heart. With his wife and daughter behind him, he crept toward the rowdy noise.

As she passed the gun rack, Ellie lifted a loaded rifle with shaky hands.

The door shuddered under a fresh wave of pounding.

"Who's there?" Ellie called, dread thick as porridge in her throat. Mama gripped her arm and yanked her two feet away.

"Open up this instant."

Ellie squealed. Her fear lifted and comfort took its place as she hurriedly lifted the bar.

Hooper stormed inside with an angry scowl. "Who locked this blasted thing?"

Mama burst into tears. "Oh Hooper."

His startled gaze swung to Pa and shock paled his features. "Thunderation! What happened here?"

Shouldering his gun, he hurried to Papa and touched his battered face. "Who did this?"

Trembling, Ellie pulled Dawsey and Tiller past the threshold and slammed the bar home. "They're still out there somewhere. Mama got a shot off, but it didn't slow them down."

"Bounty hunters?"

"One of them. The other wore a cheap star on his vest."

Chest heaving, Papa groped the empty space behind him. Dawsey dashed for his chair and they lowered him down.

"Let me catch my breath, son," he begged in a raspy croak. "Then I'll tell you what we need to do."

They had him seated near the window beneath the last rays of the setting sun. The eggplant-colored marks seemed to glow, lining his swollen neck like a hand still gripping his throat.

Wincing, Hooper touched them then smoothed Papa's grizzled head with an unsteady hand. "We both know what I have to do. For now, you need to rest."

Watching Hooper, Ellie shivered. She'd seen him this way before, with black rage simmering beneath a quiet voice and calm manner.

He motioned to Tiller. Between them, they herded Papa on shuffling feet to his bed. Ma flitted around him, pulling the covers to his chin and tucking him in on both sides.

Lying still, he gazed fretfully at Hooper. "Wait for Duncan."

Hooper's jaw formed a grim line, and he wouldn't meet Pa's searching eyes. "Some things won't wait."

One of Papa's long feet stuck from under the quilt, the dingy toenails like talons. Hooper patted his foot then moved for the door.

"Son?"

He turned.

"Don't go alone. Fetch Henry or Boss to go with you."

The glint of unshed tears in his eyes, Hooper nodded.

Ellie followed him to the gun rack. "I'm going."

Dawsey gasped and covered her mouth.

Shoving a long-barreled handgun into his waistband, Hooper shook his head. "Don't be daft."

"It'll be dark soon. I'll hide out in the brush and pick them off. You know I'm the best shot in this family."

"No."

"But it makes no sense not to take me. I can cover for you."

She'd gone too far. He whirled and gripped her arms, his face twisted into a stranger's ugly mask. "If you leave this cabin, you'll have a price to pay."

Shrinking away from him, she nodded.

Tiller jostled close. "Can I go?"

Hooper lifted his Spencer from the rack. "I need you to look after the women."

Drawing the false veil of calm around him again, he crossed to Dawsey standing near the door and cupped her face in his palm.

In that moment, Ellie knew Hooper loved her.

The way Dawsey gazed at him left no doubt which brother she preferred. "You will be careful." Her quiet words were not a request.

Hooper patted her cheek and nodded. "I'm always careful."

Before the heavy door closed behind him, Ellie dashed to sling it wide. "You'd best do like Papa said, Hooper McRae! Take Henry. . .or Boss. Don't you dare go alone!"

Dawsey's hand touched Ellie's shoulder and she spun. In a tearful daze, she stumbled headlong into her sister's comforting arms.

Chapter 36

Dawsey tugged Hooper's blanket closer and willed his knock to sound. Stretched out on his mat, she'd tossed like a landed trout through the night, sleeping in drips and dabs. Dilsey's rest appeared even more fitful, so Dawsey welcomed the soft, steady breaths coming from her direction.

The hushed whispers that carried to her long into the night drifted out to her now from Silas and Odell's room, and she wondered if they'd slept at all.

The cabin seemed to yearn for any sign of Hooper. Only Tiller, with a youth's blind trust in fate, slept from the instant his tangled red hair hit the pillow. Cutting holly branches must've worn him to a frazzle.

Dawsey rolled off the mat, wincing when she put weight on her injured leg. She'd done too much the day before but wouldn't trade her day in the holly grove for two strong limbs.

With an absent rub, she put the pain aside and lifted Dilsey's shotgun from beside her on the floor. Tiptoeing past her sister, she eased the bar from its hooks, turned the knob, and tugged on the door.

"Dawsey?"

She spun, her hand clutching her heart. "Goodness, you startled me."

Dilsey sat up on her mat, her brows drawn in suspicion. She pointed at the shotgun. "Where do you think you're going with that?"

"Out back. I was afraid to go alone, but I didn't want to wake you."

Dilsey stood and crossed to her. "You'd best let me have the gun.

You don't even know how to shoot."

She gladly handed it over. "Maybe not, but I'm a pretty fair bluff."

Leaning on the wall, Dilsey struggled into her boots. She straightened and nodded at Dawsey's bare feet. "Were you going like that?"

She shrugged. "I was trying to be quiet."

Shaking her head, Dilsey held Dawsey's boots while she slid them on. Easing the door open a crack, she peeked out.

Dawsey pressed closer. "What are we looking for?"

"Anything out of place. You get a feel for it after a while." She pointed to the porch. "Look there. Ma shot that rascal after all."

Dark splotches, trampled in some places, led from the door to the ground. Dawsey frowned. "What is that?"

"Blood." Dilsey backed away from the door and pointed. "See, there's some in here, too. In all the commotion, we didn't notice."

Dawsey looked under her feet and shuddered. Rusty-brown footprints led through the door then scattered over the wood floor. Prints she, Hooper, and Tiller had tracked inside last night.

Dilsey stepped outside and she hurried after her.

"There's a lot," Dilsey said, worry creasing her forehead. "Ma may've killed him."

Her eyes flickered, and she gripped Dawsey's shoulders. "If the sheriff comes for her, we'll say I did it. You'll back me up, won't you?"

"No!" The word shot from Dawsey's mouth. "I—I mean, then they'll take you, won't they? I can't see anything happen to you."

Dilsey gave her a shake. "Ma shot a lawman. Some cruel drunk sworn in at the last minute, but that won't matter in Robeson County. If he's dead, they'll come for her."

"We'll pray it won't come to that."

Her trembling lips rimmed in white, Dilsey gazed toward the swamp. "Don't bother. Prayers uttered in Scuffletown never reach heaven. God forgot us a long time ago."

Shame coursed through Dawsey. Whatever warmth she'd missed in Father's absent parenting, thankfully, Aunt Livvy had honored Mother's wish to pass along her abiding faith in God. Affection had its merit, but assurance of God's protective love was a priceless gift.

Sudden longing filled her heart to see Dilsey with the same assurance. She took her hand. "You're wrong, Dilsey. God hasn't forgotten. He cares about you very much."

Dilsey flinched. "About you, maybe."

Drawing her sister to the rail, she pulled her close. "God calls Himself our refuge and fortress. Does that sound like an uncaring God?"

Dilsey shrugged.

"Have you ever watched a hen defending her brood?"

"We have a chicken yard, silly. Lots of times."

"In the same way, God promised to deliver us from the snare of the fowler, to tuck us under His wing and cover us with His feathers."

She had offered the perfect example. Hope shone from Dilsey's eyes. "He said that?"

Dawsey nodded and squeezed her arm. "Yes, so trust Him. He'll take care of you if you let Him. The same scripture says, 'Only with thine eyes shalt thou behold and see the reward of the wicked.'"

Dilsey tensed. Tugging free, she started down the steps. "That's our problem in Scuffletown. Sometimes it's hard to tell the wicked from the just."

She turned at the bottom step, grief etched in her face. "If you need to go to the outhouse, then come on."

Blinking back tears, Dawsey hurried to catch up.

They spoke very little on the way down the trail and back. Dawsey mentioned the warm day. Dilsey nodded and said it wouldn't last. A curtain had dropped, shutting them off from each other, as if the comforting whispers and gentle hugs of the night before had never happened.

They rounded the house, and Dilsey spun toward the porch, raising the barrel of her shotgun. "Pa, for heaven's sake, I nearly shot you."

He poured out a steaming pan of water and set to whisking with Odell's yard broom, slinging gory splatter. "I have to clean this mess before your ma sees it. She thinks that varmint got away."

Dilsey rushed up the steps and took the broom. "You're making a mess. Beside, you're not supposed to be out of bed. Go inside and keep Ma busy. I'll clean this up."

"She's still resting, bless her. Didn't sleep a wink all night with fretting over Hooper."

Dawsey took Silas's arm to steady him. "Shouldn't Hooper be here by now?"

He glanced at her with red-rimmed eyes. "He won't come home until he finishes what he left here to do."

At the door, he looked back at Dilsey. "Make sure you get it all. Your ma don't need more fear added to her plate."

"Yes, Pa."

"I know it won't be easy, but I'd be beholden to you girls if you'd conduct yourselves today like nothing's wrong." He lifted his chin toward the wagon. "Go on with your plans for sprucing up the house. It'll take her mind off things."

Hooper had unhitched Old Abe before he left, but the load of colorful boughs still sat in front of the house. For Dawsey, all the joy had gone out of decorating for Christmas. By the look of her, Dilsey felt even less inclined, but she bit her lip and nodded. "Yes, sir. We'll do it."

Dawsey tugged on Silas's arm. "Let's go inside. I'll fix you a nice breakfast."

"Did somebody say breakfast?" Tiller stood on the threshold rubbing sleepy eyes. Bare from the waist up, a lone suspender held up his britches.

Silas hustled forward, his bulk driving Tiller inside. "You heard right. Dawsey's offered to cook for us." Staring at the soiled planks at his feet, concern wrinkled his shaggy brows. "After she mops, that is. You boys have tracked in mud."

A willing conspirator, Dawsey whirled for a damp rag—and nearly tripped over Odell standing behind her.

Wearing a white cotton dressing gown, she stood with her shoulders back, her head high. Her serenity and strength brought to mind an angelic queen. For a moment, Dawsey forgot she was short.

On the porch, Dilsey stilled with the broom in hand and stared through the open door at her mother.

Odell glanced at her then back to Silas. "Did you really think I wouldn't notice blood stains on my own floor?"

"Now, Odie," Silas soothed, his eyes bulging. "Go back to bed, darlin'. I'll bring you some breakfast in a bit."

A smile tugged the corners of her mouth. Gliding to him on bare feet, she pinched his face and kissed him. "I saw how bad I shot him, Silas. The lead tore holes in his shirt."

Tears welled, her brave front slipping. "They'll come for me today."

Silas drew her to his chest. "They'll haul you out over my dead body."

Dilsey slung the broom and ran inside, her arms enveloping her mother. "Over mine, too."

"And mine," Dawsey vowed, stretching to hug them all.

Tiller slammed and locked the door. "I have a better idea. Don't let 'em in."

Amused by the wisdom of his simple plan, Dawsey bit her lip to keep from smiling.

Showing less restraint, Odell's shoulders shook with laughter. "Oh, Tiller, if only that would work. I'm afraid nothing will keep the sheriff out." She sobered. "What I won't do is cower inside my own house like I done something wrong. We'll do just like you said, Silas. We'll adorn this house and trim Dawsey's tree the way we planned."

Her trembling fingers smoothed Dilsey's hair, patted Dawsey's cheek, then clung to Silas's hand. "I just pray when the morning comes, I'm still alive to see it."

Weaving endless holly wreaths and tying sprigs to pine bough garlands had stained Ellie's hands a merry red. She had to admit, the decorations and the young Virginia pine they'd hauled from the woods gave the cabin an enchanted feel.

Dawsey had mixed dough and shaped it into cookie stars to hang on the tree, along with a long string of pinecones. She raided Mama's button box, sewing the most colorful onto scraps of cloth, and folded them into ornaments. After that, she tied fabric strips into bows of many shapes and sizes and hung them, too.

Between her and Mama, they'd turned bowls of sticky batter into cakes and cookies and rolled flaky crusts for the brown sugar pies.

Shortly after lunch, Rhoda came bearing gifts. Surrounded by Henry's men, she stayed long enough to see that her patient was well and to pass Mama a gunnysack filled with precious sugar, butter, salt, and two dressed ducks. Mama repaid her in eggs and warm smiles.

Once she left, more wonderful smells than before floated outside from the kitchen.

Ellie perched on the edge of the steps, staring toward the distant tree line. If a horse poked his nose from the brush, it could be good news or bad. With both her brothers due any minute, she hoped for the good and strained her ears for a whistle.

The day had dawned warm, but a brisk wind and a bank of clouds from the north had chased the warmth toward the coastline.

Pa sat in his chair flicking finishing pieces from the angel he whittled for Ma's Christmas present.

Ellie shivered and glanced his way. "You want me to fetch your coat?"

He grunted. "Not yet. I'm enjoying the breeze after sweating all night."

"Don't catch a chill," she warned over her shoulder then went back to scanning the trees.

His chair groaned as he leaned back, propping his boot on the rail next to Ellie. "I'm glad to see it cooling off. Fanning yourself while eating Christmas dinner just don't feel right."

"I could use a fan right now," Dawsey said behind them. "This cool hasn't reached the kitchen."

Ellie squinted up at her. "Come out and rest a spell. You look plain tuckered."

Pa twisted around to see. "She's red in the face, Ellie. Take her out to sit in the yard so the wind can cool her down."

Ellie stood. "I will, but fetch our coats off the pegs, Dawsey. From the look of that sky, you won't be hot for long."

They skirted the rain barrel and hopped puddles on the way to the shade tree, not that they needed shade with the black sky closing in. Ellie perched on her favorite stump, leaving Pa's for Dawsey.

"You're right," Dawsey said. "It is cold out here."

Ellie stood. "Let me help you with your coat."

Slipping her arm into the sleeve, Dawsey glanced at her. "May I ask a question? One that's burned in my heart for days?"

Ellie shrugged and sat down. "I suppose you'd better. A burning heart sounds a mite uncomfortable."

Smiling, Dawsey's lashes swept her cheeks. Head down, she picked at a speck of dried flour on the leg of her pants. Dawsey had taken a shine to Ellie's trousers. Since she washed them often and hung them to dry, Ellie didn't mind. Pulling clean britches off the line was easier than digging through her laundry basket for the cleanest pair.

Clasping her hands in her lap, Dawsey drew a deep breath. "Are you glad we found each other?" Her doe eyes begged Ellie to say yes.

Longing to please her, Ellie managed a sweet smile. "I'm glad you're my sister." A sprinkle of sugar on the tongue took the bite out of castor oil. "But I wish the whole thing had never happened."

Dawsey cocked her head. "Which thing? Silas taking you, or you knowing about it?"

Biting her lip, Ellie met her eyes. "If I had my way, you'd never have come. I wouldn't be wondering what my real folks were like, and I'd still feel comfortable hearing my own name."

The swirling dark clouds overhead couldn't match the distress on Dawsey's face. "You'd rather we'd gone to our graves never knowing each other?"

Ellie nodded. "That would've been fine by me."

Dawsey turned aside, pretending a sudden interest in a knobby root. Her shoulders rose and fell in deep sighs that seemed to catch in her chest.

A strange ache swelled inside Ellie. She swiveled toward the girl fate had tossed in her lap. "Are you all right, Dawsey?"

She sniffed and pulled farther away.

Ellie caught her arm. "I'm sorry. I don't mean to sound cold." She paused and swallowed. It wasn't in her nature to seek pity. "It's just been so hard since you came."

Dawsey turned, her face damp with tears. "You've grieved for a few weeks. I've suffered for years."

Ellie gaped. "You? How have you suffered?"

Standing, Dawsey loomed over her. "Don't you see? You never really left our house. You were there, every hour, every minute of the day, sucking the life from us. I just didn't know who to blame until now." She whirled to stalk toward the house.

Ellie lit out after her. Clutching her sleeve, she tugged her around. "What are you saying?"

Dawsey's face was livid. "Your disappearance stole my family's chance for happiness. I didn't have a funny, carefree father like Silas. I lived with a man consumed by rage."

"None of that was my fault."

Dawsey jerked away. "I never had a mother because your absence killed her."

The scathing words pelted Ellie like buckshot. She stumbled away from their sting and ran toward the woods.

Dawsey caught up with her, snagging her around the waist. "Please wait. I'm sorry." She dragged Ellie to a halt and threw both arms around her neck. "Forgive me. I didn't mean what I said. You must know I didn't. I was hurt and lashed out."

Before Ellie could react, a whistle sounded from the swamp.

Dawsey raised her head, her eyes searching Ellie's face. "Duncan or Hooper?"

Papa blew a sharp blast, and Duncan rode into sight.

Trotting closer, he grinned, his arm raised in greeting.

Dawsey sucked in a breath, and Ellie's heart stopped as a man slipped out of the brush behind Duncan, pointing a long-barreled pistol at his back.

Ellie's frozen feet sprang to life and she ran, remembering too late that she wasn't armed.

A shrill cry rose from Dawsey as she sprinted alongside.

With a shout, Hooper shot out of the opposite clutch of trees, waving a rifle.

The stranger turned too late and met the barrel of the Spencer with his jaw. He fell like a stone, his pistol firing to the sky.

Duncan's horse reared, unseating him.

The strangled scream that ripped from Dawsey's throat rocked the clearing, echoing through the swamp. Arms waving, she overtook Ellie and dashed toward the men.

Duncan sat up, smiling. "It's all right, honey. He didn't shoot me."

She passed him in a blur then sailed past Hooper. Shrieking like a woman possessed, she streaked to the fallen man and threw herself on the ground.

White faced, Hooper stalked to her and pulled her to her feet. "What are you doing? Get away from that stinking bounty hunter."

Struggling against him, Dawsey pulled free and fell on the limp and bleeding man. "He's no bounty hunter, Hooper." Sobbing, she raised stricken eyes. "You just killed my father."

Hooper gazed wistfully at Dawsey's Christmas tree. The cookie streamers, button ornaments, and colorful garlands brought a false cheer to the cabin. The wreaths, red with holly, reminded him of her hopeful tale of Christ's birth. Meant to bring joy, the sight of them worsened the ache in his chest.

Pa slumped before the hearth, staring into the fire. "It don't feel like Christmas Eve, does it?"

Hooper sighed. "No, sir, it sure don't." He laid a comforting hand on Pa's shoulder. "Why don't you get some rest?"

Ignoring the idea, he leaned in his chair and gripped his head. "This whole thing is my fault."

Hooper squatted beside him. "I don't see how you can think so. I'm the one who bashed in Mr. Wilkes's head."

Papa moaned. "I'm responsible, son, not you. Taking Ellie started a fire behind me, and the flames have chased me ever since." He sat up and slapped the arm of his chair. "I pray the man's all right, but by thunder, I won't let him take her away."

Ellie got up from the table and crouched at his feet. "I'm a grown woman now. No one can make me leave Scuffletown." She snorted. "I dare them to try."

"I dare them, too," Mama said, passing a tray filled with mugs of warm milk. She glanced around the cabin. "Where's Tiller?"

"He took off awhile ago," Hooper said. "Didn't say where he was headed."

Papa grunted. "He's spending too much time with those older boys. I can't shake the feeling they're up to no good."

"I'd trust those feelings if I were you." Ellie's troubled eyes said more than her words.

"I'm failing Effie," Pa said. "If I can't get a handle on Tiller, he may be better off back in Fayetteville."

Remembering Aunt Effie's shrill voice railing at Tiller, Hooper blew out a breath and stood. "I don't think so, Pa. Most anything would be better for him than that."

The door opened and Hooper turned with a start.

Dawsey slipped in quietly with downcast eyes, her red, swollen lids visible even with the evening shadows. "Rhoda needs a pan of hot water and something to use for bandages."

Mama rushed to see to her request, and Ellie ran to Dawsey. "How is he?"

Dawsey drew a deep breath. "He's still out, but Rhoda's sure he'll be fine."

Hooper stood, moving a few steps closer. "That's good news, honey."

"Thank you."

He tried not to wring his hands like a fretful woman. "I hope you know I feel awful about what happened."

"I'm sure you do."

A shock jolted Hooper. She wouldn't meet his gaze.

Mama rushed around him with a washtub. "Stay inside and eat something, Dawsey. I'll take this out to Rhoda."

"And the cloths?"

She lifted her arm, draped with cotton rags. "Right here."

Dawsey fidgeted with her nails. "I really should get back to him."

"You will. . .after Ellie dishes you a bite of supper. We'll call you if he wakes up."

Dawsey opened her mouth to argue, but she was already out the door.

Fearing for his mama's safety, Hooper glanced after her. "Shouldn't we—"

Dawsey spun with brimstone eyes. "Duncan's guarding him, if that's what concerns you. Really, Hooper, there's little to fear now that you've cracked his skull and taken his pistol."

His stomach lurched. "I meant no harm. I just—"

"I understand perfectly. You're protecting your own. It's what you do." She pointed toward Ellie's bedroom. "He's a tired old man. He'll pose no more threat to you."

Ellie fixed a plate and set it on the table for Dawsey.

Without looking up, Dawsey politely thanked her.

Something had happened between them. They pecked and strutted around each other like wary hens.

Papa looked up from the fire. "You never told us what happened, son. Did you find those men?"

Bile filled his mouth and he cleared his throat. "It's tended."

"What became of them?"

Hooper pulled in his lips then blew them out with a frustrated breath. "Pa, don't ask. Ma's safe now. That's all you need to know."

Dawsey met Ellie's gaze across the table. Both heads swung toward Hooper, but they kept their silence.

"I have a more important question." He crossed to them and pulled out a chair. Softening his tone, he sought Dawsey's eyes. "I don't mean to raise a touchy subject, but how did your pa find us?"

She paused midbite to lift one brow then finished chewing before she answered. "I would think it's obvious."

Hooper raised his chin. "Not to me."

"He followed Duncan from Fayetteville."

Speechless for once, Papa swiveled in his chair.

Ellie lowered her mug and stared.

Drumming softly on the tabletop, Hooper allowed the answer to settle in his head. "Duncan went to Fayetteville?"

She nodded.

"And you knew he was going?"

"He did so as a kindness to me. He decided if I could go out of my way for his father, he would do the same for mine."

"That's my brother," Hooper crowed in a loud voice, "noble to the core." He gritted his teeth to control his surging anger. "So Duncan traveled to Fayetteville against Pa's counsel then let a tired old man like Mr. Wilkes—forgive me, Dawsey, you said it yourself—tail him unnoticed for forty miles?"

She pushed her plate aside. "That's Colonel Wilkes to you. My father began his career as a scout with the 26th North Carolina Regiment."

He pursed his lips. "Is that a fact?"

"It is."

Spinning in his chair, he slapped the table hard. "That's it, Pa! We should send that faithless traitor packing."

"Which faithless traitor?" The lamb to the slaughter, Duncan stood on the threshold holding Ma's empty water pail.

With a roar, Hooper charged. The last thing he heard before slamming into Duncan's chest was the *crash* of the pail hitting the floor and Papa's anguished cry.

Chapter 38

An old man lived inside the moon. He walked beside a little dog carrying a bundle of thorn-twigs. As a boy, Hooper would stare out the window with one eye shut and trace the ragged figure with his finger. Some nights, when the moon perched low and full, he still saw him.

He couldn't remember who told him the fanciful story. Likely Pa, with his lively sense of humor and love of a far-fetched tale.

Hooper led his horse from the barn and swung into the saddle. Lifting his anguished face to the sky, he searched the faint yellow surface. Sure as snuff, the man still hung there, smiling down while he trod his endless path. He seemed the last friend Hooper's vile temper had left him.

Mad at himself, he swiped his damp face with his sleeve. No sense bawling. Papa had given fair warning of the cost of another fight with his brother, a warning that escaped him until Pa loomed over their sprawling bodies, ordering Hooper to leave.

Duncan's memory had served him better. He hadn't lifted a finger in his own defense but only covered his face and rolled—an act Hooper mistook for cowardice until he realized Duncan would wake up in his own bed on Christmas morn.

His stomach lurched at the memory of his fist connecting with Duncan's gut and the grunt of pain as the wind left him in a rush. He winced, recalling the shuddering *thud* against his palms as his Spencer connected with Colonel Wilkes's skull.

Staring at the hands curled around his horse's reins, he wished they weren't capable of such awful things.

Mama's gentle voice echoed in his head, reading the words of Jesus from her Bible. " 'And if thy right hand offend thee, cut it off, and cast it from thee.' "

Hooper's right hand was his worst offender, bowing too often to the whims of his rage.

He looked over his shoulder for one last glimpse of the house. The single window glowed red from the festive decorations inside, lit by the flickering fire.

Two days ago, he sat on the porch working a hide as soft as butter, imagining the family around a Christmas tree, laughing and sharing gifts.

He patted the bulge in his saddlebag, the hide meant for Dawsey, and a bullfrog swelled in his throat. Gritting his teeth, he gathered the reins and turned the horse.

Running footsteps spun him around, reaching for his pistol.

"Hooper, wait."

He released his breath and drew his hand from the gun at his waistband. "That was foolish, Ellie. It's dangerous to sneak up on me." The truth of his words rained more shame on his head.

She ran to him, gripping the saddle horn with one hand and the leg of his britches with the other. "I can't bear to see you go. Come inside and talk to Pa. If you apologize, he'll change his mind."

"I did apologize. To him and to Duncan." He glanced longingly at the house. "It's no good, honey. His mind is set. He won't go back on his word."

"Blast his word! It's Christmas Eve."

He patted her hand. "Try to make tomorrow nice for Ma and Dawsey. They worked so hard."

Ellie clung to him, stubbornly shaking her head. "Christmas won't be nice for any of us without you. We may as well tear down the holly and toss the presents in the bog."

"You'll do no such thing. In fact, I have more gifts for under that tree. Will you tend to it for me?"

"Yes, but—"

"Get them from your room. I wrapped them in newspaper and stuck them under your bed." He reached for the saddlebag. "Except for Dawsey's." He reached inside and handed the hide down to her. "Will you make sure this gets wrapped and placed under the tree?"

Ellie watched him with tearful eyes. "Where will you go?"

He shrugged. "Henry's, where else? At least for now."

"Can I come see you there?"

He shook his head. "Too dangerous. Maybe after Sheriff McMillan cools down." With a sad smile, he saluted. "Merry Christmas, Ellie. Take care of things around here."

"Hooper?" Her pout had disappeared. "What happened to those men?"

A shudder tore through him, and he glanced away. "Trust me on this, little sister. You don't want to know."

Before she could ask more big-eyed questions, he dug his heels into his horse's side and trotted from the yard.

Dawsey sat in Dilsey's room, watching the slow rise and fall of her father's chest. She struggled to focus on prayers for his recovery, but praying for anyone else came hard after watching what happened to Hooper.

When he came to himself, his face had gone slack with shock. Realizing what he'd done, he stood up, wiping his hands on his britches as if trying to remove his guilt. When Silas raised a stern finger and roared at him to go, he'd marched to the door like a soldier accepting his fate. A soldier with tears glistening in his eyes.

Hooper's rash, impulsive nature had finally gotten the best of him. The frightened girl cowering in a shed the night she arrived longed to be glad for his comeuppance, but the woman who'd come to love every line of his dear face wouldn't allow it.

Her heart aching, Dawsey glanced at her father, mumbling in his sleep. Love Hooper or not, the violent side of him scared her witless. He'd almost killed her father and, by his own near admission, had tracked down and murdered two men in the swamp.

Perhaps such acts were necessary to survive in Scuffletown. For Dawsey, accustomed to the genteel behavior of life in Fayetteville, such rampant brutality was unacceptable. She shuddered. What more might he be capable of to protect his way of life?

The door burst open, startling her out of her gloomy thoughts.

Dilsey stood just inside, a stunned look on her face. "Oh," she said. "I'm sorry. I—for a minute, I forgot he was in here."

Her eyes widened as they lit on Father. She yanked them away and backed up two steps. "Where's Duncan?"

"Inside the house."

She nodded. "Dawsey, would you mind?" She waved toward the bed. "There are some bundles under there, and I need them."

Dawsey walked to meet her. "Don't you want to see him?"

She shook her head and retreated farther.

"He's your father, Dilsey. The man who gave you life."

Leaning, she looked past Dawsey. "He's still asleep?"

Dawsey took her hand. "Yes, he is. So he can't possibly bite you." She gave a little tug. "Come along."

The frightened girl let Dawsey lead her a little closer before she stiffened. "I'm sorry, I can't." She swallowed hard. "I just can't." Her eyes pleaded with Dawsey. "Will you gather the packages from under my bed and bring them inside to the tree? I gave Hooper my word." With that, she bolted, slamming the door behind her.

Dawsey spun, wondering if the sharp noise had disturbed Father. Truthfully, she wished he had stirred, but he lay as still as death.

Frustrated with herself for letting Dilsey escape, she ran outside to call her and nearly tripped over her sitting on the steps. Dawsey eased down beside her and hugged her close. "Taking a look won't be disloyal to Silas. It's perfectly normal to be curious."

Her sister shivered. "I'm afraid."

"There's nothing to fear, I promise. He won't even know you're there." On impulse, Dawsey stood. "I'm going inside for a while. I feel the urge for a cookie and a nice glass of milk. Please don't leave him alone."

Dilsey stretched out her hand. "No, wait."

Dawsey crossed the yard with a determined step. "I won't be long." She peeked over her shoulder as she rounded the house.

Dilsey stood with one hand on the doorknob. Pulling her shoulders back, she disappeared inside.

Smiling, Dawsey decided to take time for a slice of pie, too.

Ellie leaned her head against the door, staring at the peculiar man on the bed. How would she cross the yawning space between where she stood and the truth?

Shadowed memories of her childhood filled her mind like rushing water.

Cradled in Pa's lap on the porch, the rocker gently swaying, his shining eyes caressing her.

Balanced atop the porch rail, Papa shoving sweet melon in her mouth, laughing when she spit the seeds across the yard.

Tin cans set along an overturned tree so Ellie could practice her aim, Pa crowing with pride each time she hit one.

On his belly, half drowned in the bog, fishing her out with a stick. Rocking in his lap when he pulled her free, both crying and covered in mud.

Ellie didn't need to see the man who'd given her life. The only one who mattered was the man she'd give her life for.

Turning to go, she paused when Dawsey's father moaned and began to cough. The cough turned to hoarse hacking then desperate gasps.

Ellie sailed across the room, terrified when his bulging eyes opened and fixed on her. She longed to run and fetch Dawsey, but there was no time. If she left, he'd choke to death. Yanking him by the arm, she pulled him up and pounded on his back.

Red in the face, he brayed furiously for several minutes then fell against the pillows, groaning and clutching his head. "What the devil hit me?" His watery eyes wandered the room and then jerked to her face. "Dawsey! Merciful heavens, I've found you."

Stricken, all Ellie could think to do was tell the poor man the truth. "I'm not Dawsey, sir. I'm the other one. I'm Dilsey."

Dawsey pushed the door open, juggling two mugs and a plate of sugar cookies. Joy warmed her soul at the sight of Dilsey hunched over the bed.

"Lay back and hush, old man. Dawsey will have my hide."

"Stop talking nonsense, young lady, and get out of the way. I'm taking you home."

The mugs hit the floor with a *crash*. Dilsey and Father were wrestling!

"Calm down, Father. I'm here." She rushed to his bedside and crowded in beside Dilsey. Too late, she realized the sight of them standing together might be too much for him.

His head whipped to Dawsey then Dilsey. His mouth was a yawning cavern, his eyes blazing pools of doubt. He stared from one to the other, gulping for air.

Dawsey sat down, smoothing his hair. "Don't be frightened, dear. It's all right."

"I'm seeing things, Dawsey," he cried. "Hearing them, too. Apparitions. Ghostly beings that aren't really there." His eyes pleaded with her for the right answer. "Am I sleeping?"

She laughed. "There are no apparitions, Father, and you're wide awake. What you're seeing is real." Catching her sister's reluctant arm, she pulled her close. "It's our own dear Dilsey, come back to us at last."

Slowly, carefully, he reached a shaky hand and touched Dilsey's face. With the other, he groped for Dawsey's fingers.

His tremulous smile melted into a mask of grief. With a mournful bellow of long-denied pain, he covered his face and sobbed.

Chapter 39

Dawsey awoke to the sound of quiet knocking. She longed to return to her dream, where she and Hooper strolled in the holly tree clearing. The gloom surrounding Hooper had lifted; the doubt in her heart had vanished. She trusted him again and felt no fear. No anger shone from his eyes.

The rapping came again, chasing her dream to the shadows. Throwing back the quilt, she hurried to the door before the noise disturbed her father.

Duncan stood outside, with his hat in his hand. He'd dressed in what looked like his Sunday best and wiped his boots to a shine. "Merry Christmas."

Dawsey couldn't help but smile at his freshly scrubbed face. "Merry Christmas to you." Fighting a yawn, she rubbed her sleepy eyes. "What time is it?"

He lifted his brows. "Early, I'm afraid. How's your father?"

She glanced over her shoulder. "Still sleeping."

"I'm sorry to disturb you. Ma sent me. She's been darting around the kitchen since well before dawn, rustling in cabinets and rattling pans. Something about roasted ducks."

Dawsey frowned. "She wants to go ahead with dinner?"

He smiled. "She insists. Stockings, gifts under the tree, noggins of spiced posset, the whole holly-berried shebang."

"Noggins of posset?"

He feigned alarm. "Stay away from those. Hot sweetened milk curdled with wine." He gave her a knowing look. "Rhoda's scuppernong wine."

"I appreciate the warning." She frowned. "I'm a bit surprised at your mother, to be honest. I mean, with Hooper gone and everything."

"Hooper's the reason for all the fuss. How else can she make Pa squirm? The bigger shindig she throws, the worse he'll feel about Hooper missing out." He chuckled. "If she works things just right, Pa will be blubbering and ordering me out to fetch him."

Hope stirred in Dawsey's heart. She remembered the murdered men in the swamp and pushed it down. "You're not terribly angry with him?" She wrinkled her nose. "I fear I would be, in your shoes."

Duncan waved his hand. "Nah. I'm used to his blustering." He winked. "Gives me the chance to punch him back every now and then."

He pointed over his shoulder. "Do I tell Ma you're coming?"

She paused. "Goodness, I'm not sure. I long to help, but my father was so frightened and confused last night. If he wakes and finds me gone. . ."

"When you're ready, I'll sit with your pa. I promise to fetch you the minute he stirs."

Tenderness surged for the good-hearted man. "Thank you, Duncan. You're a very special person."

He backed away, turning his hat in his hands. "So are you, Dawsey." His eyes softened. "So are you."

For privacy, Dawsey hung a sheet in front of Father's bed. She hurried to wash and dress, shuffling around the room as quietly as possible so she wouldn't wake him. Then she lifted the makeshift curtain to peek inside. He was fast asleep.

Still afraid for him, she checked his chest for movement. It rose and fell with each steady breath. Satisfied, she let the sheet fall into place. Bounding down the steps, still pinning her hair, she hurried for Odell's kitchen.

Her jaw dropped when she stepped inside the cabin. Odell had hung even more decorations than before. She'd strung more pinecones—these dabbed with flour paste to look like snow—and tied candles to the branches of the tree, placing some in a staggered row along the mantel. They'd pulled in the last of the cherry red possumhaw boughs and arranged them in brilliant clusters.

"Merry Christmas!" A chorus of voices cried.

"What do you think?" Odell called from the hearth.

Dawsey beamed. "It's lovely." She gazed in awe at the bulging sacks on the counter. "Where on earth did you get all that food?"

"Isn't it wonderful?" Odell asked. "It's a Christmas miracle. Every time I look, there's another sack on the porch."

"Henry?"

She nodded slyly.

"Don't fret about your pa. I'll keep a close watch on him," Duncan said, touching her hand lightly as he swept past.

Dilsey, wearing more flour than was mixed in her rolled-out crust, watched Dawsey from the table. "How is he?"

"Exhausted." She grimaced. "We gave him quite a shock, but he finally settled down sometime before morning."

Odell glanced up from stirring her pot. "Before morning? Then you're tuckered, too, child. Go back to your mat for a few hours."

Dawsey waved her hand. "Honestly, I'm fine." She reached for an apron and tied it around her waist. "I'd feel positively left out if I slept through all the fun."

Tiller snorted from the corner. "Fun? I'd rather have a tooth yanked." He sat on the floor peeling nuts, surrounded by bits of shell.

Dawsey leaned to inspect his bowl. "Pecans?"

Odell grinned. "Henry sent them. We'll put them in the sweet buns." She winked and nodded. "Hooper's favorite."

Silas hunched over in his chair with downcast eyes and deep furrows in his brow. He held a stray button, tumbling it absently between his fingers. It hadn't escaped Dawsey's notice that his voice wasn't part of her Christmas greeting.

She squatted in front of him. "How are you this morning?"

He averted his eyes. "Not worth the asking."

Odell lifted her simmering stew from the hook over the fire and hustled it to the counter. "Don't mind him. He's danced his jig, and now he's not keen to pay the fiddler."

His head jerked up. "It's not the waltz you're thinking, woman." His sorrowful gaze swung to Dawsey. "The debt I can't pay is to your pa." He groped for her hands. "Your forgiveness was a powerful blessing and a testament to your good nature. I ain't expecting the same from him."

She squeezed his fingers. "I'm afraid you're right. I doubt he'll be very forgiving."

He straightened. "Still, I have to ask."

She nodded. "Let's wait until he's stronger, shall we?"

"Whatever you say, darlin'."

Dilsey, her eyes flashing, banged the table with the rolling pin. "What about Hooper? He asked forgiveness, and you shunned him."

More hurt than anger sparked Silas's eyes. "It ain't the same. I wronged folks who were strangers." His eyes flicked to Dawsey. "At least at the time." He balled his fist and slammed the arm of his chair. "Hooper strikes out at his own flesh and blood."

Dilsey's hand went to her hip, dusting flour over her clothes. "Hooper protects his own in the only way he knows. Duncan had no business riding to Fayetteville after you said no." She lifted her chin. "Truth be told, Hooper was standing up for you."

Silas leaped to his feet. "With brutality and hatred toward his brother? The boy's fuse is too short," he shouted. "I won't have it in my house."

Odell's hands stilled over her mixing bowl. "Good thing I don't feel the same. Look at you, bellowing and blustering about, punishing our son for what he learned at your knee."

Silas plopped in his chair, shrinking from her words.

"What Hooper did was wrong," she continued. "But tossing our son out of the house on a cold Christmas Eve ain't right, neither. Hooper needs love and guidance to change." She pointed toward the swamp. "He won't find much out there."

Dawsey crossed her arms and huddled near the fire, praying the argument would swing in Hooper's favor. She didn't get the chance to find out.

Father's loud, frantic rant swept through the door on Duncan's heels. Wide eyed, he pointed. "He's calling for you, Dawsey." He glanced at Dilsey. "For both of you."

Dilsey's flashing eyes melted into fear. "I won't go." Her head whipped back and forth. "Last night was enough for me."

Odell laid aside her ladle. In one quick motion, she untied Dilsey's apron and placed a dishrag in her hands. "Wash up and go with Dawsey. Can't you hear the pain in that poor man's voice?"

Silas stood. "Wait, Odie. Are you sure?"

Her firm gaze bounced to him. "He's in no shape to spirit her off. If he tries, I believe Ellie could stop him." She sobered. "You want a chance to tell that man we're sorry?"

He nodded.

"It starts right here." She gave Dilsey a little shove. "Go on, honey."

Sulking like a child, Dilsey toddled to Dawsey and clung to her. "You won't leave me alone with him, will you?"

Dawsey hugged her arm. "I promise." She smoothed a flour-crusted curl from her sister's face. "There's really nothing to fear. He sounds gruff, but he's just afraid."

Dilsey inhaled sharply through her nose. "All right, then. Let's get it over with."

Arm in arm, they trudged around the house, Dilsey growing stiffer with every step.

Dawsey had to admit Father's hoarse cries raised the hairs on her arms. She could imagine how they affected her poor sister.

They reached the steps with Aunt Livvy's words about him echoing in Dawsey's head.

"Even as a child, he was gloomy and pouting. . .when he wasn't being stubborn and willful."

Dilsey trembled beside her as they opened the door, so frightened she seemed to be holding her breath.

The reunion Dawsey had dreamed of between Father and his long-lost daughter seemed doomed by his awful tirade.

Without planning her actions, she left Dilsey at the door and stalked to the bed. Clutching the makeshift curtain in both hands, she ripped it down in one fierce jerk. "I believe that's quite enough caterwauling, if you don't mind."

Pressed against his pillow, both hands clenched at his sides, he looked like the willful child Aunt Livvy remembered. Shocked into silence, mouth still wide from shouting, he stared at Dawsey as if he'd never seen her before.

She supposed, in all the years they'd spent together, he never had.

His eyes blazed and his mouth worked furiously, but nothing came out.

"That's better. Now we can hear ourselves think." She settled on the bed beside him and motioned Dilsey closer.

As she approached, Father's head swung toward her with a hoarse gasp. "I feared I'd dreamed you."

Dilsey shrugged. "No, sir, I reckon you didn't."

Blinking against sudden tears, he swallowed several times and attempted a smile. "I'd given up on ever seeing you again." He seemed mesmerized, studying his daughters with an awestruck gaze. "You're just the same. . .but different. Just like when you were babes." He stared over their heads into the past. "Other people couldn't tell you one from the other, but your mother and I could from the start." His face seemed to crumble. "Forgive me, Margaret. I failed you."

Dawsey clutched his arm. "You haven't."

His head wagged up and down. "She made me promise to never stop looking. She knew our baby was alive."

He lifted swimming eyes to Dilsey. "I failed you, too, child. Please forgive me."

She moved a rigid step closer. "Oh no, sir. You ain't failed me at all, Colonel Wilkes. Shucks, I'm real glad about all that happened."

Dawsey waved a warning finger—too late.

"Otherwise I'd never have wound up a McRae." Smiling, she shook her head. "And that wouldn't do."

Father's mournful look turned to stone. His head spun to Dawsey. "What did she say?"

"Never mind, dear." She shot up and pulled the extra pillow from behind him. "Lie back and rest. You've had a great shock."

Ignoring her, he sat up straighter and groped his head. "What hit me, Dawsey? Surely I have injuries to the brain. I thought she said she was a McRae."

Dilsey beamed. "My brother, Hooper, gave you that awful bump with the butt of his gun." She tilted her head. "But he's real sorry."

"Your b–brother?"

"And don't fret about hearing things, Colonel. I said McRae, all right." She smiled and almost curtsied. "That's my name. Ellie McRae."

Father bolted upright and roared, struggling to climb off the bed. "I'll kill them all!"

Dawsey clutched his flailing wrists. "Run, Dilsey. Send Duncan."

Her eyes impossibly round, she stumbled away. "What did I say?"

"Just go! And don't come back."

She didn't need to say it twice. Dilsey whirled on her heels and bolted. The bar slammed into place from the outside, locking Dawsey inside with her frenzied father.

She'd once wished for a genie to bring the gloomy, sullen man to life again. *Be careful what you wish for, Dawsey.*

She never expected the God-sized miracle she prayed for would show up as a backwoods version of herself.

Chapter 40

Hooper laid aside the ax and gathered the pile of kindling he'd split for Henry's woodbox. Proud people, his folks had taught him that a man should pay his own way in the world. By the look of the bounty steadily mounting on Rhoda's kitchen counters, he'd soon have a debt to cancel for a nice Christmas dinner.

He rolled the logs in the box with a clatter and stuck his head through the door. "Where does Henry keep the chicken feed?"

Rhoda waved him in. "Henry's already tended those squawking birds. Come sit a spell. I've got fresh coffee brewing."

Hooper hid a grimace. Rhoda's coffee was as strong and dark as she was but not as pretty. Oil swam in the thick cup she'd handed him when he awoke. Three hours later his ears still rang. He held up his hand. "I'll pass, thank you." He rubbed his stomach. "My belly don't appreciate good swamp coffee."

She flashed a smile. "You wanted to say swamp mud."

He grinned.

"Suit yourself, but come inside and jaw for a spell. I don't get much company out this way. Lord knows, Henry don't do enough talking."

Hooper ducked his head, his eyes combing the yard for Henry. As appealing as Rhoda was, Hooper never heard it said that her husband was the jealous sort. One thing was certain—he didn't aim to be the man to test him. "Bring your coffee out here to the porch."

"It's too chilly. Besides, I can't leave my pies."

He gulped. "It's not so bad. Slip on a shawl or something. I'll remind you about the pies."

Cold fingers the size of corncobs clamped on Hooper's neck. Their strength, helped along by his fright, lifted him from the ground.

"You'd best watch out," an ominous voice mumbled.

Hooper's body tensed, and the swamp mud he drank threatened to spew.

The hand released him and he spun.

"Is Rhoda coaxing you into her lair?" Henry's tight smile, the same as a rousing laugh for him, eased Hooper's racing heart.

"Good morning, Henry. Much obliged for the scare."

Giggling, Rhoda pointed at him from the door.

He hung his head and shot her a sheepish grin.

"Now will you come inside and stop acting foolish."

Agreeing with her estimation, he followed Henry over the threshold.

Hooper lounged at their simple table, listening to Rhoda talk, a need she seldom got to vent, living with quiet and stoic Henry. His silence was the price the Queen of Scuffletown paid for her title—along with never knowing when she would be digging her husband's grave.

The two had welcomed him to their hearth and home without a single question. Henry opened the door wide at his knock, and Rhoda sought every way to make him feel comfortable.

He'd stretched out in front of their fire all night, his head pining for home and his heart longing for Dawsey.

"My pa threw me out." The words fell from his mouth and bounced off the rafters.

Rhoda stopped talking somewhere between her winded tirade against Sheriff McMillan and her mama's gingerbread recipe. Sadness darkened her lovely face. "I figured as much, with you not keen to talk about it."

Henry looked up from weaving a leather strap. "Silas will change his mind."

"Not this time."

"What'd you do?" Rhoda asked.

Henry's head whipped around. "Rhoda."

"It's all right," Hooper said. "I don't mind saying what a fool I am."

Rhoda stretched across the table with an eager look on her face. "Go on then."

"I have a quick temper." He lifted his eyes to the man who never made a move he didn't plan. "I don't suppose you know what that means."

Henry pointed at his wife. "I've learned from watching her."

Rhoda slapped his finger aside. "Don't mistake a woman's sass for temper." Her eyes swung to Hooper. "There's nothing so terrifying as a man given to rage."

"You're not helping," Henry said, his brow cocked.

Hooper held up his hand. "Let her speak."

Rhoda snatched his fingers and drew him across the table, her pretty eyes casting a spell. "People rest within their safe borders," she said quietly. "Like us, here in the hideout. We know how far from the house we can go without worrying about getting shot."

He nodded.

"When you fly off in a fury without warning, your stakes are always moving. Folk get lost around you so they're always dodging lead." She sat back watching him. "Do you understand?"

Somehow he did. Picturing Papa's grieved face drove her point deep. "I never could make out why my anger bothered my pa so much. I think I know now. It kept him at the ready."

Rhoda pushed up from the table. "Knowing how you've gone astray is the first mile on the road to change."

He sighed. "I sure wish that road could get me home in time for Christmas."

She set a thick slice of apple pie in front of him then ruined it with a mug of her coffee. "You are home for Christmas, as far as we're concerned. Ain't that right, Henry?"

Hooper supposed an offer like that might be worth a rotted-out belly. Smiling, he forced a sip. "Thank you kindly."

"That's not true."

Hooper's head swung with Rhoda's toward Henry's quiet decree.

She blushed to her collar. "What a mean thing to say. Hooper's welcome here for as long as he likes."

Henry shook his head. "There's nothing here for him. The only place a man should be on Christmas Day is beside his own hearth, surrounded by his folks." As if spent from talking and fresh out of words, Henry winked and picked up his fork.

Hooper swallowed his mouthful of pie and stared. It was the most he'd heard him say in one breath.

Wiping her brow, Dawsey sat on the porch of the main house to rest, feeling she'd lived three days since breakfast. She longed to push her father out of Dilsey's room and lock herself away from the madness. Instead, she and Duncan had shoved him inside and bolted the door.

It broke her heart to do such a thing, but she couldn't allow him to stumble around with a wounded head trying to kill the McRaes. By the look on his face as the door swung shut, she wondered if he'd ever forgive her.

"Can I sit with you?"

Dawsey looked over her shoulder and nodded.

Dilsey took the three steps to the ground and settled between her and the rail. "Is your pa all right?"

Weary with strife, even more weary with Dilsey, she gave her a sullen glance. "He's your pa, too, you know."

Instead of a backlash of denial, Dilsey surprised her. "I reckon I should be more careful with my words." She nudged Dawsey. "But so should you. I can allow that the colonel is my father, but I only have one pa."

Dawsey gently bumped heads with her. "Point taken."

Instead of drawing away, Dilsey rested against her shoulder. "What happened back there? What set him off?"

Lifting her sister's hand, she laced fingers with her. "You have to look at things from his perspective. For nineteen years, you've been the kidnapped daughter he needed to save from a villainous man named McRae. To hear you've become one of them was too much for him to bear."

Her eyes widened. "He knew it was Pa all along?"

Dawsey shrugged. "I don't think he knew exactly, but he had somehow traced your disappearance to that name."

Little wrinkles marred Dilsey's brow as she stared toward the trees. "Ma said they fled Hope Mills in the dead of night. Maybe he got wind of it."

"If he did," Dawsey said, "it would certainly arouse his suspicion."

Dilsey nodded. "It would mine."

"Of course, then he couldn't find them. It had to be very frustrating, as well as heart wrenching, considering he was racing to bring you home in time to save our mother."

"He was?"

"Well, in his mind, at least. I'm not convinced it would've made any difference in the end. She was very weak and frail."

Dilsey's shoulders slumped. "Then I prance in there and brag about my name." She slapped her forehead. "I have mush for brains."

Laughing, Dawsey hugged her close. "Don't be silly. You didn't know." She gave her a sideways look. "Rocks, perhaps?"

Dilsey jabbed her with an elbow. They shared a laugh before she grew silent again. "Do you think he'll ever forgive me?"

"I was just wondering the same about me"—Dawsey grimaced—"considering I helped lock him up. As for you, there's nothing to forgive. None of this is your fault, Dilsey."

Smiling, Dilsey accepted her pardon. "I have another question." She pouted her mouth. "Will you ever stop calling me Dilsey?"

Grinning, Dawsey shook her head. "Not likely. It rolls so nicely off the tongue."

Dilsey punched her arm. "Oh you!"

"Besides"—she swallowed the lump in her throat—"I picture our mother selecting our names with great care. You don't really mind, do you?"

Dilsey's arm slid around her shoulders. "I reckon not."

Behind them, Duncan cleared his throat. "Your pa will be fine, Dawsey. Once he settles down."

She bounced to her feet, brushing dirt off her britches. "I don't know if he'll ever be fine again, but there's nothing I can do if he won't let me."

Duncan held the door as she passed into the house. "Don't worry," he said. "We'll take him a heaping plate of roast duck and Indian dumplings. A fine meal should mellow him some."

She paused. "I know what a duck is, but what's the other thing you mentioned?"

Odell glanced up from her mixing bowl. "The Indian dumplings? You'll know soon enough. I need you to mix them for me."

She took the apron from Odell and gathered ingredients as she called them out.

"You'll need a pint of milk and four eggs, a salt-spoon of salt, flour to dust your hands, and a pot of boiling water." She jerked her chin toward the fire. "I've already started the water heating for you." She pointed to the shelf over the counter. "Once you beat the milk and eggs, fetch that sack of meal and measure out enough to make a stiff dough. Flour your hands and roll it into balls about the size of goose eggs. Flatten them with a rolling pin, tie them into those cloths yonder, and simmer until they're done."

Dawsey cracked eggs in the bowl. "That sounds easy enough."

"Watch them close. They'll go to pieces if you leave them too long in the pot."

"Yes, ma'am."

Odell answered the question running through Dawsey's mind. "They're good alongside meat or afterwards with molasses and butter."

Duncan slid into a seat at the table. "I'll leave the Indian dumplings for all of you, to make sure your stomachs get nice and full."

Dawsey cast him a sweet smile. "That's very thoughtful."

"Don't flatter him," Dilsey said. "That's a sugarcoated trick. He means to fill us too full to eat brown sugar pie."

Duncan smacked his lips and rubbed his middle. "With toasted black walnuts."

Odell threw an apple.

It glanced off his head, and he howled with laughter.

"Go make yourself useful to that cantankerous old man in the barn. He's determined to do both his and Hooper's chores all by himself."

Duncan bounded for the door, stopping to toss the apple in a slow arc to his mother. "We should oblige him. It might make him change his mind."

Odell shook her head and pointed at her paste of flour and butter. "This should make him change his mind. Silas knows how Hooper loves my apple potpie." She raised a brilliant smile. "He'll think of Hooper the minute it hits the table. If that don't do the trick, I'll soften his tough hide with my Tipsy Parson cake."

Duncan slipped out with a rumbling laugh.

Odell raised a brow at Dilsey, seated at the table with her head idly propped, drumming her fingers. "Ellie McRae? It's Christmas Day, not your birthday. March over and stir these onions."

Chapter 41

The table was set, the rolls browned, and the last fragrant pie squeezed onto the counter. Dawsey gazed at the bountiful spread, arms linked with Odell and Dilsey. "No one will leave this table hungry."

Odell laughed. "If they do, it's their own fault."

She patted Dilsey's back. "Go tell your pa and Duncan to wash up. Christmas dinner is ready."

She sprang for the door.

"See if you can find Tiller," Odell called. "He's been missing since morning."

Dilsey poked her head back inside. "That rascal's hiding from all the extra chores. You did him in with those pecans."

Odell sniffed. "We'll see how he feels about pecans while he's shoving a bun down his throat."

"One bun? Not a chance." Dilsey grinned and disappeared.

Odell handed Dawsey a broad plate. "Load this up for your pa, honey. I'll have Duncan take it out back."

She shook her head. "I'll take it myself. I'd like to eat my meal with him, if you don't mind."

Odell's eyes softened. "I think it's a fine idea." She paused and squinted. "Don't go by yourself, if your pa's still feisty. He might get loose and wind up lost in the swamp."

She sighed. "I suppose you're right. I'll wait for Duncan."

While Dawsey waited, she lovingly filled the plate with a sample of each dish. When nothing else would fit, she covered it with a dishcloth and laid it aside to serve herself.

Duncan breezed in drying his hands, and his mother him asked him to walk with Dawsey.

"Sure thing," he said. "Let me carry one of those plates for you, Dawsey." He raised the cloth. "You're planning to eat all of this?"

Odell laughed. "Don't listen to him. You won't be here to watch, so he'll eat three times that much."

It felt wrong to be laughing, teasing, marching across the backyard laden by a feast, with Father lost and broken inside Dilsey's bedroom. "I'm a little scared," she confessed outside the door.

"Don't be. I'll go in with you."

"That's not a good idea." She touched his arm. "Wait for me, though? At least until I give the all clear."

He smiled. "I won't leave this step."

Expecting a war whoop and a hurtling body, Dawsey braced herself and sucked in a breath as the bar lifted. Her legs tensed.

Nothing.

Duncan raised questioning brows.

She shrugged.

Dread trickled down her back as they stepped inside the dim, hushed room.

Father lay on his back with one arm resting on his forehead. He stared intently at the ceiling and didn't acknowledge their presence.

She took the food from Duncan and nodded.

He retreated to the steps to wait.

The brooding figure on the bed reminded her of the father she'd left behind in Fayetteville. His mouth was set in a grim pout and defeat lined his face.

Dawsey approached with caution. "I've brought your lunch."

Hoping he'd forgotten, she decided to forego any mention of Christmas. "You've missed two meals at least. You must be starved."

He rolled his tongue in a slow arc across his bottom lip. "If it's all the same to you, I'm a trifle more interested in a drink."

"You've had no water?" She whirled to check the pitcher by the bed. Gone.

"I don't understand. I filled it myself."

She searched the floor and found the handle next to her feet and shards of pottery in a heap between the table and the bed. "I'm so sorry.

I had no idea. It must've been broken in the struggle."

She hurried to ask Duncan to bring a new pitcher. While she waited, she wet his lips with a dish towel dipped in applesauce.

Duncan returned, striding boldly into the room.

Father's hate-filled eyes tracked him across the floor.

"Can I bring you anything else, sir?" Duncan asked.

"Yes. My pistol."

He chuckled. "That might be bad for my health, Colonel." Smiling, he nodded at the covered plate. "Enjoy your meal." With a wink for Dawsey, he strolled out whistling.

Father crossed his arms in a huff. "Who is that insufferable whelp?" He glared. "A McRae, no doubt?"

Ignoring the question, Dawsey gave him a drink then removed the dishcloth and held the food under his nose. "Look what I've brought you. Roast duck, gravy, and all the trimmings." She held up a thick slice of sweet potato bread. "Look. I even made your favorite."

His hungry gaze roamed the plate before suspicion clouded his eyes. "Do you mean to say you've been cooking with them? Standing shoulder to shoulder with our enemy?"

Her spirits drooped. "It's not what it seems."

"What then?" He shoved the plate away. "Dawsey, I find all this quite confusing."

"Of course you do, but—"

"When those men took you, I knew in my gut they were the same scoundrels who took your sister. The knowledge frightened me, stirred me from the dark abyss where I'd fallen. I had purpose again, to find you since I failed in finding Dilsey."

"You seem much more alert. I'm very grateful."

He waved his hand. "Then why do you have me questioning my sanity again? We should be on our way home to Lavinia. Instead, my own daughter has me locked in a makeshift prison while she bakes bread with her captors." His outburst ended with a hoarse shout.

Wincing, Dawsey gripped her forehead. "I know it's difficult for you to understand."

"Difficult?" The strain of his voice brought him up off his pillow. "No, daughter, impossible."

"I can explain." She wiped sweat from her top lip. "You see, I've been here for weeks, living among them and learning their ways."

He gaped. "In that short time you've forgotten who you are?"

"They've been very kind to me."

"Kind?" His eyes bulged.

"Yes. They saved my life. I was snakebit, and—"

"They've bewitched you. Your sister, too." He pointed an accusing finger. "That man took Dilsey from her crib."

"It was a long time ago. He made a mistake." The ridiculous words sounded hollow and trite. Why couldn't she find the right ones?

Tears pooled in Father's eyes. "Then the vipers came for you." He shifted his gaze to the wall. "And you've crawled into the pit with them."

"No, I—"

"Just go."

Dawsey clutched his chest. "Please give me a second to collect my thoughts. I know I can make you understand." She licked her dry lips. "I made a deal with Silas. He promised to take me home right after Christmas. It was the only way I could bring Dilsey."

He held up his hand. "I said go—back to your blasted McRaes." He flicked her away like a bothersome pest. "I imagine they're holding Christmas dinner for you."

Dawsey stumbled away, shaking her head. Bursting into tears she fled, nearly falling over Duncan outside the door.

He pulled her to his chest with one strong arm and locked the door with the other. Leading her toward the house, he tucked her closer. "It's all right, honey. He'll feel better soon, and you can take him home." He smiled down at her. "Away from us blasted McRaes."

She lifted soggy lashes. "You heard?"

Duncan shrugged. "You gave me the best seat in the house."

Guilt lay heavy on her chest. Why *did* she feel more comfortable, more at ease with the McRaes than with her own father?

Perhaps his accusation held merit. The enchanting McRaes had woven a spell on her mind from the first, a hex that grew stronger and more deceptive each day, wooing her until she couldn't tell right from wrong.

If so, Hooper possessed the most beguiling spirit, since his charms held sway over her heart.

"Don't you worry about what your father said. No one could understand how things fell unless they'd walked it out in your shoes."

Staring into Duncan's sincere gray eyes, watching the set of his handsome jaw, she wondered why quarrelsome, hotheaded Hooper had invaded her thoughts and not his good-natured, dependable brother.

Had her heart made the wrong choice?

"Honestly, Duncan, I don't understand it myself. How can I expect my father to?"

He gave her shoulders a squeeze. "Put it out of your mind for now. Let's enjoy Christmas, since it will be our last. I expect you'll be going home soon."

The thought saddened her, adding to her guilt. "I don't know if I can contribute much cheer. I'm terribly worried about him."

He cupped her face. "That won't do. I'm afraid Ma's happiness depends on us having the time of our lives." He winked. "It's all part of her big plan to bring Hooper home."

She smiled.

"Besides"—he peered at her from the corner of his eye—"I get the feeling you've spent too many holidays worrying about your pa."

She shrugged. "I don't think I know how to stop."

"Come inside with me, and I'll show you." Tugging her arm, he led her up the steps.

Dawsey couldn't help but feel better as they entered the festive cabin.

Odell turned from the hearth. "At last, here's Duncan." She lifted her brows. "And Dawsey, too?"

Dawsey nodded and took a seat.

"That just leaves Tiller, wherever he is." She cast a pitiful glance at Silas. "Of course Hooper's chair will be empty."

Silas grumbled in his wife's direction, but Dawsey saw through his blustering. She caught the look of disappointment when she and Duncan came in, and he still watched the entrance closely.

Dilsey glanced up from buttering rolls. "Should I go find Tiller?"

Her father waved his fork. "He'll turn up when his bloodhound nose catches wind of this grub. If not, it's his fault. He's supposed to stay close to home."

He gave Dilsey a teasing look. "Where's Wyatt, Puddin'? I figured he'd be at our table this year."

She blushed. "He's coming this afternoon. Says he has a special gift for me."

Dawsey shared a knowing glance with Odell. Earlier, they'd held a whispered conversation about Wyatt's intentions over a roiling kettle of dumplings.

Bowls, platters, and pitchers made the circuit until everyone filled their plates and cups to overflowing. Dawsey stared at the wonderful bounty with a ball of lead in her stomach. How could she eat and pretend to enjoy her food? Every nerve in her body jangled, every thought hovered over her father in Dilsey's room. She prayed he'd settled down to eat before his food got cold.

Silas slightly bowed in her direction, yanking her from her brooding. "Dawsey, we're pleased as peacocks to have you with us for this occasion."

She clutched her napkin in her lap. "Thank you, Silas."

"Would you honor me by asking a blessing over our meal?"

Dawsey squirmed like a netted fish and blinked up at him. How could she give thanks without a single thread of gratitude in her heart? Silas had asked her to converse with God when they weren't on speaking terms. In the muddle of confusion and pain, in the turn her life had taken, she'd somehow left God by the wayside. She couldn't even dredge up a fitting psalm for the occasion. Sweat beaded her top lip, and her breath quickened. "Silas, I—"

Dilsey pushed to her feet. "Pa, I want to say the blessing."

Every head swung her way.

Silas frowned. "That's nice, Puddin', but I've already asked Dawsey." He leaned and lowered his voice. "She's our guest."

Dilsey lifted her chin. "She won't mind." She glanced at Dawsey. "Will you?"

Dawsey recognized a lifeline when it landed in her hands. Her sister, convinced her prayers never reached heaven, had offered one in Dawsey's stead to save her.

Silas's wizened eyes watched them. "Dawsey?"

She flashed a grateful smile at Dilsey. "I won't mind a bit."

Dilsey folded her hands and bowed her head. Cracking one lid, she wiggled her finger. "Well, go on everybody, close your eyes."

Dawsey quickly obliged and the room stilled.

"Well God," Dilsey said, "I reckon You're surprised to hear from me after all this time. In case You don't remember, I'm the one who pestered You for a pony till You brung me Toby. That was a long time ago, but I ain't forgot Your kindness."

She cleared her throat. "About this meal. . .it's a fine spread, one we wouldn't have without land to farm and the strong backs of Pa and my brothers, so I'm grateful." With a sigh of resignation she continued. "I don't know if You can accept our thanks for these fine ducks and the other pilfered things. If not, at least bless Henry for his kindness in sharing and send an angel to keep him safe. Scuffletown needs him."

She drew a ragged breath. "And, Sir, I've never once thanked You for my folks, so I'm thanking You now. Please don't be mad at Ma and Pa for what they done. They were young and foolish and didn't mean no harm."

She paused for so long, Dawsey stole a peek.

Her eyes were squeezed shut, and tears rolled down her cheeks. "I know I claimed I wasn't," she said, "but I'm powerful glad You gave me a sister."

Dawsey bit her trembling lip.

"I saved the last part for Hooper." Her shoulders jerked with choking sobs. "Please bring him home where he belongs." She dropped into her chair and hid her face in the crook of her arm, her "amen" a muffled cry against the table.

Odell stood and rushed to Dilsey, smoothing her hair and cooing in her ear.

Silas pushed away his mounded plate. "Odell, cover this food and keep it warm." He turned to Duncan who had already leaped to his feet. "Son?"

"I'm on my way." He hustled to his peg and pulled on his coat. "You reckon he's at Henry's?"

"Where else would he go?" Silas stood. "Wait, I'm coming."

The sound of approaching riders stilled the scene like one of the pictures in Father's books. Dawsey didn't know to be afraid until she read fear on their faces.

Odell stared at her husband, her mouth ajar. "Silas?"

He pointed at Duncan as footsteps hit the porch.

Lifting a shotgun from the rack, Duncan whirled and aimed it at the opening door.

Hooper stood on the threshold, Henry Lowry looming at his back. Men on horseback filled the yard, evidently Henry's escort.

With a tight smile, Hooper held up his hands. "Don't shoot until I've had my say, brother."

Grinning, Duncan dropped the barrel and leaned the gun against the wall.

The room seemed to heave a relieved sigh, and butterflies tumbled in Dawsey's stomach.

Dilsey spun around the table and threw herself at Hooper.

Henry's bulk, as he squeezed past them, jostled Hooper and Dilsey further into the room.

Dawsey stared, struck again by the uncommon good looks of the big man and intimidated by the arsenal he wore.

Two ammo belts crisscrossed his chest, and two more rode his hips. He wore a holster strapped to his side and the handle of another pistol peeked out from his waistband. He carried a rifle in one hand, another slung across his back by a shoulder strap.

"Merry Christmas, folks." He slid off his hat and nodded at Odell, but it was clear who he'd come to see. "Silas?"

Silas pumped his hand. "Merry Christmas, Henry."

Odell crept around the table with her hands clasped. "We were about to sit for the holiday meal, Henry. We'd be pleased to have you join us."

He declined with a smile. "I come to plead for Hooper."

Short in stature, Silas craned his neck at Henry. "What do you mean?"

Henry motioned at the table, the festive walls, the cheery fire, and the mantel, red with holly. He paused at the tree, staring with glowing eyes and a determined nod. "He belongs here." He pointed at Dilsey, still clinging to Hooper's shirt. "With his family."

"You're right about that." Beaming, Silas jerked his thumb at Duncan. "We were just on our way to fetch him."

Hooper's head came up and his eyes shone. "You were?"

Silas clutched his sleeve. "We're going to help you get a handle on that temper, son. We'll work at it together until we beat it."

Odell hugged Hooper and got Dilsey in the bargain. "You won't be asked to leave home again, no matter what."

Silas shook a warning finger. "But I may lock you in the shed next time."

Henry gave Silas's shoulder a firm pat. Angling past the clustered family, he strolled across the porch to the yard and mounted a large horse. He disappeared from sight as the wave of men closed in around him.

Hooper eased his mother and sister aside and crossed to Duncan.

Smiling, Duncan met him with his hand out.

Hooper gripped it and pulled him close for a hug. "I'm sorry, brother. I give you my word, I'll never raise a hand to you again."

Chapter 42

Ellie led Hooper to his place at the table. Handing him a napkin, she waited while their mama filled his plate then set it down in front of him with a merry chuckle. "There," she cried. "Now it's Christmas."

Smiling, he winked at her and tucked the square of cloth around his collar. "I was just thinking the same." He gazed at each of their faces, lingering a bit on Dawsey. "There's no place I'd rather be than seated at this table."

He tilted his head at Tiller's chair. "Where's the boy?"

Papa scowled. "Someplace he shouldn't be, I'm sure. We'll wait on him like one hog waits on another." He cut into his roasted duck and gave Ma a crinkled grin. "This meal is fit for a sovereign, Odie."

Comparing them to pigs proved more truthful than Pa intended. When Ellie leaned back, two plate loads and a slice of pie later, the table looked like a herd of swine had rooted down the middle.

Pa held his stomach and groaned. "I'm not sure if that was a blessing or a curse, family."

A dreamy look on her face, Ma wiped her mouth and smiled. "An uncommon blessing for me."

Pain tugged Ellie's heart. Mama didn't often get the chance to eat her fill.

Duncan wrinkled his nose. "Why doesn't the food look good anymore?"

Reaching around him, Dawsey stacked his empty plate on the rest.

"It's to protect you from yourself."

Mama laughed and patted Pa's rounded stomach. "I can boil up some sassafras tea. It'll ease your bloat."

He shook his head. "No thank you, darlin'. I couldn't truck it in sideways. There's not a smidgen of room left."

Ellie leaped up clapping her hands. "Time to open presents."

Pa moaned. "Not yet, honey. Let's give our duck time to settle." He belched. "See? Mine's still quacking."

"You won't have to do a thing." She kissed his cheek and hurried to sit cross-legged on the floor by the tree. "I'll pass them out."

Hooper turned his chair around to watch. "Looks like you're outnumbered, Pa."

Mama cast a worried glance at the door. "We should wait for Tiller. He should be here by now. He's missing Christmas."

"You're right, darlin'," Pa said. "It's not like him to miss a meal."

Ellie slumped, frustrated with her harebrained cousin.

"He should be here and not out gallivanting," Duncan said. "I say we go ahead without him."

Hooper winked at Ellie. "Let's get started, at least. If he's not here soon, I'll go find him."

Ma bit her lip. "All right. I suppose so."

Ellie whooped and gathered an armload of presents. She picked through, reading the names. "There you go, Pa, and here's one for you, Duncan." She smiled at Hooper. "I think this one's yours." Tilting her head, she grinned at Ma. "Papa made this himself. You're going to love it."

When she'd handed out everything under the tree, stacking Tiller's near the hearth, she carried the last two bundles to Dawsey. With a grateful smile at her mama, Ellie slid the first neatly wrapped package into Dawsey's hands. "Careful, it's very old and fragile."

Stunned, Dawsey gently turned it over in her hands. "Goodness, what could it be?"

"You'll see. I didn't make yours or anything, but I think you'll like it."

Placing the second package in Dawsey's lap, she gave her a knowing wink. "Hooper worked on this for weeks."

Chattering like excited children, they took turns opening their gifts.

Duncan pulled on the sweater Ma had knitted, colored gray like his eyes, and pranced around the room to hearty laughs and teasing.

Grinning, Pa clutched a new hat from Hooper to his chest.

Ma shrieked with joy when she pulled back the paper on the angel

Pa had whittled, holding up her prize for them to see.

With little else to work with, Dawsey had strung buttons into colorful necklaces for Ma and Ellie and made candy for the men. Her chocolate buckeye kisses for Hooper brought a secret smile to Ellie's lips.

Dawsey opened Hooper's first. She squealed with pleasure and ran her hand along the deer hide then draped it around her shoulders. "Thank you, Hooper. It's lovely."

His face shone brighter than the candles on the tree.

Ellie bounced up from her place on the floor. "Now mine."

Flashing a nervous smile, Dawsey picked up the bundle and untied the string. Frowning slightly, she didn't seem to understand until she held up the dress and read Dilsey's name along the hem.

"I'm sure you had one just like it, with your name and everything." She shrugged. "I thought you might like a tie to our past."

Dawsey laid aside the garment and gathered Ellie in her arms. She cried so hard, Ellie began to wonder if she'd done the wrong thing.

"Oh, Dilsey, it's the most precious gift I've ever received. I'll treasure it always."

Ellie heaved a relieved sigh and pretended to wipe sweat from her forehead.

Dawsey laughed, and the others joined her.

A thin cry, like that of a bleating lamb, faded with the end of their laughter.

Ellie looked around the table. "What was that?"

Duncan shrugged. "I didn't hear it."

She held up her hand. "Be still for a second."

Tiller's shrill voice, calling for Pa, echoed in the distance.

Duncan chuckled. "That, I heard."

Papa straightened in his chair. "Brace yourselves, folks. Yonder comes Tiller, and he sounds hungry."

Closer to the porch, Tiller shrilled Pa's name in a choked voice.

Hooper whipped around. "That's not hungry. That's scared." He sprang from his chair at the same time Tiller blasted through the door.

The window exploded into the room. Hooper dove and rolled Tiller to the floor. Covering the boy's slender body with his own, he kicked the door shut with a *crash*.

"Down!" Pa shouted, pulling Mama and Ellie to their knees.

Duncan caught Dawsey around the waist and spun her beneath the table as a storm of gunfire cut across the back wall of the cabin.

The room leaped to life in a dizzy, bouncing spray of wood chips, shredded holly, and shattered dishes. One blast toppled Dawsey's tree, sending cookie stars flying in crumbled pieces.

"Led them straight down on us," Pa roared, his angry gaze on Tiller.

Dawsey pulled away from Duncan and gathered Ellie to her with grasping hands, breathing Bible words in her ear. " 'He that dwelleth in the secret place of the most High—' "

Ellie lunged. She had to get to the gun rack.

" '—shall abide under the shadow of the Almighty.' "

Dawsey held her and Duncan shouted, "No!"

" 'I will say of the Lord, he is my refuge and my fortress' "—

Ellie fell against Dawsey again as a fresh volley ripped through the air.

—"my God; in him will I trust.' "

Pa belly-crawled to Hooper. "We're doomed, son. Do something."

No Pa! Ellie's heart cried. *You'll get him killed.*

" 'Surely he shall deliver thee from the snare of the fowler, and from the noisome pestilence. He shall cover thee with his feathers. . .' "

Hush Dawsey.

" 'A thousand shall fall at thy side, and ten thousand at thy right hand; but it shall not come nigh thee.' "

"Wait." Hooper held up his hand. "Do you hear that?" Blessed hope oozed from his voice.

Ellie strained to hear. The gunfire hadn't stopped, just moved away from the house. Angry, threatening voices faded to the distance.

The battle had turned. The ambushers had been ambushed.

"We're saved!" Duncan shouted.

Dumbfounded, Ellie turned to stare at Dawsey.

Dawsey smiled through her tears, as if they shared a secret. She tucked Ellie's hair behind her ear. " 'Only with thine eyes shalt thou behold and see the reward of the wicked.' "

They heard familiar voices, and the door flew open. Henry and Boss stood on the porch, guardian angels with weapons drawn.

Henry stepped inside. "Everyone all right?"

Ellie rushed the gun rack.

Hooper beat her there. "Who are they, Henry? They followed Tiller to the house."

Henry's eyes turned black with a mixture of sadness and rage. "The Guard." He nodded at Tiller. "Young pups walked into a trap."

Boss looked mad enough to spit. "They've been raiding for profit, Silas. Pedaling their goods in town." He glared at Tiller. "Hit the wrong house this time. Scared the dickens out of a county official's wife."

Pa glared. "Who told you this?"

Boss pointed behind him. "We've got the Carter boys outside, quivering in their britches. Wyatt threatened the truth out of his brother. He was on his way here to tell you himself when he ran into us. I sent him home to tell his pa instead."

Ellie's heart lurched. Everything she and Wyatt feared had happened. She should've told Pa the truth instead of tossing gutless hints.

She gazed around at their shattered celebration. The candy Dawsey spent so much time making for the boys lay scattered over the floor. A bullet had blazed a hole through Papa's new hat. Ma's angel lay at her feet with a broken wing.

Filled with dread, Ellie's eyes jumped to the table where Dawsey had placed the little dress. It was gone.

She hurriedly searched the floor around the chairs. Nothing.

Frantic, she kicked through the rubble that had been their cozy Christmas. Against the back wall, she saw what she'd dreaded. With a gasp, she ran to the riddled paper, holding it up with an anguished cry.

Dawsey caught her arm from behind. "Looking for this?"

Ellie stared as she smiled and held up the dress.

"Oh, Dawsey, I thought it was lost."

"I couldn't bear the thought, so I pulled it under the table with us."

Weak with relief, she melted into Dawsey's hug.

"Ellie?" Scowling, Hooper motioned with his head.

Henry, Boss, and Papa were watching her, too.

Flushed with embarrassment, she hurried to join them. Had she gone soft, fussing over a baby's frock while her family needed her? She raised her chin and steeled her back. "Yes, Hooper?"

"It's not safe for you women with us here. We're going with Henry."

Ellie's throat tightened. "All of you?"

He nodded.

"Pa, too?"

"If you want him to stay alive."

Dawsey pushed past her. "What are you saying? You're leaving us here alone?"

His eyes softened. "Those men are no threat unless you have a price on your head." He touched her shoulder. "They won't waste time coming here once they get wind that we're gone."

"And they will get wind of it," Boss said. "We'll make sure of it."

Hooper's hand lingered on Dawsey's neck. "Don't fret. You're as safe with Ellie as you'd be with me."

Ellie's chest swelled with pride, and her plea to ride with the men died in her throat. What was she thinking? Of course she'd stay behind to mind Ma and Dawsey and keep them safe. Her hand tightened on her shotgun. "I'll take care of them, Hooper."

He nodded and ruffled her hair. "We'll stack wood and nails on the porch. Board these windows as soon as you can."

She nodded.

Ma flitted like a bee, tying bundles of clothes together for them. She found a basket of cookies, untouched by the ruckus, and poured them inside Rhoda's gunnysack. Wrapping a brown sugar pie, she slid it in, too. At the last minute, she tucked in the Tipsy Parson cake.

Smiling grimly, she handed the sack to Pa. "You may need this."

Going red in the face each time he glanced at Tiller, Pa finally caved in to his rage and caught him by the scruff of the neck. "If we live through this, Tiller McRae, you'll be on the fastest train to Fayetteville."

Wincing, he cowered away.

The men filed out, watchful, determined looks on their faces as they scoured the distant trees. Duncan, waiting outside, had already saddled the horses.

Ellie stared from the shattered window as they mounted up, watching until the last horse rode out of sight. *Please Dawsey's God, look out for them.*

Dawsey stood next to her, her nose too close to the broken glass. "Keep them, God," she breathed. "Bear them to safety in the hollow of Your hand."

Ma lifted her broom from the corner and started sweeping. "Might as well get started on this mess. It should take me all night."

Dawsey turned. "Don't fret, Odell. I'll pitch in as soon as I help board the window."

True to her word, Dawsey held the rough planks in place while Ellie nailed, leaving a space between the last two for the barrel of Ellie's gun.

Taking the broom from Ma's hand, Dawsey patted her back. "I'll finish this. Why don't you go see to the food? Hopefully we can save most of it."

Ellie picked up Pa's new hat, now trampled as well as shot through.

"What can I do to help?"

Ma pointed. "You can hold tight to that shotgun and keep your eyes pinned to the yard."

Ellie sat on a low stool and stared through the crack in the boards until her eyes watered and her back ached.

A crash spun her around.

Dawsey had gone rigid, the broom slipped from her hand.

"Heavens," Ma cried from the counter. "That scared me blue."

Ellie frowned. "What is it, Dawsey?"

She raised stunned eyes. "My father." Tearing off her apron, she hurried for the door. "What's wrong with me? I completely forgot him."

"Wait. Don't go out there, honey."

She struggled with the locking bar. "I have to, Odell. He must be terrified."

"I'm sure he's fine," Ma assured her. "Otherwise he'd be calling for you."

"With all that gunfire? He's probably too frightened to make a sound." Dawsey paused, a look of horror in her eyes. "Unless he did start shouting and—" She wrenched the door open, looking over her shoulder at Ellie. "Is there anything I can use for a weapon?"

The men had emptied the gun rack. Even Hooper's long blade was gone.

"Take the shotgun."

Shaking her head, Dawsey started outside. "I won't leave you defenseless."

Ellie clutched her arm. "I'll go with you."

"No, you won't. Stay here and guard your mother."

Odell ran toward her with the broom. "Here, honey. Take this."

"Ma, what good will that do?"

She lifted one shoulder. "She could hit someone over the head with it."

Ellie begged with her eyes. "Don't go, Dawsey."

Dawsey squeezed her hand. "Wait here. I'll be fine." With a wary glance toward the trees, she darted off the porch and disappeared around the corner of the house, waving the broom handle.

Ellie stamped her foot and locked the door.

Ma finished clearing the food, swept the floor, then set to work scrubbing what dishes escaped the ambush.

Ellie glanced up. "You must be tuckered. Wait for Dawsey to help you."

Hunched over a pan of water, she shrugged her shoulders. "I may as well keep my hands busy. It keeps me from thinking."

Ellie knew what she meant. In her fevered mind, she'd tracked the men safely to Henry's house a dozen times. "Why don't you sit and rest? We can talk a bit to take our mind off things."

Ma poured herself a spiced posset and dragged a chair up beside Ellie. "What's keeping Dawsey? Shouldn't she be here by now?"

Ellie stared through the crack at the long shadows across the yard. "I was just thinking the same." Reluctant to raise the subject, she smoothed her mama's hand. "It'll be dark soon and too dangerous for Dawsey to go outside." She winced. "Should we bring the colonel in here with us for the night?"

Ma choked a little then swallowed her sip of spiced milk. "Is it safe?"

Ellie drew a deep breath. "I suppose we could tie him up." She ducked her head. "Or hold a gun on him."

"Oh Ellie."

They sat quietly for a spell.

Ma shot her a hangdog look. "The truth is I dread facing the man."

"Then we'll leave him right where he is."

Ma waved her off. "We'll do no such thing. As soon as Dawsey comes, we'll tell her our plan. I'm sure it will rest her mind."

Ellie peered through the opening again. "Something doesn't feel right." She shot a worried look over her shoulder. "She should be back by now."

Ma sat forward, clutching her cup. "Go out and check on them, honey."

"I can't leave you alone."

"You certainly can. I'll lock the door."

Ellie stood, kicking the stool from behind her. "Are you sure?"

"Positive. Now go."

Waiting to hear Ma slide the bar into place, Ellie climbed over the rail and hurried down the side of the cabin. Painfully alert, she scanned every bush and tree, watching for movement.

She slowed at the back corner to scour the trail leading down to the outhouse. Seeing nothing out of place, she sped up, tripping over something on the ground.

Ellie rolled to her back, waving the barrel of her gun at an unseen enemy. Feeling foolish, she stood, glancing to see what had sent her sprawling.

Prickly hairs tingled on her neck, and her feet turned to stone. The broom lay on the ground, spookily out of place.

She spun toward her room, sickened to confirm what she feared.

The bar still rested on its braces, locking the door from the outside. Dawsey had never made it to the colonel.

Eyes and ears alert, Hooper weaved through the brush, a soldier in a silent army of ghosts.

Henry's men, skilled at easing soundlessly through the swamp, rode in a protective circle around him as the fenland pulled them in and the swamp tuned up for its nightly chorus.

A quick clash with the Guard led to an ugly skirmish that left Hooper with bells in his head and Duncan a bloody ear where a bullet grazed him—a minor wound that he would moan about for weeks.

Hooper prayed they'd run their foes clear back to Lumberton. He didn't relish another scuffle.

Boss led them along the small, hidden paths between dry spots, the route a well-kept secret known only to Henry's trusted circle of friends. They'd spend the next few nights at Henry's hideout, the last place Hooper expected to see again so soon. His heart ached with gratitude for the Lowrys, but the idea of leaving home had tasted of bitter swill.

Gritting his teeth at the memory of the smashed decorations and ruined tree, the broken dishes and the wide swath of ripped-up wallboards, he wondered if home would ever feel the same.

Anxious thoughts drifted to Dawsey. He regretted leaving the women alone with night approaching, but he trusted Ellie with his life. He knew she'd give hers to protect them.

Pa moaned behind him. "Is that a light I see?" His question was more of a grateful announcement.

Hooper looked over his shoulder. "Are your knees bothering you again?"

Soft laughter rumbled. "I'd use a stronger word to express it, but yes, they hurt. I'm not as young as I used to be." He grunted. "Paining me or not, I'm going down on these knees as soon as I get off this horse."

Duncan chuckled. "To thank God you're alive?"

"No, son." Pa's voice matched the mournful sigh of the wind. "To beg safety for my gals."

The men ushered Henry to his door then fanned out and merged with the swamp to keep watch.

Guilt tickled Hooper's conscience as he swung off his horse. They'd sleep safely that night. Could he hope the same for Ma and the girls? Weary of second-guessing himself, he caught hold of Pa's saddle. "Did we make a mistake, leaving them behind?"

Pa settled stiffly to the ground before he answered. "I've been wondering the same, but it's too late to fix it now. We'll send someone in the morning to fetch them."

Hooper nudged his hat aside and scratched his dampened head. "Should we wait that long?"

Rhoda appeared at the door. Backlit by lantern light, every line of her body showed beneath her thin nightdress.

Hooper yanked his gaze to the ground.

"What's wrong, Henry?" she called. "I feel a spirit of unrest over the earth."

"You're causing most of it," Henry growled. "Get inside and cover up."

"Don't know about the whole earth, Rhoda," Boss called as she ducked from sight. "Most of Scuffletown is a bit uneasy tonight."

Rhoda returned wrapped in a quilt. She shaded her eyes against the light pouring out behind her and searched the yard, her head bobbing. "Who you got out there? Do I see Silas McRae?"

Pa chuckled. "Evening, Rhoda."

"Merry Christmas, Silas. Don't stand out there in the damp. Come on in."

Papa hobbled toward her.

"I see my warning came too late." Rhoda rushed to take his arm and she and Henry helped him up the steps. "Don't fret. I have just the remedy for those stiff knees."

Duncan touched Hooper's arm. "We going back for the women?"

With a sigh, Hooper stared at the ground. "I don't know. My head tells me Ellie can handle things. My heart yearns to mount a fresh horse and race home."

Duncan idly ground the toe of his boot in the dirt. "Would Dawsey have anything to do with what your heart wants?"

Hooper's head jerked up. "What sort of question is that?"

He lifted both hands. "Just curious. You've followed her around like a nursing pup." Before Hooper could answer, Duncan gave a harsh laugh. "I must be mistaken, though. That would be awfully strange considering she's the image of our sister."

Hooper tensed. "Those two are nothing alike, and you know it."

"Nothing alike?" Duncan snorted. "Brother, they're exactly the same."

Struggling with his newfound control, Hooper handed off the reins and shoved past him. "I don't have time for this. You and Tiller bed down the horses while I sort out what to do."

Seething inside, he sprang up the steps.

"Hooper?" Duncan's eerie voice stopped him cold.

"Now what?"

"Tiller's gone."

Hooper's hand slid off the doorknob. "What do you mean?"

"Do you see him anywhere? The boy's not here."

Hooper cleared the porch in one leap. "Did he ride off with Boss and the others?"

"No," Duncan said. "That much I'm sure of."

"When was the last time you saw him?"

Duncan rubbed his chin and stared, his color in the dusky light a sickly pale. "He was there during the scuffle with the Guard."

Hooper gripped his shoulder. "Are you sure?"

"Yes." He brushed the hand away. "I saw him myself."

"Tiller wouldn't wander off alone in all that gunfire." Sickness surged in Hooper's stomach. "That means the Guard has him."

Another dreadful possibility kicked him in the teeth. He clutched Duncan's arms. "You don't think he was hit?"

Fear sparked in Duncan's eyes. "What are we waiting for? Tiller could be lying out there with a bullet in him." He waved toward the house. "Get Henry. Have him round up his men."

Pacing now, Hooper shook his head. "We won't pull Henry from his house again tonight." He spun in the direction Boss Strong had gone. "Saddle three fresh horses and fetch some lanterns," he called over his shoulder. "I'm going for Boss. He'll help us search."

"Hoop?"

He turned.

"What will we tell Pa?"

"The truth, I reckon. Unless you have a better idea."

Cursing under his breath, Duncan struck out for the barn.

At Ellie's whistle, Mama nearly ripped the door from its hinges. "For corn's sake! What took you? I was worried sick."

"I'm dreadful sorry, Ma. I was searching the woods for Dawsey."

"What?"

Ellie's jaw ached from gritting her teeth. "She's gone."

"She can't be," Ma whispered. She shook her head as if she could make Ellie's words not so. "Where would she go?"

Ellie stood near the gun rack, filling a drawstring bag with shells. "The Guard took her. One of them ambushed her behind the house. She never had a chance."

Ma sucked in a breath. "Oh, Ellie, how do you know?"

"I tracked them as far as I dared. Two sets of prints, one of them Dawsey's. The other a fairly big man."

"What are we going to do?"

"What else, Ma? I'm going after Hooper."

Mama untied her apron. "You mean *we're* going. If I stay here alone, I'll be next."

Ellie started to argue, to tell her she'd be safer locked inside the cabin. One look at the fear in her eyes changed her mind. "Are you sure, Ma? They took all the horses."

She cast an anxious glance toward the barn. "Even the colonel's?"

"Tiller rode him."

She nodded thoughtfully. "I see."

Ellie touched her arm. "This won't be an easy trip. It'll take hours to get there on foot, and we can't leave until it's good and dark."

Clenching her jaw, Ma flicked her hand. "What of it? I've run these woods for years. I could find Henry's house with my eyes closed."

Beaming with pride, Ellie hugged her.

They paced and planned, Ellie keeping watch through the slats, until night settled firmly over the yard. Gathering her courage, she glanced up. "It's time. You don't want to change your mind?"

"I'm going," Ma said.

Ellie had to ask. "Are you sure you can keep up?"

Ma drew back, insulted. "Can you keep up with me?"

If their present troubles weren't so dire, Ellie would slap her knee and howl at the challenge shining from her mama's bright eyes. She slung her shotgun over her shoulder. "I fear you may get the chance to prove yourself. Fetch a canteen and let's go."

Ma spun and hurried for the water.

Ellie carefully opened the door, scanning the yard as far as she could see in the moonlight. She shuddered, partly for Ma's sake, when she imagined stepping past the rim of trees lurking in ominous shadows. She longed for daylight, but they needed the cover of night.

"I'm ready." Ma appeared at Ellie's elbow, startling her from her thoughts. She'd dressed herself in work boots and Pa's long-sleeved shirt. She pressed floppy hats on both their heads and wrapped scarves around their necks.

Ellie narrowed her eyes and took one last look before they slipped on their coats and stepped out on the porch.

Ten feet from the house, Mama stopped and tugged at her. "What about the colonel?"

Groaning, Ellie tapped her forehead with her knuckles. "He completely slipped my mind."

"Should we take him with us?"

Ellie thought for a minute then shook her head. "Too risky."

Mama pursed her lips. "After all that gunfire, he's bound to be beside himself. Can't we at least tell him we're going?"

"And you'll explain to him why Dawsey's missing?"

She wagged her head. "Not for money."

"Let's go then. We'll be back before morning. He'll be fine until then."

Gripping each other's hands, they darted across the yard and slipped into the yawning darkness.

CHAPTER 44

There was no convincing their pa to stay behind once he learned Tiller was missing. While Rhoda wrapped a poultice on his knees to help him bear the ride, Papa gripped his head and moaned over the last words he'd said to him. "Blast this too-quick tongue in my head. If anything happens to the boy, I'll never get the chance to tell him I didn't mean what I said." His sorrowful eyes jumped to Hooper. "I wouldn't send him to Fayetteville, no more than I meant for you to leave home."

Hooper gripped his shoulder. He could understand Pa's regret. Not so long ago, he'd sat under a full moon mourning his own rash deeds. "No sense in fretting too soon. When the shooting started, Tiller likely ran home to hide behind Mama's skirts." He tried to smile. "After all, he was hungry, and home is where he can fill his stomach."

Rhoda stood up from wrapping Pa's leg. "Hooper's right. A boy that age has a bottomless belly and two hollow legs." She glanced at her brother, slouched against the wall. "Remember, Boss? You used to clean out the larder back home."

Henry sat forward at the table. "He does a fair job of it now."

She touched his arm. "You should go with them, Henry. I'd expect as much if it was Boss."

Hooper shook his head. "He offered, Rhoda. With all the trouble stirring tonight, it's best if he gets some rest. We may need him worse tomorrow."

She nodded and handed him a filled waterskin. "Be careful," she whispered. "My spirit is heavy."

He nodded grimly, wishing she'd kept the news to herself.

Duncan paced outside near the horses. "What took so long? Let's go." His gaze jumped to Papa easing off the steps and his jaw tightened. "He has no business going, and you know it."

Hooper raised his brow. "Go ahead and tell him. He won't listen to me."

They mounted their horses, and Boss led them back through the swamp the way they'd come.

They rode in silence, Hooper's anxious thoughts mingling with the night sounds. Tiller was a willful handful, no doubt, but he had a good heart. Hooper hoped no harm had come to the spirited lad.

The search party, made up of Hooper, Duncan, Pa, Boss, and three volunteers from Henry's gang, spread out over the site where they'd fallen upon the ambushing Guard. Knowing the risk they took was great, they combed the brush and called Tiller's name, shining lanterns in dark thickets and shadowed places.

At least an hour passed with no sign of him, and Hooper's spirit grew heavy.

Boss sidled up to him, breathing hard. "He's not here."

Hooper nodded. "Then he's at home, like I said."

Their eyes met, and Boss tried to hide his doubt. "Sure thing, Hoop. He's rocking by the fire right now, nursing a hearty slice of your mama's pie."

They both knew he lied.

Pa rode up panting. "What are you doing lolling about when we haven't yet found him?"

Lifting his hat, Hooper wiped the sweat off his brow. "It's no use, Pa."

He bristled. "What do you mean? That's my nephew we're looking for."

Hooper rolled his neck to ease the kinks. "I'm not done looking for him, just done searching here." He softened his voice. "We'll retrace our steps to the house. If he's not there, at least we'll feel better after checking on the women."

Pa leaned his head to gaze at the starry sky. "All right, son. It'll be a treat to lay these old eyes on my Odie again."

"Then turn and look, old man. I'm right behind you."

Hooper whipped around to stare as Ma and Ellie appeared in the circle of light.

"By crick," Pa bellowed. "It's really them." He slid from the saddle and hobbled to wrap them in his arms. "How did two little women manage to slip up on seven wary men?"

Ma lifted her chin. "We're Lumbee gals, that's how."

In the low light, Ellie squinted up at Duncan, who still had bloodstains running from his ear. "Gracious, what happened?"

His hand groped his head. "Had a run-in with the Guard. They thought I'd look better with one hat catcher, but I outsmarted them and ducked."

Ma sucked in a breath. "Oh, Duncan."

Pa glanced past them. "Is Tiller with you?"

Her eyes roamed his face. "He's supposed to be with you."

Hooper's eager gaze sought for Dawsey but didn't find her. Had Ellie left her and the colonel alone? Scowling, he dismounted. "What are you doing here? I left you to guard the house."

Ellie pulled herself from Papa's smothering grip. "We were on our way to Henry's cabin to get you." Frowning, she turned in a little half circle, gazing at each of the men. "Does this have something to do with Tiller?"

Fear niggling at his gut, Hooper turned her around. "I asked first. Where are Dawsey and the colonel?"

She bit her bottom lip and tears sprang to her eyes. "I failed you. You put your trust in me, and I let you down."

Dread seized him. He fought the urge to shake the rest out of her. "It can't be that bad, honey. Go on, tell me what happened."

Her chin wobbled out of control. "They took Dawsey."

Hooper's hands bore down on her shoulders, his fingers biting her flesh. "Who took her?"

"The Guard." Ellie winced but stood her ground. "They snatched Dawsey right out of our yard."

They raced for the house in darkness. Ellie clung to Duncan on Toby. Ma rode behind Pa on Old Abe.

"If they have Dawsey, they likely have young Tiller, too. Don't you reckon, Hooper?" Pa had asked. The hope shining from his eyes told how scared he was of being wrong.

When Ellie heard Tiller had gone missing, her heart filled with despair—until she remembered Dawsey's God.

He had granted safety for the men, even protecting them through a skirmish with the Guard. Though He likely granted Dawsey's fancy prayer and not her own, it filled Ellie with hope that He seemed to hear at all. Enough hope to dare pose two more requests.

"Please God," she whispered into the wind at her face, "bring Dawsey home. I should've mentioned my cousin by name before, since he's so much extra trouble. I'm fixing my blunder now by asking you to keep Tiller safe."

Duncan squeezed her hand, and she blushed to think he heard.

Ellie ached to start the search for Dawsey. Every muscle strained toward home, so the ride seemed to take longer than their grueling walk. Relieved tears stung her eyes when they reined up in front of the porch.

Hooper dismounted and strode her way. "Is the colonel still out back?"

Her stomach lurched and she nodded. She dreaded telling Dawsey's father that she was gone. "I expect he needs water by now." She swung from behind Duncan. "Hand me a lamp. I'll take him the flask and break the news to him."

Papa caught her by the arm. "I'll go."

She sought his face in the dim light. "You, Pa?"

He firmed his jaw. "Can you think of anyone who deserves the dreadful task more?"

"We'll all go," Hooper announced. "The colonel may've heard a struggle or voices, something to help us find Dawsey."

Ellie led them to the back of the house by lantern light. The broom still lay where she'd left it, the evidence of her stupidity. She kicked it out of the way. "They got her right here."

Hooper nodded. "Did they leave up the trail?"

She shook her head and pointed to the evergreen scrub to the left of her room. "They cut out through there."

Reaching the steps, Hooper paused and cocked his head. "Two sets of prints? You're sure?"

She nodded, fear setting in. What thoughts haunted him behind his darting eyes?

"We'd best pray the colonel heard something, then. Dawsey would've raised a ruckus struggling against one man." He paused, his face stricken. "Unless she couldn't." He yanked the bar loose and took Ellie's lantern. Holding it high overhead, he shoved the door open and pushed into the room. "Colonel Wilkes? Sir?"

Ellie crowded in behind him with the others close behind. When she reached Hooper's side in the shadowy room, he stood with one hand on his hip, gazing at the emptiness. "That shrewd old dog." He spun to face them. "The Guard didn't snatch Dawsey. Her pa did."

Hooper didn't know whether to be relieved or more afraid. The Guard at least had some experience in the swamp. Dawsey could be in serious danger traipsing about with a dizzy old man.

"Her pa?" Ellie stared dumbly at the empty bed. "How can that be? What about the locked door?" She wiggled her finger behind them. "The broom beside the house?"

Duncan laughed. "Pretty smart thinking, really. The colonel set the whole thing up to throw us off for as long as possible." He shot Ellie a teasing glance. "I reckon he never expected his tricks to buy him a four-hour head start."

Ellie scowled and looked away.

Hooper blew a ragged breath. "If you ask me, his idea was dim-witted. They have to trek for miles out of here on foot. Treacherous miles in the dark. I can't believe the old man would try such a thing."

"I can," Ellie said. "Don't forget, he was an army scout."

Duncan nodded. "The old coot tailed me all the way here from Fayetteville."

"On horseback," Hooper reminded him.

Boss leaned against the doorsill. "He didn't carry the girl away from here. Would she go willingly?"

Sadness tugged at Hooper. Was Dawsey still that eager to get away from them? He shrugged. "I suppose she must have." He glanced at Ellie. "Why would she brave the swamp a second time after what happened to her?"

"Because Dawsey—"

"She wouldn't have," Pa said, interrupting Ellie. "Not after I promised I'd take her home."

"Did she believe you?" Boss asked.

Ellie nodded. "She—"

"I think she did," Hooper said.

"I'd stake my life on it," Pa said.

Ellie stamped her foot. "If you'd all hush and listen, I'll tell you what happened."

Their attention swung to Ellie, staring back in bug-eyed frustration.

Hooper nudged her. "Go on then. Tell us."

She took a deep breath. "Dawsey went to protect the colonel. Knowing her, she refused to go, but if he struck out on his own, she'd follow. Who knows better than Dawsey how treacherous the swamp can be?"

Mama pulled her close and patted her back. "That's exactly what happened. Dawsey has a tender heart toward her pa."

Hooper pushed past them. "Either way, she's in danger. We can talk about it all day or go find her." He paused at the door. "Ellie, trim a lamp. I'll need you riding up front."

She touched her throat. "You want me?"

"Is there a better tracker in this room?"

She looked at him from under her lashes. "I wasn't sure you'd ever trust me again."

He pulled her close and kissed her cheek. "I never stopped."

Boss, his lanky body still draped against the door, caught Hooper's arm. "How much head start do they have?"

Hooper searched Ellie's face in the lantern glow.

She scratched her brow. "The sun had just set when she left the cabin. I'd say they have four or five hours on us."

Boss uncrossed his ankles and stood upright. "It's an old man and a woman, stumbling through unfamiliar terrain in the dark. They're making roughly a mile an hour, if they're lucky. We can double or triple that distance." He gripped Hooper's shoulder. "But only by daylight with fresh men and horses."

Hooper frowned. "Are you suggesting we wait?"

"Those poor animals are spent," Boss said. "My men need food. I'm asking an hour, two at the most."

"The colonel and Dawsey could be on the train in Moss Neck by then."

"Maybe." Boss quirked his lips. "If they're traveling in a straight line, which I doubt."

"A couple of hours?" Hooper shook his head. "The trail will get cold."

Grinning, Boss lifted his chin. "With Scuffletown's two best trackers on it?" He shrugged and cocked his head. "We'll help you, Hoop. Whichever way you decide."

Pa touched Hooper's back. "Boss has a good argument, son. I'm long past tuckered, and this knee of mine could use the rest."

Ma took his arm. "Who said you're going anywhere, Silas McRae?"

He jabbed his chest. "I said. Tiller's out there somewhere, too. I don't aim to rest until I find him."

Hooper's heart sank. The thought that Dawsey might be with Tiller had eased his troubled mind a bit. If she was with the colonel instead, that left the boy to face the Guard alone.

He patted Papa's shoulder. "Don't fret, we'll find them both and bring them home."

Ellie clutched Hooper's sleeve. "You're not thinking of waiting, are you? I think we should go now." Her searching gaze begged him to agree.

Pulling free of her tight hold, he wrapped his arm around her shoulder. "We're going to go along with Boss's plan this time. Go help Ma fix food for the men."

Panic blazed in her eyes. "But, Hooper—"

He leaned to whisper in her ear. "If you don't trust Boss, then trust me. Dawsey will be fine, I promise."

Mama herded Ellie and Pa out the door. "Let's go, you two. After traipsing across Robeson County, I could eat a bite myself."

Hooper offered Boss his hand. "I want to thank you again for helping my family."

He smiled and lowered his head. "Anytime, Hooper. You'd do the same for us."

"I didn't just lie to my sister, did I?"

Boss fixed him with a steady gaze. "The swamp comes with no guarantees."

Hooper tightened his grip. "Right now, I'd settle for half a chance."

Chapter 45

In the hours since the sky turned black as pitch, Dawsey had tried her best to lure her father in a gradual circle. Unfortunately, he wasn't easy to sway from his course. She wondered if he knew his way any better than she did. For all Dawsey knew, they could be miles away from Scuffletown or stumbling right past the McRaes' little shack. She longed to part the brush and see the cheery lights of the cabin in the distance, prayed to spot the darting points of searchlights.

Where could they be, the unlikely band of bandits who'd wormed their way into her heart and somehow become her family? Surely they were looking for her by now.

Lead thudded to the bottom of her stomach as she faced the truth. Her father stopped every few yards to cover their tracks, so it was possible the McRaes wouldn't find her.

"Keep up Dawsey, or we'll never get there. We've lost too much time already."

Father's voice floated back to her from somewhere up ahead. With a shudder, she hurried to catch up. It wouldn't do to be separated from him and find herself alone in the dark.

They carried a lantern, but he hadn't allowed her to use it in case the McRaes were behind them. Instead, they picked their way along by the bright moon overhead.

She trudged up behind him and tugged on his shirt. "Never get where? You can't possibly know where we are."

"Of course I do." He pointed. "Moss Neck is a couple of miles that way."

Her heart lurched. He really did seem to know which direction they traveled, as if he followed a built-in compass.

What had happened to her father? A month ago, he hardly knew who he was, much less where.

"And if we really are close to Moss Neck? What then?"

"What do you think? We'll contact the nearest officials and have that band of ruffians arrested."

Clutching his arm, Dawsey dug in her heels and pulled him to a stop. "Arrested?"

He shifted the strap of his canteen to the other shoulder. "Of course, dear. First, the elder McRae for taking my sweet Dilsey from her crib. Then the heartless cur who stole into my house and kidnapped you."

Aghast, she stared. "You can't mean it, Father."

He glanced at the starry sky then set off again. "I've never meant anything more."

Dawsey scurried behind him with her heart in her throat. "But I've explained everything, don't you remember? The McRaes made a mistake." She picked up the pace. "An absolutely horrid mistake, but they're sorry."

Father stopped so fast she plowed into his back. He spun with his hands in the air, his simpering smile frightening in the moonlight. "Oh I see. They're *sorry*. Thank you, dear, for clearing things up." He clutched his chest. "I feel so much better about them now."

Struck dumb, she gaped.

"Do you hear yourself? Defending your abductors?" He crossed to cup her chin in his hand. "What have they done to you?"

She closed her eyes and wagged her head. "I know how it sounds."

He grunted. "I'm not sure you do."

Dawsey wracked her mind. No matter what they'd done in the past, she couldn't allow her father to turn in the McRaes. Especially Hooper.

Wrapping his arm around her waist, Father pulled her along beside him. "Come, Dawsey. We grow closer to help with every footfall."

She tugged away from him. "I'm sorry, Father. I can't go another step without rest."

He struggled to hide his irritation. "I know the trek is grueling, dear, but we rested not twenty minutes ago."

"But I'm starving and limp with thirst." She let her shoulders sag. "And my leg hurts."

All of her excuses were true. Dawsey was tired and hungry, and her calf ached in the spot where the rattler had "kissed" her, as Duncan teasingly called her warning bite.

Wincing, Father gingerly groped behind his hat. "What a sorry lot we are. I fear my head hurts something fierce." He heaved a defeated sigh. "Very well. I suppose a short rest won't hurt."

He led her to a stump and spread his coat. Dawsey insisted he light the lamp and check the ground for snakes before she agreed to sit. He reluctantly complied then set the lantern away from them.

Easing down beside her, he handed over the canteen then pulled a bundle of food from his knapsack. Dawsey recognized Odell's dishcloth, filled to overflowing with sweet potato bread, Indian dumplings, and pecan-crusted buns.

She watched him, struck again at his shrewdness. "You planned this all along, didn't you?"

He kept his head down, his eyes on rationing their bounty.

"You thought of everything, the food, the water." She held up the flask and shook it. "The pitcher didn't get broken in the scuffle, did it? You were hiding the fact that you'd emptied it inside here."

"One of us had to think rationally," he said quietly.

Her mind went to the night she'd clawed the cold ground for hours and dug her way out of the shed. She'd been willing to risk her life to escape the McRaes and return to her father.

Whatever dizzy circumstances had changed Dawsey's mind, her father believed he was saving his daughters, and she respected his efforts tremendously. Somehow, she had to change his mind, too.

She longed to rest her head against his shoulder the way she'd watched Dilsey do with Silas. Not sure how Father would react, she leaned against the stump instead, chewing thoughtfully on a bun. "What if I told you Dilsey is gloriously happy?"

He laughed scornfully. "In that mud-soaked hovel?"

Trying to make light of her pain, Dawsey laughed, too. "Scandalous, isn't it? I was quite surprised to find that love could thrive in such an environment." She swallowed hard. "Even more surprised to see love so freely expressed."

She glanced at the side of his face. "The truth is the McRaes love Dilsey very much. Furthermore, she loves them. You won't change that, no matter how many charges you level against Silas and Hooper."

He tilted his head. "Turning in those monsters is how we get our little girl back."

She clutched his arm. "You're wrong. She'll be distraught. The McRaes are the only family Dilsey's ever known. If you hurt them, we'll lose her for good."

With a determined sigh, he patted her face. "You have to allow me to handle this. I know what's best for my girls."

Gazing around at the brush, he handed her a dumpling. "Finish eating, dear, then lie back and enjoy your rest. We can't dawdle here for long, so make the best of it."

Ellie slid off her horse and carefully scoured the ground. They'd lost the trail again, and Dawsey's life depended on finding it. Down on her knees, Ellie studied every patch of dirt, every shriveled leaf with a practiced eye.

The colonel turned out to be quite a match for her and Hooper. Over the past few hours, they'd tracked him in bits and pieces between home and Moss Neck, their search running hot and then cold.

They'd finally split up. Boss and his men searched toward Lumberton. Papa and Duncan made their way along the river. She prayed they were having more luck.

Hooper stood. "None of this feels right. I think we're off the mark."

Ellie stood, slapping her gloves against her leg. "I told you we shouldn't wait, Hooper. Why did you listen to Boss?"

He stared at the awakening sky. "Those few hours didn't make a difference. Time's not our problem. It's that wily old man."

Ellie bent her back to stretch out the kinks. "We've been all over this ground, from here to Moss Neck. They must've slipped into town." She glanced up. "If so, they're on the morning train."

Hooper's eyes looked hollowed out, his mouth white with strain. "Unless the colonel hangs around to see us arrested." He gripped his head. "I think I'd prefer that to Dawsey leaving."

"I'd prefer her leaving to being lost." Ellie moaned. "We have to make sure she's not out here somewhere."

"Don't worry," he said. "I won't stop searching until I know for sure."

"Wait a second." She brushed past Hooper and walked a few feet beyond him. In the first light, her skillful eye spotted an area that didn't look quite right. To anyone else it would appear to be a low spot, a shady hole. Ellie skirted the bed of scattered pine straws, a few of them flipped to their damp sides. "Over here, Hooper. They passed through here."

He came and squeezed her shoulder. "Good job, honey. Let's go."

They left their horses and continued on foot. Ellie quickly found a partial footprint then a patch of broken twigs.

"He's getting tired," Hooper said. "And careless."

They'd gone a quarter mile before Pa and Duncan slipped up quietly from behind. Pa placed a finger to his lips and pointed with a tilt of his head. "Trouble yon way," he whispered.

Ducking low, Hooper watched Sheriff McMillan and three deputies riding toward them in the distance. At the same instant, a flash of color caught his eye through the brush.

Dawsey awoke with a start, amazed to find they'd fallen sound asleep.

Her father leaned against her, snoring softly, looking more like the broken man she'd left in Fayetteville. His chin had gray bristles and his silver hair stood on end, aging him ten years in the morning light.

Watching him sleep, she ached for him. At the same time, she rejoiced over more time to reason with him.

Thankful they'd made it through the night, she yawned and stretched—until a rush of noise and motion bore down on them, nearly jolting Dawsey's heart from her chest.

The clearing erupted with loud, angry voices and pounding hooves. Cringing in fear, she huddled protectively around her startled father as strange men swooped down to encircle them.

A scowling man on horseback swung alongside and glared down at her. "Ellie McRae!" His eyes burned with sadistic pleasure, like those of a cat pouncing on a mouse. "You need to tell me where your menfolk are hiding."

Stunned, Dawsey stared up at the strange man who thought she was Ellie.

She glanced at her gasping, wild-eyed father. *Please forgive me for what I'm about to do.*

Hooper clutched Ellie's sleeve and ran, dodging young trees and leaping over bushes. They slowed near the clearing and slid down on their bellies. He motioned for her to stay put and be quiet, praying for once she would listen.

Crawling close to the ground, he reached the last patch of heavy cover and carefully parted the brush. What he saw was far worse than he'd imagined.

He reached for his gun then cursed himself for a fool. He'd left it on his horse. A rogue band of outlaws, he could outsmart. A bounty hunter or two, he could overtake. Sheriff McMillan and his gang of sworn men meant a trip to the gallows, a threat he might risk for Dawsey's sake. . .if not for Ellie.

He gritted his teeth. This was Dawsey's chance, and no doubt, she'd take it. One word against him and he'd be on the way to Lumberton Jail—no less than a hotheaded firebrand deserved—and she'd be on her way home to Fayetteville.

Desperation squeezed his insides. Once they took her, he'd never see her again. Gritting his teeth, he waited.

The sheriff sat tall in the saddle, towering over Dawsey to frighten her. In case that didn't work, he had a gun pointed straight at her head. "We know Hooper's here somewhere, Ellie. Go on and call him out."

Started, Hooper realized the sheriff's mistake. With Dawsey dressed in Ellie's clothes, he could see how easily a man might mix them.

"Be sensible, gal," the sheriff wheedled. "It'll go easier if you cooperate. If not, I can't promise to protect your ma and pa."

Dawsey unfolded from the ground and faced McMillan dead-on.

Hooper tensed. Now she would set him straight.

"Ain't seen my witless brother in a month." She propped both hands on her hips. "If you lay a hand on my folks, you'll have half the county down on your head."

Hooper's stomach jerked like Old Abe had kicked him.

"What's she doing?" Ellie whispered at his side.

He jumped then shushed her.

Colonel Wilkes found his wits and his feet. "Sheriff, you're just the man I need to see." His deep voice boomed in the clearing. "I seek justice in a matter of foul play"—he draped his arm around Dawsey's shoulder—"and protection for my daughter."

Hooper held his breath.

McMillan's puzzled gaze swung around to the colonel. "Who are you, sir?"

Dawsey pulled free and patted his back. "Don't mind him, he's. . ." She raised her brows and touched her temple. "You know."

The colonel's eyes widened. "What are you saying, Dawsey?"

The sheriff looked him over. "Who is this man?" He glanced at

Dawsey. "What are the two of you doing way out here?"

Dawsey's father stood at attention. "My name is Colonel Gerrard Wilkes, from Fayetteville. This young lady is Dawsey Elizabeth, my daughter. We're fleeing our captors, the McRaes. The scoundrels ambushed me two days ago." He pointed at Dawsey. "They've held her prisoner for weeks."

McMillan scowled. "What's going on here, Ellie?"

She jumped in front of the colonel. "Sorry, Sheriff. This here is Ma's brother, come from South Carolina for Christmas. He got away from us, and I've been tracking him all night." She shook her head. "I'm afraid he's having one of his dizzy spells."

"Dizzy spells?" her father asked.

"There, there, Uncle Jerry." Dawsey leaned toward the deputies, speaking in a loud whisper. "Injured in the war, you know."

They nodded in sympathy.

"Look here, Dawsey—" the colonel blustered.

"See?" She pointed. "He don't even know my name."

Red in the face, the colonel charged the sheriff. "Sir, I demand that you help us. The McRaes must be arrested at once and brought to justice."

McMillan's horse danced nervously and the sheriff turned his gun. "Stand back, you dotty old fool."

Dawsey clutched the back of her pa's shirt and held on. "Please don't hurt him. He don't know what he's saying."

McMillan gazed around their camp with a sneer. "You expect me to believe you're out here all alone?"

Her shoulders squared. "Why not? You ever heard of me backing down from anything?"

One of the riders laughed. The rest shook their heads.

"Besides," Dawsey continued in a voice closer to Ellie's than Ellie's. "It's a free country, ain't that right?"

One of the deputies pushed back his hat and leered. "Suppose we take you with us? Hold you until Hooper turns himself in?"

Without a trace of visible fear, she swayed her hips toward him. "Suppose Hooper sends Henry and his men to fetch me?"

The man eased back in the saddle. The others cast nervous glances. Hooper could've whittled their fear with Pa's carving knife.

A challenge in her eyes, Dawsey hooked her arm in the colonel's and pulled him toward his coat lying on the ground. Speechless, he let her slide his arms in the sleeves then took the canteen and wadded dish towel she shoved at him. "If you boys will excuse me, I need to get Uncle Jerry on home. Ma's powerful worried about him."

The sheriff nudged up the brim of his hat. "I'll eventually find Hooper and your trouble-making little cousin." He flicked his first two fingers at her. "You tell him that, you hear?"

Pulling the defeated old man by the arm, Dawsey stumbled toward the woods.

"Ellie?" McMillan called, his eyes narrowed with suspicion.

She turned.

"You're going the wrong way."

Cool as springtime, she smiled and pointed. "I reckon I know that. I left my horse over yonder."

The milling men watched her in silence, until she slipped into an oak grove and disappeared.

"She's leaving," Ellie hissed.

Hooper slapped his hand over her mouth and held it there while the posse's last horse faded with a swish of its tail into the far side of the clearing. Pulling her face around, he stared into her wild eyes. "When I take my hand away, you don't talk. Just listen. Is that clear?"

She nodded.

He let go of her mouth, pressing a finger against her lips one last time for safe measure. "We'll circle around and cut her off," he whispered.

She nodded.

Tugging her sleeve, Hooper sprang off the ground.

They ran as fast as they could and still move with stealth. Passing the thicket where they'd left Pa and Duncan, they found them gone.

His heart lifted when he spotted them standing with Dawsey in the brush. The sight of Duncan's arms around her pierced his heart, but not as much as her red nose and wet cheeks.

The colonel had sunk to the ground, staring straight ahead. Pa squatted next to him, concern lining his face.

As he reached Dawsey, Hooper softly called her name.

She turned and melted against him, furiously wiping her tears. "Oh, Hooper, I was so frightened."

Chest heaving, his arms slid around her. "Then why, Dawsey? You could've told them everything and been on your way home. Why did you face down those men?"

"I had to." She lifted swollen eyes. "I wasn't afraid for me."

CHAPTER 46

Dawsey stared through the bars on Dilsey's window, watching her and Silas warming in a bright patch of sunlight. They sat as straight as posts and as solemn as death on a bench seat next to the corncrib. She watched their lips, trying to read them, but couldn't make out a single word. By their somber expressions, she gathered Tiller had yet to come home.

"Every day a mother's son disappears in Bear Swamp."

Hooper's words floated up from her memory. Hearing him speak of such things had broken her heart at the time. Witnessing the loss firsthand brought terrible pain.

Silas had grasped his knees and mourned when he learned Tiller wasn't with Dawsey. "Oh, Lord, let the Guard have him, and not the gators," he'd wailed.

A sick look on his face, Hooper assured him that Tiller would turn up by morning.

Dawsey glanced at the sky. By the position of the sun, she'd slept right through morning with no sign of poor Tiller.

Her father, hunkered behind Dilsey on the way to the cabin the night before, had ranted at Dawsey about her betrayal most of the way. Too tired to try to appease him, she'd let him vent his rage.

Before he would step one foot inside Dilsey's room, Dawsey had to swear on her mother's grave to go home with him as soon as possible. He vowed never to sleep another night under a McRae roof and had kept his word by raving like a lunatic all night. By dawn, he finally succumbed to exhaustion and curled on Dawsey's mat where he still lay.

The door creaked open, streaming afternoon sunlight on the mud-tracked floor. Odell peeked inside holding a steaming tray. "You're awake, I see."

Taking the welcome food, Dawsey glanced toward her father. "I'd like for him to rest as long as possible." She didn't bother confessing that his welfare wasn't her only concern. She dreaded reliving his fury.

"Sorry, child." Odell ducked her head and grimaced. "Is he all right?"

Dawsey sighed. "As well as can be expected, but he's very angry with me."

"I can imagine." Odell patted her back. "Don't fret, honey. He'll come around. We'll make him understand." She turned to go but paused on the doorstep. "Will you tell us when he wakes up? Silas is so anxious to talk to him he's jumping right out of his skin." Her eyes softened. "He wants to apologize." She made a face. "Again."

For all the good it will do him, Dawsey thought. She smiled. "Of course, I'll call you."

Odell ducked back in. "Are you sure you want this door unlocked?"

"I promised him," Dawsey said. "Besides, he's not going anywhere." She cautiously approached the mat on the floor and leaned to see her father's face, cringing when he stiffened.

"I'm awake," he growled at the wall. "No one could sleep through all that mindless chatter."

Dawsey perched on the edge of the bed, her hands folded. "I plan to keep my word, Father. Just as soon as you're strong enough, Duncan will take us home."

He grunted.

"Do you think you'll ever forgive me?"

He lay so still and quiet, her heart raced with fear. Was it possible he wouldn't?

She refused to accept it. "Father, I—"

"Your mother took her own life, Dawsey."

The room swirled as his words sunk in, hateful words hurled in anger.

In her mind, she leaped to her feet, denial on her lips, but her shaky legs wouldn't hold her. "You're lying."

Father turned over and sat up, running his hands through his tousled hair. "Am I?" He waved his hand. "She didn't take too many pills or shoot herself. That would be too vulgar. She knew deliberate suicide was wrong, might cancel her ticket to heaven."

"Then she didn't—"

"She let nature do the dirty deed for her." He released a bitter laugh. "All it took was neglecting her medicine, not following the doctor's orders."

Tears flowed down his cheeks. "Margaret claimed she didn't believe in suicide. She swore she'd never do such a thing, but she lied." He clutched his forehead, his lips trembling. "Your mother simply sat down and died, Dawsey. She may as well have placed a gun to her head."

She longed to comfort him. Instead, she wrung her useless hands and let him cry out his heartbreak. When he quieted and raised his head, she whispered, "Why?"

The peaceful release on his face disappeared. He pointed toward the door. "Your beloved McRaes. There's your reason."

"Mother decided to die because Silas took Dilsey?"

"Yes." He glared at her from the floor until a shadow crossed his face. Glancing away, he repeated the answer with more force. "Yes, because they took our baby."

Dawsey watched him closely. "There's something you're not telling me."

His bottom jaw worked while he tried to hold on to his anger. Dawsey waited until he lifted sad eyes. "Your mother lived with terrible pain, arthritis in her joints. The disease led to other things—fevers, lung infections, weak blood." He sighed. "She suffered greatly, mostly because she couldn't care for her girls."

Deeply troubled, Dawsey stood and crossed to the window. "I had no idea."

Odell had joined her family outside, lightening the mood past the window.

"Your mother wouldn't want you to know," Father said. "She was determined to withstand all of it for your sakes."

The contrast between the carefree teasing outside the room and the tragedy unfolding inside tore at Dawsey's heart. She felt suspended between two worlds, two separate realities.

"When Silas McRae took Dilsey, the stress was too much. Your mother gave up the fight." Father's voice hardened. "What sort of person is capable of such a thing?"

Dawsey turned and reached out her hand. "Come here, please."

Father frowned. "What?"

"Come over here. I want to show you something."

Grumbling, he struggled to his feet and joined her at the window. Outside, Odell stood behind Dilsey, smoothing her long curls into a horse's tail with loving hands. Pulling her head back, she leaned to plant a kiss on her forehead.

Silas said something and Dilsey whirled, wide mouthed with laughter, to punch his arm.

Grabbing her hand, he tugged her onto his lap. Dilsey wrapped him in a tight hug, kissing both his cheeks, then rested her head on his shoulder.

Dawsey pointed. "That sort of person, I suppose."

He stared, his darting eyes taking in the loving scene.

"You have every right to be angry that Silas took Dilsey from her crib that night." She clenched her fists. "I'm angry, too, but it happened, and we have to be grateful her life turned out so well. It could've been far worse."

Father glanced her way. "You mean if they'd been harsh and cruel?"

Fighting tears, Dawsey shook her head. "If she'd been the one left behind." She spun away from the window and sailed out the door, running straight into Duncan's waiting arms.

Rounding the shed with a headless chicken in each hand, Hooper stopped so fast his boot heels plowed twin rows.

Duncan stood at the bottom of Ellie's steps, holding Dawsey against his chest.

Stunned, Hooper watched his conniving brother lead her gently away. He hurried closer to watch where they were going.

Halfway along the path, Duncan pulled aside a low branch and they ducked into the woods.

Blistering, bottomless fury rose inside his chest. Duncan had tried to shame him for loving Dawsey, as if his feelings were dishonorable, when all the time he had plans of his own.

"You squeeze those birds any tighter, they'll squawk."

Loosening his grip, Hooper glanced down at the dangling necks and exhaled some of his rage. "I'd pay to see that trick."

Mama waltzed closer and touched his arm. "You're flushed. What's ailing you, son?"

He handed her the chickens. "Better get these plucked."

Careful of the claws on the gnarled toes, she gathered their legs into one hand and pulled at his sleeve with the other. "Walk with me?"

Hooper dutifully fell into step beside her.

Ma seemed to smile at a private joke. "Back there, you looked ready to do some plucking yourself. Whose feathers are you gunning for?"

"I wouldn't stop at feathers," he said. "I'd go ahead and skin him, too."

"What did Duncan do now?"

He waved her question aside. "Can I ask you something, Ma?"

They reached the tub of hot water and she dunked the hapless chickens. "Ask me anything you want. I'll decide if I want to answer."

His face warmed. "Do you reckon it would seem, I don't know. . . indecent for Duncan and me to court Dawsey?"

Ma pulled in her lips then released them. "One thing's certain, both at once would be highly improper."

"All right, then." He rested his hands on his hips. "Would it be wrong for me to court Dawsey?"

She gazed at him, the picture of innocence. "What do you think?"

He jutted his chin. "Is that your way of saying yes?"

"Dawsey's a wonderful person." Yanking a handful of feathers, she tossed them behind her. "So is your sister."

Hooper's heart sank at the comparison.

"They're a lot alike—both loyal, honest, and hardworking."

Sighing, he held up his hand. "I see where you're going."

"Do you?" She laid aside the first bird and fished for the second. "I said alike, Hooper, but not the same girl."

Ma stood, shaking water from her hands. "It's all right to choose a mate who reminds you of a loved one, a person who bears traits you admire in, say, a mother or a sister." She shrugged. "I reckon we all do it. Your papa has always reminded me of my own dear pa. They have the same kind eyes and tender ways."

It was true, though he'd never noticed until she said so.

"Besides," she added grinning. "In most things those two girls are like night and day."

A weight lifted from around Hooper's heart. Avoiding her hands, covered with stink, he leaned to kiss her cheek. "Excuse me, ma'am, but I've got a rooster to pluck."

She caught his sleeve. "You don't need to fret over Duncan's flashy feathers. I've seen how Dawsey looks at you." Her smiling face turned grim. "It's that tough old bird in Ellie's room who might pose a problem. Even with your winsome ways, how will you ever sway the colonel?"

Ellie knocked at the door of her bedroom and waited to hear the colonel's muffled reply. Peeking inside, she found him slumped at the edge of the bed, his hands clasped in front of him. "Can we come in?"

Hope sparked in his eyes. "Is Dawsey with you?"

She shook her head. "Just me and Pa."

His body swiveled to the wall. "I don't want to see him."

Ellie motioned for Papa to wait. Moving soundlessly across the floor, she knelt in front of the colonel. "He's really keen to apologize. I wish you'd heard him out last night."

The colonel sniffed like he smelled something bad. "I have no interest in his apology."

Ellie sighed. "I can see you're awful mad, sir. I don't reckon a single soul could blame you." She fell back and sat on her heels. "I know his words won't bring back the chance to raise me like you done Dawsey."

"A job I failed miserably."

She tilted her head. "Huh?"

"Never mind." Swatting his words, he turned his head to watch her. "Go on."

"I was trying to say that I got powerful mad, too, when I heard."

He scooted closer. "You did?"

"Why, sure. Until Dawsey, I had nothing but two stinking brothers. What are they good for when you get right down to it, except teaching you how to hunt and track."

She paused for a breath. "Don't get me wrong, I love Hooper and Duncan an awful lot, but they ain't worth spit at girl stuff."

The colonel smiled. "I don't suppose they are."

"I always wanted a sister." She stared dreamily at the ceiling. "Not many folks can brag about having a twin, so I figure I got cheated out of a lot of years of boasting."

He perked up. "Are you saying you wish Silas had left you with us?"

She gasped and held up her hands. "Oh no, sir. I could never wish for a thing like that."

He scowled. "What then? Do you wish he'd taken Dawsey, too?"

She settled to her behind and crossed her legs. "How could I ask you to part with Dawsey? She belonged with you just like I belong here."

"That's not true," he said with a long face. "You belonged with us."

Ellie shrugged. "Once you bust a watermelon, you can't put it back the way it was, but it's still awful sweet."

He huffed. "A stolen melon may be sweet, but it deprived the rightful owner." He shook his finger. "You were meant to bring pleasure to the Wilkes family, not the McRaes."

"Now, Colonel, don't go twisting my words." She cocked her head. "You wouldn't drop a melon on purpose, would you? You'd place it on the table and cut it nice."

He nodded.

"What Pa done left us without pretty slices." She raised her brows. "Do we throw the whole thing away or take pleasure in the scattered pieces?"

Tears flooded Ellie's eyes, and she swiped them away. "Don't you see? I don't count it an accident that we all came together at last. I thank Dawsey's God every day for helping me find her." Sniffing, she wiped her nose on her sleeve. "And for giving me the chance to know you." She ducked her head. "If you don't mind, that is."

The colonel lowered himself to the floor and stretched his trembling hands to her. "Come here, child."

She scooted close and laid her head against his shoulder while he rocked her.

"I have a lot of this sort of thing to make up for." His sigh seemed to rise from the depths of his soul. "Not just with you, I'm afraid. I've been sinfully negligent at showing Dawsey how precious she is to me."

"Dawsey loves you."

He rubbed her back. "I suppose she does." Ducking to look at her, he made a face. "I can assure you I don't deserve it."

Heart pounding, Ellie sat up and gripped his arms. "Please don't put my pa in jail, Colonel Wilkes. I can't tell you how much we need him."

He went stiff and his jaw tightened.

Ellie's pleading eyes held his gaze. "What he did happened a long time ago. He ain't the same man he was then." She pressed closer to study his angry, darting eyes. "No more than you are."

His rigid chin relaxed. Staring over her head, he chewed the side of his mustache.

She waited as long as she could then waved her hand over his face. "Are you all right, Colonel?"

He blinked, his gaze wandering to hers. "Help an old man off the floor, will you?"

She stood and pulled him to his feet.

The colonel straightened his shirt and smoothed his silver hair. "I'm not sure I'll ever be ready to hear the man's apology." He patted her shoulder. "For your sake, I'll hold off on any charges."

Squealing, she wheeled for the door.

"Dilsey?"

She turned.

"Is there any chance you'll come home with us to Fayetteville? I can't make up for the years you lost, but I'll spend the rest of my days trying."

"Scuffletown is my home, sir. It's part of me." She shrugged. "If I was younger, things might be different, but. . .you understand, don't you?"

The corners of his mouth drooped, and the hopeful light left his eyes. "Of course, dear. I suppose I'm still trying to patch that melon."

"You'll come for my wedding, won't you?"

He leaned back, a stunned haze in his eyes. "You're getting married?"

She nodded.

"Do you love him?"

Her cheeks warmed. "I reckon I do."

The colonel rubbed his temples with the tips of his fingers. "Ah, Dilsey, I've missed out on so much." He sighed. "Might I hope that you'll visit on occasion? I'm sure your aunt Lavinia would love to meet you."

Ellie's heart fluttered. Seeing firsthand the life she might've had was an option she hadn't considered. "I think I'd like that very much."

She turned to go, but he held up his hand. "Tell Dawsey we're leaving first thing in the morning."

Her shoulders slumped. "So soon?"

"It's long past time." He smiled. "I have years of heartache to mend."

Chapter 47

Dawsey wiped her eyes on Duncan's handkerchief. "We'd best get back to the house now. They'll be looking for us." She touched his hand. "Thank you for listening to me whine. It seems you're always rescuing me."

Embarrassed to admit her jealous self-pity, she'd never mentioned why she was crying. Being a gentleman, he hadn't asked.

"Anytime you need a shoulder, honey, I'm your man." He gazed at her boldly, and the intimacy in his look brought a rush of warmth to Dawsey's cheeks.

"Thank you, Duncan. That's very kind of you." She presented her face for inspection. "Is my nose red?"

He grinned. "Like a holly berry."

Surprising herself, she laughed. "Oh you." Dawsey peered at him from under damp lashes.

Though Duncan was seldom serious about anything, no one could cheer her heart like him. From her first frightened day locked in Dilsey's room, the sweet, gentle man had been a comfort.

She wondered again why she felt so irresistibly drawn to Hooper when he made her feel the opposite of comfortable and safe, especially when she imagined what he'd done to those men in the swamp.

"Are you lost, brother?"

Her shudder leaped into startled dread at Hooper's voice.

He stood just inside the little clearing, his white-fisted hands gripping his suspenders and a cocky smile on his face. "You're a little turned around, I guess." He pointed over his shoulder. "The cabin's that way." Without an invitation, he sauntered closer. "Not that I blame you. I suppose Dawsey's smile has you blinded, but don't let her dimples muddle your mind. Pa would pitch a right fit if he caught you two spooning in the woods."

Dawsey shot to her feet. "How dare you?"

His anxious gaze flickered her way, but his anger with Duncan won out. "But then, you couldn't be spooning, could you, brother? Not when Dawsey reminds you so much of Ellie."

Duncan stood, his stance defiant. "All right, I admit it. She's nothing like Ellie. Dawsey makes a man want to shield her from all the evil in the world."

Hooper sneered. "You can start by protecting her from yourself."

Thrusting out his chin, Duncan poked Hooper's chest with his knuckle. "I aim to court her."

"Court her?" Hooper snorted. "I aim to marry her."

Dawsey gasped. "Stop it, both of you." Whirling, she ran for the trail.

Hooper caught up with her and spun her around. "Don't go, honey. We need to talk."

She ducked her head. "There's nothing to talk about."

"I meant what I said back there," Hooper said, twirling her away as Duncan snatched at her.

Duncan danced and bobbed, trying to see her better. "I want to marry you, too, Dawsey. I'm fairly certain of it."

Eyes veiled with passion, Hooper lifted her chin and pressed his lips to the corner of her mouth. "Say you'll be my wife, Dawsey," he whispered, just a warm breath away. "I love you with all of my heart."

Love for him surged in her chest, nudging her closer. She longed to say yes while her mind scrambled for strength to resist him. *"Deliver me, O Lord, from the evil man: preserve me from the violent man."*

As if sensing he couldn't compete with the strong feelings passing between them, Duncan hung back gaping in disbelief.

Dawsey's deliverance came in the form of footsteps, running up the trail behind them. She turned her head to watch Dilsey sail past, slowing when she caught sight of them.

She veered and hurried their way, her brows drawn into a frown. "Ma said I might find you down here." A puzzled look crossed her face. "What's wrong? You all look like you're choking on something."

Pulling free from Hooper's grip, Dawsey shook her head. "We're fine. Is something wrong at the house?"

She nodded. "Mama just noticed that Tiller's things are gone."

Hooper walked to meet her. "Everything?"

"His clothes, shoes, and Mama's gunnysack to put them in." She jerked her head toward the house. "She wants us there when she tells Pa."

Hooper nodded grimly. "We'll come right now."

Her eyes lit up and she clutched his sleeve. "There's good news, too. The colonel said he won't bring charges against Pa."

Duncan let out a *whoop* that echoed in the treetops.

Hooper beamed and hugged her close. "Are you sure?"

"He told me himself."

A jostling brother on each side, Dilsey started up the rise.

Duncan paused to cast a sheepish glance at Dawsey. She lowered her eyes, so he loped on without her.

Hooper, his mind firmly on the trouble at the house, wrapped his arm around Dilsey and never looked back. A little offended after his heartfelt proposal, Dawsey followed in a sulk.

She caught up with them near the porch, and Dilsey turned with a troubled frown. "I almost forgot. The colonel said to tell you it's time to go. His mind is set to leave in the morning."

Hooper stopped walking so fast he nearly toppled his sister. He caught Dawsey's arm and studied her face, his eyes full of questions.

With her heart on fire, she pulled away and angled past him, up the steps.

The family crowded around the table while Ellie broke her happy news. "The colonel practically promised me. He meant it, too. I could tell."

Dawsey smiled at her. "If Father said he wouldn't bring charges, he meant it."

Papa had grateful tears in his eyes. "I'm indebted to the colonel for his kindness, though I know I don't deserve it." His chest rose and fell. "I just wish he'd let me apologize."

Ellie's heart ached for him. "Maybe someday, Pa."

Mama stood in the corner, wringing a dish towel nearly to shreds. At Hooper's nod, she stepped forward and cleared her throat. "I don't mean to spoil the happy news, Silas, but I brought us together for a different reason."

One look at her face brought him to his feet. "What is it, wife?"

She waved him away. "Sit down. I can't talk with you hanging on me."

Pa sat, but he squared his chair around and didn't take his eyes off her.

Fidgeting with the ragged edges of the towel, she smiled, but it looked painful. "It's good news and bad, darlin'. Which do you want first?"

He cocked his brow. "I'm surprised at you for asking. I favor good over bad any day."

"Tiller's not lost in the swamp," she blurted.

Papa took a minute to soak up her words. Braying like a mule, he reared back and clapped his hands so sharply it rang Ellie's ears. "This is a fine day, Odie McRae." He beamed toward Ellie. "First the colonel grants me a pardon, and now I get my boy back. Where is the scalawag? We need to go bring him home."

Her throat working furiously, Ma's pleading gaze sought Hooper.

He stepped forward and touched Pa's shoulder. "That's the bad news. Tiller's gone. He left us."

Papa's eyelids fluttered. "Say again?"

"Gone, sir. Likely for good. He took all his things."

Braver now, Mama supplied more details. "He even took his Christmas presents. Packed everything in a gunnysack. Stole some food, too."

"That little rodent," Duncan said. "He had it planned all along."

Pa's face sagged with the sadness Ellie had dreaded. "It's my fault. I told him I meant to send him back to his ma."

Duncan whistled. "Tiller would do most anything to keep that from happening."

Mama swatted him with her dish towel. "You ain't helping."

Hooper squatted in front of Pa's chair. "Don't let it burden you so. You had no way of knowing."

Pa raised haunted eyes. "Still, I shouldn't have told him something I didn't mean."

Ellie jumped at a knock on the door.

"Are we expecting company?" Hooper asked, standing and reaching for the gun at his waist.

Duncan leaned to peek through the boarded window. "It's all right. It's Boss"—he looked again—"and Wyatt."

Ellie's heart took a breathtaking leap. She hadn't seen Wyatt for days—her face warmed—not since they'd kissed.

Duncan swung the door open on Boss's lanky body, slouched against the side post. "Afternoon, folks."

Wyatt's head ducked in, his eyes sweeping the room for Ellie. When he found her, his broad smile said he'd missed her.

She tried to say the same with her answering grin.

"I've brought some good news and bad," Boss said in his relaxed drawl.

Duncan chuckled. "Seems to be the day for it."

"The good first," Ellie called, watching Papa. "We could use some just now."

Mama took off her apron. "Where are your manners, children? Invite them inside first."

Beaming like a simpleton, Duncan bowed and waved them in.

Wyatt didn't wait for a second invitation. He scooted past Boss and worked his way around the room to stand by Ellie. Hidden behind their legs, his groping fingers found her hand and held on. He leaned to whisper, his breath warm in her ear, "I've got a special surprise for you."

"Later," she murmured, fighting a grin.

Boss took off his hat. "Miss Wilkes," he said to Dawsey, "I was glad to hear they found you in one piece."

"Thank you," she said. "It felt good to be found."

Ellie squirmed with impatience. "What's your news, Boss?"

Mama shot her a frown. "Mind your manners, girl."

Boss laughed and winked at Ellie. "All right then, the good first." His merry gaze swung to her parents. "Folks, I think you've seen the last of your troubles with the sheriff."

Papa leaned forward in his chair. "How's that, son?"

"Because Henry. . ." Boss stared at the floor by Papa's feet, his long fingers fumbling with his hatband. "Let's just say Henry *borrowed* the sheriff's wife overnight. Sent her home with a stern message about what fine fellows the McRaes are." He glanced up. "From what I hear, McMillan will give your boys a wide berth from now on."

Duncan broke the stillness with a rousing howl.

The family cheered and passed grateful hugs all around, a happy uproar that Wyatt used to his benefit. He pulled Ellie close and planted a thrilling kiss on her neck then stood back as blameless as a lamb.

Dawsey's mouth stood ajar. "That poor woman. She must've been frightened out of her wits."

His eyes shining with happy tears, Hooper patted her back. "Don't worry. They didn't lock her in a shed." He smiled. "The only frightening thing inside Henry's house is Rhoda's coffee."

The men hooted, Boss, the loudest of all.

Dawsey scowled. "Still, it doesn't seem right."

Papa tilted his head up at her with a thoughtful look. "You're dead-on, honey, and this family won't waste the turn of fortune that came at her expense." He shook his finger in Hooper's face. "From now on, we'll show our thanks to the sheriff's wife by staying out of trouble. Is that clear?"

Hooper nodded. "Yes, sir. I'll do my best."

Papa pinned Boss with wary eyes. "Let's get on with the bad news. I'd like to get it behind me so I can celebrate."

The weight of a serious matter smoothed the jolly lines on Boss's face. He cleared his throat. "It's about Tiller."

A hush fell over the room. Ellie wished just once that the news could stop at good.

"What now?" Hooper asked.

Boss nodded at Wyatt. "You want to tell them?"

Wyatt looked grim. "My brother's gone, too, Mr. Silas. Packed up his things and took off for the Natchez Trace. I reckon Nathan took Tiller and the other boys with him."

Papa stood on shaky legs and crossed the room. "How do you know that's where they're headed?"

Wyatt's fingers slipped away from Ellie's hand. "They heard about the looting along the Trace, and the brainless whelps figured on making a quick fortune. It's all they've talked about for weeks." He shrugged. "I chalked it up to bold talk. Never expected them to try it."

Pa seemed so wobbly, Ellie and Wyatt led him back to his chair and eased him down.

Ellie's heart caught when Wyatt hung his head. "I'm dreadful sorry, sir."

"Don't be," Pa said. "You're not to blame for my foolhardy nephew. Or for your reckless brother. You tried hard to turn him around." He slapped his leg. "Blast it! I dared to hope I might set Tiller on the straight and narrow. Instead he chose a violent path to destruction."

"That's right," Hooper said. "Tiller made his choice. There's nothing we can do about it now."

"Yes, there is," Dawsey cut in, wiping her eyes. "We can pray every day that he'll realize his mistake and come home."

Chapter 48

Ma's distress over Papa wearied Hooper to watch. She hovered around him most of the day, concern etched deep in her face. During supper, she stayed so busy pouring water in his cup and dishing ladles filled with seconds on his plate, she hardly took a bite herself. Tuckered out from fretting over him all day, she insisted they turn in early.

After she ushered him into their room and shut the door, Hooper took his coffee and went outside to watch the sunset.

Dawsey looked up from where she sat on the edge of the porch then lowered her gaze to her fidgety hands. Most likely for the colonel's sake, she'd traded Ellie's britches for one of Mama's too-short dresses, so she tugged on the skirt, trying in vain to cover her bare ankles.

Hiding a grin, he swung down beside her. "It's too quiet tonight. Where is everybody?"

She wouldn't meet his eyes. "Duncan's in the barn, I think, preparing the wagon for tomorrow. Dilsey and Wyatt took a walk. My father turned in early to rest up for our trip." She finally looked at him. "He suggested I do the same."

Hooper cocked his head. "You're not tired?"

"A little." Her gazed wandered the yard, from the shed and chicken coop on the right to the grove of sugar maples on the left, their trunks black with last spring's oozing sap. "I'm trying to take it all in. It's the last time I'll see this yard."

"It doesn't have to be."

She jerked her head to the side, her fingers gripping the porch so hard her knuckles turned white.

Blast it, Hooper. Slow down. "Say, that reminds me." He rummaged in the drawstring pouch at his waist and fished out a branch, clusters of holly berries still clinging to their stems. He handed it over. "This one somehow escaped Ma's broom." He smiled. "I thought you might like to have it, to remember our picnic in the grove."

His heart soared when she ducked her head and smiled. "We had a lovely day."

Hooper swallowed hard and reached for her hand.

She tensed but didn't draw away.

"I'll never forget your song about holly trees and the babe born to die. The story it told will set a man to thinking. I'd like to hear more someday."

Her head jerked up. "Would you really?"

Heat spread up his neck, but he nodded.

Dawsey studied him, a puzzled look in her eyes. "You're two men at once, Hooper McRae. Did you know that?"

He grinned and shook his head.

"One of you is charming and tender, like you were that day." She took a deep breath. "Like you are now."

He tucked his chin. "And the other?"

"The other is harsh and cruel, and too frightening to be around."

The bitter edge to her voice brought his head up. "That's how you see me?"

She squared around to face him. "You have to control your passions, Hooper. It's not wrong to defend your people, but it is wrong to lose yourself in the process."

"I disagree, Dawsey. Some things are important enough to die for."

She stood, her eyes flashing fire. "And to kill for?"

Why was she so angry? Hooper squinted up at her, his head spinning. "If it came to that."

Bright red blotches appearing on her cheeks, she shook her finger in his face. "There, you see? That's why I can never marry you." Though the end of Mama's dress fell far shy of the ground, Dawsey lifted the hem and sailed around the side of the house.

Hooper rested his arms on his knees and glared across the yard. It seemed whichever way he turned, she wound up mad at him. He wracked his mind to understand where he'd gone wrong.

Beginning to think the problem lay with Dawsey's temper and not his own, he picked up the holly branch she'd flung to the porch and twirled it between his fingers. She believed in a babe born to die for those He loved, yet Hooper's willingness to do the same angered her. The hardheaded woman made no sense, and he'd run short of time to sort her out. At dawn, she would climb aboard a rig bound for Fayetteville—unless he found a way to stop her.

Dread crowded his throat. Even worse, she'd sit next to Duncan the whole way. With Hooper's recent turn of luck, his simpering brother could return home engaged to the woman he loved.

He dashed the twig to the ground and pushed off the porch. Dawsey Wilkes said she could never marry him, but he knew different. Whatever it took, he'd make sure she saw things his way.

Dawsey charged around the back corner of the cabin, her eyes welling. Dilsey sat on the bottom step of her room, her upturned face glowing with pent-up bliss.

The news her sister waited to share could be only one thing, and Dawsey wouldn't spoil it. Her throat tight with pain, she blinked back her tears and smiled. "Goodness, you look like a child at Christmas." She laughed. "A bit late for Yuletide glee, aren't you? Or awfully early."

A tiny frown crept over Dilsey's forehead, marring her look of perfect joy. "You look like you're ready to cry. Is something wrong?"

Dawsey smoothed her skirt and sat, forcing a big smile to her face. "Of course not. I gazed too long at the setting sun perhaps." She clutched her sister's hands. "Now, tell me what's made you so happy."

Before Dilsey could answer, Dawsey drew back with a surprised little cry and gaped at her finger. "Oh honey, what's this?"

Dilsey's happy grin transformed her. "Wyatt gave me a betrothal ring."

"So I see."

"He rode clear to Charlotte to have it made special."

"Ah." Dawsey nodded. "That's why we haven't seen him around."

Dilsey held up her hand to admire the gold band. "It's a poesy ring. That means there's something written inside."

"Yes, I know. What does it say?"

"Just my name and some pretty words." She blushed and squirmed. "It says, 'Ellie.' I hope you don't mind. That's the only thing Wyatt knows to call me."

Dawsey scooted closer. "Of course I don't mind." She cupped Dilsey's chin. "In fact, I've been meaning to start calling you Ellie myself—since you prefer it."

Dilsey's long lashes, the matched set to Dawsey's own, swept her cheeks. "I wouldn't prefer it one bit." She glanced up shyly. "Not coming from you."

"Are you sure?"

Dilsey bit her lip and nodded.

Dawsey laughed. "All right then. Dilsey it is."

"If we have that settled, can I ask a favor?"

"Of course," Dawsey said.

She wiggled the ring off. "Will you keep this safe for me?"

Dawsey took it from between her fingers. "You're taking it off?"

"Wyatt hasn't asked Papa for my hand yet. He meant to on Christmas, before those men shot up the place."

Dawsey grinned. "He's not good at keeping a secret, is he?"

Laughter bubbled out from Dilsey. "It was burning a hole in his pocket." She sobered and closed her hand over Dawsey's fist. "I wouldn't trust another soul with this ring."

Warmth stole over Dawsey's heart. "That means the world to me." She tilted her head. "You do remember I'm leaving tomorrow?"

She nodded. "Wyatt's planning to ask Pa right after breakfast. I'll put it on once he says yes."

"You're awfully sure he will."

"Pa likes Wyatt as much as I do." She giggled. "Well, almost."

Pushing down a wave of jealousy, Dawsey bit back a sigh. Even if she could allow herself to be with someone as dangerous and explosive as Hooper, her father would sooner die than give his blessing.

Dilsey wrapped both arms around her neck. "I wish you wouldn't leave. I'll miss you something fierce."

Smoothing her hair, Dawsey's grateful heart whispered thanks to God for the gift of a sister. "I'll miss you, too, terribly, but we'll see each other often."

Dilsey sat up. "Will you come for my wedding? And bring the colonel?"

"I wouldn't miss your wedding for anything. I'm sure Father will feel the same." She offered a wry smile. "As long as he doesn't have to speak to your father."

Developing a sudden interest in the tattered hole in her britches, Dilsey bent to pick at the fraying threads stretched across her knee. "You don't have to go at all, if you don't want to."

Angling her head to watch her sister's face, Dawsey frowned. "Of course I do."

Still pulling at strings, she wagged her head. "Not if you and Hooper—"

Dawsey's hand came up. "I don't want to talk about him."

Dilsey scowled. "Why not?"

"He terrifies me."

"Dawsey Wilkes! Hooper would never lay a hand on you."

"That's not what scares me." Feeling helpless, she decided to trust her sister. "None of this is easy for me. I've fallen in love with Hooper. Leaving him is breaking my heart."

Dilsey clutched her hands. "Then don't go. Hooper can't hide how he feels about you. I've seen it all over his face."

The tears Dawsey had denied earlier welled again. "We both know what Hooper did to those men in the swamp. Every time I look at his hands, I'll remember." Her stomach quivered and she felt sick. "I can't live with him, knowing what he's capable of."

Dilsey withdrew. "We don't know what happened out there."

"What he said left little doubt." Dawsey pressed her fingers to her temples. "He practically confessed it again just now."

Glaring, Dilsey stood up ramrod straight. "If Hooper did something bad, it was to protect our ma. It's the way things are in Scuffletown. We got no choice."

Dawsey rose, too. "Well, it's savagery, and it's not how things are done in Fayetteville."

Red in the face, Dilsey stalked toward the house. At the corner, she spun on her heels and came back. "Then why did the colonel come here looking for blood? If we hadn't locked him up, my pa would be just as dead as those men in the swamp."

Dawsey's mouth fell open. She sputtered, struggling for something to say.

Dilsey jutted her hip. "You want to be careful casting judgment. In the same fix, you might be just as capable as Hooper." She thrust out her hand. "Give me my ring."

Words wouldn't come to Dawsey's defense. She dropped the gold band in Dilsey's outstretched palm and watched her flounce away.

Hooper caught Ellie's arm as she swept by the porch. "Slow down, squirt. Are your britches on fire?"

She fell against him, trembling. "Oh, Hooper."

Alarm shot through him. "What happened?"

"It's Dawsey." She clenched her fist and brought it down on his chest. "She makes me so mad."

He led her to the steps and sat her down. "What happened? I just saw you two hugging and laughing."

"You watched us?"

"For a minute. I was waiting to talk to her, but"—he lifted Ellie's chin with his finger—"I saw you waving that ring around and decided my business could wait."

She held it up for him to see. "Don't tell Pa. Wyatt hasn't asked him yet."

Smiling, he placed his finger to his lips. "Our secret. Now tell me why we're mad at Dawsey?"

"You're mad at her, too?"

He tightened his lips. "Some days I could strangle her."

Ellie's eyes widened, and she peered behind them. "Whatever you do, don't let Dawsey hear you say such a thing."

Hooper drew back frowning. "I didn't mean it, honey. Dawsey knows I'd never hurt her."

"I'm not so sure." Pain flashed in her eyes. "She called us savages, Hooper."

He stared, unable to accept it.

"It's true. She don't understand our Scuffletown ways, and she never will."

"Savages?" The word sounded ugly. "Are you sure?"

Tears streaked Ellie's cheeks. She swiped her nose and nodded.

Hooper kicked at a clod of dirt. "I asked her to marry me." He gave a bitter laugh. "Practically begged her. That makes me a fool if she feels that way about me."

"That's the crazy part. Dawsey loves you. She told me herself. The trouble is she's too stubborn and narrow minded to give in to it. She claims she's afraid of you."

The words Dawsey flung at him rang in his ears. She'd called him harsh, cruel, and frightening.

Ellie fell against him, sobbing in little broken cries. "Let her go back to her fancy life in Fayetteville. She'd never fit in here anyway."

He'd never seen Ellie so hurt. He tightened his arm around her, ready to fight the world for her sake. "That's right, honey." His chest ached, but he forced out the words. "We'll let Dawsey go back where she belongs."

Go ahead, Father. I'll be right along."

"Don't dawdle. We've a long ride ahead." He stiffened beside her then leaned to drop a quick kiss on her cheek. "There," he said, blushing, then hustled out the door.

Surprised, but pleased to the core, Dawsey stared after him, smiling.

She walked to the bed and ran her fingers over the freshly washed and folded stack of clothes loaned to her by Dilsey, while images swirled of her many days spent inside the rustic little room.

In the early days, Odell's chatty visits and Duncan's long talks provided lifelines.

Hooper's bungled apology, one she'd never officially accepted, had forced her to see him in a different light, at least for a time. Her heart ached to go back to those innocent days, before she learned the truth about him.

The most precious recollection was the day Dilsey barged in demanding to know about the life she'd missed. They'd stared at each other in wonder, giggling like children.

Cringing, she sensed God's displeasure. She'd allowed strife to mar the miracle of their reunion, and now she didn't know how to fix things.

Dawsey looked around one last time. She'd come to Scuffletown with nothing more than a ripped blue blanket and a tattered gown. She would leave in a borrowed dress. There was nothing left to take except her memories. Shrugging her empty hands, she crossed to the door and took the steps to the waiting wagon.

She rounded the house, and Duncan smiled at her from the driver's seat. "Morning, Dawsey." His brows drew together. "I hope you feel rested for the trip."

She'd hardly slept at all, and looked it, by his concerned remark. "I'm sure I'll be fine."

"Ma and Pa thought it best to stay inside." He dipped his chin. "For the colonel's sake. They said to tell you good-bye for them."

"Of course." Disappointed, she glanced toward the house. A figure ducked into the shadows beside the window. Somehow, she knew it was Odell.

Duncan held up a bulging dishcloth. "She packed a breakfast for us."

Dawsey nodded and forced a smile. Her traitor heart searched for Hooper but found Dilsey, strolling across the yard leading Father's horse.

"Why thank you, dear," he called as she grew near. "I nearly forgot him."

Dilsey tied the gelding near the tailgate then hurried around to wind both arms around his neck. "I'll miss you, Colonel."

Even Father's stoic demeanor couldn't withstand the force of a Dilsey hug. His stern face melted with surprised pleasure then heart-wrenching pain. "Come see us soon?" His deep voice wavered. "Won't you?"

She backed away and nodded. "I promise. Good-bye, sir."

The lump in Dawsey's throat grew unbearable. "Dilsey, come here, please. I need to speak to you."

With trembling chin and clenched fists, her sister looked up for the barest second before she spun and bolted.

"Dilsey!" She raised the hem of her skirt to run after her, but Hooper appeared from behind the shed and drew her out of sight.

Blinded by tears, she allowed Father to help her into the wagon.

Patting her hand so hard it stung, he tried to comfort her. "There now, don't fret. The poor little thing couldn't bear to say good-bye is all."

She didn't bother to correct him.

Gazing around the familiar, waterlogged yard, achingly empty without the bright-eyed, laughing McRaes, Dawsey fell back against the seat. "Take me home, please, Duncan. Get us there as fast as you possibly can."

He flicked the reins and Old Abe Lincoln surged forward. The wagon shuddered into motion, each turn of the wheels taking her that much farther from Dilsey and Hooper.

Hooper and Ellie reached the cabin just as Ma and Pa stepped out onto the porch. Shading his eyes against the early sunlight, Hooper watched the swaying wagon reach the end of the lane and turn onto the dirt road.

Every nerve in his body strained to leap on Toby's back and cut them off, to pull Dawsey down from her seat beside Duncan and beg on bended knee for her to stay.

"There she goes," Pa said in a hollow voice, his declaration searing Hooper's heart. "It seems a lifetime ago that she came."

Mama sighed. "Because of her, our lives will never be the same." Her arm slipped around Ellie's waist. "Especially yours, honey. I know you'll miss her."

Before Ellie spun off in a fit of tears, Hooper caught the back of her neck, kneading with gentle fingers. "We'll all miss Dawsey, but some things can't be helped." He tugged Ellie loose from Mama and held her close. "I reckon we'll get past the pain somehow."

Ma shot him a sideways look. "I'd come to hope she might stay in Scuffletown for good."

He shook his head. "It wouldn't have worked out. Dawsey's better off where she's going."

Papa idly drummed his fingers on the rail. "They could at least have stayed through Hogmanay like Dawsey promised. It's only four days away."

"Don't be an old fool, Silas. Your bargain with Dawsey ended the second the colonel arrived. I'm sure she'd rather celebrate the dawn of a new year with her own family."

"And her own kind," Ellie whispered, drawing worried looks from both their folks.

Before they could ply her with questions, a sudden motion in the yard drew their eyes. Hooper tensed, but thankfully, he didn't draw his gun. A young girl, barely ten years old, ran barefoot out of the sugar maple grove and came to stand by the bottom step.

Hooper recognized her, but not by name or face. She could easily belong to any family along the Lumber River. The girl's badge of loyalty was her high cheekbones and straight black hair.

"Mornin'," she called in a clear voice. "All is well?"

Papa smiled and nodded. "All is well, honey."

She darted back to the trees, returning with Henry's wife at her heels.

Weariness marked Rhoda's shuffle, but her eyes darted warily along the far trees until she reached them. Mama hurried inside for an extra chair, but Rhoda waved it aside and stood at the edge of the porch. "I can't stay, Odell. I've come to see Hooper, but I reckon you've all earned the right to hear."

Hooper stepped up and gripped the rail. "Has something happened?"

"Not yet," she said, her eyes veiled. "We don't want you taken by surprise when it does."

Poor Papa groped for his chair and sat. "Go on. Tell us."

Rhoda raised her proud head. "Henry's going away. He's leaving Scuffletown."

Hooper's mouth sagged. With a quick glance, he counted more flycatchers open for business. "What do you mean? For good?"

She nodded. "He's weary. What started as a fight for justice became a bloodbath with no end in sight. The balance between right and wrong shifted on us. We have no peace, day or night."

Rhoda stared over the treetops. "Henry feels, with him gone, things will settle down in Scuffletown. As long as Sheriff McMillan and the Guard are after him, the swamp will run red with bloodshed."

"And you?" Mama asked. "You'll go with him, of course."

She bit her lip. "It's better if I stay. Give Henry his fresh start."

"But honey—"

Rhoda shook her head. "I walked into my marriage with wide-open eyes. I knew what I'd gotten myself into." She sighed. "What's best for Henry is the way it will be." Her haunted eyes turned to Hooper. "I've delivered Henry's message. What I say next comes from me."

He took the steps to the ground. "I'd be proud to hear it."

She touched his arm. "Lay it down, Hooper. You've done all you could for our people without your soul turning black. If Henry's right, things will settle down once he goes." Nodding around at the circle of watchful eyes, she challenged them. "No more fighting and stealing. Do your best to be a good neighbor. Share what you have with those in need. Let's take care of our own." Tears spilled onto her cheek. "Otherwise, I'll lose Henry for nothing."

Hooper gave her a solemn nod.

She smiled through her tears and returned it. With an overhead wave, she led the girl to the grove and slipped from sight.

It had been two weeks, two days, and enough tears to fill the rain barrel since Dawsey rode out of their lives for good. As long as Ellie was awake, the insufferable pain and loneliness stayed with her. Each morning when her eyes opened, she probed her heart for tender spots, praying her grief had lessened. She decided God had hitched a ride with Dawsey, because the hurt stayed the same.

Duncan returned, spouting whimsical stories of the big house in Fayetteville with its immense rooms and towering gables. "The bed was three foot high," he boasted, "with scented sheets and down quilts as soft as a bed of feathers."

"A down quilt *is* a bed of feathers, son," Pa had teased.

When he began to speak in hushed tones about holding the magic lantern, Ellie covered her ears and ran for the shed. Hooper found her there, with Duncan in tow, and pinched the braggart's ear until he begged forgiveness and swore to say no more.

Ellie wasn't used to carrying grief tucked inside. Even Mama's boundless joy in planning her wedding couldn't reach through Ellie's sorrow to help her feel again.

With a heavy heart, she dressed and trudged to the house to help Ma with breakfast. The dark belly of the sky matched her mood but didn't bode well for the swollen creeks and rivers, overfed by yesterday's sheets of rain. Needed or not, they'd see a storm before the eggs were good and scrambled.

Just as predictable, Mama hovered near the counter cutting biscuits, and Papa sat at the table with a cup of coffee.

"Mornin', sunshine."

Mama fired him a warning glance.

"Well, a man can hope, can't he? I miss my Ellie. She's the only hope of sunshine we'll have today."

Mama popped him with a mixing spoon.

He howled and rubbed his arm. With a scowl in her direction, he pushed out the chair next to him. "Come sit by me, Puddin'. Let's you and me come up with some games to play. I reckon we'll be rained in for a spell."

He'd barely finished speaking before the bloated clouds burst with a crash of thunder. The rain battered the boarded window so hard, it sounded like pounded drums.

A war cry sounded from the yard. Seconds later, Hooper and Duncan skidded across the porch and fell through the door laughing.

"By thunder!" Duncan cried. "It's a downpour."

Mama rushed to them with dish towels.

Hooper took one, but Duncan dodged and flicked water in her face.

Mama squealed and chased him in circles. "Come here, you batty boy. You're mussing my floor."

A grin tugged Ellie's lips at their larking about, and she longed to join in. The sight of Hooper, smiling for the first time since Dawsey left, swelled her heart.

"Get over here, boys," Papa called. "You're just in time to help me find a game."

Hooper sat across from him with a somber face. "We'll be playing bob the bounty hunter, if that storm floods the yard."

Pa's cup stopped halfway to his mouth. "What do you mean, son?"

Hooper took a sip of the coffee Ma poured him. "If his body surfaces, he could float right up to the house."

Ellie gaped. "Hooper! How can you joke about such a thing?"

He frowned at her over his cup. "I'm not joking."

Duncan swung into his chair and leaned across the table. "They're in the bog?"

Hooper nodded. "One of them."

Ellie's mouth turned to soot. She forced her tongue from the roof of her mouth. "Where'd you put the other one?"

He glanced at her casually then lifted the dish towel and pilfered a slice of bacon. "I didn't put him anywhere."

Gracious, Hooper! You boast of murder then eat with the same mouth? Her hands clenched in her lap and her stomach felt queasy. Had Dawsey been right all along?

With a quick glace at Ma, standing at the hearth, she lowered her voice. "So you only killed one of them?"

She'd wasted her whisper. Mama's ears were too good. Her skillet hit the floor with a *crash*, and she spun toward the table. "Hooper?"

He lifted his gaze from the spilled eggs and stared back at her. "Yes, ma'am?"

Her eyes and nose turning red, she came toward him, wiping her hands on her apron. "I won't have my hide safe at your expense. Please tell me you didn't kill those men."

He calmly sat back in his chair. "I didn't kill those men."

Ellie barely heard him. "What did you think, Ma? They just decided they wouldn't come back?"

Mama studied the floor with darting eyes. "I just figured Henry took care of them or one of his men." She swiped her mouth with the back of her hand. "Dear Lord, anyone but Hooper."

Hooper stood up so fast, his chair crashed to the floor. "I didn't kill those men!" A deafening peal of thunder put a period on his denial. Lightning flashed, throwing flickering light on their startled faces.

In the silence that followed, bacon sizzled and spilled drops of egg sputtered in the fireplace. Ellie smelled the biscuits burning.

Hooper picked up the chair and plopped it down at the table. "They're dead, but I didn't kill them. No one did."

Ma sagged into her place beside Ellie. "Then how?"

His hand went to his hip and he shook his head. "Like I said, one stumbled into the bog."

Ellie flinched. "You didn't try to save him?"

"I wasn't there. I tracked his footsteps to the quicksand, and none came out the other side. That and his hat floating nearby were enough clues to his fate."

"And the other man?" Ma asked.

He sat down across from her again. "Gators. They smelled the blood and closed in on him. I'd guess he was at the water's edge, washing his wounds."

She moaned. "You're certain?"

Grimacing, he pushed away the plate of bacon. "I had the misfortune to stumble onto their picnic."

Mama stared at her open palms. "I killed him, then. I may as well have baited him and tossed him in the pond."

Hooper leaned to gather her hands. "He met a bad end, but it's not your fault. Those men came out here looking for trouble. They found it with no help from you."

Ellie slung her arm around Ma's shoulders. "Picture his hands tightening on Papa's neck. You had no choice but to pull that trigger."

She shook her head, a hollow look in her eyes. "It's not so, Ellie. He let go of your pa and ran. I shot him out of pure blind rage, and I'll answer to God for my sin."

Papa gripped her wrist. "Don't you mourn over this, Odell McRae. If I'd held the gun, I'd have blasted him myself."

Duncan nodded. "He's right. Any one of us would've done the same."

"If you want to unburden to the Almighty, go ahead," Papa said. "After that, we'll talk no more about it." He released her and gave her a tender smile. "Now go tend my breakfast before it turns to coal."

Ellie watched her go then poured her fury out on Hooper. "All this time I thought you killed them. How could you make me think such a thing?"

He tilted his head. "How could you think it?"

She hit the table with her fist. "Pa asked you what happened to those men, and you said—"

"I said not to ask, because their deaths were gruesome. You chose to think the worst."

She ducked her head.

"Ellie, I might engage someone in a fair fight if he wronged one of you, but I'd never hunt down a defenseless man. You should know that."

Relief flooding her limbs, she ran around the table and wrapped her arms around his neck. "I'm so sorry. It haunted me to think you could do such a thing, even for Ma."

Standing, he returned her hug. "How about showing a little more trust in me?"

She lowered her chin. "I'm not the only one who believed it. Even Dawsey—" She slapped her hand over her mouth. "Oh, Hooper."

He pushed her to arm's length. "What about Dawsey?"

"She thinks you ambushed those men and killed them."

Pain flashed in his eyes. "That's why she's afraid of me?"

Ellie nodded. "I think so."

His hands fell away. "How could she think me so ruthless?" He bit his bottom lip, his throat working. "But then, you all believed it, too."

With a knot forming in the pit of her stomach, Ellie clutched his sleeves. "It was a mix-up, that's all. We thought you confessed. Even then, I found it hard to believe."

"Dawsey didn't." He blinked back his tears. "With the way I've behaved, it's no wonder all of you thought the worst."

The cabin went silent as Hooper stood staring at his feet. With a ragged sigh, he hooked his arm around Ellie's neck. "If it takes the last ounce of my strength, I'm going to win this family's faith in me again."

Papa beamed, and Duncan leaped up to pat Hooper's back. The women crowded around, smothering him with kisses.

"But first"—he drew back and rubbed his chin—"Ellie, I need to borrow Toby. He's young and strong. He'll make good time."

Ellie danced an eager jig. "But I want to go with you. Take Duncan's horse. He's nearly as fast."

Pa looked back and forth between them. "Where are you going, son?"

"I have to go see Dawsey and set things right."

Duncan squirmed. "You can't, Hooper. The colonel said I was welcome anytime, but he wants nothing to do with you and Pa."

"I'll deal with that problem when I get there."

"He'll shoot you on sight."

Hooper pushed up his sleeves. "It's a risk I'll have to take."

"Well, you can't take my horse."

Papa glared. "Why not?"

Duncan slapped the table. "It ain't right," he shouted and wheeled away from them in a sulk.

Papa followed him to the hearth and slid one arm around his shoulders. "I know you fancy Dawsey. If you're honest with yourself, you'll admit you don't love her the way your brother does."

Duncan shrugged his arm off. "Who says I don't?"

"I know my boys," Pa persisted. "It may be winter outside, but in here"—he patted Duncan's chest—"there's a touch of spring fever." He turned Duncan to face him. "Are you prepared to marry Dawsey Wilkes? Give her a home and a passel of babies?"

Duncan dropped his gaze.

"That's what I figured." Pa patted his shoulder. "Unless I need eyeglasses, Dawsey loves Hooper, too. There's not much you can do to change her feelings, so why don't you step out of their way and wish them well?"

Duncan stole a shamefaced glance at Hooper. "Go on and take my horse. He's faster than your old nag."

"Thanks." Hooper grinned. "I'll take good care of him."

Mama worried her dishcloth. "You'll wait until it stops raining, won't you, children?"

Hooper crossed to the window. "It's not going to stop anytime soon, and I can't wait." He glanced over his shoulder at Ellie. "Bring a change of clothes. We're going to get wet."

Papa banged his empty cup. "Nobody's leaving this cabin just yet. I hereby call a McRae family meeting to order." His piercing gaze locked on Hooper. "There's some important business we need to discuss with you, son."

Chapter 51

Fayetteville, North Carolina, January 1872

Dawsey carried a tray holding two cups of chamomile tea into the parlor. Handing one to Aunt Livvy, she kicked off her slippers and curled her legs beneath her in the chair. The rain, relentless throughout the day, still fell against the windows with a comforting murmur. "Do you think it will ever let up, Auntie?"

Her aunt's red-tinged cheeks glowed in the lantern light. "Let it flood if it wants to, dear. Nothing could douse my joy. Each time these old eyes see you again, I praise God afresh." The eyes in question shone with tears. "I had feared you were lost to us forever."

Dawsey swallowed her sip of tea. "I'm sorry you experienced such a trying time. However, I did send word that the McRaes promised to bring me home."

Aunt Livvy's expressive brows dipped and her china rattled as she laid aside her cup. "My milk curdles every time I hear that dreadful name. Lord knows, your father cursed it in blasphemous rants for days." She took a quick breath. "I'm telling you, he turned into a madman."

Dawsey leaned toward her nodding. "When I saw him ride up, sitting tall and sure in the saddle, I couldn't believe my eyes. He'd been so befuddled when I left."

Aunt Livvy swept her hand. "Like the raising of Lazarus. When those awful boys took you, fear and grief drove your father beyond his limits. The more desperate he grew to find you, the stronger and clearer he became—almost like the old Gerrard again."

She sat back, remembering. "The fog lifted from his eyes, replaced by a glint of purpose. Each dawn he saddled his horse and searched for you long into the night."

Dawsey groaned. "Poor Father."

"One morning, a girl no older than twelve appeared on our doorstep. The poor thing was sickly and dirty like one of those pitiful little wretches along the river." She huffed scornfully. "I'm sure it's where he found her, that. . .that. . ." Her finger danced. "Was his name Duncan?"

Dawsey nodded.

Aunt Livvy drew herself up and sniffed. "Whatever his name, he sorely underestimated your father. Gerrard simply paid the girl double to betray her deceitful benefactor. When he left the front stoop with her, we didn't see him again until he returned with you." Smiling, she lifted her cup. "A happy trade that was, I might add."

Gazing at the flickering fire, Dawsey sighed. "I suppose she led him straight to poor Duncan."

Sputtering tea, Aunt Livvy slid her wavering saucer to safe ground again. Coughing, she held her napkin to her mouth and stared.

"I'm sorry, Auntie, but he was on a mission of mercy on my behalf. Duncan McRae is a very nice man."

Her aunt's hand shot up, still clutching the lacy cloth. "Please, dear, I can't bear to hear you say such things. How your father allowed him to sit at our table was more than I could fathom." She shifted in the chair. "Let's change the subject, shall we?"

Dawsey lifted her chin. "As you like." If the very mention of the McRae name upset her, Dawsey didn't dare voice her true feelings.

She missed pausing at the door of the cabin to soak up the laughter echoing from inside, missed Duncan's teasing banter and Odell's childlike ways. She longed to slip into a pair of Dilsey's britches and sit in the swirling mists, immersed in one of Silas's charming tales.

Her heart ached for every second spent with Dilsey and mourned every second lost, but her traitorous thoughts turned most often to Hooper, no matter how hard she fought to resist.

She'd told him he frightened her. The pain and confusion on his dear face when she said it had become a constant companion.

Her emotions tempted her to put her fear aside and allow love for him to overtake her doubts. No matter how difficult, she had to stand fast in her resolve. If she allowed herself to dwell on his proposal, on his passionate plea and warm breath on her lips, she'd be undone.

Father appeared at the door with a big smile. "Is this a private hen party?"

Aunt Livvy glowed with pleasure. "We'll allow one old rooster, dear. Come in and pull up a seat." She curled her long fingers around the arms of her chair and pulled to her feet. "Visit with Dawsey while I go brew a fresh pot."

She'd hardly risen before a loud knock sounded at the front door. Her startled gaze jumped to Father. "At this hour?" She glanced at Dawsey. "Hide in the pantry. It could only mean trouble."

Dawsey laughed, but her stomach tightened. "Auntie, I'll do no such thing."

"Calm down you two," Father ordered. His wary glance toward the hall belied his steady tone.

Her eyes wellsprings of alarm, Aunt Livvy clutched at the air with both hands, as if to draw Father to her. "Don't go, Gerrard. Let Levi answer."

"Don't be silly, Lavinia. Levi and Winney have retired for the night. Besides, I'm perfectly capable of answering my own door."

The rapping grew louder and more persistent as they followed Father, skulking like thieves, into the foyer. One hand on his back, Dawsey drew a quick breath. "This is silly. It doesn't have to be trouble, does it? Perhaps Mrs. Gilchrist is down in her back again."

Aunt Livvy gripped Dawsey's hands, her anxious gaze fixed on the knob. "Not this time. I have a sense of foreboding."

The women clung together as Dawsey's father swung open the door.

"You," he growled, clenching his fists. "How dare you come here?"

His gaze jumped to the pitiful wretch next to Hooper, and he let out an agonized cry.

The specter of Dilsey leaned in the hollow of Hooper's arm, her lips blue and her hair streaming in rivulets. Drenched to the skin, her meager garments clung to her shivering body.

"Merciful heavens," Aunt Livvy croaked, gaping from Dilsey to Dawsey.

Dawsey hurried forward. "Hooper, for goodness' sake, bring her in."

As he gently handed off his sister, Dawsey felt his hands trembling.

She pointed toward the parlor. "Go sit by the fire. Once we get her settled, I'll bring you some dry clothes."

Between Dawsey and her father, they got Dilsey upstairs to

Dawsey's room. He hovered outside while she and Aunt Livvy changed the soaking waif into a dry dressing gown and slid her between the sheets.

Aunt Livvy peeked out. "Go and fetch Winney, Gerrard. Have her prepare hot tea and broth." She ducked out again. "And hurry!"

Dawsey leaned to plump the pillows. Her sister's grasping fingers closed around her hand. "I—I'll be all right now," she chattered. "P–Please go see to Hooper."

Dawsey shook her head. "I won't leave you."

Frantic hands threw back the covers. "Then I'll do it myself."

They caught her and eased her shoulders down.

"Very well," Dawsey said. "If you're sure you're all right, I'll take him some dry things then come right back."

Aunt Livvy frowned but nodded her approval.

Dawsey hustled down the hall to her father's room, emerging with clothing and a warm woolen sweater. Stopping for a towel in the hall closet, she bolted down the stairs.

Hooper hovered in a tight ball before the fire, as if unwilling to soil the parlor rug. He whirled when she rushed in, worry etched in his forehead. "Is she all right?"

"She's dry and beginning to warm. We can only pray she doesn't become ill." She handed him the towel. "What were you thinking to bring her out in a storm? Or yourself for that matter?"

His eyes flickered with guilt. "It wasn't a storm when we left. I thought it would pass."

She took the cloth from his hands. "You might've caught your death. What on earth are you doing here?"

He stood like a shearing lamb and let her roughly dry his hair. Of their own accord, her hands drew him closer until he nearly toppled into her, gripping her arms to stay upright. "Dawsey, I had to come." His piercing brown eyes studied her from under wet stands of hair. "I had to see you."

She stared up at him, her staunch resistance melting. "I've missed you."

"Deliver me, O Lord, from the evil man."

"I'm not as bad as you think."

Had she spoken her prayer aloud?

"I'm a man of strong convictions. I'll admit they've had the best of me lately, but I didn't ambush those men in the swamp."

She blinked at him. "You didn't?"

Gentle fingers lifted her chin. "No, honey. They were already dead when I found them."

"But I thought—"

"You thought wrong."

Confused, she rubbed her forehead and tried to think. "You as much as admitted it. You said your mother didn't have to worry because the problem was tended."

He squeezed her arms. "Think hard. Did I once say I stalked those men and killed them?"

Dazed, she shook her head.

"I'd never say so, because I didn't. I left home intending to put the fear of God in them and drive them from Scuffletown for good. The swamp exacted a much higher price."

"And the heavens shall declare his righteousness: for God is judge himself."

She had haughtily spouted scripture at Hooper. Now one of her beloved Psalms brought swift conviction. "Can you forgive me for misjudging you? Especially without all the facts?"

Hooper smoothed her hair. "Yes, because I earned your distrust." His eyes glowing, he cupped her face with both hands. "I love you, Dawsey. If you'll give me a chance, I'll prove I can control my foul temper. You don't have to marry me until you're sure."

She bit her lip. "What about the raiding with Henry?"

"Over and done. We're going to find a better way."

She leaned into his wet embrace. "Then I don't have to wait. I'm sure now."

His hand slid up her neck to tilt her face. "You'll marry me?"

She rose on her tiptoes and kissed him. "Yes. As soon as possible."

"Dawsey Elizabeth!" Father's bellow ricocheted off the four corners and rattled the chandelier.

Dawsey and Hooper leaped apart.

"Oh, Lord, be merciful," Winney moaned. She paused long enough to peek around the doorframe with owl eyes then streaked past.

Thoughts of murder danced on Father's face as he strode into the room. "What is this madness?"

Hooper faced him. "It's not madness, sir. I've come to ask permission to marry Dawsey."

Father sucked an indignant breath. "You what?" His cheeks seemed to pulse beneath their purple hue. "I'll die first."

Dawsey felt pride in Hooper's control. With a sincere smile, he tilted his head. "I hope not, Colonel, but if we have to wait that long, I'm willing."

A raging bull, Father charged.

Dawsey screamed, but Hooper sidestepped, catching the back of his shirt before he lunged headfirst into the fireplace.

"Father, that's enough."

Three sets of astonished eyes swung to Dilsey, leaning on the threshold in Dawsey's dressing gown. Aunt Livvy's arm around her slender waist helped her to stand.

Forgetting Hooper, Father pulled free and straightened, smoothing his hair into place with a shaky hand. "What did you call me?"

Dilsey limped toward them. "That's who you are, I reckon." She sat, motioning him to do the same. "I'm calling a Wilkes family meeting to order." She glanced at Dawsey. "I think my sister has something she'd like to say."

Weak with gratitude, Dawsey moved to stand behind her chair. "Yes, I believe I do."

Father glared at Hooper. "Not until I've tossed this ruffian outside on his ear."

"If Hooper goes, I go," Dilsey said, scooting to the edge of the cushion.

Dawsey drew herself up. "And so do I."

Father's throat worked furiously. "Don't be silly, Dawsey. Where would you go?"

"Ma and Pa will be happy to take her in," Dilsey said. "They miss her something awful."

With a fond glance at the top of her sister's head, Dawsey's fingers tightened on the upholstery. "You're outnumbered, Father. You may as well sit down and hear me out."

Aunt Livvy stretched to full height. "You heard your daughters, Gerrard. Dawsey has something to tell you. Now sit."

He stared. "Lavinia? What's come over you?"

With a tender look at Dilsey, she smiled. "We've had us a little talk upstairs. Dilsey's an insightful girl."

Over the next few minutes, Father sat like he'd been told, sipping Winney's broth and bravely taking his medicine. He barely sputtered when Dawsey informed him that she longed to have his blessing, but she'd marry Hooper without it.

"I love you very much and always have," she reminded him. "Even when you didn't offer the same devotion. Now I'd like for you to accept the man I'm going to marry." She shifted her attention to Aunt Livvy. "The same goes for you. Hooper did a terrible thing when he took me that night, but if he hadn't we'd never have found Dilsey."

Aunt Livvy nodded. "Yes, I can see that. Perhaps it was meant to be."

Dawsey tended to agree. Her fanciful mind wanted to believe the impish McRaes held some magic charm to make them irresistible. Her heart knew that God had mended the broken pieces and woven His will through all of their lives.

Still unaware of divine intervention, Father hung his head. "Yes, we found her, but now I'm losing you both. Dilsey's marrying a Scuffletown man, and now Dawsey will go live there, too."

Hooper took a hesitant step. "Not necessarily, sir. There's more news I haven't yet shared with Dawsey."

Turning, he stroked her cheek. "My folks own one hundred acres in Hope Mills. They abandoned it years ago when they fled to Scuffletown." His fingers traced her neck to her shoulder. "It's not what you're used to, and the house will need some work, but they've offered it to us."

Her arms went around his neck. "It sounds wonderful."

Aunt Livvy brightened. "Hope Mills is only seven miles away."

Father slapped his knees and stood. "An old soldier knows when to retreat." His eyes still veiled, he held out his hand to Hooper. "I surrender, son. I have no choice but to offer my blessing."

Beaming, Hooper pumped his hand. "I promise you won't regret it, Colonel."

Crossing to Dilsey, Father reached for her hand. "Will you allow me one request?"

She tilted her head. "I'd need to hear it first."

"Fair enough," he said, chuckling. "Will you bring your young man to Fayetteville and let me throw you and Dawsey a proper wedding?"

Always up for a party, Aunt Livvy squealed. "We can plan a double ceremony. I'll throw a grand celebration. . .Fayetteville-style."

In the clamor that followed, Dilsey stared holes through the floor.

Dawsey held up her hand. "Be quiet, everyone. I think it's my sister's turn to speak."

Dilsey lifted grateful eyes then sighed. "It's not that I don't appreciate it, Father. It's a wonderful offer, but I'm afraid I have to say no. My ma has a shindig all arranged. She's fretted over it for weeks." She smiled. "This one is Scuffletown-style, which I think will be more to my liking."

She gave Aunt Livvy a shy glance. "I'd be proud if you both would come."

Father and Aunt Livvy shared a look. Then with tears in her eyes, she took Dilsey's hand. "Of course we'll come to your wedding, honey."

"We wouldn't miss it for the world," Father said. His head came up suddenly, the spark of an idea dawning in his eyes. "Don't move a muscle, little lady. I have something for you."

Chapter 52

The colonel spun away so fast Ellie jumped. She stared after him as he sailed from the room, moving quicker than she thought possible. She questioned Dawsey with her eyes, but her sister only shrugged.

He returned as fast as lightning and stepped into the room smiling, a treasure cradled in his hands.

Behind her, Hooper gasped.

The magic lamp was the most fetching thing Ellie had ever seen. Golden fingers of fire leaped on its sides, reflected from the hearth, no doubt, but they lured her with a spellbinding dance. She longed to hold it, yearned to touch the flickering light.

No wonder Papa had grieved for so many years.

The colonel handed her the gold lantern then wiggled his fingers at it. "You may keep it, dear. A wedding gift."

Ellie's breath caught. "Oh no, sir." She leaned and held out his offering—but not too far. "I couldn't keep something as fine as this. Pa claims it's worth a fortune."

"And he's right," the colonel said, a distant look in his eyes. "When I found it in your crib, I realized Silas had laid aside his plunder and took you instead. For years, I held out hope that he would someday return for it and thereby lead me to where he'd taken you." He shook his head. "In my befuddled state, I began to believe I could lure him into offering an exchange."

Dawsey touched his shoulder. "So you placed the bait in the window every night and waited."

Rubbing his face with both hands, he nodded. "Delusions of a silly old fool," he mumbled between his fingers.

"Not necessarily," Aunt Livvy said, nudging him. "Both of your daughters are here in this room, and it's because of that bauble, if I heard the story straight. I'd say that means you netted your fish in the end."

He stared at her until the truth sank in. "I believe you have a point, Lavinia." Smiling, he swept his hand at Ellie. "Consider it my gift to you, dear. Sell it with my blessing, and put the money to good use."

Dawsey crossed to Ellie and closed her hands around the lamp. "Please take it. I'd love to see the blasted thing do some good."

Hefting her prize, Ellie felt like an unworthy trade for the splendid piece. She smiled through her tears. "There are a lot of memories tied up in this lantern. I hope I can bear to part with it." She lifted her eyes to the colonel. "I won't agree without telling you my intentions. If I sell it, I'd like to use most of what it's worth to give me and Wyatt a good start"—she paused—"but I'll use the rest to help the widows and orphans in Scuffletown."

The colonel settled into his chair with a satisfied nod. "Even better."

Laughing merrily, Hooper crouched beside her. "Wait till Pa sees you with that thing. I suppose he can die happy now."

Ellie grinned. "All those years ago, he thought he traded me for the magic lantern. Won't he be surprised to learn he left it for me instead?"

Dawsey knelt beside Hooper. "But, honey, it was your inheritance all along."

Ellie's grin slowly died and her stomach tightened. "That's true. It wasn't a trade. Pa had no right to either one, did he?"

Biting her lip, Dawsey shook her head.

Tears burned Ellie's eyes. "Will you ask your God to forgive my pa for all the hurt he's caused?"

Hooper gripped her wrist. "Only Pa can ask God for pardon, Ellie. Just like we both have to ask Him for our own, but Pa's been talking an awful lot about forgiveness lately, so it's on his mind."

Dawsey patted her knee. "Maybe you need to call a McRae family meeting about God's mercy when you get home."

Frowning, Ellie swiveled her head to Dawsey. "What Pa did was extra bad. Will God be able to forgive him?"

She smiled. "I have a psalm to answer that question. Would you like to hear it?"

"I'd like it very much."

"All right, it goes like this: 'If thou, Lord, shouldest mark iniquities, O Lord, who shall stand? But there is forgiveness with thee. . . .'"

Ellie frowned. "Is that a yes?"

Laughing, Dawsey stretched to kiss her cheek. "Not just a yes, sister dear. A resounding yes."

Dawsey nodded at the lamp, tucked in Dilsey's lap. "It's good that you've come into possession of that portion of your birthright, but there's more laid up for you, Dilsey."

She tilted her head. "What more could I ask than what you've already given me?"

Dawsey gathered her hands. "God's promises are an inheritance more enduring and a treasure far more valuable than anything this world affords. That's the legacy left to us by our mother. I hope you'll allow me to share with you the riches she wanted us to have."

"I reckon I'm willing," Dilsey said. "But how?"

"We can start by teaching you the Psalms."

"I'll help," Aunt Livvy said, sniffing.

Dilsey smiled. "Ma used to read them to us, so that'll give me a head start. We can teach Hooper, too."

The colonel cleared his throat. "Girls, I wouldn't mind sitting in on those lessons myself. It's been too many years since I opened a Bible."

Aunt Livvy leaned her head against his shoulder, fishing her handkerchief from her waistband. "I think that's a fine idea, Gerrard. An absolutely fine idea." Wiping her eyes, she held out her hand to Dilsey. "But first, we need to adjourn this meeting and get you upstairs into bed."

Dawsey took Hooper's arm. "And you may come with me. I'll show you where to get a hot bath and a change of clothes."

With a slight tug on her sleeve, he held his ground until the others had filed from the room.

When the last of their footsteps reached the top of the stairs, she gave him a questioning look. "What are you up to, Hooper? Are you trying to catch lung fever?"

Laughing, he spun her around. "Nonsense, I'm practically dry." He touched her nose. "We still have one matter left to settle, Miss Wilkes. I figure today's as good a time as any."

She wiggled her finger. "Not so formal, Mr. McRae. Now, what is your pressing business?"

Sobering, he wrapped his arms around her waist. "You never accepted my apology."

"Apology?"

A slight frown creased his brow. "For dragging you out of a window, hauling you off to Scuffletown against your will."

Touching her chin, she pretended to ponder. "That was quite a ruthless thing to do."

Shame crossed his face. "I'm not proud of it."

"However, I realized something tonight," she said, "with all the talk of trading Dilsey."

He cocked his head. "Go on."

"In a way, I got traded, too. You came here to see the lantern, but you got me instead."

A roguish grin lit his handsome face. "Is it too late to change my mind?"

She squealed and swatted him then whirled for the door.

Laughing, he caught her before she got away. Pulling her so close she felt his heartbeat, his dark eyes pierced her soul. "That would be a foolish exchange, now wouldn't it, Dawsey? With my fondest wish already granted, I have no need for Aladdin's lamp."

EPILOGUE

Robeson County, North Carolina, February 1872

Silas leaned against the new windowpane watching Ellie and Duncan play a muddy game of chase. Hooper stretched across the top step, trying his hand at whittling and laughing at their tricks.

The long-awaited return of his children from Fayetteville hadn't come soon enough for Silas. They'd stayed with the Wilkes family while Dawsey nursed Ellie back to health and Hooper prepared the old home place for his bride-to-be.

Ellie's wedding would commence on schedule, despite the recent news of Henry's death. Boss came early one morning, shifting his eyes and shuffling his feet, to tell them Henry blew his face off while drawing a load from his shotgun. Silas never believed it for a minute.

Rhoda's casual style of mourning was the first clue that he was right. Rumors of a cloaked woman, seen scurrying toward the hideout late at night, confirmed his suspicions—Henry Lowry had staged his demise. Further proof was her heartfelt insistence to forego her husband's mourning period and proceed with Ellie's nuptials.

Henry had simply gone away, as Rhoda foretold. She said herself that Henry didn't want the McRaes taken by surprise at the news of his departure.

Ellie's upcoming wedding would give Silas the chance to see young Dawsey again and hopefully make amends with her pa. Following his children's lead, he'd hauled his many sins to the foot of the cross where they belonged and hoped to unburden himself to Colonel Wilkes, as well.

"What are you mooning at, husband?" The warmth of Odell's shoulder against his arm drew him from his hopeful thoughts.

Silas chuckled. "Watching our fine brood of children and thinking how blessed I am." He put his arm around her and hugged her close. "They're all handsome rascals like me. Don't you agree?"

She nudged him with her pointy little elbow. "That ain't a bit funny." Her wary eyes darted over his face. "The boys must never know, Silas. We learned firsthand how much trouble the truth can bring."

"It's not trouble that concerns me, love. That much I deserve, but it would do no good to tell them now. There's little hope they'd ever find their families."

"Hush, we *are* their family," she scolded.

He smiled. "I once feared we'd wind up childless in our waning years, with no one to tend our needs, but it's a fine bunch we wound up with, Odie."

She cut her eyes at him, her hard look meant to shame him. "At what cost to their parents?"

"Wife, I'm convinced I saved those boys from harsh and loveless lives." He pointed past the tattered drapes at their laughing brood. "Would you turn back the clock now?"

Pulling in her bottom lip, she followed his finger with her eyes then shook her head. "I couldn't part with a single one."

Silas glanced at Hooper, so handsome that some folks called him pretty, just not to his face. With his black hair and blacker eyes, he never once doubted where he belonged and would never guess he'd been lifted from a passing Gypsy wagon.

His gaze moved to good-natured Duncan, spinning Ellie around the yard. Short and stocky, lighter skinned than all the rest, his eldest son suspected what the others never questioned.

"Look at me," he'd cry. "Show me another Lumbee as fair as me."

"It's the Scot come out in you, boy!" Silas would lie. "Look at young Tiller. He got a double dose."

"But Pa," he protested, and rightly so. "My eyes are so different from yours and Ma's. They're clear and gray like a wolf's."

What could he tell the lad? *Son, I plucked you from a basket beneath a spreading oak while your ma pounded laundry on a riverbank?* The poor widow had a passel of mouths to feed and likely never noticed he was gone.

Ellie shoved Duncan aside and raced for the porch. Jumping

Hooper's prone body, she hit the door like a sudden gust of wind. "She's here! Dawsey's come for my wedding." Her excited face glowed. "The colonel and Aunt Livvy, too."

Silas stepped outside with Odell on his heels and shaded his eyes. Hooper loped like a spirited deer toward the fancy carriage jostling down the lane.

"Well, this is it, Odie, my love. Another chance to ask Colonel Wilkes to forgive me."

Ellie wrapped her arms around his waist and squeezed. "Suppose he won't?"

"Then I'll bide my time and try again. Maybe at Hooper's wedding."

She lifted her pretty face. "What if he chooses to never forgive you?"

Without waiting for his answer, she beamed like a sunray and sailed off the top step. Dawsey's carriage had arrived.

Silas watched the colonel climb stiffly from his coach. He smoothed his long coat and ran one hand across his silver hair. Smiling fondly at the girls, who stood laughing and clinging to each other, his gaze lifted past them to the porch. The smile faded, but he didn't flinch.

A good sign.

"Well?" Odie asked quietly behind him. "What if?"

Silas glanced over his shoulder. "For both our sakes, I pray he won't make that decision." He cocked his head. "If he does, I can't blame him, but I'll go to my grave trying to persuade him. Any reckoning due after that will be between the colonel and God."

He lifted his hand in greeting and crossed to meet the Wilkes family coming up the steps. "Don't stand there gawking, Odie McRae. Put some coffee on the fire. Ellie's folks have come to call."

Cherokee Indian Sweet Potato Bread

1 quart cornmeal
1 teaspoon soda
3 cups diced sweet potatoes
12 corn husks

Mix cornmeal, soda, and potatoes with enough boiling water to make a stiff dough. Knead well to make firm bread. Wash cornhusks and scald them in hot water. Put dough on large end of blade and be sure all sides are covered with blade and tie end of blade in a loop. Drop bread in boiling water. Boil 45 minutes.

From the Museum of the Cherokee Indian in Cherokee, North Carolina

Indian Dumplings

1 pint milk
4 eggs
¼ teaspoon salt
Sifted Indian meal
Flour

Take a pint of milk, and four eggs well beaten. Stir them together, and add a salt-spoon (¼ teaspoon) of salt. Then mix in as much sifted Indian meal as will make a stiff dough. Flour your hands; divide the dough into equal portions, and make it into balls about the size of a goose egg. Flatten each with the rolling pin, tie them in cloths, and put them into a pot of boiling water. They will boil in a short time. Take care not to let them go to pieces by keeping them too long in the pot.

Serve them up hot, and eat them with corned pork or with bacon. Or you may eat them with molasses and butter after the meat is removed.

If to be eaten without meat, you may mix in the dough a quarter of a pound of finely chopped suet.

From the book *Directions for Cookery* by Eliza Leslie

Marcia Gruver

Marcia is a full-time writer who hails from Southeast Texas. Inordinately enamored by the past, she delights in writing historical fiction. Marcia's deep south-central roots lend a southern-comfortable style and touch of humor to her writing. Through her books, she hopes to leave behind a legacy of hope and faith to the coming generations.

When she's not plotting stories about God's grace, Marcia spends her time reading, playing video games, or taking long drives through the Texas hill country. She and her husband, Lee, have one daughter and four sons. Collectively, this motley crew has graced them with eleven grandchildren and one great-granddaughter—so far.
